Whistle-Binkie

**Whistle-Binkie**

The piper of the party, etc. - Vol. 1

Whistle-Binkie

**Whistle-Binkie**
*The piper of the party, etc. - Vol. 1*

ISBN/EAN: 9783337340049

Printed in Europe, USA, Canada, Australia, Japan

Cover: Foto ©Andreas Hilbeck / pixelio.de

More available books at **www.hansebooks.com**

# WHISTLE-BINKIE

OR

# THE PIPER OF THE PARTY

BEING

## A Collection of Songs for the Social Circle

VOL. I.

GLASGOW

DAVID ROBERTSON & CO.

1878

*Printed by* R. & R. CLARK, *Edinburgh.*

# NOTE BY THE PUBLISHERS

OF THE

## NEW (1878) EDITION.

——◆——

THE present Edition is, with some verbal corrections, a reprint of that published in 1853, and to it
are added brief Memoirs of some of those connected
with the work who have died since then.

The explanatory notes are given, with the ex-
ceptions above referred to, as they were written in
1853, and regard must be had to this date in perus-
ing them.

# PREFACE.

—◆—

THE Songs contained in WHISTLEBINKIE were published in distinct Series throughout a period of fifteen years, the first having been issued in 1832.

The Publisher has confidence in asserting that so large a body of original Songs has never before been offered to the public in one volume.

Although, as might be expected, the Songs are of different degrees of merit—a few exhibiting more marked felicities than others—it will be found that most of them express some feeling or sentiment which the heart delights to cherish.

Looking to the number of contributors, it will readily be conceded, it is presumed, that the work, taken altogether, presents a remarkable instance of the universality of that peculiar talent for Song-writing for which Scotland has always been distinguished, and that it will be considered a favourable specimen of the national genius in that pleasing department of literature.

# A WORD AT PARTING.[1]

———✦———

IT has been often objected to this work, that it was too squat and cube-like in appearance—the publisher resolved, in consequence, to make two volumes of it. This has been done, and is largely supplemented by Biography and new pieces. Each volume is complete in itself; the only connection is the running title.

The memoirs of deceased contributors are supplied by parties who personally knew the individuals whose history they give; the Memoirs may therefore be implicitly trusted. The new pieces introduced are those left over of the last issue, series fifth, of this work, and which had the editorial imprimatur of the lamented editor, from the last edition of Motherwell's Poems, which underwent the critical inspection of the poet's friend, William Kennedy.

A large number also are from the prolific pen of that Son of Song, James Ballantine, one of the original staff of Whistlebinkians, and who is now

---

[1] Preface to volume second of the previous edition of "Whistlebinkie."

the only one remaining among us who wrote
expressly for this work at its starting; he is by far
the largest contributor of any of his gifted brethren.
The lion's share of the labour and honour is his,
in giving material, and also critical advice in the
selections and prunings to which the compositions
were subjected.

In taking farewell, the publisher cannot refrain
from wishing that this highly-gifted child of song
may long be spared to the public. He and his
publisher, greatly his senior in years, are only left
to cherish the memory of those whose " Lyres lie
silent now and sad."

He who gave publicity to this work has followed
the remains of many of these minstrels to " The
dusty house of Death," and felt the wheel working
at life's cistern, troubled when that hollow booming
key-note of death was struck, as the soil fell on the
casing which contained the unconscious remains of
those whom he loved, reflecting that he soon, too,
must return to mix with kindred dust.

GLASGOW, *June* 1853.

# CONTENTS.

## WHISTLE-BINKIE.

# CONTENTS.

# CONTENTS.

# BIOGRAPHICAL SKETCHES.

## JOHN DONALD CARRICK.

As the Editor of the First Series of "Whistle-Binkie," and as a man of considerable literary reputation, we think some account of this amiable and lamented gentleman will be acceptable to our readers.

John Donald Carrick was a native of Glasgow, and was born in April 1787. His mother is reported to have been a woman of superior powers of mind, and, in particular, to have possessed a fund of humour, with great acuteness of observation, qualities for which her son John was very remarkable. Carrick's education was necessarily limited, from the narrow circumstances of his parents; but in after life, when he had raised himself into a respectable station in society, the activity and vigour of his mind enabled him to supply in a great degree the deficiencies of his early education. When very young he was placed in the office of Mr. Nicholson, an architect of considerable eminence in Glasgow; and he continued to feel a partiality for that branch of art during his lifetime.

Young Carrick possessed great resolution of character, at times amounting to obstinacy. This quality of mind accompanied him through life, and if it now and then communicated a rather too unbending turn to his disposition, was undoubtedly the origin of that vigour and independence of mind which never deserted him.    Whether influenced by this feeling, or impatient of the uncertain and cheerless character of his youthful prospects, the rash lad determined on sallying forth alone into the world, to push his fortune, as the phrase is.    Accordingly, some time in the autumn of 1807, without informing anyone of his intentions, he set off for London, full of adventurous hope and courage.    This, be it remembered, was a journey of four hundred miles, to be performed on foot, for the few shillings which constituted his worldly wealth precluded any more expensive conveyance ; and whatever may be our opinion of the prudence of such a step, we cannot but feel respect for the stout-heartedness of the mere youth who could undertake it.    The first night our youthful adventurer arrived at Irvine, in the county of Ayr, and prudently economising his limited means, instead of putting himself to expense for a lodging, he took up his abode in the cosy recess of a " whinny knowe," where he was awoke in the morning by the roar of the ocean-tide, which was rapidly advancing on his heathery couch. Strong in the sanguine hopefulness of youth, he pursued his solitary way, living on the poorest fare, and sleeping sometimes in humble road-side hostels ; but more often encamping under the kindly canopy of heaven, amid the sheaves with which an early harvest had covered the ground, or nestling snugly in some green and leafy nook, on he went, we may be sure, fatigue-worn, and perhaps heart-worn, until he reached the town of Liverpool.

In after life he often reverted to his feelings on entering that town, and meeting with a recruiting party, gay with ribbons, and enlivened by the sound of fife and drum. The animating sight suggested to him the idea of enlisting, and so strong was the temptation, that, unable to decide for himself, he threw up his stick in the air, to be guided in his decision by the direction in which it should fall.    As his cudgel fell in the direction of London, he resolved to follow its prudent dictates, and girding up his loins, manfully continued his journey to the metropolis, where he soon after arrived, with only half-a-crown in his pocket. Carrick delighted in after years to refer to this ambitious sally of his wayward youth—his bivouac at night in the snuggest retreat he could find, with the solemn quiet of the green woods above and around him, and the gentle breeze of an autumn evening to lull him to rest,—or sometimes the doubtful shelter that he found in humble alehouses and bush-taverns.

Arrived in London, the friendless youth offered his services as a shopman. His Scottish accent and rough appearance after such a journey, with awkward, unformed manners, would no doubt operate against him with the more polished citizens of the capital. At length a shop-keeper, himself a Scotchman, captivated by the music of his mother tongue, engaged him in his service. He appears to have been employed in this way by various individuals until the spring of 1809, when he obtained a respectable situation in an extensive establishment, in the Staffordshire pottery business. His stay altogether in the metropolis appears to have been about four years. He returned to Glasgow early in the year 1811, and opened a large establishment in the same line of business, which he understood thoroughly, from having been employed for a considerable time in the great house of Spodes and Co., of London. In this occupation Mr. Carrick continued for fourteen years, with various success. His prospects at one period were of the most flattering kind, but becoming unfortunately involved with a house in the foreign trade, of which a near relative was a partner, these promising hopes were blasted.

The leisure which his business afforded him had, for some years, been diligently and profitably employed by Mr. Carrick in mental culture, to supply the deficiencies of his early education. The bias of his taste led him to cultivate an acquaintance with our older Scottish literature, and in 1825 the fruit of these studies appeared in the "Life of Sir William Wallace," which was published as one of the series of Constable's Miscellany. It has continued a favourite with the public ever since, and has lately been reprinted in a new edition. He began about the same time to throw off some of those humorous songs and pieces which, when sung or recited by himself, used to form the delight of his private friends. In 1825 he commenced business as a travelling agent, and his affairs leading him frequently into the Highlands, he acquired that knowledge of the Gaelic character, in its minuter shades and peculiarities, which overflowed so richly in the conversation of his later years, and gives such a zest to many of his comic and graphic sketches. This business not being so remunerative as he had expected, he finally abandoned mercantile pursuits, and devoted himself to literary composition. He engaged about this time as sub-editor of the *Scots Times*, at that period a journal of high standing in Glasgow. In 1832 a literary journal called "*The Day*" was published in Glasgow, to which he contributed many admirable pieces. One of his co-labourers in this pleasing and popular miscellany was the highly-gifted William Motherwell, a poet of no common elevation, and a person of a genial and kindly temperament. The eccentric and well-known Mr. Andrew Henderson was another intimate friend and associate of Carrick's; and these three richly-endowed individuals, though of characters and habits of mind very opposite to each other, lived in the warm enjoyment of mutual friendship; and, it is painful to add, followed each other to a premature and lamented grave within the brief space of two years.

In 1832 the First Series of this work was published, which was edited by Mr. Carrick, who also contributed several excellent songs and humorous poetical pieces, as well as an admirably written introduction, in which the etymology of the term "Whistle-Binkie" is pleasantly and humorously set forth. Early in 1833 he became the editor of the *Perth Advertiser*, a newspaper of liberal principles. For this situation he was admirably fitted, not only from his acquired experience in the *Scots Times* office, but still more from his extensive general information, the soundness of his judgment, and the calm, clear sense which his writings as a politician always exhibited. He did not, however, long retain this office, for, finding himself subjected to the indignity of being superintended by a committee of management, who interfered in the most summary and vexatious manner with his independence as an editor, he indignantly threw up his engagement, and bade adieu for ever to the Fair City. During his brief sojourn in Perth, Carrick wrote several humorous pieces of various kinds, his kindly and joyous temperament finding always some congenial escapement, notwithstanding the disagreeable circumstances in which he was placed. Of these pieces, one of the best is the well-known letter from " Bob, " to his friend in Glasgow, which appears in the last edition of the " Laird of Logan," at page 224. He does not seem to have thought much of the citizens of St. Johnstoun, remarking, with caustic severity, that "the last thing a true man of Perth would show you was the inside of his house."

At this critical period of his fortunes, some individuals in Kilmarnock, of liberal opinions, had projected a newspaper, and were looking out for an editor ; immediate application was made by Mr. Carrick's friends, the result of which was successful. He was powerfully supported in this object by his generous friend Motherwell, who, though differing widely in politics, gave a strong but honest recommendation of his general talents, as well as fitness for the situation, stating at the same time, " He (Motherwell) had never concealed his most rooted hostility to what was called Liberal or Reform principles."

Carrick left Perth in February 1834, and immediately proceeded to Kilmarnock, to enter on his duties as editor of the *Kilmarnock Journal.* It was fondly hoped by the friends of this warm-hearted but ill-starred man of genius, that here, at last, he might set up the staff of his rest ; but a short period served to dispel these pleasing hopes, and to cast a shadow over his prospects, which was never to pass away till it darkened down into the gloom of the grave. Here, too, Carrick was subjected to the annoyance and torture of a committee of management, many of whom were persons the most incompetent for such a delicate duty as the superintendence of a public journal. The members of this junta were, moreover, divided into parties, in a state of bitter hostility with each other, so that, when, urged by some of them, he had written a few lively, satirical articles, of local application, which severely galled sundry individuals in the town, the parties who had suggested them, alarmed for the consequences, withdrew their countenance equally from the editor and his journal.

Previous to his leaving Perth, there is reason to believe that the disease which brought on his death had evinced its existence by slow and insidious approaches, at first in the form of partial paralysis of the nerves and muscles of the mouth, issuing finally in tic douloureux, one of the most excruciating diseases to which the human frame is liable. The annoyance to which he was incessantly subjected induced a severe attack of this complaint, and obliged him to apply for a temporary leave of absence, engaging to find a substitute to do duty for him during its continuance. This reasonable request was refused by the *humane and enlightened* committee of management, and the wretched state of his health leaving him no alternative, he resigned his situation, and returned to Glasgow in the month of January 1835. During his stay in "Auld Killie," notwithstanding the painful visitations of disease, and the annoyances to which he was subjected in the exercise of his editorial duties, he never exhibited more affluence of mind, or a more perfect command over his rich and various powers. Besides various literary compositions, he exercised the duty of editor to the first edition of the "Laird of Logan," which appeared in June 1835. After this, Carrick went to Rothesay for the benefit of his health, but found it declining so rapidly, that he had given up all hopes of continued activity, and actually had fixed upon a spot in which to lay his weary and worn-out frame. Recovering, however, he returned to Glasgow, and resumed his literary pursuits. He contributed, about this time, some admirable papers to the *Scottish Magazine*, rich in humour and in happy traits of Scottish habits and peculiarities entitled, "Nights at Kilcomrie Castle, or the days of Queen Mary." Occupied with these and various other compositions, some of which are still in manuscript, and at times suffering acutely from the attacks of the painful disease, which now seldom, for any length of time, intermitted its visitations, and which, from its effect on his power of speech, was peculiarly obnoxious to a person of his social habits and character, Carrick continued to mix occasionally in society, and enjoy the fellowship of his friends. But a severe attack of inflammation coming on, aggravated by the weakening effects of a recent course of depletion, suggested by his medical attendant, proved too much for his enfeebled frame to resist, and, after a few days' suffering, he expired on the 17th of August 1835.

As a literary man Carrick's peculiar forte lay in the rich and humorous resources of a lively and salient mind and imagination. In broad humour he was singularly effective, and the edge of his satire was keen and biting. He had a quick perception of the ridiculous, coupled with much observation and knowledge of mankind. As a describer of old manners and customs he is remarkably happy ; and there is a graphic truth and beauty, enchased in a fine vein of drollery, in his descriptive sketches. The excess of his humour was ever ready to overflow in a stream of pleasant waggery, which the kindness of his nature, with his gentlemanly habits and self-respect, prevented from degenerating into broad or offensive caricature. As the editor, and a principal writer in the first series of the "Laird of Logan," he will long be remembered. Of this admired collection of Scottish and Gaelic stories, Carrick was the original projector, and he also contributed the excellent biographical sketch of "the Laird," with the greater part of the anecdotes of that celebrated humorist.

In concluding this brief memoir, we may observe, generally, that as a descriptive painter of the comic and ludicrous aspects of man and society, and as equally skilful in the analysis of human character, combined with a rare and never-failing humour, a pungent but not malicious irony, and great ease and perspicuity of expression, few writers have surpassed John Donald Carrick.

---

## ALEXANDER RODGER.

ALEXANDER RODGER was born in the village of Mid-Calder, Mid-Lothian, on the 16th July 1784. His father occupied the farm of Haggs, close by the small village of Dalmahoy. The weak health of his mother for several years consigned him to the care of two maiden sisters, of the name of Lonie ; and it was not till he had attained the age of seven years that he returned to the parental roof. His father appears at this time to have given up farming, and to have kept an inn in Mid-Calder. Up to that period the young bard had not received any regular education, but now he was put to school in the village. And this, as far as we have learned, was the only education he received, except what he may have acquired for himself, in after life, during the few hours he could steal from laborious employment.

Shortly after this his father removed to Edinburgh, where Alexander was sent to learn the trade of a silver-smith, with a Mr. Mathie. He continued a year in this employment, when his unfortunate father became embarrassed in his affairs, and, in consequence, emigrated to Hamburg, whence he sent for his son ; but his relations by the mother's side, being strongly attached to the boy, persuaded him to accompany them to Glasgow, where, in 1797, he was apprenticed to a respectable weaver of the name of Dunn, who resided at the Drygate Toll, in the near neighbourhood of the ancient Cathedral of Glasgow. We may be sure so venerable a relic of antiquity would be often visited by the youthful poet, and contribute, by its solemn magnificence and historical interest, to fan the flame of his poetic genius.

In 1803 the loyal fever, universally prevalent, infected our friend Sandie, who celebrated his connection with the Glasgow Highland Volunteers in a satirical poem of considerable merit, in which he employed the powers of his Muse in what became afterwards a favourite amusement with him, hitting off the peculiarities of his Celtic brethren. The corps, being principally composed of Highlanders, furnished ample scope for the keen edge of the poet's wit, and he seems then to have imbibed that attachment to the mountaineers which has led him so often to embalm their colloquial humours and foibles in his poetic effusions. Rodger continued in this volunteer regiment, and in another which rose out of it after its dissolution, called the Glasgow Highland Locals, for no less than nine years.

In 1806 the poet, then only twenty-two years of age, married Agnes Turner, by whom he had a large family. After his marriage Rodger removed to Bridgeton, a suburb of Glasgow, where he continued to solace himself, from time to time, in poetical composition and the exercise of his musical talents. His knowledge of the science of music enabled him to compose for his own amusement, and qualified him for imparting a knowledge of its principles to others, which he prosecuted for some time, the emoluments from which assisted him considerably in maintaining his young and growing family. Amongst the earliest efforts of his poetic vein is a poem entitled "Bolivar," written on the occasion of seeing in the *Glasgow Chronicle,* in September 1816, that this distinguished patriot and soldier had emancipated the negro slaves in the districts of. Carraccas, Venezuela, and Cumana, to the number of seventy thousand.

The peaceful tenor of the poet's life continued unbroken by any material event until the year 1819 when local and general politics ran so high, and the fever of radicalism, at times so endemic among the working population of this country, was at its height.   In that year a weekly newspaper called *The Spirit of the Union*, was started in Glasgow, by a person of the name of Gilbert M'Leod, which was conducted with some considerable ability, but with very little discretion.   The political and satirical propensities of Rodger having found in its columns a frequent and congenial vent, the editor took him into his service.   Thus, the poet, somewhat rashly, in our opinion, exchanged the calm obscurity of a peaceful, and then not unprofitable occupation, for the more conspicuous but more doubtful and hazardous theatre of political warfare. He did not, however, remain long in this situation, for within a few weeks, owing to his indiscreet violence, and that of the party with which he was concerned, the editor was apprehended on a charge of sedition, and soon after tried, found guilty, and sentenced to transportation for life.   The establishment being broken up, Rodger returned to his loom ; but having become, from his connection with this journal, considered as a disaffected person he was apprehended, on the 8th of April following, with many other individuals, on the alarm occasioned by the publication of the famous "treasonable Address," purporting to be issued by "a Provisional Government." Into the political history of these melancholy times we do not feel called upon any farther to enter.   Rodger was confined in the city Bridewell, and used with most reprehensible harshness, being treated like a common felon, and placed in solitary confinement.   The spirit of the indignant poet rose, however, superior to the petty malice of the small-souled officials of the day ; and he used to solace himself in his seclusion, by singing, at the top of his lungs, his own political compositions ; some of which were undoubtedly sufficiently well spiced, and could not therefore be very grateful to the ears of his

jailors.   To silence the obstreperous indignation of the
bard, he was removed to a back cell, where he gave vent
to his lacerated feelings in the indignant " Song written
in Bridewell."   The poet often used to relate many
entertaining anecdotes of this stormy and eventful period
of his life.   Amongst others, when his house was searched
for seditious publications (terrible bugbears at that time
to the local authorities of Glasgow), Sandie handed the
Family Bible to the sheriff's officer who was making
search, it being, as he said, the only treasonable book in
his possession ; and for proof of this, he referred the
aghast official to the chapter on kings, in the first Book
of Samuel.

In 1821 the late amiable Mr. George Rodger, manager
of Barrowfield works, and whose eminent skill and
scientific acquirements may be said to have laid the
foundation of the prosperity of that extensive establishment, got him employed as an inspector of the cloths
used for printing and dyeing.   In that situation he continued eleven years.   Here, his employment being less
severe, and more remunerative, Rodger produced some of
his best pieces.   In 1822, when George IV. visited Scotland, the poet indited his celebrated lyric of " Sawney,
now the King's come," which, having been published in
the *London Examiner*, made its appearance in Auld
Reekie, just as his Majesty had enriched his subjects
there with the sight of his royal person.   From that
sarcastic effusion having appeared simultaneously with
Sir Walter Scott's well-known piece, " Carle, now the
King's come," no little speculation was created as to the
author, and, in particular, it was said, by its unlucky
opposition, to have much annoyed the sensitive loyalty
of Sir Walter.   It is not to be denied that the humour of
this political and social satire is rather too broad for
general circulation.   About this time Rodger exhibited
his public spirit in a form more generally popular.
Thomas Harvie of West-Thorn having blocked up a
public foot-path on his property by the river side, which

had been long in use by the inhabitants of Glasgow and its vicinity, Rodger, by extraordinary exertion, organised and directed a public opposition, which ultimately proved successful.

In 1832 a new phase of Rodger's many-coloured life opens upon us. A friend, who had recently commenced business as a pawnbroker, requested the poet to take the management of it for him, to which he unfortunately agreed, and thus lost an excellent situation, with the prospect of further advancement, under the kindly auspices of his friend, Mr. George Rodger. Little was such an employ-ment adapted for the heart of a poet like Rodger, over-flowing with human sympathy, and sensitively shrinking from the scenes of misery and want with which it neces-sarily brought him into contact. In a few months he felt compelled to abandon it, and was soon after engaged by the late Mr. Prentice, Editor of the *Glasgow Chronicle*, as a reader and reporter of local news. He remained there about a year, when the late John Tait, an intimate friend of his, having started a weekly newspaper on Radical principles, he was employed by him as general assistant. The premature death of Tait, with the pecu-niary embarrassments in which the establishment had become involved, led to the dissolution of this connection. Rodger was again thrown upon the world; but in a few months after he obtained a situation in the *Reformers' Gazette* office, in which he continued till his death, highly esteemed by his employer, and respected by a wide range of friends and admirers. In 1836 he received a public dinner in the Tontine Hotel, when above two hundred gentlemen, of all varieties of political complexion, assembled to testify their respect for the poet and the man; and he was presented with a silver box filled with sovereigns—a fruit not found in much profusion on the barren though sunny sides and slopes of Parnassus.

Mr. Rodger's first appearance as an avowed author was in 1827, when a small volume of his pieces was published by David Allan and Co., of Glasgow; but, although this publication contributed to make him more generally known, it did not improve, in an equal degree, his pecuniary and private comforts. In 1838 Mr. David Robertson, Glasgow, published a volume containing a new and complete collection of our poet's compositions. This seasonable and agreeable publication has had an extensive sale, and contributed to diffuse the reputation of the author. Another small volume of his pieces was also unwisely published in Glasgow, entitled "Stray leaves from the Portfolios of Alisander the Seer, Andrew Whaup, and Humphrey Henkeckle." The poems in the latter are almost entirely political, and had previously appeared in various Glasgow journals, under the cognomens above noted. Some of these pieces are of great merit, but the unalloyed zeal and warmth of the author's feelings occasionally break out into rather too much acerbity and vigour of expression, thereby weakening the truth and force of their general effect.

Of Rodger's poetry, we may observe that his forte is undoubtedly a mixture of humour with satire, finely compounded, and powerfully and gracefully expressed. Even in those poems in which the humour is most kindly and gentle, and devoid of all political malice, there is a lurking vein of satirical truth and feeling flashing up at every turn. The two pieces, entitled "Colin Dulap," and "Jamie M'Nab," are full of a delicate and racy humour—finely descriptive of the parties, and warm with genuine feeling and truth. "Peter Cornclips," is Mr. Rodger's longest and most ambitious poem, but we do not think it by any means the best. It is deficient in dramatic truth and interest—in character and incident; but it contains many vigorous lines. Some of his songs have become very popular, in particular that of "Behave yoursel' before folk," which had the rare distinction of being quoted in the "Noctes Ambrosianæ" of *Blackwood's Magazine.*

Rodger cannot be called a descriptive poet : it is with living man, and not with inanimate nature, that he chiefly deals. Even in his lighter pieces he seldom indulges in mere description, but gaily touching the material world, his yearning sympathies bear him away to the haunts of men, kindly to survey and ponder over the panoramic succession of life's weary round,—now revelling in the enjoyment of the pleasing and hearty aspects of our common nature, and now rising up in honest indignation, tempered by his habitual kindness of nature to expose in biting, sarcastic verse, the meanness of the great, the poverty of soul of the proud, and the many oppressions and "ills that flesh is heir to." Modest and unassuming in manner, but observant in habit, with a fine hearty humour floating about him like an atmosphere, under the correction, however, of strong common sense and self-respect, none ever left his company without delight, and a warm wish for the prosperity of the favourite lyric bard of the west country.

Mr. Rodger's health began to give way in the summer of 1846. Unable to discharge the duties of his situation in the *Gazette* office, he went to the country, to try whether a change of air would brace his relaxed frame ; but he returned to Glasgow unimproved by the change. He gradually sunk, and passed away from this shifting scene, 26th September 1846.

Some of Mr. Rodger's friends exerted themselves in procuring from the Merchants' House a burying place for Mr. Rodger's remains in our own Necropolis. Mr. Leadbetter, the then Dean of Guild, was so obliging as to go and select the spot where the poet's ashes were to unite with the soil from which they came. A sweeter or more picturesque spot could not have been selected to receive a poet's remains. It constitutes a portion of the steep bank of MNEMA, and behind it the ground rises abruptly to the top of the tall cliff, crowned with a circular mausoleum, which forms so conspicuous an object from different points of view. A stately tree, blasted in its upper extremities, but otherwise still leafy and vigorous, flings its long shadow over the poet's grave when the sun is declining in the west; and a little above, on a green and sloping bank, is a venerable double thorn, with other trees and shrubs, diffusing a sylvan atmosphere around the spot.

A very tasteful monument has been erected over his grave, executed by the late Mr. Mossman, sculptor, on which is the following inscription, written by William Kennedy, author of "Fitful Fancies," etc. etc., and a quotation from one of Mr. Rodger's own poems :—

To the Memory of
ALEXANDER RODGER,
A POET
Gifted with feeling, humour, and fancy ;
A MAN
Animated by generous,
Cordial, and comprehensive sympathies,
Which adversity could not repress,
Nor popularity enfeeble ;
This Monument
Is erected in testimony of public esteem.
BORN
At Mid-Calder, 16th July 1784 ;
DIED
At Glasgow, 26th September 1846.

What though with Burns thou could'st not vie,
In diving deep or soaring high,
What though thy genius did not blaze
Like his to draw the public gaze ;
Yet thy sweet numbers, free from art.
Like his, can touch—can melt the heart.—RODGER.

Mr. Rodger regretted publishing the volume entitled "Stray Leaves." The parties who advised the publication of this collection wished, while the poet was on his death-bed, to get possession of some other MS. pieces which had been composed for the purpose of enlivening some of their convivial club meetings. As soon as the party in quest of these compositions left the house, Sandy rose from his sick-bed, and searched the drawer where they had been deposited, and, gathering them together, committed them to the flames.

It must not be concealed that the generous, facile, disposition of the poet exposed him to the solicitation of parties too convivial in their habits, and that he had not the fortitude to say " No." This often led him to keep late hours, and, consequently, the children had not the father's presence at night, when the family, relieved from the labours of the day, are collected around the domestic hearth, where, above all places, the parental advice and sympathy in joy and sorrow has such a happy influence.

## WILLIAM MOTHERWELL.

WILLIAM MOTHERWELL was a native of Glasgow, where he was born on the 13th October 1797. He was of a Stirlingshire family, possessed of a small property in that county, called Muirmill, and which had been in their possession for some generations. At an early age he was sent to live with an uncle in Paisley, where he received a respectable education, and was bred to the profession of a lawyer, or, as they are generally termed in Scotland, "a writer." His abilities, as well as his diligence, must have early attracted notice, as he was appointed, when only twenty years of age, Sheriff-Clerk Depute in Paisley, an office equally honourable and responsible, though not of great emolument. His literary tastes and habits had previously been exhibited in various anonymous pieces of considerable merit; and in 1828 he undertook the editorship of the *Paisley Advertiser*, and launched out fearlessly into the heaving sea of party politics. At an early period of his life his political principles and tendencies are said to have been liberal; but they soon hardened down into a determinate Toryism, in which they continued during his whole life. In 1828 he also assumed the management of the *Paisley Magazine*, a periodical, as we have been informed, of considerable merit, and which various of his own lyrical effusions, as well as sundry compositions in prose, contributed to adorn and enrich.   In the following year he resigned the office of Sheriff-Clerk Depute, and confined his attention to his literary pursuits and the editorship of the *Paisley Advertiser*.

In the early part of 1830 he was engaged as editor of the *Glasgow Courier*, a newspaper of considerable local influence and repute, and conducted on principles of a high church-and-king Toryism ; and thus the poet-politician was introduced into a new and wider field of interest and competition.   In the hands of Motherwell the *Courier* fully sustained its character as a fierce and uncompromising champion of ultra Tory opinions ; and during the excitement of the struggle for Parliamentary Reform in 1831-2 it was especially fierce and violent in its political denunciations.   We believe, however, that Motherwell was not much of a politician himself, and that the enthusiasm of his party politics was derived more from his fancy than his judgment—the product, in fact, of his poetical and indiscriminate admiration of everything con-nected with a chivalrous antiquity.   He held this situa-tion for about five years, and notwithstanding the occasional effervescence of his strongly expressed political opinions, retained to the last the general respect of society, with the hearty good will and esteem of his many friends.

In person, Motherwell was short in stature, but uncom-monly muscular and vigorous, with a large head, and short neck and throat, a conformation fatally inadequate to resist the character of the apoplectic seizure which finally carried him off.   On the 1st of November 1835, in company with his friend, the late Mr. Philip Ramsay, he had been dining in the environs of the city, and after his return to town, feeling oppressed and unwell, he went to bed.   Sleep, however, did not diminish the oppression, and in a short time he lost the power of speech.   Medical assistance was immediately obtained, but unfortunately too

late to be of any avail, and this sweet singer, and genial
and kindly hearted Scotchman, was blotted out of the
ranks of the living by a blow equally sudden and unex-
pected.   Deep and general were the regrets and sympathies of his friends, and of society at large, when this
premature and unlooked-for event became known, and
the general esteem in which he was held was manifested
by a public funeral, which was attended by many persons
of opposite political opinions, and by more than one of
his most determined political opponents.   He was buried
in the Necropolis of Glasgow, in the Fir Park, supposed
to have been in very remote times a Druidical grove, a
fit resting-place for the remains of a poet, whose soul
sought and found its highest consolations in the glowing
memories of the dim and shadowy past.   With a becoming
liberality, the merchants' house of Glasgow, the proprie-
tors of the ground, bestowed a site, in a beautiful situation,
for the poet's grave, near to the spot where reposes his
life-long and congenial friend, Andrew Henderson, author
of a collection of Scottish Proverbs.   An elegant monument has recently been erected to his memory by some
of his literary and personal friends, from a design by his
friend, the late James Fillans ; and, from within a screen
the bust of the poet, by the same tasteful artist, an
admirable likeness, looks forth upon one of the most
impressive and unique scenes to be met with in any place
of sepulture in the world.   The following exquisite lines,
from a Monody on his death by William Kennedy, an
intimate friend and congenial spirit, are inscribed on the
Monument :—

> " Not as a record, he lacketh a stone !
> 'T is a light debt to the singer we've known—
> Proof that our love for his name hath not flown,
>     .   With the frame perishing—
>     That we are cherishing
> Feelings akin to the lost Poet's own."

Such is a brief outline of the personal history of
William Motherwell, the incidents of which are few, and

in themselves unimportant. It is in their works, and in the progressive development of their genius, that the true history of literary men is to be found. We shall now proceed shortly to sketch out the more salient points of Motherwell's literary career, of which the incidents are comparatively brief and meagre. In 1827, whilst residing in Paisley, he published his "Minstrelsy, Ancient and Modern," a work of great merit and research, and which gave him permanent rank and influence as a literary antiquarian. In the introduction to this publication the writer has exhibited a thorough acquaintance with the ballad and romantic literature of Scotland, as well as great powers of research and antiquarian discrimination. Besides its merits as a historical and critical disquisition, it is a piece of a chaste and vigorous character, as well as eloquent composition. It is now very scarce, and much sought after by the lovers of our olden literature and poetry. Whilst he was Editor of the *Paisley Magazine* he enriched its pages with various of his poetical compositions, the pathos, grace, and beauty of which attracted public attention to the rising poet. In 1832 a volume of his poetical pieces was published by Mr. David Robertson of Glasgow, whose shop, for many years, was the resort of the poet and a select circle of congenial spirits, "the keen encounter of whose wits" rendered it classic ground, and still enrich it with memories alike mournful and pleasant. With the publication of this volume the name and fame of Motherwell will be chiefly connected. Many of the pieces are of exquisite beauty; and the lyrics, "Jeanie Morison," "My heid is like to rend, Willie," and "Wearie's Well," will take rank with any similar compositions in the English language. In a soft melancholy and touching tenderness of expression they have never been excelled. We are happy, at finding our opinion of these beautiful lyrics supported by so competent a judge as Miss Mitford, who, in a recent publication by her, comments thus gracefully and discriminatingly upon them :—"Burns is the only poet with whom, for tenderness and pathos, Mother-well can be compared.   The elder bard has written much more largely, is more various, more fiery, more abundant ; but I doubt if there be in the whole of his collection any-thing so exquisitely finished, so free from a line too many, or a word out of place, as the two great ballads of Motherwell.   And let young writers observe that this finish was the result, not of a curious felicity, but of the nicest elaboration.   By touching and re-touching, during many years, did ' Jeanie Morrison ' attain her perfection, and yet how completely has art concealed art !   How entirely does that charming song appear like an inexpressible gush of feeling that *would* find vent.   In ' My heid is like to rend, Willie,' the appearance of spontaneity is still more striking, as the passion is more intense—intense, indeed, almost to painfulness."   About the same time, his friend, Andrew Henderson, published his well-known collection of Scottish Proverbs, to which Motherwell contributed an introductory treatise, which showed him to be extensively read in Scottish proverbial antiquities, and is, besides, a piece of eloquent and vigorous composition.   In the year 1835, in conjunction with the Ettrick Shepherd, he edited an edition of the works of Burns, to which he contributed the principal part of the biography, with copious notes.   The edition, however, never became popular, chiefly owing to the absence of good taste and sound judgment in his brother editor.   Motherwell was, about this time, connected with a literary periodical published in Glasgow, with the euphonious title of *The Day*.   To this publication he contributed various excellent papers, and some rich poetical pieces.   His Adventures of Bailie Pirnie, a Paisley dignitary, exhibit great power of humour and playful fancy.

In 1846 a second edition of his poems was published by Mr. Robertson, with a memoir of his life by Dr. M'Conechy of Glasgow, containing twenty additional poems ; and in 1849 a third edition was issued, and which contained no less than sixty-eight pieces never before published. So it may now be considered that the best fruits of Motherwell's genius have been carefully selected and set before the public. The selection of these additional pieces was entrusted chiefly to the poet's personal friends, Dr. M'Conechy and Mr. William Kennedy. In the third edition the following beautiful and touching poetical tribute to his memory by Mr. Kennedy most appropriately closes the volume :—

Place we a stone at his head and his feet ;
Sprinkle his sward with the small flowers sweet ;
Piously hallow the poet's retreat !
    Ever approvingly,
    Ever most lovingly,
Turned he to nature, a worshipper meet.

Harm not the thorn which grows at his head ;
Odorous honours its blossoms will shed,
Grateful to him—early summoned—who sped
    Hence not unwillingly—
    For he felt thrillingly—
To rest his poor heart 'mong the low-lying dead.

Dearer to him than the deep Minster bell,
Winds of sad cadence at midnight will swell,
Vocal with sorrows he knoweth too well,
    Who—for the early day—
    Plaining this roundelay,
Might his own fate from a brother's foretell.

Worldly ones treading this terrace of graves,
Grudge not the minstrel the little he craves,
When o'er the snow-mound the winter blast raves—
    Tears—which devotedly,
    Though all unnotedly,
Flow from their spring, in the soul's silent caves.

Dreamers of noble thoughts raise him a shrine,
Graced with the beauty which glows in his line ;
Strew with pale flowrets, when pensive moons shine,
    His grassy covering,
    Where spirits hovering,
Chaunt for his requiem, music divine.

Not as a record he lacketh a stone !—
Pay a light debt to the singer we've known—
Proof that our love for his name hath not flown,
    With the frame perishing —
    That we are cherishing
Feelings akin to our lost poet's own.

As a poet, Motherwell was perhaps deficient in that
robust vigour of opinion necessary for long and sustained
flights.  His muse had not the majestic pace, or "the
long-resounding line," of the higher class of poets.   But
in the utterances of the heart, borne up and sustained by
a sweet-toned fancy—in natural gushes of feeling—and in
a rich mental and poetical sympathy with the sights and
sounds of living nature, few have risen to an equal pathos,
and a descriptive beauty more touching and telling.   Such
pieces as, "In the quiet and solemn night," "The midnight wind," "The water, the water," "The solemn song
of a righteous heart," "A solemn conceit," etc., possess a
generic character, and are especially imbued with a pensive and querulous melancholy, and a pathetic quaintness
of expression, strikingly original.   It is as if the shadow
of his early fate had fallen at times on the soul of the poet,
and touched a chord in his muse, attuned to finer issues
and higher inspirations than ordinary.   In another and
very different style of composition he has produced various
pieces of great beauty and elegance of thought and expression.   In light and graceful *vers de société*, sparkling with
sentiment, and richly inlaid with the gems of a playful
fancy, such pieces as, "The serenade," "Could love
impart," "Love's diet," are perfect bijoux of their kind,
and dazzle the imagination with their brilliant affluence
and concentrated elegance of thought.   His Norse songs
of war and chivalry possess a wild, bold bearing and
character, which have made them much admired.   Various
of his imitations, too, of the olden ballad are beautifully
executed, and breathe the free, wild spirit of the greenwood, and tell pathetically of the agonies of young hearts
that "loved not wisely, but too well."

Such was the poet—let us briefly consider the man. In general society Motherwell was reserved ; but with his intimate friends he let himself out freely into the whim or enjoyment of the hour.    Amongst his intimate associates were John D. Carrick, Andrew Henderson, and John Howie, all of whom have passed away, like himself, from this mortal scene.    In company with these and other select friends his natural reserve gave place to a rich enjoyment of the sly quips and drolleries of the first of these, or the more boisterous and explosive humours of the second ; and we ourselves have enjoyed, more than once, the company of these three rich-minded, but oddly-paired men, in a well-known tavern in the Trongate—the Swan with Two Necks—which was their favourite resort.    In this cosy howf we have listened with delight to the delicious chirping of these congenial souls, when they had washed their eyes in a tumbler or two, and were hitting right and left in the unrestrained glee and social abandonment of mirth and good fellow-ship.    They are all gone, and so are some others who were members of that brilliant brotherhood which once graced and enriched our city ; but there still linger in many a heart pleasing though mournful reminiscences, which cluster around their rich memories, associated as they now are. with the name and fame of William Motherwell.

---

## EDWARD PINKERTON.

EDWARD PINKERTON was a son of the Rev. Mr. Pinker-ton, minister of what was then called the Relief Church, in Campbelton, Argyleshire, and dates his birth December 1798.    He was sent, in due time, to the High School, Edinburgh, to receive the elements of a classical education ; and he afterwards matriculated in the Glasgow University.

The celebrated Professor Sandford, of the Glasgow University, was a fellow-student with Mr. Pinkerton, and their standing in the class, under Dr. Pillans, was nearly on a par. He afterwards joined the medical classes, and obtained his diploma in 1817. His youthful appearance, it was considered, might militate against his obtaining that confidence so necessary in the treatment of the varied maladies to which frail man is subjected ; and he did not consider it prudent to enter into public practice, but took charge, meantime, of a subscription school in his native town, Campbelton. He afterwards taught the classical department of a boarding-school at Galashiels. He obtained the appointment of assistant surgeon in the Royal Navy in 1825, in H.M.S. " Warspite," under command of Commodore Brisbane. The " Warspite " was ordered to India, and returned to this country in 1827, after performing a voyage round the world. Mr. Pinkerton had suffered a severe shock of paralysis, and was laid up in Chelsea Hospital ; but his intellect was unimpaired by the attack, though his frame was so shaken that he was unable to return to public duty, and he retired on Government allowance. Mr. Pinkerton came to reside in Glasgow amongst his friends, and was almost a daily visitor, as long as he was able, at the levées of wit and humour in the shop of our publisher. He died in 1844.

The pieces contributed by him to this work have his name attached. No one at all competent to judge of lyric compositions will fail to see in them no ordinary ability.

He published, in 1832, a small volume of poetry, entitled " The Propontis," which was well received by the public.

Mr. Pinkerton occupied his time between literary pursuits and giving instructions in Greek to students attending the University. He was considered a very excellent scholar—few, indeed, surpassed him in the knowledge of this elegant language, and he appeared sometimes a little vain of this acquisition.

## JOHN GRÆME.

JOHN GRÆME, whose numerous unacknowledged contributions to this work will be afterwards noticed, was born in the city of Glasgow, on the 19th of May 1797. His father, after whom he was named, was by profession a hair-dresser. The maiden name of his mother was Janet Williamson. The relations of John Græme were in very respectable circumstances—his uncle, Robert Græme, some of whose family still survive (1852) was Sheriff-Substitute in Glasgow : his name appears as one of the witnesses at the record of Græme's birth.

The subject of our memoir was sent by his parents to learn weaving, the practical knowledge of which was considered indispensable to fit him for a manufacturing establishment.

His parents died while he was young, and the property left by them, or to which they expected to succeed, became the subject of a law-suit, and went against Græme, which fell with a crushing blow on the family. This calamity left on the mind of John an impression which was never erased—melancholy, to which he was very subject, it was feared would have settled down on his mind, and his friends sent him for part of the summer to the neighbourhood of Bucklyvie, so as to change the scene and break off the train of thought which was coursing through his mind with the greater danger as it was confined to one channel, disappointment. The change had the desired effect, and he returned to Glasgow renewed in bodily health, and with a new and healthy tone imparted to his mind.

He obtained employment in a warping room in St. Andrew's Square for some time ; afterwards he pursued the same mode of obtaining a living with Mr. Lawson, at that time an extensive manufacturer in Glasgow, afterwards the honoured manager of the Glasgow Provident Bank. Græme always spoke of Mr. Lawson with almost the affection of a son.   While turning the warping reel, etc., Græme formed the idea of qualifying himself for the profession of medicine, and after labour hours studied Latin with Mr. James Stirling (now Rev. Mr. Stirling, United Presbyterian Church, Kirriemuir), to enable him to understand the mysteries of the art, whose vocabulary is expressed in that noble language.   He also had a private class, in which he taught his pupils the elements of geography.

It is said that he accepted the office of tutor in the family of a farmer, in the upper ward of Lanarkshire, the very farm-house to which, as the story goes, Morton was carried prisoner by the Covenanters, after their disastrous defeat at Bothwell Brig.   We never heard Mr. Græme allude to this tutorship ; his stay must have been but short there, and we should think the coarse modes of living in these sequestered places would but ill accord with the sensitive mind of Græme.   In struggling to get on with his medical classes he had much privation, but honourably and creditably obtained his diploma in 1826.   His knowledge of pharmacy was acquired under Mr. John Wallace, a surgeon in Glasgow of amiable memory.

He opened a small shop in Trongate of Glasgow, which had been previously occupied by a medical gentleman.   The young lancet-bearer expecting that a certain amount of his predecessor's practice would fall into him, for which he paid more, perhaps, than the intrinsic value of medicines, etc., etc., were worth.   This turned out an unprofitable beginning : he then removed to the Gallowgate, where he remained but a short time.   His next place for administering medicine and advice was the High Street, where he continued till he died, which melancholy event took place 11th February 1852.

Græme was one of the original staff of Whistlebinkians, and whose humorous contributions at its first publication assisted to give the work the popularity it very soon acquired.

Græme would never allow his name to be attached to his compositions ; but, now that his rebuke need not be

feared, we give a list of his contributions to this work :—
" The Fruit of Old Ireland," " Kate M'Lusky," " Irish
Love Song," " Kilroony's visit to London," " Young
Paddy's Tutor," " The Herring-head Club," " Pat
Mulligan's Courtship," and " Kitty O'Carrol."

We quote a notice of John Græme, contributed by an
intimate friend, and which appeared in the *Glasgow
Citizen* :—

" Few men were better known, or held in higher
respect, not less for his genial and lovable qualities as a
private friend, his rich and racy humour, strong sense,
and general information, than for the active benevolence
and enlightened philanthropy which formed the basis of
his character. We believe that in early life his circumstances were not promising ; but the vigour of his mind
enabled him to acquire, almost self-taught, the elements
of a medical education, to which profession he finally
devoted himself, and in which his practice, though limited,
was respectable. The educational deficiencies of his opening years, although remedied to a considerable extent by
an astute and manly intellect, and by varied and general
reading and inquiry, were never sufficiently repaired to
place him in a high literary position. The rich natural
resources of his mind found a vent, however, in various
prose and metrical compositions, which he contributed
to those well-known collections of Scottish song and
social *facetiæ*, 'Whistle Binkie' and the ' Laird of Logan,'
and also, we have reason to believe, in other channels of
which we have no personal knowledge.

" It was in the society of private friends, however, of
whom he had many, who continued their attachment to
him through life, and whose kindness soothed and
ministered to him in the lingering hours of mortal sickness, that the kindly and genial qualities of his nature
broke forth in their full lustre and perfection. A rich
flow of humour, never degenerating into mere buffoonery
or vulgar personalities, rendered him the soul and centre
of the social circle, and his sudden bursts of impromptu

drollery, happily conceived and felicitously expressed, never failed to set the table on a roar. Those who, like the writer, have often listened to his songs (generally of his own composition), or witnessed his dramatic and imitative powers in his extemporaneous exhibitions, will not soon forget the man any more than the genial humorist and friend. His memory will long be cherished by many surviving friends, associated as it will be with other rich and pleasant memories floating around the congenial names of Motherwell, Carrick, and Henderson, of which bright, though narrow circle, he was long a member."

How often has he set the table on a roar! We have seen him put gentlemen into nervous fits with his imitations both of the rational and the irrational portions of creation. Poor Carrick, when unable to take any part in the amusements of the social party—"Never mind," said he, when sympathised with that he could not aid as he was wont in keeping up the hilarity, "you have Græme with you : you should learn to appreciate him." His remains are deposited in the paternal burying-place, north-east corner of the Cathedral, the footpath only between his grave and the abutments of its walls. There in peace rest his ashes, mixing with those of his mother and a beloved sister who predeceased him.

---

## CAPTAIN CHARLES GRAY, R.M.

AMONG the many who, in Scotland, have piped sweetly in the sunny nooks of poesy, without attaining any very dazzling height, was Captain Charles Gray, R.M. The Captain was a native of Anstruther, in Fifeshire, renowned likewise as the birthplace of Dr. Chalmers, the glory of the Scottish pulpit, and of Professor Tennant, who immortalised in verse the hilarities of "Anster Fair." For thirty-six years he had served in the Royal Marines, but of flood or of field he appeared to have scarcely a tale to tell. With his soldier's uniform he contrived to lay aside the soldier. His talk was of Scottish song. Scottish song was the one unchangeable hobby of his life. While yet a lieutenant he sung of Scotland on the blue waters of the Mediterranean. He was engaged in several years in the blockade of Venice, but his heart, in the midst of every excitement, continued true to Anster, and Fife, and Scotland. Many of his pieces bear foreign dates, but their theme is almost uniformly Scotch. His admiration of Burns, and indeed of all the great lyrists of his homeland, partook of the familiar fondness of a love, and the engrossing enthusiasm of a worship ; and his soul gave out echoes as sleepless as those which dwell near mighty cataracts, of the wondrous music with which it was filled unceasingly as with an inspiration.

Some dozen or fourteen years have now passed since we numbered Captain Charles Gray among our close friends. At first we saw him only during his occasional visits to Scotland ; but latterly he had retired on full pay, and taken up his permanent residence in a quiet suburb of Edinburgh, lying to the south of Heriot's Hospital. We enjoyed his society from the simplicity, good faith, and heart-warmth which were his unvarying characteristics. Like a veteran tree-trunk sprouting, the old man exhibited the verdurous freshness of boyhood. He had long been a widower, and his only son was, as he had himself been, a Lieutenant in the Royal Marines. But he had companions in his books ; and, so long as he had a genuine old ballad to rehearse, he could never feel weary or alone. At the sound of ancient melody he would break through any conceivable fortification of cobwebs ; and ramble in a very rapture of enchantment in the midst of old-world haunts—wherever, indeed, human hearts had, in times long lapsed, either bounded with uproarious humour or melted with mellifluous pathos.

There was not, perhaps, in all broad Scotland a man, in all respects, more happily constituted than Captain

Charles Gray.   In his case the spirit of the poet seemed,
like the person of the soldier, to have passed through
all perils without receiving a single wound or leaving a
single scar.   Like *Autolycus*—to whom, however, he
bore no other resemblance—he went on his way singing,
as it were,—

> " Jog on, jog on, the footpath way,
>     And merrily hent the stile-a ;
> A cheery heart goes all the day,
>     Your sad tires in a mile-a. "

Several of his " Lays and Lyrics" his friend, Mr. Peter
M'Leod, had winged with appropriate music, and the
secret feeling lay cosy at his heart that these, at least,
would go down the sunny slopes of posterity ; and this
gracious fancy cheered him through years which knew
neither eves nor winters, with darling glimpses of a
bright poetic immortality.   Among his intimate literary
friends were Professor Tennant, whom he describes as

> " —— reserved and shy,
> With humour lurking in his eye,"

and Professor Thomas Gillespie of St. Andrews, with
whom he was wont to correspond in rhyme.   He was
likewise on terms of friendship with Mr. Robert Chambers,
whose larger range of faculties did not carry him beyond
the enjoyment of kindred pursuits.   Mr. Patrick Maxwell,
the biographer of the sweet poetess Miss Blamire,—a
man after his own heart, and with all his time on his
hands, was his daily companion.   Poor Gilfillan, with
his plaintive " Why left I my hame !" and satiric " Peter
M'Craw ;" Mr. David Vedder, with his many manly
lyrics, like gusts from his own native Orkneys ; Mr. James
Ballantine, with his graphic and sturdy vigour of expression and sentiment ; and Mr. Thomas Smibert, whose
polished and eloquent strains have long enriched our
periodical literature, and been recently given to the world
in a collected shape, were among his congenial associates.
Who among his friends can forget the gusto with which

he used to sing, in spite of a somewhat croaky voice, his own excellent ditty of "When Autumn has laid her sickle by," or Tannahill's fine roystering burlesque of "Barochan Jean"? A fish-dinner at Newhaven with a select party of such spirits, and with Donaldson—well known in Edinburgh circles—to sing "Caller Herring," as no other man could, and Peter M'Leod to rise in his enthusiasm to the full height of "I am a son of Mars," is a reminiscence "to dream of, not to tell."

The closing decade of the last half-century has stolen away since the days of which we speak ; but Edinburgh sociabilities still come back upon us, from time to time, if only in intimations of change. Robert Gilfillan has "left his hame," and gone to rest underneath the flowers of which it was his joy to sing ; and our warm-hearted friend Captain Gray no longer enlivens, with his radiant good-humour, the social circles of the beautiful city of his adoption. Some years before his death he was a zealous contributor to "Whistle-Binkie," in which he took a lively interest. He likewise published in the columns of the *Glasgow Citizen* newspaper an elaborate series of "Notes on Scottish Song," displaying much careful re-search, and acute and curious criticism. With such love-labours, relieved by an occasional attendance at a "Burns Anniversary" at Irvine, or "Nicht in Glasgow" with his west country *cronies*, glided away the latter days of Captain Charles Gray, like a stream singing its way cheerily to the sea. The last time we saw him he was an invalid indulging in daily carriage airings. Lunch was laid out in anticipation of our visit, and we found his faithful friend, Mr. Patrick Maxwell, enlivening the pale valetudinarian with his good company. He looked thin and shaken, but the old embers glowed within him, and his kindly blue eyes brightened with their wonted lustre as he de-scanted on his favourite theme. His end, it would appear, was rapidly approaching ; and on the morning of Sunday, April 13, 1851, the good Captain closed his eyes on this world at the age of sixty-nine.

Captain Gray was not gifted with high genius.   He had, nevertheless, amassed such wealth of genial and harmonious fellowship in his life as to enable him to bequeath to his friends a memory which none of them will willingly let die.   As a poet he lacked imaginative brilliancy, nor was he master of any profound strain of pathos.   The characteristics of his muse was exuberance of animal spirits.   Had he been a musician his forte would have been reels, strathspeys, and polkas.   His verses were poured out, not from a torn heart, but from a buoyant and healthy nature.   The stream of his song has neither breadth nor depth, richness nor magnificence, but it has a pleasant warble and a bright sparkle of its own, and its course is through meadows, graced with all flowery embroidery, and under skies which wear their clouds only for adornings.   The passing of such a man from the festive circle and the busy street into the unseen world leaves a strange gap in the dread unlifted veil, through which we seem, for a moment, to catch a wild wide glimpse of the BEYOND.

---

## ALEXANDER FISHER.

ONLY a few days have elapsed (8th Nov. 1852), since we returned from the grave of another contributor to our pages.   Alexander Fisher was born in Glasgow in 1788. His father was a tobacconist, to which profession he also bred his son.   His father gave him an excellent education, which Alexander afterwards improved by very diligent and extensive reading.

He married, in 1811, Helen Campbell, sister to James and William Campbell of Candleriggs Street, Glasgow, justly celebrated for the large extent of their private and public charities, and an extensive business connection. Several of Mr. Fisher's family predeceased their father, others of them, with his partner in life, survive to lament his loss, the eldest of whom, Dr. A. Fisher, enjoys an extensive and very respectable medical practice in Glasgow.

Mr. Fisher's contributions are all of a humorous description, and his muse never seemed so much in her element as in describing the awkward misplacings of the adjuncts of nouns, which Highlanders beginning to speak English always exhibit. The pieces of his in this work are almost all of this description. They are, " The Twal o' August ;" " Ta offish in ta mornin', or Duncan Grant her Cousin's son ;" " Ta praise o' Ouskie ;" " Ta gran Highland bagpipe ;" " Shean M'Nab ;" " I'se red ye tak' tent ;" " I never will get fu' agin." For a few years preceding his death, he and Mrs. Fisher and the youngest unmarried daughter lived in a cottage on the seaside at Ardrossan.

---

## JOHN SPIERS.

John Spiers, our most endeared and intimate friend, requires a notice, however brief, at our hand. He was born at Alexandria, Dumbartonshire, in 1798. His father was connected with the Excise. Mr. Spiers came to Glasgow when a young lad, and entered the warehouse of Messrs. James and Morris Pollock. He was partner with Mr. James Pollock after the partnership of the two brothers had been dissolved. When Mr. Pollock died, Mr. Spiers continued the business on his own account. In 1836 he married Amelia Baxter, fourth daughter of the late Mr. Isaac Baxter, Italian warehouse, Buchanan Street.

His early death was occasioned by his connection with those speculations in railways, etc., which have sent so many to premature graves, and involved families in irretrievable ruin. Mr. Spiers' sensitive frame could not bear up under the prospective ruin which stared him in the face. He had a very severe attack of British cholera, from which the medical gentleman had at first no fears of danger; but his mental anxiety induced convulsive attacks, which carried him away to happier and better scenes, in the hope of which he even triumphed while in the last grasp of the Terrible King. He was withdrawn from the conflict 21st July 1846. His amiable partner followed him about four years afterwards, leaving a family of four children, three daughters and one son. The care of these orphans devolved on their uncle, Mr. Walter Baxter, who, with his partner in life, are (1852) with the most exemplary diligence acting the part of parents to them.

Mr. Spiers only contributed one piece to this collection, though he was a large contributor to the Laird of Logan. He was possessed of a very superior taste and sound judgment, to which we very generally deferred. He was always one of the group who assembled in our publisher's, and whose laugh, fresh from the heart, made all joyous about him. Peace to his memory, which will be cherished by the writer while the hand-breadth of his days are continued to the limit—" Hitherto shalt thou come and no farther."

## JOHN HOWIE.

JOHN HOWIE, though not a contributor to this work, deserves a niche in it. His name is associated with those of the Motherwell coterie. He was born in the parish of Eaglesham, where his father was an extensive farmer. The family is descended from an ancestry celebrated in the annals of those conscientious sufferers who were prosecuted for their adherence to the Presbyterian cause, in opposition to Prelacy.

Mr. Howie received a liberal education—he attended the Glasgow College for some years, but did not prosecute any of the learned professions ; he devoted himself to mercantile pursuits. His senior brother, James, studied with him, and is now (1852) one of the most respectable members of the Faculty of Procurators. It ought not to be concealed that Mr. James Howie raised amongst his friends, after Motherwell's demise, four-fifths of the sum then subscribed to assist in defraying his debts, and aiding Motherwell's only remaining sister, who died at Rothesay, in 1850. We do not over-state the matter when we say that Mr. Howie raised above a thousand pounds.

John Howie was connected with the house of Dennistoun, Buchanan, and Co., of Glasgow. A predisposition to pulmonary complaint rendered it necessary for Mr. Howie to seek a milder clime, and he left this country in 1835, and resided principally in Jamaica till his death in 1847. Mr. Howie made a journey home in 1846, his medical adviser thinking that his native air might brace up his sadly relaxed and debilitated frame. He reached London, but was ordered back to Jamaica, as his life, it was thought, could not be preserved any time in this northern climate. When the writer called for him, on a Wednesday, at Furnival's Inn, High Holborn, in August 1846, expecting to see his old and endeared friend, he was told that he had left on the previous Saturday for Jamaica.

Mr. Howie was possessed of a very vigorous, clear, cool, philosophical judgment, and of a fine literary taste ; we thought sometimes others got the credit for compositions which were written by Mr. Howie. Motherwell uniformly deferred to his taste and judgment. The following is an extract from a letter addressed to the writer on the melancholy occasion of Motherwell's death, which for taste and feeling is not often surpassed :—

" You need not, I daresay, be told with what distressing astonishment the announcement of our cherished friend, Motherwell's death came upon me. The bitterness of my own regret was, in my own case, greatly aggravated in reflecting upon the number of sympathetic souls in your own circle, who would be equally heart-stricken by his untimely doom. His career has been mournfully brief, though, happily, not barren; and I cannot doubt that his works will yet rise to a far more estimable popularity than they have hitherto done, and chiefly with that portion of his kind for whom he had ever the heartiest regard—song-loving and simple hearts. To the rugged mass he was, as you are aware, but half known; and some there are who will *pet* his memory who cared but coldly for the living man. But the brief fever is over, and his life I know was not unhappy, although it was rather a fit than a term—more a passion than an existence. But, was it ever otherwise with true genius! The crust that covers it is almost always prematurely cracked by the very intensity of the flame that glows within."

———

## JAMES SCOTT.

JAMES SCOTT was born at Lanark, November 1801. His parents removed to Glasgow when their son was little more than four years of age. He was sent back again to Lanark, to reside with his maternal grandmother, who taught him to read. At the age of seven years he entered the Grammar School, where he remained about four years. On leaving Lanark he came to Glasgow, and entered the *Glasgow Chronicle* office, for which journal he reported for some considerable time.

In June 1826 he left for Canada, to edit the *Montreal Herald*, and returned to this country in September 1831. While in Canada he established the *Montreal Weekly Gazette*. Early in 1832 Mr. Scott joined the *Greenock Advertiser*, a connection that continued till his death on 1st December 1849.

Mr. Scott was much esteemed in Greenock, and took a patriotic lead in all public movements. He had a memory of extraordinary tenacity, and could have reported from memory, almost verbatim, speeches of any ordinary length. He suffered, for a considerable time before his death, by that malady fatal to physical and mental effort—softening of the brain. His amiable partner watched over him, and nursed him with the most pious care, during his painful and protracted illness. A large family predeceased him. Mr. Scott contributed one piece to Whistlebinkie.

## ROBERT CLARK.

ROBERT CLARK, author of "Kate Macvean," and "Rhymin' Rab o' our Toun," was born in Paisley, in 1810. He was early apprenticed to the trade of weaving, at which he became a proficient workman. From his youth he was remarkably fond of reading, especially poetry. He had a taste for the sister art, music, the study of which he pursued, and became a tolerable performer on the flute and the clarionet. A small collection of Scottish Songs, etc., was published, with his name, entitled "The Thistle." He was married in August 1832.

Having a strong inclination to try his fortune in America, Robert sailed from Liverpool for Philadelphia in 1844, and resided there for above two years. His principal employment was at his own trade, with occasional engagements at the theatre as a performer on flute and clarionet. In Philadelphia Clark rallied around him a number of young men from his native town, and formed them into a society for instrumental music, under the name of the *Paisley Band*. He was attacked by a severe fever and ague, and, for the recovery of his health, he re-visited his native country in 1846, and entered into business, on his own account, as a broker ; but such a profession did not suit his disposition, and he resolved to return to America. He embarked for New York in the ship Merlin, on the 23d of April 1847. The Merlin is supposed to have been lost on her voyage, and Robert to have perished, with the whole passengers and crew, as no tidings of them ever reached this country.

----

## ROBERT GILFILLAN.

SOME half dozen of years have scarcely elapsed since the former complete edition of " Whistlebinkie " was issued ; yet, during that comparatively brief interval, death has removed several of the sweet singers to whose combined genius its pages are indebted for their choicest effusions. Among others by whose contributions the present work has been enriched, was Robert Gilfillan, a brief outline of whose humble and somewhat uneventful life, compiled from various authentic sources, is here given.

Robert Gilfillan was born on the 7th of July 1798, at Dunfermline, in the county, or, as it is sometimes called, the " Kingdom," of Fife. His parents, who were persons of humble rank in society, were generally respected in their own sphere, for their industry, intelligence, and moral worth. The poet's mother, especially, is represented as having been a woman of more than ordinary endowments. For several years during the boyhood of the future bard his father was rendered unable by ill health to provide in an adequate manner for the necessities of his young and helpless family. In this period of trial, the mother, from whom her gifted son inherited a considerable portion of his intellectual vigour and strong love of independence, exerted herself in the most praiseworthy manner to give her children " a decent upbringing." Hardships and privations there must have been in that

lowly home ; yet, under that admirable mother, they
never ceased to form

"A virtuous household, though exceeding poor."

Of the first twelve years of the poet's life little is
known. When a mere child, we are told by one who
knew him well in after days, Robert toiled manfully to
assist his mother. His aid was needed to swell the
family store, and the boy rendered it ungrudgingly.
While other children of his age were at school, or sport-
ing themselves over the sunny braes, he was already
engaged in the serious struggle of existence ; yet was he
not a stranger to the 'enjoyments which, happily, even
under the most adverse circumstances, are incident to the
morning of life. At a very early age he began to practise
the art of song-writing ; and it is related, that when
engaged on one occasion during the Christmas holidays,
in a *guising* excursion, he sang some verses which he
had written on the death of Abercromby with so much
effect, as to win unprecedented supplies of "bawbees
and blauds o' bread and cheese" from the guidwives of
Dunfermline.

In 1811, when only thirteen years of age, Robert
Gilfillan left his native town to serve an apprenticeship
in Leith as a cooper. To this handicraft, however, he
seems never to have taken kindly ; yet he faithfully fulfilled his engagement, punctually giving his earnings from
week to week to his beloved mother, and enlivening his
leisure hours by the composition of poetry and the practice of music on a "one-keyed flute," which he purchased with a small sum of money which he found one
morning while passing along an obscure street in Leith.
The song of "Again let's hail the cheering Spring,"
according to a manuscript journal of the poet, was one
of the early effusions of this period ; while "The yellow-
haired laddie," as we learn from a passage in one of his
letters, was among the first airs that he learned upon the
flute, "*under his own tuition.*"

At the termination of his apprenticeship, Mr. Gilfillan, then in his twentieth year, returned to Dunfermline, where he was engaged for nearly three years as shopman in a grocery establishment. During this period he formed the acquaintance of a number of young men, possessed, like himself, of literary tastes, who held occasional meetings for mutual improvement in literature, science, and art. At the sederunts of this congenial society, the productions of the poet were either read or chanted; while they were, at the same time, subjected to a friendly criticism. This period, the poet frequently remarked, was the happiest in his life.

Mr. Gilfillan afterwards returned to Leith, where he filled, for many years, the responsible situation of clerk to Mr. M'Ritchie, an extensive wine merchant. While fulfilling the duties of this office, to the satisfaction of his employer, he found time also to keep up an intimate correspondence with the Muses. His songs, through the medium of newspapers and magazines, gradually attracted public attention and admiration. At length, in the year 1831, he was induced by the solicitations of his friends, and his now numerous admirers, to publish a collection of his productions. The volume, which was entitled "Original Songs," contained about a hundred and fifty pages. It was dedicated to Allan Cunningham, and was received by the public in an exceedingly favourable manner. Encouraged by the success of this, his first literary venture, Mr. Gilfillan subsequently published, in 1835, another and enlarged edition, containing fifty additional songs. Soon after this volume saw the light, he was entertained at a public dinner in Edinburgh, at which Mr. Peter M'Leod, who had composed the music to some of his finest songs, presided as chairman.

In the year 1837 Mr. Gilfillan was appointed Collector of Police Rates at Leith, an office which he continued to occupy until the period of his death. In the same year, on the motion of Sir Thomas Dick Lauder, he was installed as Grand Bard to the Grand Lodge of Free Masons in Scotland.

He also contributed a number of poetical pieces to the pages of the *Dublin University Magazine*, and other periodical works ; while, for the lengthened period of twenty years, he wrote the principal portion of the Leith news for the *Scotsman*, besides enriching the columns of that and other journals with original communications in prose and verse.

In 1850 Mr. Gilfillan and others, who regretted to see the dilapidated condition into which the monument had fallen, which was erected to the poet Fergusson in the Canongate churchyard, by Robert Burns, originated a subscription for the purpose of having it put into a proper state of repair. The appeal was liberally responded to, and the monument was effectually repaired. On Monday, the 2d of December 1850, he attended a dinner of the Grand Lodge of Scotland, where he sang several of his own songs, and appeared in his ordinary health and spirits. Next day he was slightly unwell, but was able to take a walk in the open air. On Wednesday morning, however, shortly after he had risen from bed, he was seized with a violent fit of apoplexy. Medical aid was immediately called, and he subsequently rallied so far as to be able to converse. A second fit then supervened, and in the forenoon of that day the poet was no more. He died in the fifty-second year of his age. His remains were accompanied by a numerous and highly respectable company to the place of sepulture, in the churchyard of South Leith, where an appropriate monument, erected by public subscription, has since been placed, to mark the spot where his earthly remains are deposited.

His own songs, although neither gifted with a voice of great compass or power, he always sung with a degree of feeling and taste which seldom failed to charm, and which caused his society to be courted on convivial occasions to an extent far beyond what the dictates of prudence would justify. The mistaken, or it may be selfish, hospitalities of those who call themselves friends and admirers, have too often been the medium of destruction to the poet, who might well exclaim, in answer to the courtesies of such parties, with the frog in the fable, "What is sport to you is death to us."

Among the song-writers of his country, Robert Gilfillan is undoubtedly entitled to an honourable position. His effusions are uniformly pervaded by tenderness of feeling, appropriateness of imagery, and that genuine simplicity of expression which forms one of the principal elements of lyrical success. He has not the vigorous passion and manly energy of a Burns, nor the descriptive truthfulness and freshness of feeling which are so sweetly combined in a Tannahill, but his verses are ever musical and soft, while he has touched, in various instances, on chords which had escaped the ken of his great predecessors in the art of song. "Why left I my hame?" a strain which is indeed full of pathos, at once found its way to the popular heart ; while the "Happy days of youth," "Fare-thee-well, for I must leave thee," "Peter M'Craw," and many other productions of his genius, are characterised by merits of a high order, and have already attained a place among the lays which the world "will not willingly let die."

### LAMENT FOR ROBERT GILFILLAN.

O Mourn, Scotland, mourn, for thy sweet poet gane ;
Thy children, far distant, shall swell the sad strain ;
By hearth and by homestead, in cottage and ha',
Are lorn hearts deploring poor Robin awa'.

Where glen-burnies wimple, where hill-torrents flow,
Where gowden whins blossom, and strong thistles grow,
Where merles greet the gloamin', and larks hail the daw',
They've lost their fond lover, poor Robin awa'.

Old age totters feebly, and youth paces slow,
They linger, to mourn o'er their bard lying low,
While angel tears hallow the turf, as they fa'
Frae beauty's eyes streaming, for Robin awa'.

O gen al the feeling his mem'ry imparts,
For deeply his lyrics are shrined in our hearts,
And rich as the fragrance when southlan' winds blaw,
The flower posie left us by Robin awa'.

JAMES BALLANTINE.

## JOHN IMLAH.

JOHN IMLAH was born in North Street, Aberdeen, about
the end of the year 1799. He was the youngest of seven
successive sons—a circumstance which he used jocularly
to boast of, as conferring on him, according to the old
freet, supernatural powers of some sort or other ; although
what they were "he could not undertake to say." His
parentage was respectable—the Imlahs having been
farmers for several generations in the parish of Fyvie ;
and the poet's father, although only a publican, or rather
a country innkeeper, must have been a man of some
standing and influence, as he enjoyed the title, and
exercised the authority of Bailie of Cuminestone, a popu-
lous village, where his house long continued to be known
as "the bailie's house." Nor after his removal to Aberdeen, which took place at Whitsunday 1798, could the
Bailie have been in straitened circumstances, for he
brought up the four of his seven sons who lived to man-
hood in a comfortable way ; and John, at least, had the
advantage of a pretty fair education, including attendance
for a year or two at the grammar school. Ultimately,
however, he had to abandon his literary studies, for
which he evinced both liking and capacity, and betake
himself, as his brothers had done before, to a trade. He
was apprenticed to Mr. Allan, a pianoforte maker, to
learn the higher, or finishing branches of the business ;
but he was soon removed from the bench altogether.
Having given evidence of the possession of a good musical
ear, his master initiated him into the mysteries of tuning,
at which he speedily became an adept. On leaving Mr.

Allan, he proceeded to London, where his qualifications procured him almost immediate employment ; and in the course of a few years he entered into an engagement with the leading firm, Broadwood and Co., which lasted till he left this country to visit his brothers, and would probably have been renewed again had he lived to return. His connection with the Broadwoods was on the whole a very agreeable one, and suited well his character and tastes. During the season, or rather, from the beginning of the year to the middle of June, he performed the duties of a regular town and house tuner, on a fixed salary ; and from June to December he was allowed to travel in the north-east of Scotland, working on his own account, and eking out his income by an occasional commission on the sale of a piano.

Mr. Imlah spent his five or six months in Scotland in a pleasant roving manner. There is hardly a town between Edinburgh and Inverness, where he had not a circle of attached friends, who were always delighted to see him ; then he was a welcome guest when he appeared professionally at the mansions of the nobility and gentry ; and, to crown all, he had a host of cousins and second cousins in the parish of Methlic, near Aberdeen, on whom he delighted to lavish the strong natural feelings which he had no other outlet for—being an orphan and a bachelor, and the only two of his brothers who were in life having emigrated to distant climes so long before that he had but a faint impression of having ever seen them.

Mr. Imlah was perhaps better known and more generally liked than any other person in the same sphere of life. His lively and social disposition, based on intelligence, uprightness, a nice sense of honour, a real goodness of heart, made him a general favourite with all classes. His claims as a poet can be judged of by the specimens in this work. He published two volumes, and was a regular contributor to the newspapers of his native town. Some of his sweet and simple lyrics have

been set to music by eminent composers, and have been
sung occasionally by our most distinguished Scottish
vocalists.

Mr. Imlah possessed a great deal of nationality —
nationality of the right kind ; not the ignorant assump-
tion of undue superiority, but a rational apprehension of
the real excellences of the character and position of the
people to whom he belonged.   In England he was ever
foremost to defend Scotland and Scottish habits from
prejudiced assailants ; while in Scotland, on the other
hand, he was equally ready to point out our short-
comings, and wherein we might advantageously take
lessons from our southern neighbours.   To all the metro-
politan associations established for the benefit of his
poorer countrymen, he was, according to his means, a
cheerful and liberal contributor ; and, in his private
capacity, he was never found wanting when the claims
of the needy, the unfortunate, or unrequited merit, came
before him.

Mr. Imlah was cut off prematurely, in the vigour of life,
while performing a duty of affection which he had long
looked forward to with a mixture of melancholy and plea-
surable anticipations.   His two remaining brothers—the
one resident in Nova Scotia, the other in the West Indies
—had been separated from him for a period of thirty years.
At length an opportunity occurred of meeting them together at Halifax.   After a joyful, and, to him, most com-
plimentary, parting with his friends in London, he set sail,
and had a delightful meeting with his relations.   He
spent some time in Nova Scotia, and then accompanied
one of his brothers and a nephew to Jamaica, where,
after a brief period of enjoyment he fell a victim to the
fatal disease of the island.   He died on the 9th of
January 1846, having just entered his forty-eighth year.
The *Cornwall* (Jamaica) *Chronicle* paid a just tribute to
his memory ; and we think we cannot better conclude
our brief notice, than by quoting the opinion which only
a short intimacy enabled our Colonial brethren to form

of Mr. Imlah. The *Chronicle* says, "He is deeply lamented by his relations and friends, and sincerely regretted by a numerous circle of acquaintances. He was a man of unaffected manners and great singleness of heart, who, to a lively imagination and versatile talent, added a ready store of general knowledge, which rendered his society very acceptable to those whose congeniality of mind led them to similar pursuits. He died in Christian hope and resignation, and, we trust, in an odour of mind which dictated, in one of his sacred poems, the following lines :—

" ' O, dark would be this vale of tears—more dark this vale of death—
Had we no hope through Godward thoughts — no saving trust
    through faith ;
Where tear shall never dim the eye, nor sob disturb the heart,
Where meet the holy and the just, and never more to part.' "

---

## WILLIAM FINLAY.

WILLIAM FINLAY was born at Paisley in the year 1792. At an early age he attended Bell's school, at that time a well-known seminary in the town, and, subsequently, the Grammar School, where, under Mr. Peddie, he made such progress, that at nine years of age he could read and translate Cæsar with facility. Bred to the loom, he was for twenty years a Paisley weaver. Leaving that trade, he wrought for some time afterwards as a pattern setter, or "flower lasher," as it is locally termed. About the year 1840 he obtained employment in the office of Mr. Neilson, printer, Paisley. He next removed to Duntocher, where he resided and filled a situation for a short period. Finally, he was employed by Mr. Stirrat, bleacher, Nethercraigs, at the base of Gleniffer Braes, about two miles to the south of Paisley. He died of fever on the 5th of November 1847, and was interred in the Paisley Cemetery on the 9th of the same month.

Such are the leading facts in the outer history of William Finlay. The character of the inner man may be gathered from his writings ; at least, it is very correctly and intelligibly indicated there.

While yet a young man, working at the loom, he became known among circles of his townsmen as a writer of verses. Some of his productions of this era, about 1812 or 1813, are lively and humorous pictures of scenes which came under his notice, with, here and there, graphic sketches of character and strokes of satire indicative of the powers which his after life developed. A few years later, about 1819 and 1820, during what is known in Paisley as the "radical time," he published some political verses, which, having a leaning to the popular side, caused him to be regarded with suspicion by those whose sympathies were all on the side of arbitrary power. Finlay, however, was no rabid or dangerous radical in politics at any time, and as he advanced in life, he became rather conservative in his views.

In course of time, Finlay became generally known as a pretty successful writer of humorous and satirical verses. As a satirist, he possessed considerable abilities ; and, although this was only one of the phases of his character, and, perhaps, not the most important, it was the one in which, from his frequent appearances in it, he was most familiar to his townsmen during his lifetime.

Numerous efforts of our author, made with little study, and under many disadvantages, indicate that, had he been in a position to cultivate his natural abilities, and to look abroad for themes of more general interest, he might have taken high rank as a satirist. It says much for the goodness of his heart and the soundness of his judgment, that, although he frequently and freely wielded the satiric pen, and set the whole community a laughing, he seldom, if ever, incurred the enmity of those of whom he wrote. His satire was never savage : it was always tempered with humanity ; and there was a drollery about it which even its victims could scarcely resist.

Some of the most agreeable of his productions are those in which there is a mixture of the descriptive, the humorous, and the kindly, mellowed here and there with the pathetic, and delicately spiced with the satirical.   " The Widow's Excuse," " My Auld Uncle John," and other specimens of this union, will occur to the reader.

In reality, it was in pathos, more than in satire or humour, that William Finlay's true strength lay.   Calls were constantly made on him by friends of one kind and another to be satirical and humorous, and to these calls his good nature, his ever ready perception of the ludicrous, and other reasons, induced him to respond.   His soul, left to its own breathings, however, like an Æolian harp to commune with the wind, gave utterance to tender, melancholy strains, descriptive of the blight of sickness, sorrow, and misfortune, or of the ever recurring visits of the angel of death to the struggling sons of clay.   His mind, although by no means gloomy, was always sensitive, and tenderly appreciated the griefs and sufferings to which mortality is subject.   On looking over his collected works, one cannot help being struck by the many sorrowful vicissitudes which have presented themselves to him, and which he has recorded.   The Destroyer, in stern reality, visited him.   He was practically "acquainted with grief."   It devolved on him to lay his wife and four of his children in their graves ; and, in the course of his life, he was called on to mourn the melancholy departure of many relatives and esteemed friends.   Every stanza which he composed on such a subject may be regarded as a veritable inscription over the grave of a lost one, little known to the world perhaps, but known, and loved, and lamented by him.   In these grave productions of his there is much simple and true pathos, calculated to surprise those who have only known him in his humorous and satirical effusions.   What may equally surprise such people, is his intimate acquaintance with, and strikingly appropriate employment of, the solemn language of Scripture.   Few could employ Bible language so effectively. Sometimes he uses little else, just connecting Scripture phrases by a few words of his own, and yet avoiding all appearance of forcing quotations into his service. Partly from temperament, and partly from early education, whatever superficial observers might think, strata of religious principle, feeling, and knowledge, formed no inconsiderable portions of his strangely mixed character.

It can scarcely have escaped the notice of any one who has looked into his writings, that these, in many instances, especially among his songs, are characterised by the most comical association of incongruities, producing very ludicrous effects. A glance at " Joseph Tuck," " Bankrupt and Creditors," etc., will illustrate this remark. This peculiarity is suggestive of his own character, which was, to some extent, a contradictory mixture, not only of grave and gay, of lively and severe, but of strength and weakness, of wisdom and folly. Like many other men of intellectual abilities and genial disposition, he wanted inflexibility of purpose, and that " prudent, cautious self-control," which, according to Burns, " is wisdom's root." Yielding to the fascinations of conviviality, he sometimes fell into excesses which no one deplored more sincerely than himself. In taking remorseful retrospects of his conduct, as he always did on such occasions, he sometimes described the exercise as looking down his own throat. Frequent and touching allusions to the sin which most easily beset him, occur in his writings. Unfortunately, the reflections which the glass produced were almost as readily effaced from his memory as in the case of the apostle James's man, who it will be remembered, after beholding himself in a *glass*, went away and straightway forgot what manner of man he was.

For the last year of Finlay's life, however—during his residence at Nethercraigs, amidst the fresh breezes, the dewy fields, the waving foliage, and the gushing streams of the country, he had completely abandoned the bottle, with all its associations, and had become temperate and

cheerful as a skylark. Poor fellow! cold water was, in
one respect, the death of him ; for during a quiet nocturnal
walk, he accidentally fell into a pond or reservoir, where
he was thoroughly drenched, and, neglecting to change
his clothes immediately afterward, a fever was induced,
which carried him off.

In his demeanour, William Finlay was very modest
and unassuming, and without a particle of affectation.
With a generally well-informed mind, a lively and playful
fancy, a sharp and ready wit, a productive vein of
humour, imperturbable good nature, and great warmth of
heart, he was a decided favourite with all who knew him.
His time and talents were perhaps too freely drawn on
by his friends ; and, although he employed them in
what he found to be agreeable occupations, these occupations must have interfered to some extent with the
other and necessary pursuits of a working man. That
he sometimes felt this to be the case, is evident from
what he has left on record ;—

> " While others have been busy, bustling
>     After wealth and fame,
> And wisely adding house to house,
>     And Baillie to their name,
> I, like a thoughtless prodigal,
>     Have wasted precious time,
> And followed lying vanities
>     To string them up in rhyme."

He contributed to the poet's corner of the *Paisley
Advertiser* for a series of years, and a great variety of
his effusions reached the public through other channels.
About the beginning of 1846 a good many of his best
pieces were collected and published at Paisley, in a
volume[1] dedicated to his friend Mr. Matthew Barr.

[1] "Poems, Humorous and Sentimental," by William Finlay.
Paisley, Murray and Stewart and William Wotherspoon, 1846.

## GEORGE DONALD.

GEORGE DONALD, author of nearly a dozen Songs in the Nursery portion of Whistlebinkie, was born in Calton of Glasgow, in January 1800. His parental ancestors belonged to the Western Highlands. At the period of the birth of the subject of this memoir his father was what is called a tenter in one of the power-loom factories in the Calton.

Alexander Crum, Esq., founder of the highly respected family of that name, so justly esteemed in Glasgow, engaged the poet's father, on the recommendation of the late Mr. Bartholomew, to whom he had woven for twenty years, to go to Thornlie Bank, in 1808.

The Factory Act was not then in existence, and he would have been thought a visionary enthusiast who would have attempted to limit the hours of labour, or the age at which young persons should be allowed to enter public factories. It is painful to contemplate a youth possessed of the tender sensibilities which distinguish those of a poetic temperament—often, also, not the most robust constitution—subjected as George was, at the early age of eight years, to the long hours which regulated these works, from six in the morning till eight in the evening six days of the week, with an interval of an hour and a half for both meals.

Having observed the eager desire which our poet began to manifest for reading, the manager of the factory very kindly allowed him to attend school for two hours each day. He had only received, previously, some elementary instruction at a school in Glasgow, taught by an old woman. By dint of close application to his favourite pursuits, he succeeded in gaining a knowledge of English and geography ; he also attained a knowledge of the rudiments of the Latin language, under the tuition of Mr. Robert Lochtie, who taught a school in the village, and who, besides, assisted and directed the studies of his young pupil.

During the period of what may well be remembered, and called the Radical rebellion, George Donald found ample scope for his poetic talent. He was an ardent advocate for civil and religious liberty. Many of his pieces, contributed to the liberal political journals of the day, show how earnestly he advocated the divine origin of liberty as the common birthright of man. His contributions to these journals were the means of introducing him to some of the leaders of the political circles of Glasgow. This acquaintanceship may be said to have been the first step that led to those consequences which were the source of his subsequent misfortunes.

In 1825 George married Mary Wallace, who was employed at Thornlie Bank with himself. In consequence of the extreme depression of trade in 1826—a year well remembered by many then engaged in commercial pursuits, in their after days—the works at Thornlie Bank were closed, and those who had been engaged at them were obliged to seek employment elsewhere.

The subject of our memoir was engaged to act as manager of a factory in the neighbourhood of Belfast; but his stay there did not much exceed a twelvemonth. He returned to Scotland in 1831, and rented a small house at the Townhead of Glasgow, and from this period, George Donald's moral descent, forgetfulness of what he owed to himself and to his family, was irremediable and rapid.

His literary and political acquaintanceships were renewed. He became a member of a political club; and the important discussions, as its members considered them, were continued till late hours, and deep libations from the inebriating bowl wound up the proceedings. For a time be attended his work and his family, but the moral poison had infected him, and very soon completed his ruin. His family became completely neglected; and, though his helpmate struggled night and day to maintain herself and family—which consisted of a son and two daughters—and employed all those means which a dutiful and affectionate wife never fails to do, to win back the partner of her life from dissipation, it was all in vain.

We quote, from a popular work of the day, a case similar to that of Mrs. Donald :—" She paced the floor of her lonely apartment with painful anxiety. Her children asleep—no living to share her woes, or sound to break the midnight silence, save the melancholy click of the old wooden clock, which might have made the lonely woman imagine that she held her finger on the wrist of old Time, and felt the pulsations which denoted his rapid progress towards the limits ' No longer ;' and as each large division in the circle of his steps had been passed over, the rusty machinery gave an alarm, as if shuddering at its own progress, and sounded the knell, delivering over another passage of Time ' To the years beyond the flood.' One struck— two followed—and still the death-like silence prevailed within the humble dwelling. Oh ! ye riotous drunkards, whose throats are as if they were parched by blasts from hell ! how many hearts are withering to death under your cold neglect ? how many tender shoots, introduced by you into this bleak world, are thus left to sicken and die ?"

He became, like his brother and contemporary, Sandy Rodger, connected with a radical newspaper started at this time, entitled the *Liberator*, which had a brief existence of some eighteen months. In this office Donald's habits may be said to have been thoroughly ruined, and those of Rodger far from being improved, besides losing a considerable sum of money, the contributions of his friends, in this slough of despond.

Our poet returned to work at his usual employment, but that had lost all its charms for him. Not though a weeping wife and helpless children mourned, could the hapless son of the muses be restrained from carousing with his boon companions. After using every endeavour to reclaim him, despair took hold of Mrs. Donald's heart, and in 1836 she abandoned him, taking her family with her to Thornlie Bank, where, under her mother's roof, she found shelter. Some have considered this as a hasty step, and that she ought to have continued with her husband, and persevered in her efforts to reclaim him ; But it is far easier to blame than to bear. Had she been alone, the case would have been different, but these children had to be cared for, and that by the mother alone. The arm on which she and her children looked to under Providence for support had become morally paralysed. The result, we think, showed the course she took was the right one, for, instead of being struck with sorrow and shame for the cause of this abandonment, and resolution to retrace his steps, he plunged deeper and deeper in the vice that had become his master, and, as the Proverbs say, "He was holden in the cords of his own sin." No doubt he had, as all drunkards have, repentant fits, and abstained from indulgence for a time, but these passed away, verifying the passage of Sacred Writ.

Donald, after this crisis, was driven hither and thither like stubble in the whirlwind, the march downwards doubly accelerated. He made a journey to America, but soon returned to his native country not much improved by his travels. Up to the period of his last illness, he continued to write both prose and verse for the journals of the day. He published "The Lays of the Covenanters," a work worthy of his name, but from which he derived very little pecuniary return. One of these Lays appeared in the *Banner of Ulster*. When Dr. Chalmers happened to be in Belfast, and "the Lays" came under his eye, he was much pleased with them, and sent, by the hand of a friend, a guinea to the author—a great boon to him at the time.

Some of Donald's happiest efforts may be seen in the

pieces he contributed to the little popular work, "Songs for the Nursery." There are ten songs of his in that collection, and the reader of critical taste for the felicitous expression of our Scottish idiom, and domestic sympathies and feelings, will not fail to say that George Donald is entitled, with Miller, Ballantine, Smart, Rodger, etc. etc., to the compliment paid to them by Lord Jeffrey.

During part of his last days Donald was employed in the office of the *Glasgow Examiner*, under Mr. Smith, who was very kind to him. A cold which he caught in 1850 settled down on his chest, and in 1851 it assumed such a serious aspect that he was advised to go into the Royal Infirmary; but his family, whose eyes watched, though unobserved, his melancholy career, took him home to Thornlie Bank, and had medical skill and nursing applied to his disease, but in vain. His lips were sealed by death 7th December 1851.

Thus passed away a hapless gifted child of song, the last passages of whose melancholy life give a fearful admonition to the tuneful tribe who come after him. In one of his notes to a gentleman who gave him assistance sometimes, he says, "My thoughts at times are fearful : may God forgive and protect me." In another "I am shoeless and shirtless, and cannot write for the cold." We consider it necessary to quote these distressing passages from his correspondence, to serve as a warning to others to beware of the Poets' slaughter-house—the Tavern.

***

## ROBERT L. MALONE.

ROBERT L. MALONE was born in Anstruther, Fife, about the year 1812, and was a younger member of a family of seven daughters and six sons, most of whom died in infancy. His father was a captain in the Royal Navy, and latterly held a command in the Coast Guard Service.

His mother was a Rothesay lady, in which town his father ultimately settled down on half-pay, but died when Robert was a child of five years of age. At fourteen, after acquiring a mere rudimental education, Robert entered the Navy, and served for three years on board the gun-brig "Marshall," Lieutenant M'Kirdy, long known in the west of Scotland in connection with the Fisheries service. He then served some time in the Mediterranean, and also in South America, on board the well-known ship Rattlesnake. At the end of ten years, declining health forced him to quit the service, and join his family at Rothesay. The fine air of that salubrious locality had a beneficial effect on him, and he rallied, but, being naturally of a delicate constitution, he never attained to anything like vigour. He had all his life been a lover of poetry, and especially that of his native land ; but it was during the solitary hours which a delicate state of health imposed on him, that he was led to give his thoughts an embodiment in song. His mode of life hitherto had given a turn to his mind and his musings, and the latter found vent in his principal poem of " The Sailor's Dream," which is full of rich imagery. " The Sailor's Funeral" is another effusion in which his early associations are evoked.

In 1836 he came along with his family to reside in Greenock, where he passed his time in quiet and unobtrusive wanderings among the fine scenery of Inverkip vale, no doubt maturing his poetical aspirations, and husbanding the portion of health which he yet retained. In 1845 he published a volume of poems, which was largely patronised, and justly appreciated, gaining him many friends. Before this time, however, he had contributed some good songs to this work. About the end of the same year he obtained a situation as a clerk in the Long-room of Her Majesty's Customs at Greenock ; and here he remained, highly esteemed, till about the middle of June 1850, when he was compelled to abandon his duties ; and on the 6th of July, three weeks afterwards, he died, in his thirty-eighth year, regretted by all who knew him, and admired and esteemed, not more for his writings than for his extreme modesty, and quiet, agreeable, retiring, and obliging disposition. His remains rest in Greenock cemetery, a locality around which he so often delighted to wander. Though so long a period of his short life was spent on shipboard, he ever delighted to dwell

> "'Mid nature's guileless joys."

Every line he has written is the emanation of a mind imbued with a keen and careful perception of all that is lofty and pure. His predilection for the muse did not lead him to neglect the more austere duties of his office— he wrote little and published less from the date of his appointment.

## WILLIAM THOM.

WILLIAM THOM was born in a house in Sinclair's Close, Justice Fort, Aberdeen, about the end of 1788 or the beginning of 1789. His father was a merchant, but died soon, and left his mother so poor that the only education she could afford her son was a short attendance at a dame's school, which, however, he seems to have improved well enough to enable him to make what he learned there the foundation for some self-tuition afterwards. At an early age he was bound apprentice to the firm of Bryce and Young, cotton manufacturers, Lower Denburn, where he distinguished himself more by his smart repartees, his audacious abuse of bigger and stronger shopmates, and his success among the female weavers, than by his skill or industry, although undoubtedly he mastered sufficiently the mysteries of his craft. He was possessed from his boyhood of a wonderful "gift of the gab," which served him well both in putting down men, and gaining over women. Original lameness from a deformed foot had been increased by an

accident, and when his sarcastic remarks were likely to
get him "a thrashing," he pawkily contrived to escape by
exclaiming, "You coward, wad ye strike a cripple?" It
is suspected that he did not always get so easily out of
the scrapes which his smooth tongue brought him into
with the gentler sex. Although short in stature, and
deformed, he could boast more conquests than the tallest
man in the factory; and it is a fact that to the end of
his days he possessed the power—however sparingly he
may have used it—of fascinating both men and women
by his conversation. He used to remark jocularly, that
the true road to success was to indulge in a sort of mys-
terious verbiage, which neither the speaker nor the listener
could understand, for that women were like seals, which
the sailors had first to astonish and then secure.

About 1817 the firm of Bryce and Young was dissolved,
and Thom, along with a number of his fellow-workmen,
went to the large weaving-factory of Gordon, Baron and
Co., where he worked for ten years, enjoying all the
time much celebrity as a boon companion. He played
the flute admirably—he sang well—he produced an
occasional original song—he was always ready with a
speech, comic or serious—and his lively, agreeable, and
shrewd talk, never failed to keep the company alive. It
is needless to say that he was much sought after, and that
the sort of life he was almost forced to lead, contributed
little either to immediate or permanent advantage. A
matrimonial engagement which he had entered into turned
out unfortunately, the fault being, perhaps, to some extent
his own; there was a sort of break-up in the circles
which he frequented; he grew lonely and dull, and, at
length, left Aberdeen for the south. After trying Dundee, he went to live at Newtyle, where he seems to have
passed some years of hard work and domestic happiness
with his Jean. The touching autobiographical episode
which he relates with so much pathos occurred at this
time. Many a reader must have wept over the tale of
utter destitution—the pawning of the last article of value

—the purchase of the small pack—the death of the child
—the flute-playing for money—and all the other details
connected with the wandering portion of the poet's life.
At last, he says, his soul grew sick of the beggar's work,
and times getting a little better, he settled down to his
loom. In January 1840 he took up his abode in Inverury, for the sake of getting the better pay of what is
called "customer work;" and here his conversational
powers secured for him again a good deal of countenance
and some substantial benefit. Still there seemed no
chance of escape from his lot of toil. But his better star,
though he knew it not, was in the ascendant; and it
shone brightly, but alas, briefly! One of the finest of his
poetical pieces—No. I. of "The Blind Boy's Pranks"—
was forwarded to the *Aberdeen Herald* with a note to
the editor, in which the author, with conscious pride,
stated that if he did not think the poetry good, he
(Thom) pitied his taste. The editor did think it good,
and inserted it in his first publication, with the following
note :—

"These beautiful stanzas are by a Correspondent who
subscribes himself 'a Serf,' and declares that he has
to 'weave fourteen hours of the four-and-twenty.' We
trust his daily toil will soon be abridged, that he may
have more leisure to devote to an art in which he shows
so much natural genius and cultivated taste."—The piece
was copied widely into the newspapers, and in the
columns of the *Aberdeen Journal* met the eye of Mr.
Gordon of Knockespock, who was so much struck with
the beauty and fancy it displayed, that he resolved forth-
with to do something for the author, and began his good
work by sending a five-pound note. This was a most
welcome present to Thom in the middle of winter, and
when his resources were at a very low ebb. He had
found a real Mecænas; for soon afterwards, to use his
own words, 'he and his daughter were dashing it in a
gilded carriage in London, and under the protection and
at the expense of Mr. Gordon, spent four months in

England, visiting and being visited by many of the leading men of the day.' Other friends sprung up, and in
1844 a small volume, entitled 'Rhymes and Recollections,' dedicated to Mrs. Gordon, was published, and
had a good sale. Thom, in the meantime, had returned
to his loom at Inverury, but in the end of the year just
mentioned he went again to London, with the view of
getting out an enlarged edition of his poems, and engaging permanently in some literary employment. He was
most cordially welcomed by a number of enthusiastic
countrymen ; and in February 1845 a grand dinner
was got up to him in the 'Crown and Anchor,' W. J.
Fox, Esq. (now M.P. for Oldham) presiding, and several
men of eminence connected with literature and art form-
ing part of the company. Some delay occurred in the
publication of his second volume, or there can be no doubt
that the favourable impression he produced at that
dinner, and in the private intercourse that ensued, would
have secured a rapid sale. As it was, his fame had
spread abroad in the world. He received from India the
proceeds of a ball got up in his favour, and chiefly
through the exertions of the late Margaret Fuller of the
Tribune, a sum of nearly £150 from New York, in
addition to £300 that had been sent to him before. The
working-classes of London, too, contributed their mite in
honour of the weaver-poet. They got up a meeting for
his benefit in the National Hall, High Holborn, which
was presided over by Dr. Bowring, and proved highly
successful. This was the culminating point of his career.
Dickens, William and Mary Howitt, Forster (*of the
Examiner*), John Robertson (formerly of the *Westminster
Review*), Eliza Cook, his friend Fox, and a host of other
literary celebrities, paid him every attention. Several of
our leading statesmen took an interest in him, and he had
an opportunity of seeing and enjoying all that the best
society in London could produce. He visited Paris at a
later period, along with Mr. Mowatt—a warm-hearted
Scotchman who, for many years, has always had at Tower

Hill a hearty welcome for those of his countrymen who can show any claim to the possession of talent or genius, no matter how humble their circumstances otherwise—and was highly delighted with all he saw. But in London he found parasites, even among the literary class, as well as friends : his pecuniary means melted rapidly away—the delay in the publication of his book prevented it from being so profitable as it might have been—he either did not find suitable literary employment, or did not get paid for it—the temptations of the great city, in some respects, proved too strong for him—he began to lose caste, and fairly lost heart. Starvation was almost staring him in the face, and he resolved to return to Scotland. At this juncture Mr. Fox stood his friend, and partly by private subscriptions, and partly by a grant from the Literary Fund, procured him the means of travelling, with his family, to Dundee.

For the incidents connected with the poet's early life we are indebted to William Anderson, a brother bard in Aberdeen, who has done much to illustrate the scenery and characters of his native town ; to Mr. John Robertson of Lower Thames Street, London, a warm and disinterested friend of Thom's, and a rhymer too, we owe the details of the London visit ; and a kindred spirit in Dundee, Mr. James Scrymgeour, has enabled us to complete our brief sketch by furnishing the following melancholy account of Thom's last days. He had expected, or hoped rather, that his health and spirits would recover if he removed to some spot familiar in former times, and he took up his abode at Hawkhill, a suburban district of Dundee, where he had once worked at the loom ; but he soon discovered, though heartily welcomed, that his was a malady which no change of scene could alleviate or cure—the vital spring was affected, he suffered from the

> "——desolating thought which comes
> Into man's happiest hours and homes,
> Whose melancholy boding flings
> Death's shadow o'er the brightest things.

There were many in Dundee who did all they could to lift the weight from his heart, and dispel the gloom from his countenance, but all in vain. He walked about, as brother poet Gow said, "with his death upon him." He was present at the Watt Institution Anniversary Festival (of 19th Jan. 1848), and was introduced to a large assembly, by the president, Lord Kinnaird. His reception was hearty, but his words were few; he was not at home; the fountains of poetry and pleasure were dried up in him; the zest of life was quite gone. He could neither sit, nor walk, nor read, nor write with any comfort. On the 29th of February he died. On the 3d of March following his remains had the honour of what may be called a public funeral. The town's officers and the guildry officers in their liveries headed the cortège. "Dark ee'd Willie," the poet's son, acted as chief mourner, and the hearse was followed by the provost and many of the principal inhabitants of Dundee. The coffin, when bared, exhibited the letters W. T., aged 59, and amid the sympathies of the crowd was lowered into the earth at a spot where, oftener than once, during his last days, its occupant said he would like to be buried. A warm admirer, Mr. Geo. Lawson of Edinburgh, author of "The Water Lilies," as a farewell tribute of respect, planted the grave with wild flowers, and during the snow-storm of the present year (1853), the writer of this notice having sent to Dundee to make inquiries about the poet's death, received from his correspondent a snowdrop, one of many which had reared their heads in the form of a T over the poet's last resting-place.

We must leave it to the reader to draw his own moral from the sad history of Thom. If he had faults, his merits were not few. The circumstances of his early life were not calculated to give much firmness to his character, and his sudden blaze into notoriety helped perhaps to carry him off his feet a little. But he never lost his fine sensibilities; he could appreciate what was good, and sensible, and just, if he did not always practise it, and he was as generous to others as he was reckless of his own interests.

It only remains to mention that Thom's children, two boys and a girl, are in a fair way of getting on in the world. The oldest son, through the assistance of Mr. Gordon of Knockespock, got a good education, and is now, we believe, a tutor at one of our Scottish Universities ; the second had, through Dr. Bowring, a situation on the Blackwall railway, but left it to go to sea, where he is doing well ; the daughter, a handsome young woman, has gone to Australia.

---

## R. A. SMITH.

SMITH had passed into the spiritual world several years preceding the publication of the first series of this Work, but his name will ever be associated with our national music. The following notice is extracted from "M'Conechy's Life of Motherwell ;"—

" Smith was born at Reading, in Berkshire, in 1779. His father was a native of West Calder, in Lanarkshire, and his mother an Englishwoman of respectable connections. In the year 1773 his father emigrated to England in consequence of the dulness of the silk-weaving trade, but returned to Paisley after an absence of seventeen years, bringing with him his son, whom he intended to educate to the loom. This, however, was found to be impossible. Nature had furnished the lad with the most delicate musical sensibilities, and after an ineffectual struggle with the ruling passion, music became the business of his life. He attained to considerable provincial distinction, and composed original music for the following songs of the poet Tannahill, whose intimate friend he was :—Jessie the Flower o' Dumblane, The Lass of Arranteenie, The Harper of Mull, Langsyne beside the Woodland Burn, Our Bonnie Scots Lads, Despairing Mary,

Wi' waefu' heart and sorrowin' ee, The Maniac's Song,
Poor Tom's Farewell, The Soldier's Widow, and We'll
meet beside the Dusky Glen.

"In 1823 he removed to Edinburgh at the solicitation
of the late Rev. Dr. Andrew Thomson, where he led the
choir of St. George's Church, of which Dr. Thomson
was the incumbent, and where he died in January 1829.
Between him and Motherwell there existed a warm
friendship, arising no doubt from a congeniality of tastes
on many points ; but, on the part of the latter, strength-
ened by a sincere respect for the virtues as well as the
genius of the man. Smith had to contend through life
not only with narrow means and domestic discomfort,
but against the pressure of a constitutional melancholy
which occasionally impaired the vigour of his fine faculties. His real griefs—of which he had a full share—
were, therefore, increased by some that were imaginary ;
and he was obviously accustomed not only to lean upon
the stronger mind of his friend in his moments of depression, but to seek for sympathy in his distress, which, it
is needless to add, was never refused. In November
1826 Smith thus writes to him :—

"'I would have written you long ere this, but have
been prevented by an amount of domestic distress sufficient to drive all romance out of the mind ; and you
must be aware that without a considerable portion of
that delightful commodity no good music can be engen-
dered. To be serious, my dear friend, two of my family,
my eldest daughter and youngest son, are at this moment
lying dangerously ill of the typhus fever. I hope that I
may escape the contagion, but I have sometimes rather
melancholy forebodings ; and in the midst of all this, I
am obliged to sing professionally every day, and mask
my face with smiles to cover the throbbings of a seared
and lonely heart.'

"To this sad effusion Motherwell returned the following characteristic reply :—

"'Your domestic afflictions deeply grieve me. I trust

by this time, however, that your children have mended, and that you are no sufferer by their malady. Kennedy and I have been shedding tears over your calamities, and praying to Heaven that you may have strength of spirit to bear up under such severe dispensations. We both, albeit we have no family afflictions to mourn over, have yet much to irritate and vex us—much, much indeed, to sour the temper and sadden the countenance—but these things must be borne with patiently. It is folly of the worst description to let thought kill us before our time. . . . . I hope to hear from you soon, and to learn that your are in better spirits, and that the causes which have depressed them are happily removed. Kennedy joins me in warm and sincere prayers that this may speedily be the case.'"

The following very characteristic document was found among Motherwell's papers, and its publication may induce our dear friend, James Ballantine, to reconsider the opinion he gave in his otherwise admirable Lectures on Scottish Song, in which he asserted that to be successful as a writer of song, it is necessary that the poet should be able to sing himself ;—

" At Edinburgh, the twentieth day of October, eighteen hundred and twenty-eight years, and within the New Slaughter's Coffee-house there—

" In presence of Mr. R. A. Smith and other gentlemen, who subscribe as witnesses to this document—

" Appeared William Motherwell, who solemnly affirms and declares, that not having been blessed with a voice or ear, he is utterly incapable of singing any song, holy or profane, for the delectation of any compotators. And this is truth.

"WILLIAM MOTHERWELL."

" I, R. A. Smith, of Edinburgh, hereby certify, that having made a trial of the above William Motherwell his singing abilities, I declare that the statement put forth by him is strictly true. And I beg leave to express a hope that this testimonial under my hand may be a means of saving him from persecution in all companies of honest fellows partial to song, for the poor rascal cannot utter a note.

"Given under my hand, place and date first above-mentioned, before these witnesses—Mr. P. Buchan of Peterhead, and Messrs. John Stevenson and Sandy Ramsay, booksellers in Edinburgh—all being at this time quite comfortable, and able with me to form a due appreciation of the musical talent of Turk or Christian.

"R. A. SMITH.

" P. BUCHAN, witness.
" JO. STEVENSON, witness.
" A. RAMSAY, witness.

" P.S.—With feelings of the deepest regrèt I have this evening signed the above document ; but the strict regard I entertain for truth, and the utter abhorrence I have for FICTION, oblige me to set my hand and seal to what is positively a notorious fact.

"R. A. SMITH."

## DAVID ROBERTSON.

DAVID ROBERTSON, the projector and publisher of "Whistle-Binkie," was born in 1795, at the farm of Easter Garden, in the parish of Kippen, Perthshire. His forefathers had been settled there for many generations. Coming to Glasgow in 1810, he served his apprenticeship with William Turnbull, whose premises in the Trongate fronted the Tron Kirk. Mr. Turnbull was one of the old, stately school of booksellers, and his business was a leading one in "the trade" of Glasgow in his day. He died in 1823. Mr. Robertson, who had remained in his employment after completing his indenture, continued the business in partnership with the late

Mr. Thomas Atkinson, a gentleman widely known for his social and literary accomplishments. The co-partnery subsisted for seven years, and in 1830 was dissolved of mutual consent. Mr. Robertson removed to 188 Trongate, which soon became the literary lounge of the city. Here Motherwell, Carrick, Andrew Henderson, William Kennedy, and many other authors and wits were wont to meet and interchange the news and gossip of the day; and during well-nigh a quarter of a century he gathered round him in the same premises not only the local *literati*, but also a circle of congenial acquaintances who, from their social gifts or peculiarities of talent, might deservedly be classed under the designation "Characters." His own innate love and keen appreciation of the humorous and the pathetic, made him a good listener to narrations of either complexion, one bright saying capping another while the conversation lasted, and in this way he came to accumulate an exhaustless store of anecdote and story, which, in congenial company, he was always ready to communicate.

"Whistle-Binkie" was originally published in a small volume, not a fourth of the size of the completed work. It was printed at the celebrated press of Hedderwick and Son, and was edited at first by J. D. Carrick, afterwards under the editorship of Alexander Rodger, it evoked a crowd of poets and poetasters, the plenteousness of the supply running to the extent of a *sixth* series, adapted specially for the young, which appeared under the title of "Songs for the Nursery," and includes many gems which have made the names of James Ballantine, William Millar, and others, famous as lyrists for Scottish childhood. This series attracted the favourable notice of Lord Jeffrey, who, in a letter to Mr. Robertson, wrote of it as follows :—

*Craigcrook, 26th May* 1844.

"In returning you my thanks for your pretty little book of *Nursery Songs*, I cannot resist expressing the great pleasure and *surprise* which I experienced in finding so much *original Genius* in a work ushered in under a title, and in a form, so unpretending.

" There are some merely childish pieces no doubt, some that are rather vulgar, several that are too long and dwell too much on common-places.   But there are more touches of genuine pathos, more felicities of idiomatic expression, more happy poetical images, and above all, more sweet and engaging pictures of what is peculiar in the depth, softness, and thoughtfulness of our *Scotch* domestic affections in this extraordinary little volume than I have met within anything like the same compass since the days of Burns.

" Though I have a due sense of the merits of our Doric dialect, I cannot help thinking that some of your authors have a little caricatured it, and aspired to being more purely Doric than the Dorians themselves.   I doubt at least whether the language in which some of these pieces are composed be now a spoken language among any class of the community, or will appear natural and easy throughout, even to those who perfectly understand it.

" But I have no right (and certainly no inclination) to find fault with a gift for which I feel myself to be much obliged, and from which I have derived so much gratification ; and therefore, wishing and predicting much success to your publication, and to your authors large increase of fame,—I remain, your obliged and faithful servant,

F. Jeffrey."

Whistle-Binkie became, in its way, during the currency of its publication, a museum in which the minor song-writers of Scotland could have the progeny of their muse collected and preserved, and they availed themselves of it to a gratifying extent.   As they wrote in their native Doric, they must have helped in some measure to conserve and fix a language, which, in the changes of modern life, was in danger of passing away from the literature of the country.

Following this poetical contribution to the cherished

vernacular of Scotland, Mr. Robertson issued a prose collection, "The Laird of Logan," which, from a tiny volume grew to the substantial dimensions in which it appeared latterly. Every story offered for insertion in its pages was subjected to a rigid scrutiny, to test its genuineness, humour, and pith. No revived "Joe Millar" was entertained for an instant as a candidate for a place in "the Laird." The book represents the lights and shadows of Scottish wit and humour, and as a collection of original anecdotes, stories, and witty sayings, has probably never been surpassed. Its first editor was John Donald Carrick, but, for the larger portion of its contents, the superintendence of the press devolved on Mr. Robertson, who, besides, was himself the *raconteur* of many of its raciest passages. The publication of these and other volumes illustrative of Scottish life and character caused him to be well known here at home, and wherever Scotsmen are to be found.

In 1837 Mr. Robertson was appointed Her Majesty's bookseller for Glasgow, an honour all the more distinguished, in that he was the first on whom it was conferred, and that it was unsolicited on his part.

It remains to be stated that from his youth up, David Robertson, though an unpretentious, was a pronounced and consistent Christian, taking an active share in the religious and philanthropic work going on around him. He commended his religious beliefs by a pleasant word, a judicious advice, and, according to his means, an open hand for all who sought his help. His wit had the indispensable grain of salt, but not a drop of vitriol. His relations to the song-writers and other authors who came about him were of the most pleasing kind. With them, as in his general social intercourse, he ever comported himself as a Christian gentleman, and obtained on all sides an amount of hearty affection such as falls to the lot of few. Repeatedly during his lifetime, public testimony was borne to the esteem in which he was held by those who knew him longest and best; and after his decease, a number of his friends united in raising to his memory, in Glasgow Necropolis, an obelisk and medallion portrait, with an inscription which may appropriately close this sketch :—

## To the Memory of

### DAVID ROBERTSON,
#### Bookseller, Glasgow.

His kindly nature, approved integrity,
consistent piety, and rare worth
endeared him to numerous friends,
and gained him universal esteem.
A warm-hearted Scotchman,
he keenly relished the national characteristics
in poetic and humorous literature,
and authors in both walks found in him
a genial and generous patron.
As a publisher,
he introduced to the world several volumes
rich in Scottish Song, and
illustrative of native manners, genius, and humour.
His sudden death
cast a shade over a wide circle,
and was mourned as a public loss.
Born at Carden, Perthshire, MDCCXCV
Died at Glasgow MDCCCLIV.

———

Attached friends
raised this monument.

# DISSERTATION ON WHISTLE-BINKIES.

DR. JAMIESON, in defining "Whistle-binkie," thus illustrates the term in its application : "One who attends a penny wedding, but without paying anything, and therefore has no right to take any share of the entertainment ; a mere spectator, who is, as it were, left to sit on a bench by himself, and who, if he pleases, may whistle for his own amusement." If the Doctor's explanation were correct, the race of Whistle-binkies would long ere this have become extinct in the country, as we cannot suppose the treatment he describes much calculated to encourage their growth ; but, as we observe the meaning of the term is only given as understood in Aberdeenshire, we presume he means to avail himself of the County privilege, and retract it when he finds it convenient.

As names in Scotland are held in estimation according to their antiquity and respectable standing, it may not be amiss to inform our readers that the Whistle-binkies in the present day can vie with most names in Europe, not only in a numerical point of view, but also in heraldic importance. It has, however, been alleged, that the Whistle-binkies of the North arose, at first, from what some consider to be rather a low origin ; this, were it true even to the fullest extent, is no disparagement, since the acorn must mingle with the earth before the oak is produced. According to the most pains-taking among our etymologists, the name was first conferred upon one who, in his attendance upon weddings and other convivial occasions, rendered himself so agreeable to the company by his skill in whistling, that he was allowed to sit at the Bink or board, and partake of the good things free of all expense ; an honour, in the early ages of our history, which was only conferred on the highest degree of merit. In process of time, the cognomen of Whistle-binkie, which arose in a rude age, came to be applied to men whose intellectual powers were either put forth in whistling, singing, story-telling, or any other source of amusement that caught the fancy and received the encouragement of their fellow-men, while engaged in their convivial orgies. In the present times the profession is divided into so many castes that we find it no easy task to assign them their proper places. In our endeavour to effect this, however, we shall begin with the sons of the " sock and buskin," with the celebrated Mr. Matthews at their head, whom we take to have been the most renowned Whistle-binkie of his age. In the next rank to the votaries of Thespis, we would place all professional singers who appear at public dinners, and receive the run of their teeth, and a per contra *mair attour* for their attendance. After them comes a class of a more modest description, to whom a dinner ticket is considered a remuneration sufficiently liberal, and whose powers of song, like the captive tenantry of the grove, is poured forth for the slender consideration of seed and water. Though, in these three classes, may be comprised a great proportion of those who are justly entitled to belong to the fraternity of Whistle-binkies, yet there are fractions of the great body-politic which we cannot properly assign to any of the above castes ; some of these we would arrange under the head of amateur Whistle-binkies. This description, though not so numerous, perhaps, as any of the others, are much inclined to consider themselves superior in point of personal respectability to any we have mentioned : this, however, is a point which does not lie with us to decide. Suffice it to say, that an amateur Whistle-binkie is one whose acquaintance is courted on account of his possessing the talents we have described, and whose time is occupied in fulfilling an eternal round of dinner and tea-party engagements, not that his entertainers have any personal regard for his character, but merely because they can make him a useful auxiliary in amusing their friends. Those men who relish this mark of distinction can easily be known by their perpetual attempts to divert, and the delectable expression of conviviality which is ever and anon lighting up their countenances, where may be seen, traced in the legible hand of joyous dame Nature herself, " Dinner, Tea, or Supper parties, attended in town or country, on the shortest notice." There is also another description of the same genus, which may be called hooded Whistle-binkies ; these gents are invited out for the same purpose as the former, but perhaps, from the delicate management of their host, or the obtuseness of their own perceptions, they are prevented from discovering that they are present for a motive. All lions, in our opinion, whether they belong to science, literature, or the arts, if they accept an invitation for the purpose of allowing themselves to be stirred up with the long pole, and shown off for the amusement or gratification of old ladies, young ladies, little masters or misses, come under the denomination we have so often referred to. Even the clergyman who attends a public dinner, and says grace as an equivalent for his ticket, may be considered (with reverence be it spoken) as coming under the designation of a respectable, well-disposed, time-serving Whistle-binkie.

As we do not wish, however, to draw too largely on the patience of our readers, we shall conclude by noticing another set of men, which we have not yet enumerated : these we shall term saucy Whistle-binkies, and to the conduct of two of this class, we may safely aver, the present little publication owes its existence. The case was this :—a much respected friend of ours, whom we shall call Mrs. Petticraw, had a large party about a month ago, to which we, among many others, were invited. The good lady had no resources within herself, and afraid to trust to chance for the amusement of her company, had very considerately invited two noted Whistle-binkies to attend ; the one celebrated for the sweet, chaste, and melodious style in which he warbled forth the sentimental minstrelsy of the day ; and the other equally famed for the fine vein of rich, racy, laugh-exciting humour, which he threw into his songs, which were all as comic in conception, as if they had been genuine castes taken from the interior of the harns-pan of Momus himself. In the prospect of meeting two such worthies, curiosity stood, most ladylike, on tiptoe. She might as well, however, have kept her seat ; neither of the gentlemen made their appearance, and their absence formed an ever-recurring topic of sorrowful remark. Seeing the disappointment which the conduct of these popular favourites occasioned to our kind hostess and her fair friends, the thought struck us, that it would be doing a service to a number of our female acquaintances, and perhaps to the public at the same time, if we could manage to get up a sort of substitute for such saucy Whistle-binkies, in order that—when they happened to be taken ill with the whippertooties or mullygrubs, two complaints to which they, above all other men, are particularly exposed—their absence in any party where they had been invited might not be quite so severely regretted as in the instance we have just noticed. With this view, therefore, and in order to enable every gentle-man and lady to become, to a certain degree, their own Whistle-binkies, we have selected, chiefly from unpublished manuscripts, the following collection of Comic and Senti-mental Songs, which, as we have been particularly careful in excluding all pieces of an indelicate or immoral description, we respectfully present to the notice of the public, confident if it does not excite the smiles of the fair, that the most fastidious among them will never find herself a blush out of pocket by a careful perusal of its pages. J. D. CARRICK.

# WHISTLE-BINKIE

# WHISTLE-BINKIE.

---

## SCOTTISH TEA-PARTY.

Now let's sing how Miss M'Wharty,
T'other evening had a party,
　　To have a cup of tea ;
And how she had collected
All the friends that she respected,
　　All as merry as merry could be.
Dames and damsels came in dozens,
With two-three country cousins,
　　In their lily-whites so gay ;
Just to sit and chitter-chatter,
O'er a cup of scalding water,
　　In the fashion of the day.

(*Spoken in different female voices*). "Dear me, how hae ye
been this lang time, mem?" "Pretty well, I thank ye, mem.
How hae ye been yoursel?" "O mem, I've been vera ill wi' the
rheumatisms, and though I were your tippet, I couldna be fu'er o'
*stitches* than I am ; but whan did ye see Mrs. Pinkerton?" "O
mem, I haena seen her this lang time. Did ye no hear that Mrs.
Pinkerton and I hae had a difference ?" "No, mem, I didna hear.
What was't about, mem?" "I'll tell you what it was about, mem.
I gaed o'er to ca' upon her ae day, and when I gaed in, ye see,
she's sitting feeding the parrot, and I says to her, ' Mrs. Pinkerton,
how d'ye do, mem?' and she never let on she heard me ; and I says
again, ' Mrs. Pinkerton, how d'ye do?' I says, and wi' that she
turns about, and says she, ' Mrs. M'Saunter, I'm really astonished

you should come and ask me how I do, considering the manner you've ridiculed me and my husband in public companies.' ' Mrs. Pinkerton,' quo' I, ' what's that ye mean, mem?' and then she began and gied me a' the ill-mannered abuse you can possibly conceive. And I just says to her, quo' I, ' Mrs. Pinkerton,' quo' I, ' that's no what I cam to hear, and if that's the way ye intend to gae on,' quo' I, ' I wish ye gude morning ;' so I comes awa. Now I'll tell ye what a' this was about. Ye see, it was just about the term time, ye ken, they flitted aboon us, and I gaed up on the term morning to see if they wanted a kettle boiled or anything o' that kind ; and when I gaed in, Mr. Pinkerton, he's sitting in the middle o' the floor, and the barber's shaving him, and the barber had laid a' his face round wi' the *white* saip, and Mr. Pinkerton, ye ken, has a very *red* nose, and the red nose sticking through the white saip just put me in mind o' a *carrot* sticking through a *collyflower;* and I very innocently happened to mention this in a party where I had been dining, and some officious body's gane and tell't Mrs. Pinkerton, and Mrs. Pinkerton's ta'en this *wonderfully* amiss. What d'ye think o' Mrs. Pinks?" "Deed, mem, she's no worth your while ; but did you hear what happened to Mrs. Clapperton the ither day ?" "No, mem. What's happened to her, poor body ?" " I'll tell you that, mem. You see, she was coming down Montrose Street, and she had on a red pelisse and a white muff, and there's a bubbly-jock[1] coming out o' the breweree—and whether the red pelisse had ta'en the beast's eye or no, I dinna ken, but the bubbly-jock rins after Mrs. Clapperton, and Mrs. Clapperton ran, poor body, and the bubbly-jock after her, and in crossing the causey, ye see, her fit slippet, and the muff flew frae her, and there's a cart coming past, and the wheel o' the cart gaes o'er the muff, and ae gentleman rins and lifts Mrs. Clapperton, and anither lifts the muff, and when he looks into the muff, what's there, but a wee bit broken bottle, wi' a wee soup brandy in't ; and the gentlemen fell a looking and laughing to ane anither, and they're gaun about to their dinner parties and their supper parties, and telling about Mrs. Clapperton wi' the bubbly-jock and the bottle o' brandy. Now it's vera ill done o' the gentlemen to do anything o' the kind, for Mrs. Clapperton was just like to drap down wi' perfect vexation, for she's a body o' that kind o' laithfu' kind o' disposition, she would just as soon take aquafortis as she would take brandy in ony clandestine kind o' manner !"

---

[1] Turkey-cock.

Each gemman at his post now,
In handing tea or toast now.
  Is striving to outshine ;
While keen to find a handle
To tip a little scandal,
  The ladies all combine ;
Of this one's dress or carriage,
Or t'other's death or marriage,
  The dear chit chat's kept up ;
While the lady from the table,
Is calling while she's able—
  " Will you have another cup ? "

" Dear me, you're no done, mem—you'll take another cup, mem—take out your spoon." "Oh no, mem, I never take mair than ae cup upon ony occasion." "Toots, sic nonsense." "You may toots awa, but it's true sense, mem. And whan did ye see Mrs. Petticraw, mem?" "Deed, I haena seen her this lang time, and I'm no wanting to see her ; she's a body o' that kind, that just gangs frae house to house gathering clashes, and gets her tea here and her tea there, and tells in your house what she hears in mine, and when she begins, she claver clavers on and on, and the claver just comes frae her as if it cam' aff a *clew*, and there's nae end o' her." "Oh you maun excuse her, poor body, ye ken she's lost a' her *teeth*, and her tongue *wearies* in her mouth wantin' *company*." "Deed they may excuse her that wants her, for it's no me. Oh ! ladies, did ye hear what's happened in Mr. M'Farlane's family? There's an awfu' circumstance happened in that family, Mr. and Mrs. M'Farlane havena spoken to ane anither for this fortnight, and I'll tell you the reason o't. Mrs. M'Farlane, poor body, had lost ane o' her teeth, and she gaed awa to the dentist to get a tooth put in, and the dentist showed her twa-three kinds o' them, and amang the rest he showed her a Waterloo ane, and she thought she would hae a Waterloo ane, poor body. Weel the dentist puts in ane to her, and the tooth's running in her head a' day, and when she gangs to her bed at nicht, as she tells me—but I'm certain she must have been dreaming—just about ane or twa o'clock in the morning, mem, just about ane or twa o'clock in the morning, when she looks out o' her bed, there's a *great lang* sodger standing at the bedside, and quo' she, ' Man, what are ye wanting?' she says. Quo' he, ' Mrs. M'Farlane, that's my tooth that ye've got in your mouth.' ' Your tooth !' quo' she, ' the very tooth that I bought the day at the dentist's?' ' It does

na matter for that,' quo' he, 'I lost it at Waterloo.' 'Ye lost it at
Waterloo, sic nonsense !' Weel wi' that he comes forret to pit his
finger into Mrs. M'Farlane's mouth to tak' the teeth out o' her
mouth, and she gies a snap, and catch'd him by the finger, and he
gied a great screich, and took her a gowf i' the side o' the head, and
that waukened her, and when she waukens, what has she gotten but
Mr. M'Farlane's finger atween her teeth, and him roaring like to
gang out o' his judgment ! ! Noo, Mr. M'Farlane has been gaun
about wi' his thumb in a clout, and looking as surly as a bear, for
he thinks Mrs. M'Farlane had done it out o' spite, because he
wadna let her buy a sofa at a sale the other day ; noo it's vera ill-
done o' Mr. M'Farlane to think onything o' that kind, as if ony
woman would gang and *bite* her ain *flesh* and *blood* if she *kent o't.*"

> Miss M'Wharty, with a smile,
> Asks the ladies to beguile
>     An hour with whist or loo ;
> While old uncle cries "Don't plague us ;
> Bring the toddy and the negus—
>     We'll have a song or two."
> " O dear me, uncle Joseph !
> Pray do not snap one's nose off ;
>     You'll have toddy when your dry,
>     With a little ham and chicken
>     An' some other dainty pickin'
>     For the ladies, by and by."

"Weel, mem, how's your frien' Mrs. Howdyson coming on in thae
times, when there is sae muckle influenza gaun about amang families?" "Mrs. Howdyson ! na, ye maun ask somebody that kens
better about her than I do. I hae na seen Mrs. Howdyson for three
months." "Dear me ! do ye tell me sae ? you that used to be like
twa sisters ! how did sic a wonderfu' change as that come about?'
"'Deed, mem, it was a very silly matter did it a'. Some five months
since, ye see, mem (but ye maunna be speaking about it), Mrs.
Howdyson called on me ae forenoon, and after sitting awhile she
drew a paper parcel out o' her muff ;—'Ye'll no ken what this is?'
said she. 'No,' quo' I, 'it's no very likely.' 'Weel, it's my worthy
husband's satin breeks, that he had on the day we were married ;
and I'm gaun awa' to Miss Gushat to get her to mak' them into a
bonnet for mysel', for I hae a great respect for them on account of
him that's awa'.' Respect ! thinks I to mysel (for about this time

she was spoke o' wi' Deacon Purdie), queer kind o' respect !—trying
to catch a new guidman wi' a bonnet made out o' the auld ane's
breeks !—but I said naething. Weel, twa or three weeks after this
I was taking a walk wi' anither lady, and wha should we meet but
Mrs. Howdyson, wi' a fine, flashy, black satin bonnet on ! So we
stopped, and chatted about the weather and the great mortality
that was in the town, and when shaking hands wi' her at parting,
I, without meaning ony ill, gae a nod at her bonnet, and happened to say, in my thoughtless kind o' way, 'Is that the breeks !'
never mindin' at the time that there was a stranger lady wi'
me. Now, this was maybe wrang in me, but considering our
intimacy, I never dreamed that she had ta'en't amiss—till twa three
Sundays after, I met her gaun to the kirk alang wi' Miss Purdie,
and I happened to hae on ane o' thae new fashionable bonnets—
really, it was an elegant-shaped bonnet ! and trimmed in the most
tasteful and becoming manner—it was, in short, such a bonnet as
ony lady might have been proud to be seen in. Weel, for a' that,
mem, we hadna stood lang before she began on my poor bonnet,
and called it a' the ugly-looking things she could think o', and
advised me to gang hame and change it, for I looked so vulgar and
daftlike in't. At length, I got nettled at her abuse, for I kent it
was a' out o' spite ; ' Mrs. Howdyson,' says I, 'the bonnet may be
baith vulgar and daftlike, as you say, but I'm no half sae vulgar and
daftlike as I wad be, if, like *some folks*, I were gaun to the kirk wi'
a *pair o' auld breeks on my head !*' So, I turns on my heel and left
them ; but though it was the Sabbath-day, I could not help thinking
to mysel—my lady, I trow I've gien you a lozenge to sook that'll
keep you frae sleeping, better than ony confectionery you've ta'en
to the kirk wi' ye this while."

"Weel, ladies, there are some strange kind o' folks to be met with
after a'. I've just been listening to your crack, and it puts me in
mind of a new-married lady I was visiting the ither day. Before
she was married, she was one of the dressiest belles we had about
the town, and as for changing bonnets, you would seldom meet her
twice wi' the same ane on. But now, though she has been little
mair than three months married, she has become one of the most
idle tawpie drabs that ever was seen, and has so many romantic
fancies and stupid conceits about her, that I often canna help pitying
the poor husband. Besides, she kens nae mair about house matters
than if she had never heard o' sic things. She was an only dochter,
you see, and, like the ewe's pet lamb, she got mair *licking* than
*learning*. Just to gie ye an instance o' her management—she told
me she was making preparations for a dinner that her husband was

going to give in a day or twa, and, amang ither things, she said that
he wanted a turkey in ruffles ! 'Turkey in ruffles !' quo' I, 'that's
a queer kind o' dish !' 'Queer as it is, I'll manage it.' 'I would
like to see it,' quo' I. So wi' that, she rings the bell and orders the
servant to bring it ben. Weel, what's this but a turkey ; the
feathers were aff, to be sure, which showed some sma' glimmering
o' sense, but the neck o' the beast was a' done up wi' fine cambric
ruffles ; these were to be ta'en aff, it seems, till it was roasted, and
then it was to get on a' its finery again, so as to appear in full puff
before the company ; and this was what she called a turkey in
ruffles ! 'Dear me !' quo' I, 'this is a way o' *dressing* a turkey I
never saw before—I'm thinking the guidman must have meant
turkey and truffles.'—'Truffles !' cried she, looking like a bewildered
goose, and 'what's truffles in a' the world ?' 'Just look your cookery-
book,' quo' I, 'and you'll find that truffles are no made o' cambric
muslin.' Now, ladies, did you ever hear such ignorance ? but,
better than that, she went on to tell me how she had sent the servant to
the market to buy a hare, to mak soup o't ; 'but,' says she, 'what
do you think the stupid creature did ? instead of a hare, she brought
me twa rabbits ; now, ye ken, mem, rabbits dinna mak guid hare-
soup.' 'No,' quo' I ; '*hare-soup* made o' *rabbits* may be a rare dish,
but it's no to my taste.' 'That's just my opinion ; so, as they're
gay and white in the flesh, I'm thinking just to make a bit veal-pie
o' them :—what do you think o' that for economy ?' 'Excellent,'
quo' I, 'if you can *manage* it.' 'But,' said she, 'I'm to hae a
haggis too, as a novelty to some English gentlemen that are to be
of the party ; now, I'm thinking of having the bag of the haggis
dyed turkey-red ; its a fancy o' my ain, and I think it would
astonish them ; besides, it would cut such a dash on the table !'
'Dash on the table !' quo' I, 'nae doubt it would cut a dash on the
table ;—but wha ever heard o' a turkey-red haggis before ?' Now,
I think, ladies, if my frien' can either make *hare-soup* or a *veal-pie*
out of a pair of *rabbits*, she'll be even a greater genius than Mrs.
Howdyson, wi' her new bonnet made out o' a pair of auld breeks !"

> So thus to sit and chitter chatter
> O'er a cup of scalding water,
>    Is the fashion of the day.

CARRICK.

## THE PARTING.

OH ! is it thus we part,
And thus we say farewell,
As if in neither heart
Affection e'er did dwell !
And is it thus we sunder,
Without or sigh or tear,
As if it were a wonder
We e'er held other dear ?

We part upon the spot,
With cold and clouded brow,
Where first it was our lot
To breathe love's fondest vow !
The vow both then did tender,
Within this hallow'd shade—
That vow, we now surrender ;
Heart-bankrupts both are made !

Thy hand is cold as mine,
As lustreless thine eye ;
Thy bosom gives no sign
That it could ever sigh !
Well, well ! adieu's soon spoken,
'Tis but a parting phrase—
Yet said, I fear heart-broken
We'll live our after-days !

Thine eye no tear will shed,
Mine is as proudly dry ;
But many an aching head
Is ours, before we die ?
From pride we both can borrow—
To part, we both may dare—
But the heart-break of to-morrow,
Nor you nor I can bear !

MOTHERWELL.

## COURTING AND CAUGHT.

My heart was joyous as a summer mead
    All clad in clover,
When first I felt that swimming in my head
    That marks the lover.

The wildest waste a Canaan was to me
    Of milk and honey ;
Farther, I had not learn'd to sipple tea,
    Or count my money.

The future lay before my longing eyes
    In warm perspective,
When straight I set about to exercise
    The right elective.

Sweet Sarah Tims, a killing, cutting thing
    (Who now my lot is),
With eye-lid drooping like the turtle's wing,
    Soon caught my notice.

At first, I felt it was a cramping task
    To pop the question ;
I fear'd the answer I might wish to ask
    Would need digestion.

But, no indeed—my dove was on the wing ;
    I said, " Wilt do it ?"
" I care not," quoth she ; " 'tis a pleasant thing,
    Though one should rue it !"

## THE ROSE OF THE CANONGATE.

There lived a maid in Canongate—
    So say they who have seen her ;
For me, 'tis by report I know,
    For I have seldom been there.

But so report goes on, and says,
  Her father was a Baker ;
And she was courted by a swain
  Who was a Candle-maker.

'Tis said she long had lov'd the youth,
  And lov'd him passing well ;
Till all at once her love grew cold,
  But why, no one could tell !
At first he whin'd, then rav'd, and blam'd
  The fair one's fickle fancies ;
For miss's heart was led astray
  By reading of romances.

She dream'd of lords, of knights, and squires,
  And men of high degree ;
But lords were scarce, and knights were shy,
  So ne'er a joe had she !
Alarm'd at last to see old age
  Was like to overtake her,
She wrote a loving valentine
  Unto the Candle-maker.

" She hoped," she said, " for her disdain
  He did not mean to slight her ;
As she but meant to *snuff* his *flame*,
  To make it *burn* the *brighter !*
You know Love's *taper* must be *trimm'd,*
  To keep it brightly *blazing ;*
And how can that be better done,
  Than by a little *teazing ?*"

He own'd " her arguments were good,
  And *weighty* as a feather ;
But, while in *snuffing,* she had *snuff'd*
  The *flame* out altogether !
And, what was worse, 'twas very plain,
  Her charms were sadly blighted ;
And there was little hope that now
  Love's *taper* could be *lighted.*"

With grief this *billet-doux* she read,
    And, while her heart was bleeding,
Took three-and-ninepence from the till,
    And paid her quarter's reading.
The stings of humbled female pride,
    Embittered every feeling,
And next day poor Miss Rose was found
    Suspended from the ceiling !

Now, ladies all, of every grade,
    I hope you'll here take warning ;
And when you meet with lovers true,
    Please show some more discerning.
You're not aware how much by *scorn*,
    The *flame* of true love suffers ;
Yet, should you think it fit to *snuff*,
    Be *gentle* with the *snuffers*.

CARRICK.

## MO LAOGH GEAL !¹

WILT thou go, mo laogh geal,
Mo laogh geal, mo laogh geal !
Oh, wilt thou go, mo laogh geal !
    And roam the Hielan' mountains?
I'll be kind as kind can be,
I will daut thee tenderlie,
In my plaid or on my knee,
    Amang the Hielan' mountains.
      Oh, wilt thou go, mo laogh geal, etc.

Heather-beds are saft and sweet,
Mo laogh geal, mo laogh geal !
Love and ling will be our meat,
    Amang the Hielan' mountains.

¹ *Mo Laogh Geal*, literally means, My White Calf. This expression, however ludicrous it may seem to the mere English reader, is to the ear of a Highlander replete with the tenderest affection.

And when the sun goes out o' view
O' kisses there will be nae few,
Wi' usqueba and bonnach dhu,
   Amang the Hielan' mountains.
     Oh, wilt thou go, etc.

Neither house nor ha' hae I,
Mo laogh geal, mo laogh geal !
But heather bed and starry sky,
   Amang the Hielan' mountains.
Yet in my lee you'll lye fu snug,
While there is neither flae nor bug,
Shall dare to nip your bonny lug,
   Amang the Hielan' mountains.
     Oh, wilt thou go, etc.

Berries, now by burn and brae,
Mo laogh geal, mo laogh geal !
Are sweet'ning in the simmer ray,
   Amang the Hielan' mountains.
For thee the blackest I will pu',
And if they stain your bonny mou',
I'll bring it to its rosy hue,
   Wi' kisses 'mang the mountain
     Oh, wilt thou go, etc.

Your mither's dozin' at her wheel,
Mo laogh geal, mo laogh geal !
The boatie waits, then let us steal
   Awa to the Hielan' mountains.
Look cross the sea to Brodick Bay,
The moon with silver paves the way,
Let's keep her path, we canna stray,
   'Twill lead us to the mountains.
     Oh, wilt thou go, etc.

CARRICK.

## WEE TAMMIE TWENTY.

Tune—*Gee Wo, Neddy.*

There's Wee Tammie Twenty, the auld tinkler bodie,
Comes here twice a year wi' his creels and his cuddy,
Wi' Nanny his wifie, sae gudgy an' duddy,
It's hard to say whilk is the queerest auld bodie.
   *Chorus*—Sing gee wo, Neddy,
      Heigh ho, Neddy,
      Gee wo, Neddy,
      Gee hup an' gee wo.

He works brass and copper an' a' sic like metals,
Walds broken brass pans, southers auld copper kettles ;
Wi' ilka auld wifie he gossips and tattles,
An' ilka young lassie he coaxes an' pettles.
  Sing gee wo, Neddy, etc.

Fou stievely he clouts up auld broken-wind bellows,
Or mends, wi' brass clasps, broken-ribb'd umbrellas ;
An' sic sangs he can sing, an' sic stories can tell us,—
I trow but Wee Tammie's the king o' guid fellows.
  Sing gee wo, Neddy, etc.

Auld Nan's second-sighted, she sees far and clearly,
Foretells ilka waddin' a towmond or nearly ;
Can tell ilka lad the bit lass he lo'es dearly,
An' gin the bit lassie lo'es him as sincerely.
  Sing gee wo, Neddy, etc.

She tells ilka auld maid she yet may recover ;
She tells ilka gillflirt some slee chiel will move her ;
Ilka dark black-e'ed beauty she spaes a wild rover,
An' ilka blue-e'ed ane, a true-hearted lover.
  Sing gee wo, Neddy, etc.

Ilka wanton young widow she spaes a brave sodger,
Ilka thrifty landlady her best paying lodger,

Ilka fat-legget hen-wife an auld dogin' cadger,
An' ilka yillhouse wife an' auld half-pay gaudger.
 Sing gee wo, Neddy, etc.

At night they get fou in auld Watty Macfluster's,
Whaur a' the young belles sparkle round them like lustres,
An' a' the young beaux gather round them in clusters,
An' mony braw waddin's made up at their musters.
 Sing gee wo, Neddy, etc.

They'd a humph-backit laddie, they ne'er had anither,
Could coax like the faither, an' spae like the mither ;
He'd the craft o' the tane, an' the wit o' the tither,
There ne'er was sic mettle e'er souther'd thegither.
 Sing gee wo, Neddy, etc.

He could spout a' last speeches, could sing a' new ballants,
Could mimic a' tongues, frae the Highlants or Lawlants,
Grew grit wi' the lasses, an' great wi' the callants,
An' a' bodie laugh'd at the wee deilie's talents.
 Sing gee wo, Neddy, etc.

But what think ye the gillie did here the last simmer ?
He ran aff wi' Maggy, the young glaikit limmer,
Syne stole a bit pursie to deck out the kimmer,
An' was sent ower the seas to the felling o' timmer.
 Sing gee wo, Neddy, etc.

[*Slow and with feeling.*]

Nae mair the aul' bodies look hearty an' cheerie,
For the loss o' their callant they're dowie and eerie ;
They canna last lang, for their hearts are sae weary,
An' their lang day o' life closes darksome and dreary.
 Sing gee wo, Neddy, etc.

     JAMES BALLANTINE, Edinburgh.

## A BRITISH SAILOR'S SONG.

A SHIP! a ship! a gallant ship! the foe is on the main!
A ship! a gallant ship; to bear our thunder forth again;
Shall the stripes and stars, or tricolor, in triumph sweep
    the sea,
While the flag of Britain waves aloft, the fearless and the
    free?

Nobly she comes in warlike trim, careering through the
    wave,
The hope, the home, the citadel of Britain and the brave.
Well may the sailor's heart exult, as he gazes on the sight,
To murmur forth his country's name, and think upon her
    might.

How proudly does the footstep rise upon the welcome
    deck,
As if at every pace we trod upon a foeman's neck!
Hurrah! hurrah! let mast and yard before the tempest
    bend,
The sceptre of the deep from us, nor storm nor foe shall
    rend.

Our country's standard floats above, the ocean breeze to
    greet,
And her thunder sleeps in awful quiet beneath our tramp-
    ling feet;
But let a foeman fling abroad the banner of his wrath,
And a moment will awake its roar to sweep him from our
    path!

No foreign tyrant ever through our wooden bulwarks
    broke,
No British bosom ever quailed within our walls of oak;
Let banded foes and angry seas around our ship conspire,
To tread our glorious decks, would turn the coward's
    blood to fire!

Out every reef! let plank, and spar, and rigging crack
    again,
Let a broad belt of snow surround our pathway through
    the main ;
High to the straining top-mast nail the British ensign
    fast—
We may go down, but never yield, and *it* shall sink the
    last.

Our country's cause is in our arms, but her love is in our
    souls,
And by the deep that underneath our bounding vessel
    rolls—
By heaven above, and earth below, to the death for her
    we'll fight ;—
Our Queen and country is the word!—and God defend
    the right !               E. PINKERTON.


## THE FRUIT OF OLD IRELAND.

SOME sing of roast beef, and some sing of kail brose,
And some praise plum-pudding the Englishman's dose ;
Such poets, we think, should be counted our foes
When they name not the fruit of old Ireland—the beauti-
    ful nice Irish fruit.

This sweet little plant is the choicest of fruit,
It grows not on branches, but lies at the root,
So modest and humble, its just at your foot—
The elegant fruit of old Ireland—the beautiful sweet Irish
    fruit.

When evening sets in, Paddy puts on the pot,
To boil the dear praties and serve them up hot ;
His sweet little hearth-stone is then the dear spot
Where you meet with the fruit of old Ireland—the beauti-
    ful nice Irish fruit.

And then he sets out full of praties and love,
To court his own Judy the sweet turtle-dove ;
One would think him inspired by young Cupid above,
But its nought but the fruit of old Ireland—the beautiful
    nice Irish fruit.

For down by her side he so bouldly will sit,
And tell how his heart has been bothered and smit,
Peace or quiet in this world he can ne'er get a bit,
For she's loved like the fruit of old Ireland—the beautiful
    nice Irish fruit.

So the heart of poor Judy is melted like fat,
When thus it's besieged by young flattering Pat,
Och ! he swears that his life is not worth an old hat,
For she's dear as the fruit of old Ireland—the beautiful
    nice Irish fruit.

Have ye e'er been in Ireland, at Dublin or Clare,
Or passed half a night at a wake or a fair ?
Oh ! the beautiful fruit that we often see there,
Is the pride and the glory of Ireland—the elegant nice
    Irish fruit.

If e'er in that country you go to a feast,
Or sit down to dinner with bishop or priest,
Be assured that at table there's one dish at least,
Containing the fruit of old Ireland—the elegant nice Irish
    fruit.

But to sing all the wonders produced by this root,
How it's prized by each man, woman, child, and poor
    brute,
Would require Homer's powers, then, hurra, for the
    fruit,
The beautiful fruit of old Ireland—the elegant nice Irish
    fruit !

## KATE M'LUSKY.

Air—"*St. Patrick was a Gentleman.*"

TALK not of Venus, or the love of any heathen creature,
Of nightingales, or turtle-doves, that bother human
    nature ;
But talk to me, and don't depart from morning till it's
    dusky,
Concerning her who stole my heart, the charming Kate
M'Lusky.
        She's never absent night or day,
            As through the world I wander ;
        And thus I pine my time away,
            Like any gooseless gander.

Oh ! Kitty's eyes are black as jet, her cheeks are red as
    roses,
Her lips with pearls round are set, her ringlets are like
    posies ;
Her praises I could sit and sing, till roaring make me
    husky,
I never, never shall forget the darling Kate M'Lusky !
        She's never absent night or day, etc.

Sweet Kitty, dear ! when first we met, ye were so young
    and simple,
You had a most bewitching step, and on each cheek a
    dimple ;
And then the fragrance of your breath, it was so sweet
    and musky,
Oh, murder ! but she'll be my death, the jewel Kate
M'Lusky,
        She's never absent night or day, etc.

I've wander'd many a weary mile, around the Irish nation,
And hundreds I have made to smile, of the female gene-
    ration ;

But Kitty, she has made me weep, in sorrow's weeds I'll
    busk me—
My heart is broken most complete, with cruel Kate
    M'Lusky.
        She's never absent night or day, etc.

O Kitty ! if ye wont relent, ye will commit a murder,
My ghost will make the jade repent, at midnight I'll dis-
    turb her ;
I'll search me out a great big tree, and hang on't till I'm
    fusty,
That all the gaping world may see I'm killed with Kate
    M'Lusky.
        She's never absent night or day, etc.

Good people all, both great and small, behold my situa-
    tion,
Just kick'd about like some foot-ball, for Kitty's recrea-
    tion ;
Oh ! may the wicked heartless jade be single till she's
    musty,
And at fourscore be still a maid, the unmarried Miss
    M'Lusky.
        Then should she haunt me night and day,
          As through the world I wander ;
        If I be gooseless, folks will say,
          Ould Kate has got no gander.

## JAMIE M'NAB.[1]

GAE find me a match for blythe Jamie M'Nab ;
Ay, find me a match for blythe Jamie M'Nab ;
The best piece o' *stuff* cut frae Nature's ain *wab*,
Is that Prince o' gude fallows—blythe Jamie M'Nab.

In her kindliest mood Madame Nature had been,
When first on this warld Jamie open'd his een,

---

[1] Connected with the *Glasgow Herald* newspaper, and well entitled
to the high praise awarded to him by the poet.

For he ne'er gied a whimper, nor utter'd a sab,
But hame he cam' laughin'—blythe Jamie M'Nab.

In process o' time Jamie grew up apace,
And still play'd the smile on his round honest face,
Except when a tear, like a pure hinny-blab,
Was shed o'er the wretched by Jamie M'Nab.

And Jamie is still just the best o' gude chiels—
Wi' the cheerfu' he laughs, wi' the waefu' he feels ;
And the very last shilling that's left in his fab,
He'll share wi' the needfu'—blythe Jamie M'Nab.

Blythe Jamie M'Nab is sae furthy and free,
While he's cracking wi' you, while he's joking wi' me,
That I ne'er wad wish better than twa hours' confab
Ower a horn o' gude yill wi' blythe Jamie M'Nab.

Blythe Jamie M'Nab is nae thin airy ghaist ;
For he measures an ell-and-twa-thirds round the waist ;
Yet a wittier wag never trod on a slab,
Than that kind-hearted billie—blythe Jamie M'Nab.

Yes, Jamie has *bulk*, yet it damps not his glee,
But his flashes o' fancy come fervid and free ;
As bright frae his brain, as if lively " Queen Mab "
Held nightly communings with Jamie M'Nab.

He tells sic queer stories, and rum funny jokes,
And mak's sic remarks upon a' public folks,
That Time rattles by like a beau in a cab,
While sitting and list'ning to Jamie M'Nab.

I carena for Tory —I carena for Whig—
I mindna your Radical raver a fig ;
But gie me the man that is staunch as a stab
For the rights o' his CASTE, like blythe Jamie M'Nab.

Amang the soft sex, too, he shows a fine taste,
By admiring what's handsome, and lovely and chaste ;

But the lewd tawdry trollop, the tawpie, and drab,
Can never find favour wi' Jamie M'Nab.

Some folks, when they meet you, are wonderfu' fair,
And wad hug you as keen as an auld Norway bear ;
The next time they see you, they're sour as a crab—
That's never the gate wi' blythe Jamie M'Nab.

No !—Jamie is ever the same open wight,
Aye easy, aye pleasant, frae morning till night ;
While ilk man, frae my Lord down to plain simple Hab,
Gets the same salutation frae Jamie M'Nab.

Had mankind at large but the tithe o' his worth,
We then might expect a pure heaven on earth ;
Nae rogues then would fash us wi' *grip* and wi' *grab*,
But a' wad be neebours—like Jamie M'Nab.

Lang, lang hae blythe Jamie and Samuel[1] the sage,
Together sped on to the ripeness of age ;
But "*live by the way*"—(we must needs pick and dab)
Is the motto of Samuel and Jamie M'Nab.

And on may they speed as they've hitherto done,
And lang rin the course they have hitherto run ;
Wi' a pound in their pouch and a watch in their fab ;
Sage Samuel the sonsy—blythe Jamie M'Nab.

Yes—lang may the SONSY GUDEMAN o' the *Herald*,
Wi' Jamie M'Nab, wauchle on through this warld ;
And when, on life's e'ening, cauld death steeks his gab,
May he mount up on high—wi' blythe Jamie M'Nab.

                                        ALEX. RODGER.

---

[1] Samuel Hunter, Esq., late Editor.

## LOVE'S DIET.

TELL me, fair maid, tell me truly,
 How should infant Love be fed ;
If with dew-drops, shed so newly
 On the bright green clover blade ;
Or, with roses pluck'd in July,
 And with honey liquored !
  Oh, no ! oh, no !
  Let roses blow,
 And dew-stars to green blade cling ;
  Other fare,
  More light and rare,
 Befits that gentlest nursling.

Feed him with the sigh that rushes
 'Twixt sweet lips, whose muteness speaks
With the eloquence that flushes
 All a heart's wealth o'er soft cheeks ;
Feed him with a world of blushes,
 And the glance that shuns, yet seeks :
  For, 'tis with food,
  So light and good,
 That the Spirit-child is fed ;
  And with the tear
  Of joyous fear
 That the small elf's liquored.   MOTHERWELL.

## THE BUMPER.

SOME rail against drinking, and say 'tis a sin
 To tipple the juice of the vine ;
But as 'tis allow'd that we all have our faults,
 I wish no other fault may be mine.
But mark me, good fellows, I don't mean to say,
 That always to tipple is right ;
But 'tis wisdom to drown the dull cares of the day,
 In a bowl with old cronies at night.

See yon husbandman labours with care on the plain,
 Yet his face is lit up with a smile,
For the whisp'rings of hope tell again and again,
 That harvest rewards all his toil.
Just so 'tis with us, tho' we labour with pain,
 Yet we hear with unmingled delight,
The whisperings of hope tell again and again,
 Of a harvest of pleasure at night.

How soothing it is, when we bumper it up,
 To a friend on a far distant shore,
Or how sweetly it tastes, when we flavour the cup,
 With the name of the maid we adore !
Then here's to the maid, then, and here's to the friend,
 May they always prove true to their plight,
May their days glide as smooth and as merrily round,
 As the bumpers we pledge them to-night.

CARRICK.

## A MOTHER'S ADVICE.

DONAL's her pairn, no more sons will she had,
 He'll pe laird o' the stirk whan her's gane,
An' that will pe soon, for her's doitet and done,
 And the preath in her throat made her grane ;
  Deed, ay, my good lad !
 The preath in her throat made her grane.

My poor poy ! there's a lump in her throat, that she's sure will
turn't out a presumption !—an' all the doctors in the college canna
tak' it out.

Now Donal, poor lad ! you'll never pe blate,
 But teuk your auld mither's advice ;
Mark weel what ye say, her commands weel obey,
 An' I'll warrant I'll got her a wifes !
  Deed will I, my good lad !
 An' I'll warrant I'll got her a wife.

Her praw new hose she'll maun be surely put on,
   She'll sure tey're no tatter nor torn ;
Her braw new hose will suit her new clothes,
   An' they'll thocht her a shentlemans born !
     Deed will they, my bonnie pairn,
     They'll thocht you a shentlemans born.


When Donal, poor lad ! put on her new clothes—
   Hooh, wow ! but the laddie look spree !
He'll roar an' he'll dance, an' he'll kicket an' he'll prance !
   Hugh ! there's nocht but a ladies for me !
     Deed no, my good lad !
     There's nocht but a ladies for thee.


Now Donal, poor lad ! he'll gone up the street,
   An' he'll meet farmer's tochter called Grace,
He'll no pe shust taen ony kisses but ane,
   Whan she'll teuk him a slap on the face.

   Deed did she, ta vile jade ! she'll teuk him a slap on the face. Oh
the drunken trouster, to offer so to my Donal, decent lad ! She
should be catch and procht to shail, and put shame on her face for a
years to come.


But now sin' my Donal a-wooing has gane,
   To muckle Meg Dhu o' Loch-sloy ;
She's blin' o' an e'e, an' her mouth stan's a-jee,
   An' a hump on her shouther like buoy.

   Deed has she, poor creature ! She has a hump on her shouther,
like ta ship's buoy ; but never mind, Donal, shust got ta money, a
great daud o' grund to buy, though she's as ugly as ta *foul tief.*


Now she'll pray, an' she'll wish tat weel she may be,
   Since Donal ta wifes now has got ;
Although she's no beauty, she can do her duty,
   An' Donal's content wi' his lot !
     Deed is he, good lad !
     And Donal's content wi' his lot.

## SHON M'NAB.

TUNE—"*For a' that an' a' that.*"

NAINSEL pe Maister Shon M'Nab,
  Pe auld's ta forty-five, man,
And mony troll affairs she's seen,
  Since she was born alive, man ;
She's seen the warl' turn upside down,
  Ta shentleman turn poor man,
And him was ance ta beggar loon,
  Get knocker 'pon him's door, man.

She's seen ta stane bow't owre ta purn,
  And syne be ca'd ta prig, man ;
She's seen ta Whig ta Tory turn,
  Ta Tory turn ta Whig, man ;
But a' ta troll thing she pe seen,
  Wad teuk twa days to tell, man,
So, gin you likes, she'll told your shust
  Ta story 'bout hersel, man :—

Nainsel was first ta herd ta kyes,
  'Pon Morven's ponnie praes, man,
Whar tousand pleasant tays she'll spent,
  Pe pu ta nits and slaes, man ;
An' ten she'll pe ta *herring-poat*,
  An' syne she'll pe fish-cod, man,
Ta place tey'll call Newfoundhims-land,
  Pe far peyont ta proad, man.

But, och-hon-ee ! one misty night,
  Nainsel will lost her way, man,
Her poat was trown'd, hersel got fright,
  She'll mind till dying day, man.
So fait ! she'll pe fish-cod no more,
  But back to Morven cam', man,
An' tere she turn ta whisky still,
  Pe prew ta wee trap tram, man :

But foul pefa' ta gauger loon,
  Pe put her in ta shail, man,
Whar she wad stood for mony a tay,
  Shust 'cause she no got bail, man ;
But out she'll got—nae matters hoo,
  And came to Glasgow town, man,
Whar tousand wonders *mhor* she'll saw,
  As she went up and down, man.

Ta first thing she pe wonder at,
  As she cam down ta street, man,
Was man's pe traw ta cart himsel,
  Shust 'pon him's nain twa feet, man ;
Och on ! och on ! her nainsel thought,
  As she wad stood and glower, man,
Puir man ! if they mak you ta *horse*—
  Should gang 'pon a' your *four*, man.

And when she turned ta corner round,
  Ta black man tere she see, man,
Pe grund ta music in ta kist,
  And sell him for pawpee, man ;
And aye she'll grund, and grund, and grund,
  And turn her mill about, man,
Pe strange ! she will put nothing in,
  Yet aye teuk music out, man.

And when she'll saw ta peoples walk,
  In crowds alang ta street, man,
She'll wonder whar tey a' got spoons
  To sup teir pick o' meat, man ;
For in ta place whar she was porn,
  And tat right far awa, man,
Ta teil a spoon in a' ta house,
  But only ane or twa, man.

She glower to see ta Mattams, too,
  Wi' plack clout 'pon teir face, man,
Tey surely tid some graceless teed,
  Pe in sic black disgrace, man,

Or else what for tey'll hing ta clout,
  Owre prow, and cheek, and chin, man,
If no for shame to show teir face,
  For some ungodly sin, man?

Pe strange to see ta wee bit kirn,
  Pe jaw the waters out, man,
And ne'er rin dry, though she wad rin
  A' tay like mountain spout, man;
Pe stranger far to see ta lamps,
  Like spunkies in a raw, man;
A' pruntin pright for want o' oil,
  And teil a wick ava, man.

Ta Glasgow folk be unco folk.
  Hae tealings wi' ta teil, man,—
Wi' fire tey grund ta tait o' woo,
  Wi' fire tey card ta meal, man;
Wi' fire tey spin, wi' fire tey weave,
  Wi' fire do ilka turn, man,
Na, some o' tem will eat ta fire,
  And no him's pelly purn, man.

Wi' fire tey mak' ta coach pe rin,
  Upon ta railman's raw, man,
Nainsel will saw him teuk ta road,
  An' teil a horse to traw, man;
Anither coach to Paisley rin,
  Tey'll call him Lauchie's motion,
But oich! she was plawn a' to bits,
  By rascal rogue M'Splosion.

Wi' fire tey mak' ta vessels rin
  Upon ta river Clyde, man,
She saw't hersel, as sure's a gun,
  As she stood on ta side, man:
But gin you'll no pelieve her word,
  Gang to ta Proomielaw, man,
You'll saw ta ship wi' twa mill-wheels,
  Pe grund ta water sma', man.

Oich ! sic a town as Glasgow town,
  She never see pefore, man,
Ta houses tere pe mile and mair,
  Wi' names 'pon ilka toor, man.
An' in teir muckle windows tere,
  She'll saw't, sure's teath, for sale, man,
Praw shentleman's pe want ta head,
  An' leddies want ta tail, man.

She wonders what ta peoples do,
  Wi' a' ta praw things tere, man,
Gie her ta prose, ta kilt, an' hose,
  For tem she wadna care, man.
And aye gie her ta pickle sneesh,
  And wee drap parley pree, man,
For a' ta praws in Glasgow town,
  She no gie paw-prown-pee, man.

ALEX. RODGER.

## MAGGY AND WILLIE.

TUNE—"*Whistle an' I'll come to ye, my lad.*"

### CHORUS.

O, WHAT wud I do gin my Maggy were dead ?
O, what wud I do gin my Maggy were dead ?
This wud e'en be a wearifu' warld indeed,
To me, gin my ain canny Maggy were dead.

Bairns brought up thegither, baith nursed on ae knee,
Baith slung ower ae cuddy, fu' weel did we gree ;
Tho' I was born armless, an' aye unco wee,
My Maggie was muckle an' bunted for me.
  O, what wud I do? etc.

When she grew a woman an' I grew a man,
She graspit my stump, for I hadna a han',

An' we plighted our troth ower a big bag o' skran,
Thegither true-hearted to beg thro' the lan'.
    O, what wud I do? etc.

Tho' whiles when the skran and the siller are rife,
We baith may get fou, we ne'er hae ony strife ;
To me she ne'er lifted her han' in her life,
An' whaur is the loon that can brag sic a wife?
    O, what wud I do? etc.

O, Maggy is pure as a young Papist nun,
An she's fond o' her will as the wean o' its fun,
As the wight o' his drink, or the wit o' his pun—
There's no sic anither Meg under the sun.
    O, what wud I do? etc.

Mony big loons hae hechted to wyle her awa,
Baith thumblers and tumblers and tinklers an' a' ;
But she jeers them, an' tells them, her Willie tho' sma',
Has mair in his buik than the best o' them a'.
    O, what wud I do? etc.

I'm feckless, an' frien'less, distorted an' wee,
Canna cast my ain claes, nor yet claw my ain knee ;
But she kens a' my wants, an' does a'thing for me,
Gin I wantit my Maggy I'm sure I wud dee.

    Then what wud I do, gin my Maggy were dead?
    O, what wud I do, gin my Maggy were dead?
    This wud e'en be a wearifu' warld indeed,
    To me, gin my ain canny Maggy were dead.
            JAMES BALLANTINE, Edin.


## COME SIT DOWN, MY CRONIE.

COME sit down, my cronie, and gie me your crack,
Let the win' tak' the cares o' this life on its back ;
Our hearts to despondency, we ne'er will submit—
We've aye been provided for, an' sae will we yet.
    An' sae will we yet, etc.

Let's ca' for a tankard o' nappy brown ale,
It will comfort our hearts, an' enliven our tale ;
We'll aye be the merrier, the langer that we sit—
We've drank wi' ither mony a time, an sae' will we yet.
    An' sae will we yet, etc.

Sae rax me your mill, an' my nose I will prime,
Let mirth an' sweet innocence employ a' our time ;
Nae quarr'lin' nor fightin' we here will admit,
We've parted aye in unity, an' sae will we yet.
    An sae will we yet, etc.

Let the glass keep its course, an' gae merrily roun',
The sun has to rise tho' the moon soud gae doun ;
Till the house be rinnin' roun' about, 'tis time eneugh to
    flit ;
When we fell we aye wan up again, and sae will we yet.

An' sae will we yet, an' sae will we yet—
When we fell we aye wan up again, an' sae will we yet.
                    W. WATSON.


## THE TWAL O' AUGUST.

SHE'LL taen't ta gun upon her shouther,
A pock o' lead upon the other,
An' she'll had her horn weel fill wi' pouther,
    Upon the Twal o' August.

    For, oh but she's fond o' shooting !
      Fond, fond, fond o' shooting ;
    Oh but she's fond o' shooting,
      Upon the Twal o' August.

Twa ponny tog rin at her heel,
An' oh tey'll snock the burd out weel,
She'll no be fear for man nor Deil,
    Upon the Twal o' August.
      For, oh but, etc.

Ta first tey'll call'd her Cailach Mohr,
Ta noter's name was Pruach Vohr,
An' troth tey'll rais't a ponny splore,
   Upon the Twal o' August.
      For, oh but, etc.

Wi' pouther tan, she'll sharge ta gun,
An 'tan she'll ram't in lead a pun',
Tan threw't her gun the shouther on,
   Upon the Twal o' August.
      For, oh but, etc.

She'll gang't a bit an' rise ta purd,
Another tan, an' tan a third ;
But aye to shot, she maist turn't fear'd,
   Upon the Twal o' August.
      For, oh but, etc.

She'll teuk't ta gun up ta her shouther,
An' whether ta fright, or n'else the pouther,
But o'er she'll fa't an' maist turn smother,
   Upon the Twal o' August.
      For, oh but, etc.

She'll fa'at back on a muckle stane,
An' roar't a grunt, an tan a grane,
An' she'll thocht her back had lost ta bane,
   Upon the Twal o' August.
      For, oh but, etc.

Poor Pruach Vohr, he was 'nock plin,
An' aff his head was blaw the skin ;
He'll youll't a squeel, an' aff he'll rin,
   Upon the Twal o' August.
      For, oh but, etc.

She'll ne'er will go ashooting more,
To kill ta purds, an' tats what for ;

Ta peoples say, a plum was sour,
  Upon the Twal o' August.
    For, oh but she's tire o' shooting!
    Tire, tire, weary shooting!
    For she'll shot her tog, an' lam't herself,
    Upon the Twal o' August.
               A. FISHER.


## IRISH LOVE SONG.

OH! what a beautiful bit of mortality,
  Sweet Judy O'Flannigan is unto me;
The world must allow her angelic reality,
  The like of my Judy I never shall see.

Her manner is free from all low vulgara*l*ity,
  So politely genteel, unaffected, and free;
To see her and think of a moment's neutrality,
  You might just as well go dance a jig on the sea.

O smile on me, Judy! with some partiality,
  For the brains in my skull have been all set ajee;
Else I soon shall be dead, that's an end to vitality,
  Broken-hearted and murder'd your Paddy will be!

And pray, where the deuce did ye get your morality;
  Would you like your poor Paddy to hang on a tree?
Sure Judy, that would be a bit of rascality,
  While the daws and the crows would be pecking at me!

O name but the day, without more bother*ality*,
  Then the happiest of mortals your Paddy will be;
Ere a year will go round, ye'll have more *mothèrality*,
  And that the whole town of Kilkenny will see!

Then we'll laugh, dance, and sing, with true conviviality,
  While the rafters would ring to the noise of our spree,
And our hearts will be beating with congeniality,
  When Judy and Paddy they married shall be!

Oh what a beautiful bit of mortality,
  Sweet Judy O'Flannigan is unto me;
The world must allow her angelic reality,
  The like of my Judy I never shall see!


## BONNY FLORY.

I'VE lodged wi' mony a browster wife,
  And pree't her bonny mou';
But the coshest wife that e'er I met,
  Was Mistress Dougal Dhu.
But Mistress Dougal's no for me,
  Though always kind I've thought her;
My pleasure is to sit beside
  Her rosy-cheekit dochter.

To me, sweet Flory's wee bit mou'
  Is never out o' season;
An' if ye'll hover but a blink,
  I will explain the reason:
Her breath's the balmy breath o' *Spring*,
  Her tongue kind *Hairst* discloses,
Her teeth show *Winter's* flakes o' snaw
  Set round wi' *Simmer's* roses.

Then I'll awa to the Hielan' hills,
  Whar heather-bells are springing;
And sit beside some waterfa',
  And hear the linties singing;
And while they sing their sang o' love,
  Frae 'neath their leafy cover,
I'll press sweet Flory to my breast,
  And vow myself her lover!

The bustled beauty may engage
  The dandy in his corset;
But I'm content wi' Hielan' worth,
  In hodden-grey and worset.

And if she'll gie her wee bit han',
   Although it's hard and hackit,
Yet, heart to heart, and loof to loof,
   A bargain we shall mak it.

CARRICK.

## THE MUIRLAN' COTTARS.

" THE snaw flees thicker o'er the muir, and heavier grows
   the lift ;
The shepherd closer wraps his plaid to screen him frae
   the drift ;
I fear this nicht will tell a tale amang our foldless sheep,
That will mak mony a farmer sigh—God grant nae
   widows weep.

I'm blythe, guidman, to see you there, wi' elshin an' wi'
   lingle,
Sae eydent at your cobbling wark beside the cosie ingle ;
It brings to mind that fearfu' nicht, i' the spring that's
   now awa,
When you was carried thowless hame frae 'neath a wreath
   o' snaw.

That time I often think upon, an' mak' it aye my care,
On nichts like this, to snod up a' the beds we hae to spare ;
In case some drift-driven strangers come forfoughten to
   our bield,
An' welcome, welcome they shall be to what the house
   can yield.

'Twas God that saved you on that nicht, when a' was
   black despair.
An' gratitude is due to Him for makin' you His care ;
Then let us show our grateful sense of the kindness He
   bestowed,
An' cheer the poor wayfaring man that wanders frae his
   road.

There's cauld and drift without, guidman, might drive a
    body blin',
But, Praise be blessed for a' that's gude, there's meat
    and drink within ;
An' be he beggar be he prince, that Heaven directs this
    way,
His bed it shall be warm and clean, his fare the best we
    hae."

The gudeman heard her silentlie, an' threw his elshin by,
For his kindlie heart began to swell, and the tear was in
    his eye ;
He rose and pressed his faithfu' wife, sae loving to his
    breast,
While on her neck a holy kiss his feelings deep expressed.

" Yes, Mirran, yes, 'twas God Himself that helped us in
    our strait,
An' gratitude is due to Him—His kindness it was great ;
An' much I thank thee thus to mak' the stranger's state
    thy care,
An' bless thy tender heart, for sure the grace of God is
    there."

Nor prince nor beggar was decreed their kindness to
    partake ;
The hours sped on their stealthy pace as silent as the
    flake ;
Till on the startled ear there came a feeble cry of wo,
As if of some benighted one fast sinking in the snow.

But help was near—an' soon a youth, in hodden grey
    attire,
Benumbed with cold, extended, lay before the cottar's
    fire ;
Kind Mirran thow'd his frozen hands, the guidman
    rubbed his breast,
An' soon the stranger's glowin' cheeks returning life
    confess'd.

How aft it comes the gracious deeds which we to others
    show
Return again to our own hearts wi' joyous overflow !
So fared it with our simple ones, who found the youth
    to be
Their only son, whom they were told had perish'd far at
    sea.

The couch they had with pious care for some lone
    stranger spread—
Heaven gave it as a resting-place for their loved wanderer's
    head :
Thus aft it comes the gracious deeds which we to others
    show,
Return again to our own hearts with joyous overflow.

CARRICK.

## BEHAVE YOURSEL' BEFORE FOLK.

AIR—*Good morrow to your night cap.*

BEHAVE yoursel' before folk,
  Behave yoursel' before folk,
And dinna be sae rude to me,
  As kiss me sae before folk.

It wadna gie me meikle pain,
Gin we were seen and heard by nane,
To tak' a kiss, or grant ye ane ;
  But guidsake no before folk.
    Behave yoursel' before folk ;
    Behave yoursel' before folk ;
  Whate'er you do, when out o' view,
    Be cautious aye before folk.

Consider, lad, how folk will crack,
And what a great affair they'll mak',
O' naething but a simple smack,
  That's gi'en or ta'en before folk.

Behave yoursel' before folk.
Behave yoursel' before folk ;
Nor gie' the tongue o' auld or young
Occasion to come o'er folk.

It's no through hatred o' a kiss
That I sae plainly tell you this ;
But losh ! I tak' it sair amiss
  To be sae teazed before folk.
    Behave yoursel' before folk,
    Behave yoursel' before folk ;
  When we're our lane ye may tak' ane,
    But fient a ane before folk.

I'm sure wi' you I've been as free
As ony modest lass should be ;
But yet, it doesna do to see
  Sic freedom used before folk.
    Behave yoursel' before folk ;
    Behave yoursel' before folk ;
  I'll ne'er submit again to it—
    So mind you that—before folk.

Ye tell me that my face is fair ;
It may be sae—I dinna care—
But ne'er again gart blush sae sair
  As ye hae done before folk.
    Behave yoursel' before folk,
    Behave yoursel' before folk ;
  Nor heat my cheeks wi' your mad freaks,
    But aye be douce before folk.

Ye tell me that my lips are sweet,
Sic tales, I doubt, are a' deceit ;
At ony rate, it's hardly meet
  To pree their sweets before folk.
    Behave yoursel' before folk,
    Behave yoursel' before folk ;
  Gin that's the case, there's time and place,
    But surely no before folk.

But, gin you really do insist
That I should suffer to be kiss'd,
Gae, get a license frae the priest,
   And mak' me yours before folk.
     Behave yoursel' before folk,
     Behave yoursel' before folk ;
   And when we're ane, bluid, flesh and bane,
     Ye may tak' ten—before folk.
ALEX. RODGER.

## THE ANSWER.

   Can I behave, can I behave,
   Can I behave before folk,
   When, wily elf, your sleeky self,
   Gars me gang gyte before folk ?

In a' ye do, in a' ye say,
Ye've sic a pawkie coaxing way,
That my poor wits ye lead astray,
   An' ding me doilt before folk !
     Can I behave, etc.
     Can I behave, etc.
   While ye ensnare, can I forbear
   A kissing, though before folk ?

Can I behold that dimpling cheek
Whar love 'mang sunny smiles might beek,
Yet, howlet-like, my e'e-lids steek,
   An' shun sic light, before folk ?
     Can I behave, etc.
     Can I behave, etc.
   When ilka smile becomes a wile,
   Enticing me—before folk ?

That lip, like Eve's forbidden fruit,
Sweet, plump, an' ripe, sae tempts me to't
That I maun pree't though I should rue't,
   Aye twenty times—before folk !

Can I behave, etc.
Can I behave, etc.
When temptingly it offers me,
So rich a treat—before folk?

That gowden hair sae sunny bright;
That shapely neck o' snawy white;
That tongue, even when it tries to flyte,
   Provokes me till't before folk!
      Can I behave, etc.
      Can I behave, etc.
When ilka charm, young, fresh, and warm,
Cries, "Kiss me now"—before folk?

An' oh! that pawkie, rowin' e'e,
Sae roguishly it blinks on me,
I canna, for my saul, let be,
   Frae kissing you before folk!
      Can I behave, etc.
      Can I behave, etc.
When ilka glint conveys a hint
To tak a smack—before folk?

Ye own that were we baith our lane,
Ye wadna grudge to grant me ane;
Weel, gin there be nae harm in't then,
   What harm is in't before folk?
      Can I behave, etc.
      Can I behave, etc.
Sly hypocrite! an anchorite
Could scarce desist—before folk?

But after a' that has been said,
Since ye are willing to be wed,
We'll hae a' "blythesome bridal" made,
   When ye'll be mine before folk!
     Then I'll behave, then I'll behave,
     Then I'll behave, before folk,
For whereas then, ye'll aft get "ten,"
It winna be before folk!

ALEX. RODGER.

## JEANIE MORRISON.

I've wander'd east, I've wander'd west,
    Through mony a weary way ;
But never, never, can forget
    The luve o' life's young day !
The fire that's blawn on Beltane e'en,
    May weel be black gin Yule ;
But blacker fa' awaits the heart
    Where first fond luve grows cule.

O dear, dear Jeanie Morrison,
    The thochts o' bygane years
Still fling their shadows ower my path,
    And blind my een wi' tears :
They blind my een wi' saut, saut tears,
    And sair and sick I pine,
As memory idly summons up
    The blithe blinks o' langsyne.

'Twas then we luvit ilk ither weel,
    'Twas then we twa did part ;
Sweet time—sad time ! twa bairns at schule,
    Twa bairns, and but ae heart !
'Twas then we sat on ae laigh bink,
    To leir ilk ither lear ;
And tones, and looks, and smiles were shed,
    Remember'd ever mair.

I wonder, Jeanie, aften yet,
    When sitting on that bink,
Cheek touchin' cheek, loof lock'd in loof,
    What our wee heads could think ?
When baith bent doun ower ae braid page
    Wi' ae buik on our knee.
Thy lips were on thy lesson, but
    My lesson was in thee.

Oh mind ye how we hung our heads,
　　How cheeks brent red wi' shame,
Whene'er the schule-weans, laughin', said,
　　We cleek'd thegither hame !
And mind ye o' the Saturdays
　　(The schule then skail't at noon),
When we ran aff to speel the braes—
　　The broomy braes o' June?

My head rins round and round about,
　　My heart flows like a sea,
As ane by ane the thochts rush back
　　O' schule-time and o' thee.
Oh, mornin' life ! Oh, mornin' luve !
　　Oh, lichtsome days and lang,
When hinnied hopes around our hearts,
　　Like simmer blossoms, sprang !

O mind ye, luve, how aft we left
　　The deavin' dinsome toun,
To wander by the green burnside,
　　And hear its water croon ;
The simmer leaves hung ower our heads,
　　The flowers burst round our feet,
And in the gloamin' o' the wud,
　　The throssil whusslit sweet.

The throssil whusslit in the wud,
　　The burn sung to the trees,
And we with Nature's heart in tune,
　　Concerted harmonies ;
And on the knowe abune the burn,
　　For hours thegither sat
In the silentness o' joy, till baith
　　Wi' very gladness grat !

Aye, aye, dear Jeanie Morrison,
　　Tears trinkled down your cheek,
Like dew-beads on a rose, yet nane
　　Had ony power to speak !

That was a time, a blessed time,
　When hearts were fresh and young,
When freely gush'd all feelings forth,
　Unsyllabled—unsung!

I marvel, Jeanie Morrison,
　Gin I hae been to thee
As closely twined wi' earliest thochts
　As ye hae been to me!
Oh! tell me gin their music fills
　Thine ear as it does mine;
Oh! say gin e'er your heart grows grit
　Wi' dreamings o' langsyne?

I've wander'd east, I've wander'd west,
　I've borne a weary lot:
But in my wanderings, far or near,
　Ye never were forgot.
The fount that first burst frae this heart,
　Still travels on its way;
And channels deeper as it rins
　The luve o' life's young day.

O dear, dear Jeanie Morrison,
　Since we were sinder'd young,
I've never seen your face, nor heard
　The music o' your tongue.
But I could hug all wretchedness,
　And happy could I dee,
Did I but ken your heart still dream'd
　O' bygane days and me!

MOTHERWELL.

## JESSY M'LEAN.

OH hark! an' I'll tell you o' Jessy M'Lean,
She promis'd shortsyne she would soon be my ain,
So mind ye'll be ready to come on neist Friday,
An' see me get buckled to Jessy M'Lean.

Lang, lang, hae I lo'ed her, and faithfully woo'd her,
Yet ne'er has she treated my suit wi' disdain,
For sense an' good nature enliven ilk feature,
And guileless the heart is o' Jessy M'Lean.

Tho' nane o' your butterflee beauties sae vain,
That flutter about, aye, new lovers to gain;
Yet she has attractions to catch the affections,
And prudence, the heart that she wins, to retain.

Her mild look so touching, her smile so bewitching,
Her rich melting tones, sweet as seraphim's strain,
Rush through my heart thrilling, and wake every feeling
Of tender attachment for Jessy M'Lean.

When sitting beside her, my heart is aye fain,
To think what a treasure will soon be my ain;
Nae fause gaudy glitter, to cheat, then embitter,
But pure solid worth, without hollow or stain.

And should a bit callan' e'er bless our snug dwallin',
Or ae bonnie lassie (as heaven may ordain),
The sweet smiling creature, its *mither* ilk feature,
Will knit me still closer to Jessy M'Lean.

                                        ALEX. RODGER.


## I SEEK TO WED NO OTHER LOVE.

SING not that song again, lady!
    Look not to me with sighs;
Past feelings all are buried now,
    Ah! never more to rise.
The pledge that bound our hearts in one,
    Was register'd on high;
Nought but thy *wish* could cancel it,
    Could I that *wish* deny?

I cannot pledge *again* lady!
    Our griefs must now be borne;

The angel who records above,
  Would laugh us both to scorn :
I seek to wed no other love,
  No, no, that cannot be ;
My widow'd heart must still bleed on,
  In memory of thee !

The bliss which once you had to give,
  I covet now no more :
A few short struggles here, and then
  Life's sighs and pangs are o'er.
I seek to wed no other love,
  No, no, that ne'er can be ;
My widow'd heart must still bleed on,
  In memory of thee !       CARRICK.


## THE SERENADE.

    WAKE, lady, wake !
    Dear heart, awake
    From slumbers light,
For 'neath thy bower, at this still hour,
    In harness bright,
Lingers thine own true paramour
    And chosen knight !
    Wake, lady, wake !

    Wake, lady, wake !
    For thy lov'd sake,
    Each trembling star
Smiles from on high, with its clear eye ;
    While nobler far,
Yon silvery shield lights earth and sky,
    How good they are !
    Wake, lady, wake !

    Rise, lady, rise !
    Not star-fill'd skies

I worship now :
A fairer shrine, I trust, is mine
        For loyal vow.
O, that the living stars would shine
        That light thy brow !
        Rise, lady, rise !

        Rise, lady, rise !
        Ere war's rude cries
        Fright land and sea :
To-morrow's light sees mail-sheath'd knight,
        Even hapless me,
Careering through the bloody fight,
        Afar from thee.
        Rise, lady, rise !

        Mute, lady, mute !
        I have no lute,
        Nor rebeck small,
To soothe thine ear with lay sincere
        Or madrigal :
With helm on head, and hand on spear
        On thee I call.
        Mute, lady, mute !

        Mute, lady, mute
        To love's fond suit !
        I'll not complain,
Since underneath thy balmy breath
        I may remain
One brief hour more, ere I seek death
        On battle plain !
        Mute, lady, mute !

        Sleep, lady, sleep,
        While watch I keep
        Till dawn of day ;
But o'er the wold, now morning cold,
        Shines icy grey !

While the plain gleams with steel and gold,
  And chargers neigh !
  Sleep, lady, sleep !

  Sleep, lady, sleep !
  Nor wake to weep
  For heart-struck me.
These trumpets knell my last farewell
  To love and thee :
When next they sound, 't will be to tell
  I died for thee !
  Sleep, lady, sleep !     MOTHERWELL.


## THE UNINVITED GHAIST.

  As the deil and his dame,
  Ae nicht were frae hame,
A ghaist frae this world did tick at their door.
  A wee deil did answer
  An' roar'd, " What d'ye want, Sir !
"I want," quo' the ghaist, "just to rank in your
    core."

  " The guidman's frae hame, man,
  The guidwife's the same, man,
To admit ye mysel' is against their comman's,
  Sae slip your wa's back ;
  An' our *cork* when he's slack,
Will gie ye a hint when he's takin' on han's."

  The ghaist turn'd his heel
  Without sayin' fareweel,
An' sneak'd awa back wi' his thumb in his jaw ;
  Thinking 't was a hard case,
  That in sic a warm place,
A puir ghaistie should get sic a *cauld coal to blaw*.

  Now, let some folk reflect
  Upon this disrespect,

An' look ere they loup, whar their landing's to be ;
    For it seems there is reason
    To tak tent o' their wizen,
Since the deil's on the *shy*, and their frien's ca' them *fee*.
                    CARRICK.

## BRANDY VERSUS BEAUTY.

MISS Dorothy Dumps was a lovely maid,
    Fal lal la, fal lal di dal di de,
In nature's rarest gifts array'd,
    Fal lal, etc.

Her cheeks wore *England's* rose's hue,
Her eyes were of the *Prussian* blue,
And *Turkey* red were her elbows too ;
    Fal lal, etc.

    Now, many a youngster came to woo,
        Fal lal, etc.
    But at them all she look'd askew ;
        Fal lal, etc.

The youths all strove, but strove in vain,
The maid's affections sweet to gain;
But she answer'd still with proud disdain,
    Fal lal, etc.

    Now, we've all heard grave sages say,
        Fal lal, etc.
    That beauty's but a flower of May ;
        Fal lal, etc.

For time began her charms to crop,
Nor paint nor patch could beauty prop,
So she lost all hope and took to the *drop*.
    Fal lal, etc.

    But as we very seldom see
        Fal lal, etc.

That *brandy* and *beauty* do agree,
    Fal lal, etc.

So frequent did she ply the dose,
At last, alas ! the *faithless* rose
Gave the *slip* to her cheek, and *drew up* with her nose !
    Fal lal, etc.

Now, Miss Dolly's nose *shines* a *lighthouse*, fit
    Fal lal, etc.
To show the rock on which she has split ;
    Fal lal, etc.

For when the brandy gains the sway,
The *loves* and the *graces* all so gay,
Soon pack up their *awls* and fly away,
    Fal lal, etc.                    CARRICK.


## THE HARP AND THE HAGGIS.

AT that tide when the voice of the turtle is dumb,
And winter wi' drap at his nose doth come,—
A whistle to mak o' the castle lum
    To sowf his music sae sairie, O !
And the roast on the speet is sapless an' sma',
And meat is scant in chamber and ha',
And the knichts hae ceased their merry guffaw,
    For lack o' their warm canarie, O !

Then the Harp and the Haggis began a dispute,
'Bout whilk o' their charms were in highest repute :
The Haggis at first as a haddie was mute,
    An' the Harp went on wi' her vapourin', O !
An' lofty an' loud were the tones she assumed,
An' boasted how ladies and knichts gaily plumed,
Through rich gilded halls, all so sweetly perfumed,
    To the sound of her strings went a caperin', O !

" While the Haggis," she said, "was a beggarly slave,
" An' never was seen 'mang the fair an' the brave ;"
"Fuff! Fuff !" quoth the Haggis, "thou vile lying knave,
  Come tell us the use of thy twanging, O !
Can it fill a toom wame ? can it help a man's pack ?
A minstrel when out may come in for his snack,
But when starving at hame, will it keep him, alack !
  Frae trying his hand at the hanging, O ?"

The twa they grew wud as wud could be,
But a minstrel boy they chanced to see,
Wha stood list'ning by, an' to settle the plea,
  They begged he would try his endeavour, O !
For the twa in their wrath had all reason forgot,
And stood boiling with rage just like peas in a pot,
But a Haggis, ye ken, aye looks best when it's *hot*,
  So his bowels were moved in her favour, O !

" Nocht pleasures the lug half sae weel as a tune,
An' whar hings the lug wad be fed wi' a spoon ?"
The Harp in a triumph cried, "Laddie, weel done,"
  An' her strings wi' delight fell a tinkling, O !
" The harp's a braw thing," continued the youth,
" But what is a harp to put in the mouth ?
It fills na the wame, it slaiks na the drouth,—
  At least,—that is *my* way o' thinking, O !

" A tune's but an *air ;* but a Haggis is *meat ;*—
An' wha plays the tune that a body can eat ?—
When a Haggis is seen wi' a sheep's head and feet,
  My word she has gallant attendance, O !
A man wi' sic fare may ne'er pree the tangs,
But laugh at lank hunger though sharp be her fangs ;
But the bard that maun live by the wind o' his sangs,
  Waes me, has a puir dependence, O !

" How aften we hear, wi' the tear in our eye,
How the puir starving minstrel, exposed to the sky,

Lays his head on his harp, and breathes out his last sigh,
    Without e'er a friend within hearing, O !
But wha ever heard of a minstrel so crost,—
Lay his head on a Haggis to gie up the ghost ?—
O never, since time took his scythe frae the post,
    An' truntled awa to the shearing, O !

"Now I'll settle your plea in the crack o' a whup ;—
Gie the Haggis the lead, be't to dine or to sup :—
Till the bags are weel filled, there can nae drone get up,—
    Is a saying I learned from my mither, O !
When the feasting is ower, let the harp loudly twang,
An' soothe ilka lug wi' the charms o' her sang,—
An' the wish of my heart is, wherever ye gang,
    Gude grant ye may aye be thegither, O !"

CARRICK.

## SWEET BET OF ABERDEEN.

Air—"*The Rose of Allandale.*"

How brightly beams the bonnie moon,
    Frae out the azure sky ;
While ilka little star aboon
    Seems sparkling bright wi' joy.
How calm the eve ! how blest the hour !
    How soft the sylvan scene !
How fit to meet thee—lovely flower !
    Sweet Bet of Aberdeen.

Now, let us wander through the broom,
    And o'er the flowery lea ;
While simmer wafts her rich perfume,
    Frae yonder hawthorn tree :
There, on yon mossy bank we'll rest,
    Where we've sae aften been,
Clasp'd to each other's throbbing breast,
    Sweet Bet of Aberdeen!

How sweet to view that face so meek,—
  That dark expressive eye,—
To kiss that lovely blushing cheek,—
  Those lips of coral dye !
But O ! to hear thy seraph strains,
  Thy maiden sighs between,
Makes rapture thrill through all my veins—
  Sweet Bet of Aberdeen !

O ! what to us is wealth or rank ?
  Or what is pomp or power ?
More dear this velvet mossy bank,—
  This blest ecstatic hour !
I'd covet not the Monarch's throne,
  Nor diamond-studded Queen,
While blest wi' thee, and thee alone,
  Sweet Bet of Aberdeen !   ALEX. RODGER.


## THE NAILER'S WIFE.

AIR—"*Willie Wastle.*"

THERE lives a Nailer wast the raw,
  Wi' brain o' peat, an' skull o' putty ;
He has a wife—gude safe us a' !
  A randy royt ca'd Barmy Betty!
    O sic a scauld is Betty!
    Och hey ! how bauld is Betty !
    Xantippe's sel', wi' snash sae snell,
    Was but a lamb compared wi' Betty.

An' O but she's a grousome quean,
  Wi' face like ony big bass fiddle,
Twa flaming torches are her een,
  Her teeth could snap in bits—a griddle.
    O what a wight is Betty !
    O sic a fright is Betty!
    Wi' fiery een, an' furious mien,
    The queen o' terrors sure is Betty !

Ye've seen upon a rainy night,
　Upon the dark brown clouds refleckit,
Clyde Airn Warks' grim an' sullen light—
　Then, that's her brow when frowns bedeck it,
　　　O what a brow has Betty!
　　　O sic a cowe is Betty!
　　　Her vera glow'r turns sweet to sour,
　　　Sae baleful is the power o' Betty.

It had been good for you and me,
　Had mither Eve been sic a beauty,
She soon would garr'd *auld Saunders* flee
　Back to his dungeon dark and sooty.
　　　O what a grin has Betty!
　　　Oh how like Sin is Betty!
　　　The auld "foul thief" wad seek relief,
　　　In his maist darksome den frae Betty.

Whene'er you see a furious storm,
　Uprooting trees, an' lums down smashin',
Ye then may some idea form,
　Of what she's like when in a passion.
　　　O what a barmy Betty!
　　　O sic a stormy Betty!
　　　The wind an' rain may lash the plain,
　　　But a' in vain they strive wi' Betty.

For then the weans she cuffs and kicks,
　In fau't or no, it mak's nae matter;
While trenchers, bowls, and candlesticks,
　Flee through the house wi' hailstane blatter.
　　　O what a hag is Betty!
　　　O sic a plague is Betty!
　　　Dog, cat, an' mouse, a' flee the house.
　　　A-wondering what the deuce means Betty.

Her tongue—but to describe its power,
　Surpasses far baith speech and writing;
The Carron blast could never roar
　Like her, when she begins a flyting.

O what a tongue has Betty !
O siccan lungs has Betty !
The blast may tire, the flame expire,
But nought can tire the tongue o' Betty.

ALEX. RODGER.


## "O MITHER, ONY BODY."

AIR—"*Sir Alex. M'Donald's Reel.*

"O MITHER, ony body !
Ony body ! ony body !
O mither, ony body !
　But a creeshy weaver."

"A weaver's just as good as nane,
A creature worn to skin and bane,
I'd rather lie through life my lane,
　Than cuddle wi' a weaver."

The lassie thocht to catch a laird,
But fient a ane about her cared ;
For nane his love had e'er declared,
　Excepting, whiles—a weaver.

Yet ne'er a weaver wad she tak',
But a' that cam', she sent them back,
An' bann'd them for a useless pack,
　To come nae mair and deave her.

Their sowen crocks—their trantlum gear—
Their trash o' pirns she couldna bear ;
An' aye the ither jibe and jeer,
　She cuist at ilka weaver.

But sair she rued her pridefu' scorn,
E'er *thretty nicks* had mark'd her horn,
For down she hurkled a' forlorn,
　In solitude to grieve her.

She gaed to kirk, she gaed to fair,
She spread her *lure*, she set her *snare*,
But ne'er a *nibble* gat she there,
 Frae *leading apes*, to save her.

At last, unto the barn she gaed,
An' ilka e'ening duly pray'd,
That some ane might come to her aid,
 An' frae her wants relieve her.

An' thus the lassie's prayer ran—
Oh send thy servant some bit man,
Before her cheeks grow bleach'd an' wan,
 An' a' her beauties leave her."

A weaver lad wha ance had woo'd,
But cam' nae speed, do a' he could,
Now thocht her pride might be subdued,
 An' that he yet might have her.

He watched when to the barn she gaed,
An' while her bit request she made,
In solemn tones he slowly said—
 "Lass, will ye tak' a weaver?"

"Thy will be done—I'm now content,
Just ony body ere I want,
I'll e'en be thankfu' gin Thou grant,
 That I may get a weaver."

The weaver, he cam' yont neist day,
An' sought her hand—she ne'er said, "Nay."
But thocht it time to mak' her hay,
 So jumpit at the weaver.

Now, ye whase beauty's on the wane,
Just try the barn, at e'en, your lane,
Sma' fish are better far than' nane,
 Ye'll maybe catch a weaver.

ALEX. RODGER.

## BLYTHE ARE WE SET WI' ITHER.[1]

BLYTHE are we set wi' ither ;
   Fling Care ayont the moon ;
No sae aft we meet thegither ;
   Wha would think o' parting soon ?
Though snaw bends down the forest trees,
   And burn and river cease to flow ;
Though Nature's tide hae shor'd to freeze,
   An' Winter nithers a' below ;
     Blythe are we, etc.

Now, round the ingle cheerly met,
   We'll scug the blast, and dread nae harm ;
Wi' jaws o' toddy reeking het,
   We'll keep the genial current warm.
The friendly crack, the cheerfu' sang,
   Shall cheat the happy hours awa',
Gar pleasure reign the e'ening lang,
   And laugh at biting frost and snaw.
     Blythe are we, etc.

The cares that cluster round the heart,
   And gar the bosom stound wi' pain,
Shall get a fright afore we part,
   Will mak' them fear to come again.
Then, fill about, my winsome chiels,
   The sparkling glass will banish pine ;
Nae pain the happy bosom feels,
   Sae free o' care as yours an' mine.
     Blythe are we, etc.

[1] This song hath a right pleasant smack of boon companionship.
The lines—
     Now, round the ingle cheerly met,
       We'll scug the blast, and dread nae harm ;
     *Wi' jaws o' toddy reeking het,*
       We'll keep the genial current warm—
are worthy of Burns. The Author was Ebenezer Picken, a native of
Paisley, who was born about the year 1765, and after many vicissitudes, died in 1815 or 1816. His poems have been published.

## ADAM GLEN.[1]

TUNE—*Adam Glen.*

PAUKY Adam Glen,
   Piper o' the clachan,
Whan he stoitet ben
   Sairly was he pechan,
Spak a wee, but tint his win',
Hurklit down and hostit syne,
Blew his beak, an dightit's een,
   An' whaisl't a' forfoughten.

But his yokin dune,
   Cheerie kyth't the body,
Crackit like a gun,
   An' leugh to auntie Madie ;
Cried, My callants, raise a spring,
" Inglan John," or ony thing,
For weel I'd like to see the fling,
   O' ilka lass and laddie.

Blythe the dancers flew,
   Usquebaugh was plenty,
Blythe the piper grew,
   Tho' shaking han's wi' ninety
Seven times his bridal vow
Ruthless fate had broken thro'—
Wha wad thought his coming now
   Was for our maiden auntie.

She had ne'er been sought,
   Cheerie houp was fading,
Dowie is the thought
   To live and die a maiden.
How it comes we canna ken,
Wanters ay maun wait their ain,
Madge is hecht to ADAM GLEN,
   An' soon we'll hae a wedding.

[1] By Mr. Laing of Brechin—this is one of the best illustrations of
the *frosty-bearded* anti-Malthusian that we have met with in type.

## SANCT MUNGO.[1]

SANCT MUNGO wals ane famous sanct,
    And ane cantye carle wals hee,
He drank o' ye Molendinar Burne,
    Quhan bettere hee culdna prie ;
Zit quhan he culd gette strongere cheere,
    He neuer wals wattere drye,
Butte dranke o' ye streame o' ye wimpland worme,
    And loote ye burne rynne bye.

Sanct Mungo wals ane merrye sanct,
    And merrylye hee sang ;
Quhaneuer he liltit uppe hys sprynge,
    Ye very Firre Parke rang ;
Butte thoch hee weele culd lilt and synge,
    And mak sweet melodye,
He chauntit aye ye bauldest straynes,
    Quhan prymed wi' barlye-bree.

Sanct Mungo wals ane godlye sanct,
    Farre famed for godlye deedis,
And grete delyte hee daylye took,
    Inn countynge ower hys beadis ;
Zit I, Sanct Mungo's youngeste sonne,
    Can count als welle als hee ;
Butte ye beadis quilk I like best to count
    Are ye beadis o' barlye-bree.

Sanct Mungo wals ane jolly sanct :—
    Sa weele hee lykit gude zil,
Thatte quhyles hee staynede hys quhyte vesture,
    Wi' dribblands o' ye still ;
Butte I, hys maist unwordye sonne,
    Haue gane als farre als hee,
For ance I tynde my garmente skirtis,
    Throuch lufe o' barlye-bree.    ALEX. RODGER.

[1] The Patron saint of Glasgow Cathedral. The Molendinar burn, alluded to in the third line, is the Lethe that separates the two great repositories of mortality—the churchyard of the Cathedral and the Necropolis.

## GLASGOW PATRIOTS.[1]

*AIR—" There was a handsome Soldier."*

LOYAL hearted citizens !
Great news there's come to town ;
I have not got the particulars yet,
But they'll be in the afternoon.

Loyal hearted citizens !
Great news I've got to tell,
Of the wars in Spain and Portingall,
And how the town of Badajos fell.

There was one Aleck Pattison,
A man of great renown ;
He was the first that did mount Badajos walls,
And the first that did tumble down.

He was a handsome tall young gentleman,
As ever my eyes did see ;
A captain, colonel, or major,
He very soon would be.

I am the author of every word I sing,
Which you may very well see,
The music alone excepted,
But just of the poetree.

[1] It is not long since the turf covered the remains of the Glasgow
Homer, Alexander M'Donald, alias *Blind Aleck*, author of these
verses, who for many years perambulated our streets, and with
dexter hand directed the movements of his violin, while his lips gave
the *measured* accompaniment. A remarkably spirited sketch of his
life appeared in the Scots Times Newspaper at his death, drawn
up by our City Chamberlain, Mr. John Strang. Aleck was,
perhaps one of the readiest improvisatores of his time ; and it was
greatly to his advantage that he was not distressed by a very
delicate ear for either numbers or harmony. Whether his lines
had a greater number of feet than consisted with ease and grace, or
limped in their motion for want of the due proportion, these defects
were amply compensated for by a rapid articulation in the one
case and in the other by a strong dash or two of the bow.

I've travell'd the world all over,
And many a place beside :
But I never did see a more beautifuller city,
Than that on the banks of the navigatable river, the Clyde.

I left Inverness without e'er a guide,
And arrived in Glasgow city,
Where I've been informed that bold John Bull,
Again beat the French so pretty.

I came into the Star Inn and Hotel ;
First, they gave me brandy, and then they gave me gin ;
Here's success, to all the waiters
Of the Star Inn ———— and Hotel !

## THE TOOM MEAL-POCK.[1]

PRESERVE us a' ! what shall we do,
  Thir dark unhallowed times ?
We're surely dreeing penance now,
  For some most awfu' crimes.
Sedition daurna now appear,
  In reality or joke,
For ilka chield maun mourn wi' me,
  O' a hinging toom meal-pock.
      And sing, Oh waes me !

When lasses braw gaed out at e'en,
  For sport and pastime free,
I seem'd like ane in paradise,
  The moments quick did flee.
Like Venuses they a' appeared
  Weel pouther'd were their locks [2]—

---

[1] This capital song was written by John Robertson, Weaver, in
Paisley, about the time of the political ferments of 1793. We know
not the air to which it is sung, but believe it is an old one. Our
worthy friend, Mr. George Miller, Blantyre, sings it (1850) inimit-
ably, whether the air, or the accent, or the action, be taken into consideration.

[2] The allusion here is to hair powder, which, at the time in
question, was used by all respectable persons, *gentle and semple*.

'Twas easy dune, when at their hames,
  Wi' the shaking o' their pocks.
      And sing, Oh waes me!

How happy past my former days,
  Wi' merry heartsome glee,
When smiling Fortune held the cup,
  And Peace sat on my knee;
Nae wants had I but were supplied,
  My heart wi' joy did knock,
When in the neuk, I smiling saw
  A gaucie, weel-filled pock.
      And sing, Oh waes me!

Speak no ae word about Reform,
  Nor petition Parliament;
A wiser scheme I'll now propone,
  I'm sure ye'll gie consent;—
Send up a chield or twa like *him*,
  As a sample o' the flock,
Whase hallow cheeks will be sure proof
  O' a hinging toom meal-pock.
      And sing, Oh waes me!

And should a sicht sae ghastly-like,
  Wi' rags, and banes, and skin,
Hae nae impression on yon folks,
  Just tell ye'll stand a-hin.
O, what a contrast will ye show,
  To the glow'rin' Lunnun folk,
When in St. James' ye tak' your stand,
  Wi' a hinging toom meal-pock.
      And sing, Oh waes me!

Then rear your hand, and glow'r, and stare,
  Before yon hills o' beef;
Tell them ye are frae Scotland come,
  For Scotia's relief;—
Tell them ye are the very best
  Wal'd frae the fattest flock;

Then raise your arms, and O ! display
　　A hinging toom meal-pock.
　　　　And sing, Oh waes me !

Tell them ye're wearied o' the chain
　　That hauds the state thegither,
For Scotland wishes just to tak'
　　Gude nicht wi' ane anither !
We canna thole, we canna bide
　　This hard unwieldy yoke,
For wark and want but ill agree
　　Wi' a hinging toom meal-pock.
　　　　And sing, Oh waes me !


## I SHALL RETURN AGAIN.[1]

I WOULD not have thee dry the tear
　　That dims thine eye of blue ;
I would not that thy cheek should wear
　　A smile at our adieu :
Yet cheer thee, love, the past was bliss,
　　And though we part in pain,
A happier hour will follow this,
　　And we shall meet again.

Oh think not that the wild sea-wave
　　Shall bear my *heart* from thee,
Unless its cold breast prove my grave,
　　'Twill work no change in me.
The troubled music of the deep
　　Is now our farewell strain,
And fond affection well may weep ;
　　Yet—I'll return again.

[1] This song was one of the first written by Mr. Kennedy, and was presented by him to our publisher, who had suggested the air to which it is usually sung—The Highland Watch, or March of the 42d Regiment. We regret that a lyrist so highly gifted does not favour the world with more of his pieces.

I go to find a bower of peace,
   In lovelier lands than thine,
Where cruel fortune's frowns shall cease,
   Where I can call thee mine,
And when to crown my fairy plan,
   But *one thing* shall remain ;
Then, love—if there be truth in man—
   I shall return again.     WM. KENNEDY.


## THE ANSWER.

WHY walk I by the lonely strand ?
   He comes not with the tide,
His home is in another land,
   The stranger is his bride.
The stranger, on whose lofty brow,
   The circling diamonds shine,
Is now his bride, whose earliest vow
   And pledge of hope, were mine.

They tell me that my cheek is pale,
   That youth's light smile is gone ;
That mating with the ocean gale
   Hath chilled my heart to stone ;
And friendship asks what secret care
   There is to work me wo,
But vainly seeks a grief to share
   Which none shall ever know.

Ye waves, that heard the false one swear,
   And saw him not return,
Ye'll not betray me, if a tear
   Should start in spite of scorn.
Yet, no—a wounded spirit's pride,
   Though passions pangs are deep,
Shall dash the trait'rous drop aside,
   From eyes that must not weep.

In vain, alas ! I have no power
  To quit this lonely strand,
From whence at the wild parting hour,
  I saw him leave the land.
Though he has ta'en a stranger bride,
  My love will not depart ;
Its seal, too strong for woman's pride,
  Shall be a broken heart.   WM. KENNEDY.


## NED BOLTON.

A JOLLY comrade in the port, a fearless mate at sea ;
When I forget thee, to my hand false may the cutlass be !
And may my gallant battle-flag be stricken down in
    shame,
If when the social can goes round, I fail to pledge thy
    name !
Up, up, my lads !—his memory !—we'll give it with a
    cheer,—
Ned Bolton, the commander of the Black Snake privateer !

Poor Ned ! he had a heart of steel, with neither flaw nor
    speck ;
Firm as a rock, in strife or storm, he stood the quarter-
    deck ;
He was, I trow, a welcome man to many an Indian dame,
And Spanish planters crossed themselves at whisper of
    his name ;
But now Jamaica girls may weep—rich Dons securely
    smile—
His bark will take no prize again, nor ne'er touch Indian
    isle !

'S blood ! 'twas a sorry fate he met on his own mother
    wave,—
The foe far off, the storm asleep, and yet to find a grave !
With store of the Peruvian gold, and spirit of the cane,
No need would he have had to cruise in tropic climes
    again :

But some are born to sink at sea, and some to hang on
    shore,
And Fortune cried, God speed! at last, and welcomed
    Ned no more.

'Twas off the coast of Mexico—the tale is bitter brief—
The Black Snake, under press of sail, stuck fast upon a
    reef;
Upon a cutting coral-reef—scarce a good league from
    land—
But hundreds, both of horse and foot, were ranged upon
    the strand:
His boats were lost before Cape Horn, and, with an old
    canoe,
Even had he numbered ten for one, what could Ned
    Bolton do!

Six days and nights the vessel lay upon the coral-reef,
Nor favouring gale, nor friendly flag, brought prospect of
    relief;
For a land-breeze the wild one prayed, who never prayed
    before,
And when it came not at his call, he bit his lip and
    swore;
The Spaniards shouted from the beach, but did not
    venture near,
Too well they knew the mettle of the daring privateer!

A calm! a calm! a hopeless calm!—the red sun burning
    high,
Glared blisteringly and wearily, in a transparent sky;
The grog went round the gasping crew, and loudly rose
    the song,
The only pastime at an hour when rest seemed far too
    long,
So boisterously they took their rouse, upon the crowded
    deck,
They looked like men who had escaped, not feared, a
    sudden wreck.

Up sprung the breeze the seventh day—away! away to
    sea
Drifted the bark, with riven planks, over the waters free;
Their battle-flag these rovers bold then hoisted top-mast
    high,
And to the swarthy foe sent back a fierce defying cry.
" One last broadside!" Ned Bolton cried,—deep boomed
    the cannon's roar,
And echo's hollow growl returned an answer from the
    shore.

The thundering gun, the broken song, the mad tumultu-
    ous cheer,
Ceased not so long as ocean spared the shattered
    privateer :
I saw her—I—she shot by me, like lightning, in the gale,
We strove to save, we tacked, and fast we slackened all
    our sail—
I knew the wave of Ned's right hand—farewell!—you
    strive in vain !
And he, or one of his ship's crew, ne'er enter'd port again.

WM. KENNEDY.

## IRISH INSTRUCTION.

IN this wonderful age when most men go to college,
And every man's skull holds a hatful of knowledge,
'Twill soon be a wonder to meet with a fool,
Since men are abroad like Professor O''Toole.
    Derry down, down, down, derry down.

There are very few men like O'Toole who can teach,
When the head won't respond, he applies to the breech;
And whacking them well, till he gives them their full,
Let us knock in the larning, says Doctor O'Toole.
    Derry down, etc.

One morning the Doctor went out to his walk,
And found on the door his own likeness in *chalk,*

That morning he flogg'd every brat in the school,
It's a part of my system, says Doctor O'Toole.
    Derry down, etc.

Now get on with your larning as fast as you can,
For knowledge is sweeter than eggs done with ham ;
Fire away with your lessons, mind this is the school,
Or I'll blow ye to pot,' says Professor O'Toole.
    Derry down, etc.

And now, my dear childer, bear this in your mind,
That words without meaning are nothing but wind ;
Accept of all favours, make that the first rule,
Or you're nothing but goslins, says Doctor O'Toole.
    Derry down, etc.

When you go to a house and they ax you to eat,
Don't hold down your head, and refuse the good meat,
But say you will drink too, or else you're a fool,
Myself does the same thing, says Doctor O'Toole.
    Derry down, etc.

When father and mother have turned their backs,
Don't kick up a row with the dog and the cat ;
Nor tie the pig's tail to a table or stool,
Ye're a parcel of villains, says Doctor O'Toole.
    Derry down, etc.

But give over fighting, and think of your sins,
Or I'll break every bone in your rascally skins,
Nor try to deceive me like ducks in a pool,
For I'll find out the sinner, says Doctor O'Toole.
    Derry down, etc.

When into your grandmother's cupboard ye break,
In scrambling down from it take care of your neck—
Don't cheat the poor hangman, that crazy old fool ;
Give the *Devil* his due, says Professor O'Toole.
    Derry down, etc.

The lessons are over, so run away home,
Nor turn up your nose at a crust or a bone ;
Come back in the morning, for that is the rule ;
And ye'll get more instructions from Doctor O'Toole.
      Derry down, etc.


## MARY BEATON.

BONNIE blooming Mary Beaton !
Bonnie blooming Mary Beaton !
Could I but gain her for my ain,
I'd be the blythest wight in Britain.

I've woo'd and sued this mony a day,
  Ilk tender vow o' love repeatin',
But still she smiles, and answers "*nay*,"
    While I, puir saul ! am near the greetin'.
      Bonnie blooming, etc.
If smiles frae her can wound sae sair,
How sair were frowns frae Mary Beaton !

The lee-lang nicht I sich and grane,
  An' toss an' tumble till I'm sweatin',
For wink o' sleep can I get nane,
    For thinkin' still on Mary Beaton.
      Bonnie blooming, etc.
Poor troubled ghaist ! I get nae rest,
And what's my trouble ? Mary Beaton.

When ither youngsters blythe an' gay,
Set aff to join some merry meetin',
By some dyke-side I lanely stray,
    A-musing still on Mary Beaton.
      Bonnie blooming, etc.
A' mirth an' fun, I hate an' shun,
An' a' for sake o' Mary Beaton.

I ance could laugh an' sing wi' glee,
  And grudg'd the hours sae short an' fleetin',

But *now* ilk day's a *moon* to me,
  Sae sair I lang for Mary Beaton.
    Bonnie blooming, etc.
Till ance she's mine, I'll waste an' pine,
For now I'm past baith sleep an' eatin'.

Her fairy form sae light an' fair,
  Her gracefu' manner sae invitin',
Alas ! will kill me wi' despair,
  Unless I soon get Mary Beaton.
    Bonnie blooming, etc.
Wad she but bless me wi' a YES,
Oh how that *yes* my lot wad sweeten !

ALEX. RODGER.

## PETER AND MARY ;

### A KITCHEN BALLAD.

*Founded on Fact, and written expressly for all the Hangers-on about
the Dripping-Pan.*

THE learned have said (but who can tell
  When learned folks are right)
That there is no such thing in life
  " As loving at first sight."

But I will now an instance bring,
  You may rely upon,
How PETER BLACK fell deep in love
  With MARY MUCKLEJOHN.

He through the kitchen window look'd,
  When Mary just had got
A round of beef all newly cook'd,
  And smoking from the pot.

And aye he gaz'd and aye he smelt,
  With many a hungry groan.
Till Mary's heart began to melt
  Like marrow in the bone.

And looking up, she sweetly smiled,
　Her smile it seemed to say,
" Please, Mr. Black, if you're inclined,
　You'll dine with me to-day."

*At least* so Peter read her smile,
　And soon tripp'd down the stair ;
When Mary kindly welcom'd him,
　And help'd him to a chair.

There much he praised the round of beef,
　And much he praised the maid ;
While she, poor simple soul, believed
　Each flattering word he said.

Perhaps he made some slight mistakes,
　Yet part might well be trew'd,
For though her face was no *great shakes*,
　The beef was really *good.*

Then Peter pledged his troth, and swore
　A constant man he'd be,
And *daily*, like a man of truth,
　Came *constantly* at *three.*

And thus he dared, though long and lean,
　Each slanderous tongue to say,
That, though when present, he seem'd long,
　That he was *long* away.

*Three* was the hour when bits were nice,
　And then he show'd his face,
But show'd it there so very oft
　That Mary lost her place.

Some fair ones say that love is sweet,
　And hideth many a fault ;
Our fair one found, when *turn'd away*,
　Her love was rather *salt.*

Poor Mary says to Peter Black,
　" Now wedded let us be,

Bone of your bone, flesh of your flesh
  You promis'd to make me."

" Flesh of your flesh, I grant I said,
  Bone of your bone, I'd be ;
But now you know you've got no *flesh*,
  And *bones* are not for me."

Poor Cooky now stood all aghast
  To find him on the shy,'
And rais'd her apron-tail to wipe
  The *dripping* from her eye.

She sobb'd " Oh, perjured Peter Black,
  The basest man I know,
You're Black by name, you're black at heart,
  Since you can use me so."

Yet, still to please her Peter's *taste*
  Gave her poor heart relief ;
So Mary went and hung herself,
  And thus became *hung beef.*

That grief had *cut her up*, 'twas plain
  To every one in town,
But Peter when he heard the tale,
  He ran and *cut her down.*

Fast, fast his briny tears now flow'd,
  Yet Mary's sands ran fleeter ;
Such *brine* could not *preserve* the maid,
  Though from her own *salt Peter.*

From this let cookmaids learn to shun
  Men who are long and lean ;
For when they talk about their love,
  'Tis *pudding* that they mean.    CARRICK.

## THE DEIL O' BUCKLYVIE.

NAE doubt ye'll hae heard how daft Davie M'Ouat
Cam' hame like a deil, wi' an auld horn bouat ;
His feet they were cloven, horns stuck through his bonnet,
That fley'd a' the neibours whenc'er they look'd on it ;
The bairns flew like bees in a fright to their hivie,
For ne'er sic a deil was e'er seen in Bucklyvie.

We had deils o' our ain in plenty to grue at,
Without makin' a new deil o' Davie M'Ouat :
We hae deils at the sornin', and deils at blasphemin' ;
We hae deils at the cursin', and deils at nicknamin' ;
But for cloots and for horns, and jaws fit to rive ye,
Sic a deil never cam' to the town o' Bucklyvie.

We hae deils that will lie wi' ony deils breathing,
We're a' deils for drink when we get it for naething ;
We tak' a' we can, we gie unco little,
For no ane 'll part wi' the reek o' his spittle ;
The shool we ne'er use, wi' the rake we will rive you,
So we'll fen without ony mair deils in Bucklyvie.

Though han'less and clootless, wi' nae tail to smite ye
Like leeches when yaup, yet fu' sair can we bite ye ;
In our meal-pock nae new deil will ere get his nieve in,
For among us the auld ane could scarce get a livin',
To keep a' that's gude to ourselves we contrive aye,
For that is the creed o' the town o' Bucklyvie.

But deils wi' Court favour we never look blue at,
Then let's drink to our new deil, daft Davie M'Ouat :
And lang may he wag baith his tail and his bairdie,
Without skaith or scorning frae lord or frae lairdie ;
Let him get but the Queen at our fauts to connive aye,
He'll be the best deil for the town o' Bucklyvie.

Now, I've tell't ye ilk failin', I've tell't ye ilk faut :
Stick mair to yer moilin', and less to yer maut ;

And aiblins ye'll find it far better and wiser,
Than traikin', and drinkin' wi' Davie the guizar ;
And never to wanthrift may ony deil drive ye,
Is the wish o' wee Watty, the bard o' Bucklyvie.

CARRICK.

## A MOTHER'S DAUTY.

AIR—"*My mither's aye glowrin' ower me.*"

My mither wad hae me weel married,
My mither wad hae me weel married ;
    Na, she tries a' she can
    To get me a gudeman,
But as yet, a' her plans hae miscarried.
To balls and to concerts she hies me,
And meikle braw finery buys me ;
    But the men are sae shy,
    They just glow'r and gang by,
There's nane has the sense yet to prize me.

To ilka tea-party she tak's me,
And the theme o' her table-talk mak's me ;
    But the folks leuk sae queer,,
    When she cries " Lizzy! dear,"
That their conduct most grievously racks me.
She haurls me aff to the coast there,
Expecting to mak' me the toast there ;
    But somehow or ither,
    A lass wi' her mither,
Discovers her time is but lost there.

At the kirk, too, I'm made to attend her.
Not wholly heart-homage to render,
    But in rich " silken sheen,"
    Just to see and be seen,
And to dazzle the gowks wi' my splendour :
But for a' my sweet smirks and my glances,
There's never a wooer advances

To oxter me hame,
Wi' my dainty auld dame;
Alas, now, how kittle my chance is!

I'm sure I'm as good as my cousin,
Wha reckons her joes by the dizen;
That besiege her in thrangs,
Ilka gate that she gangs,
A' swarmin' like bumbees a-bizzin'.
And for beauty, pray what's a' her share o't?
Like me she could thole a hue mair o't?
For its granted by a',
Though she dresses right braw,
She has wonderfu' little to spare o't.

But I trow I maun try a new plan yet,
And depend on *mysel'* for a man yet;
For my cousin Kate vows,
That *some mithers are cowes*,
That wad scaur the best chiel that ever ran yet.
And gin I hae the luck to get married;
Gin I hae the luck to get married
Wi' a husband to guide,
(Let Miss Kate then deride),
I'll be proud that my point has been carried.

ALEX. RODGER.

## "HOUT AWA', JOHNNY, LAD!"

Hout awa', Johnny, lad! what maks ye flatter me?
Why wi' your praises sae meikle bespatter me?
Why sae incessantly deave and be-clatter me,
Teasing me mair than a body can bide?
Can I believe, when ye "angel" and "goddess" me,
That ye're in earnest to mak me your bride?
Say, can a woman o' sense or yet modesty,
Listen to talk frae the truth sae far wide?

Few are the flatterer's claims to sincerity,
Loud though he boast o' his honour and verity;
Truth frae his lips is a wonderfu' rarity,
    Words by his actions are sadly belied!
Woman he deems but a toy to be sported wi',
    Dawted or spurn'd at, as caprice may guide;
Blooming a while to be dallied and courted wi',
    Then to be flung like auld lumber aside!

True love has seldom the gift o' loquacity,
Lips to express it, aft want the capacity;
Wha, then, can trust in a wooer's veracity,
    Whase butter'd words o'er his tongue saftly slide?
What are loves tell-tales, that give it sweet utterance,
    Wherein the maiden may safely confide?
What—but the glances, the sighs and heart-flutterings,
    Of the loved youth who takes truth for his guide?

Yet, though I've spoken wi' seeming severity,
Made observations wi' prudish asperity,
I'd be the last ane to geck, or to sneer at ye,
    Kenning how little is made by fause pride.
Could we but then understand ane anither, then
    Soon wad my bosom the matter decide;
Leaving my worthy auld father and mither, then
    Hey, Johnny, lad! I'd become your ain bride.
                                ALEX. RODGER.


## HIGHLAND POLITICIANS.

CODE, Tougall, tell me what you'll thocht
    Apout this Bill Reform man,
Tat's breeding sic a muckle steer,
    An' like to raise ta storm man;
For noo ta peoples meet in troves,
    On both sides o' ta Tweed man,
An' spoket speechums loud an' lang,
    An' very pauld inteed, man.

'Teed, Tonald, lad, she'll no pe ken,
    For she's nae politish, man,
But for their speechums loud an' lang,
    She wadna gie tat sneesh, man ;
For gin she'll thocht ta thing was richt,
    She would her beetock traw, man,
An' feught like tamm—till ance ta Bill
    Was made coot Cospel law, man.

Hoot toot, man, Tougall! tat micht do
    When SHORDIE TWA did ring, man,
An' her fore-faiters trew ta tirk,
    To mak teir Charlie king, man ;
But tirks, an' pistols, an' claymores,
    Pe no for me nor you, man ;
Tey'll a' pe out o' fashions gane
    Since pluity Waterloo, man.

Last nicht she'll went to pay her rent,
    Ta laird gie her ta tram, man,
An' tell her tat this Bill Reform
    Was shust a nonsense tamn, man !
Pe no for honest man's, she'll say,
    Pe meddle 'ffairs o' State man,
But leave those matters to him's CRACE,
    Him's CLORY, an' ta great man.

She'll talk 'pout *Revolations*, too,
    Pe pad an' wicked thing, man,
Wad teuk awa ta 'stinctions a',
    Frae peggar down to king, man ;
Nae doubts, nae doubts, her nainsel' said,
    But yet tere's something worse man,
To *Revolations* tat will teuk
    Ta puir man's cow nor horse, man.

An' ten she'll wish ta *Ministers*
    Pe kicket frae teir place, man :
Och hon, och hon ! her nainsel said,
    Tat wad pe woefu' case, man ;

For gin ta *Ministers* pe fa',
   *Precentors* neist maun gang, man—
Syne wha wad in ta Punker stood,
   An' lilt ta godly sang, man?

Och! ten ta laird flee in a rage,
   An' *sinfu' deil* [1] me ca', man—
Me tell him no pe understood
   What him will spoke ava, man:
Ta sinfu' deil!—na, na, she'll say,
   She'll no pelang tat clan, man,
Hersel's a true an' trusty *Grant,*
   As coot as 'nitter man, man.

But, Tougall, lad! my 'pinion is,
   An' tat she'll freely gie, man,
Ta laird pe fear tat this Reform
   Will petter you an' me, man;
For like some ither lairds, she still
   Wad ride upon our pack, man;
But fait! she'll maype saw ta tay,
   Pe tell him 'nitter crack, man.

For *Shames ta feeter* [2] say this Bill
   Will mak' ta rents pe fa', man;
Pe mak' ta sneesh an' whisky cheap,
   Ta gauger chase awa, man;
An' ne'er let lairds nor factors more
   Pe do ta poor man's harm, man,
Nor purn him's house apoon him's head,
   An' trive him aff ta farm, man.

Weel, Tonald! gin I'll thochtit that,
   Reformer I will turn man,
For wi' their 'pressions an' their scorns,
   My very pluit will purn, man:
Och, shust to hae ta tay apout,
   Wi' some tat I will ken, man;

---

[1] Infidel.      [2] James the Weaver.

Tey'll prunt my house to *please la laird*,
Cot ! let them try't again, man !

ALEX. RODGER.

## O ! DINNA BID ME GANG WI' YOU.

O ! DINNA bid me gang wi' you,
   'Twould break my mither's heart ;
There's nane to care for her but me,
   Sae dinna bid us part ;
Increasing frailties tell that here
   Her time will no be lang,
And wha wad tend her deeing bed,
   Gin I wi' you should gang ?

She kens our hearts, and says she thinks
   She could our absence bear ;
But while she speaks, her aged e'e
   Is glist'ning wi' a tear.
Light waes will weet the youthfu' cheek,
   But ah ! severe's the pang
That stirs the time-dried fount of grief,
   Sae dinna bid me gang.

JAMES SCOTT.

## KILROONY'S VISIT TO LONDON.

HAVE ye heard of the excellent sport
   Afforded by Master Kilroony,
How, when he got up to the court,
   The king recognised an old crony !
" Right happy to see you I am !
   And welcome you are into Lunnan :"
The natives cried out, There is Dan,
   We scarcely believed you were comin'.

(*Spoken.*) "And so, Mr. Daniel Kilroony, how do you do ?" says
the King. "Pretty well, I thank you," says Dan, "Oxis doxis
glorioxis to your Kingship's glory, for ever, and a day after ; I hope

your Majesty is full of salubrity?" "That I am," says the King.
"Did you bring your shillelah with ye, Dan?" "I did." "And right
you were," says His Majesty, "for betwixt you and me, there is the
*ould one* to pay here, and no money to give him; depend upon it,
there will be wigs upon the grass this year, long before it grows,
Dan; but keep your mind asy, for I am determined to stand by my
loyal loving subjects, as long as they have a button on their coats."
"That's right," says Dan, "and if one of the varmint after this
presume to question your Majesty's goodness, blow me if I don't
beat their two eyes into one."

> Then the King and Kilroony down sat,
> And partook of an excellent dinner;
> There was roasted and boil'd, lean and fat,
> To comfort the heart of each sinner;
> There was brandy, and porter, and ale,
> With excellent wine and good whisky,
> All the fruits that are sold by retail;
> So the King and Kilroony got frisky.

"And how is Mrs. Kilroony and all the childer?" says the King
after the dinner was over. "Why, pretty well, thank your Majesty,"
says Dan. "How is your own good lady, the Queen, I don't see her
about all the house, at-all-at-all?" "Spake aisy," says the King,
"she's in bad humour to-day, this is Friday, and she's busy wi' washing
and cleaning; and when engaged in that sort of work, the *ould black
gentleman* with the long tail couldn't make her keep the dumb side
of her tongue undermost." "And are ye so circumstanced?" said Dan,
"it's just the same way with Mrs. Kilroony; when her blood got up,
she used to make me believe that she would fight the devil himself;
but faith I took it out of her." "And how did you manage that?"
says the King. "Just wi' the same elegant instrument you were in-
quiring after a little ago. I rubbed her down with an oaken towel,
and gave her five-and-twenty drops of shillelah oil next her stomach
in the morning." "Don't mention it," says the King. "Then don't
ax me," says Dan.

> "Arrah, murder!" exclaim'd the good King,
> "Could you cudgel the bones of a woman?"
> "I would try," says Kilroony, "to bring
> Back her sinses, and make her a true one;

For ladies, when doing what's wrong,
   Are nought but a parcel of *varmint :*"
Says the King to Kilroony, " Go home,
   I've heard quite enough of your *sarmint.*"

" Get out of my house this minute," says the King, "and never afterwards let me hear you insinuate anything against the female generation. Bad luck to you for a dirty bog-trotting-potwalloper, can't ye give out your counsel to your own beautiful *pisantry?* six millions of elegant male and female Paddies, all in a state of beautiful naturality; sure there's work enough for your patriotism. Daniel Kilroony, leave this, I say, and never be after showing yourself here as long as there's a nose protruding from your countenance." "Please your Majesty," says Dan, "might I venture to show myself should I ever happen to lose that useful appendage?" "Never," says the King. —" Leave my presence, or I'll spake ye into the earth in a moment."

So Kilroony was " *cut* at the court,
   And soon left the city of Lunnan ; "
All the Paddies had capital sport,        ·
   When they saw poor Kilroony back coming.
" Kilroony, Kilroony !" said they,
   " You would fain be a parliament *mimber*,
But the King he put *salt* in your tay
   And burn'd your nose with a cinder."
    O have you not heard, etc.


## THE DEUKS DANG O'ER MY DADDIE. [1]

THE bairns got up in a loud, loud skreech,
   The deuks dang o'er my Daddie, O ;
Quo' our gudewife, " Let him lie there,
   For he's just a paidling body, O :
He paidles out, and he paidles in,
   He paidles late and early, O :
This thirty years I hae been his wife,
   And comfort comes but sparely, O."

[1] The first two stanzas are, with a few verbal alterations, from Burns—the additional verses are by a facetious contributor to whom this publication is indebted for the graphic humour of our brethren of the Green Isle.

"Now haud your tongue," quo' our gudeman,
　"And dinna be sae saucy, O,
I've seen the day, and so hae ye,
　I was baith young and gaucy, O.
I've seen the day you butter'd my brose,
　And cuitered me late and early, O ;
But auld age is on me now,
　And wow but I fin't richt sairly, O."

"I carena tho' ye were i' the mools,
　Or dookit in a boggie, O ;
I kenna the use o' the crazy auld fool,
　But just to toom the coggie, O.
Gin the win' were out o' your whaisling hauze,
　I'd marry again and be voggie, O ;
Some bonny young lad would be my lot,
　Some rosy cheeked roggie, O."

Quo' our gudeman, "Gie me that Rung
　That's hingin' in the ingle, O ;
I'se gar ye haud that sorrowfu' tongue,
　Or else your lugs will tingle, O.
Gang to your bed this blessed nicht
　Or I'll be your undoing, O ;"
The canny auld wife crap out o' sicht,
　What think ye o' sic wooing, O ?

## LOVE'S FIRST QUARREL.

"Whar' shall I get anither love,
　Sin' Johnny's ta'en the gee ?
Whar' shall I get anither love,
　To speak kind words to me ?

To row me in his cozie plaid,
　Whan wintry winds blaw snell,
Whar' shall I get anither love ?
　Waes me, I canna tell.

Yestreen I quarrell'd wi' my love,
　　'Cause he behaved unmeet,
An' rubb'd my cheek wi' his hard chin
　　Till I was like to greet.

I flate upon him lang and sair,
　　At last he took the huff,
An' tell't him ne'er to see my face,
　　If he kept his baird sae rough.

But a' nicht lang I lay an' sigh't,
　　Wi' the warm tear in my e'e,
And I wish'd I had my Johnny back,
　　Though his baird were to his knee.

It's harsh to use a maiden thus,
　　For her simplicity,
Wha scarce can tell what loving means,
　　Or kens what man should be."

The youth ahint the hallan stood,
　　And snirtled in his sleeve,
It's cordial to a love-sick heart,
　　To hear its true love grieve.

He slipp'd ahint her—ere she wist,
　　He baith her e'en did steek,
"Now guess and tell wha's *weel shav'd* chin,
　　Is press'd upon your cheek?"

Her lips sae rich wi' *hinny* dew,
　　Smil'd sae forgiving-like,
That Johnny crook'd his thievish mou,
　　To herry the sweet *byke.*

CARRICK.

## THE GUDEMAN'S PROPHECY.

THE win blew loud on our lum-head,
    About auld Hallowe'en ;
Quo' our gudewife to our gudeman,
    " What may this tempest mean !"

The gudeman shook his head an' sich'd,
    Quo' he, "'Tween you and me,
I fear we'll hae some bluidy wark,
    And that ye'll live to see.

For just before the Shirra Muir,
    We had sic thuds o' win',
An' mony a bonny buik lay cauld,
    Before that year was dune."

" Hoot, toot ! gudeman, ye're haverin' noo,
    An' talkin' like a fule,
Ye ken we've aye sic thuds o' win',
    'Bout Candlemas or Yule."

" I'll no be ca'd a fule," quo' he,
    " By ony worthless she,
My boding it sall stan' the test,
    An' that belyve ye'll see."

" To ca' your wife a worthless she,
    Shows just ye're scant o' wit,
But if ye'll speak that word again,
    I'll brain you whar ye sit."

Now up gat he, and up gat she,
    An' till't fell teeth an' nail,
While frae the haffets o' them baith,
    The bluid cam down like hail.

Our Gutchyre now spak frae the nuik,
    A sairie man was he.
" Sit down, sit down, ye senseless fouk,
    An' let sic tuilzeing be,

An' gudewife learn an' no despise
   The word o' prophecy,
For "*bluidy wark*" this nicht has been,
   An' that ye've lived to see.

I could hae seen wi' hauf an e'e,
   The prophecy was sure,
For siccan words 'tween married fouks,
   Bring on a "*Shirra Muir.*"

An' noo I hope ilk wedded pair,
   A moral here may fin',
An' mind though tempest rage without,
   A *calm sough* keep within.

CARRICK.

## THE WEE RAGGIT LADDIE.

WEE stuffy, stumpy, dumpie laddie,
Thou urchin elfin, bare an' duddy,
Thy plumpit kite an' cheek sae ruddy
   Are fairly baggit,
Although the breekums on thy fuddy
   Are e'en right raggit.

Thy wee roun' pate sae black and curly,
Thy twa bare feet, sae stoure an' burly,
The biting frost, though snell an' surly
   An' sair to bide,
Is scouted by thee, thou hardy wurly,
   Wi' sturdy pride.

Come frost, come snaw, come win', come weet,
Ower frozen dubs, through slush an' sleet,
Thou patters wi' thy wee red feet
   Right bauld an' sicker,
An' ne'er wast kenned to whinge or greet,
   But for thy bicker.

Our gentry's wee peel-garlic gets
Feed on bear meal, an' sma' ale swats,
Wi' thin beef tea, an' scours o' sauts,
    To keep them pale ;
But aitmeal parritch straughts thy guts,
    An' thick Scotch kail.

Thy grannie's paiks, the maister's whippin',
Can never mend thy gait o' kippin';
I've seen the hail schule bairnies trippin',
    A' after thee,
An' thou aff, like a young colt, skippin'
    Far ower the lea.

'Mang Hallowfair's wild, noisy brattle,
Thou'st foughten mony a weary battle,
Stridin' ower horse an' yerkin' cattle
    Wi' noisy glee,
Nae Jockey's whup nor drover's wattle,
    Can frighten thee.

Ilk kiltit Celt, ilk raggit Paddy,
Ilk sooty sweep, ilk creeshy caddie,
Ilk tree-legg'd man, ilk club-taed laddie,
    Ilk oily leary,
Ilk midden mavis, wee black jaudy,
    A' dread an' fear ye.

Ilk struttin' swad, ilk reelin sailor,
Ilk rosin't snab, ilk barkin't nailer,
Ilk flunky bauld, ilk coomy collier,
    Ilk dusty batchy,
Ilk muckle grab, ilk little tailor,
    A' strive to catch ye.

Ilk thimblin', thievin', gamblin', diddler,
Ilk bellows-mendin' tinkler driddler,
Ilk haltin', hirplin', blindit fiddler,
    Ilk wee speech-crier,
Ilk lazy, ballant-singin' idler,
    Chase thee like fire.

Ilk waly-draiglin', dribblin' wight,
Wha sleeps a' day, an' drinks a' night,
An' staggers hame in braid daylight,
  Bleerit, blin', an' scaur,
Thou coverest him up, a movin' fright,
  Wi' dunts o' glaur.

Ilk auld wife stoyterin' wi' her drappie,
In teapot, bottle, *stoup*, or cappie,
Fu' snugly fauldit in her lappie,
  Wi' couthy care,
Thou gar'st the hidden treasure jaupie
  A' in the air.

At e'en, when weary warkmen house,
Their sair forfoughten spunks to rouse,
An' ower th' inspirin' whisky bouse,
  Croon mony a ditty,
Thou sits amang them bauld and crouse,
  Whiffin' thy cutty.

Thine education's maistly perfect,
An' though thou now are wee an' barefoot,
Thou'lt be a swankin', spunky spark yet,
  Or I'm mista'en,
Unless misfortune's gurly bark yet
  Should change thy vein.

O, why sould age, wi' cankered e'e,
Condemn thy pranks o' rattlin' glee,
We a' were callants ance, like thee,
  An' happier then
Than, after clamberin' up life's tree,
  We think us men.
    JAMES BALLANTINE, Edinburgh.

## THE QUEEN'S ANTHEM.

GOD bless our lovely Queen,
With cloudless days serene ;—
    God save our Queen
From perils, pangs and woes,
Secret and open foes,
Till her last evening close,
    God save our Queen.

From flattery's poisoned streams ;—
From faction's fiendish schemes,
    God shield our Queen ;—
With men her throne surround,
Firm, active, zealous, sound,
Just, righteous, sage, profound ;—
    God save our Queen.

Long may she live to prove,
Her faithful subjects' love ;—
    God bless our Queen.
Grant her an Alfred's zeal,
Still for the Commonweal,
Her people's wounds to heal ;
    God save our Queen.

Watch o'er her steps in youth ;—
In the straight paths of truth,
    Lead our young Queen ;
And as years onward glide,
Succour, protect, and guide,
Albion's hope—Albion's pride ;—
    God save our Queen.

Free from war's sanguine stain,
Bright be Victoria's reign ;—
    God guard our Queen.

Safe from the traitor's wiles,
Long may the Queen of Isles,
Cheer millions with her smiles ;—
    God save our Queen.
ALEX. RODGER.

## THE FORSAKEN.

O GIVE me back that blissful time,
When I so fondly gazed on thee,
And loved—nor deemed my love a crime,
Till now, too late, my fault I see.

O give me back my innocence !
Alas ! that may not—cannot be,
Too deep, too dark is my offence,
For purity to dwell with me.

Hast thou forgot the solemn vows,
So oft exchanged by thee and me,
While seated underneath the boughs,
Of yonder venerable tree ?

Those vows, indeed, may be forgot,
Or only laughed at, now, by thee,
But to thy mind they'll yet be brought,
When cold below the sod I'll be.

How could'st thou treat a maiden so,
Who would have gladly died for thee ?
Think, think what I must undergo,
Think of my load of infamy ;

O could repentance wash my stain,
What peaceful days I yet might see,
But no ;—I ever must remain
A victim of my love for thee.
ALEX. RODGER.

## OH! PRINCELY IS THE BARON'S HALL.

OH! princely is the Baron's hall,
   And bright his lady's bower,
And none may wed their eldest son
   Without a royal dower;
If such, my peerless maid, is thine,
Then place thy lily hand in mine.

A cot beside the old oak-tree,
   The woodbine's pleasant flower,
A careless heart and spotless name,
   Sir Knight, are all my dower;
Thy gold spur and thy milk-white steed,
May bear thee where thou'lt better speed.

Now, by the ruby of thy lip—
   The sapphire of thine eye—
The treasures of thy snowy breast,
   We part not company:
A sire's domain—a mother's pride,
Can claim for me no wealthier bride.

WM. KENNEDY.

## WEE RABBIE.

AE mornin', wee Rabbie, fu' canty and gabbie,
   Gat up frae his nestie an' buskit him braw;
To sweeten his lifey, he wish'd for a wifey,
   An' fix'd on tall Nelly o' Heathery Ha'.

The laughin' wee bodie soon mountit on Doddie,
   Sae sleekit, an' bridled, an' saddled, an' a';
A drap in his headie, to haud his heart steadie,
   Aff he trotted for Nelly o' Heathery Ha'.

A wooer mair vap'rin', mair paukie and cap'rin',
   Ne'er before took the road sae weel mountit an' a';

But the fowk thought him muzzy, to fix on a huzzy,
    Sae strappin' as Nell o' Heathery Ha'.

But Rabbie was happy, love smit wi' the nappy,
    Nor dream'd that his person was punylie sma';
He canter'd fu' smirky, a bauld little birky,
    Nor halted till landit at Heathery Ha'.

Wi' whip-han' he knuckled, while neighbours a' chuckled,
    An' wondered what made him sae trig and sae braw ;
Ne'er thinking that Doddie had brought the wee bodie,
    A-wooin' to Nelly o' Heathery Ha'.

But Rabbie soon lightit, without being frightit,
    An' vow'd he'd hae Nelly, or hae nane at a';
Then tiptoe in goes he, resolved to be easie,
    Before he'd leave Nelly o' Heathery Ha'.

Soon Nelly, though taller, wi' Rabbie though smaller,
    Agreed to be buckled for gude an' for a' ;
She vows he is snodie, though but a wee bodie,
    An' better a mannie than ne'er ane ava.

Sae they've remounted Doddie, lang Nell, the wee bodie ;
    'Twas sport to see Rabbie sae brisk gaun awa'.
He sat in Nell's lapie, sae laughin' an' happy,
    An' trottit hame crously frae Heathery Ha'.


## LOVELY MAIDEN.

LOVELY maiden, art thou sleeping ?
    Wake, and fly with me, my love,
While the moon is proudly sweeping
    Through the ether fields above ;
While her mellow'd light is streaming
    Full on mountain, moor, and lake !
Dearest maiden, art thou dreaming ?
    'Tis thy true love calls—awake ?

All is hush'd around thy dwelling,
 Even the watch-dog's lull'd asleep ;
Hark ! the clock the hour is knelling,
 Wilt thou then thy promise keep ?
Yes, I hear her softly coming,
 Now her window's gently rais'd,
There she stands, an angel blooming—
 Come, my Mary ! haste thee, haste !

Fear not, love ! thy rigid father
 Soundly sleeps, bedrench'd with wine ;
'Tis thy true love holds the ladder,
 To his care thyself resign !
Now my arms enfold a treasure,
 Which for worlds I'd not forego ;
Now our bosoms feel that pleasure,
 Faithful bosoms only know.

Long have our true loves been thwarted
 By the stern decrees of pride,
Which would doom us to be parted,
 And make thee another's bride ;
But behold my steeds are ready,
 Soon they'll post us far away ;
Thou wilt be Glen Alva's Lady
 Long before the dawn of day !
ALEX. RODGER.

## COME THEN, ELIZA DEAR.

DEAREST Eliza, say, wilt thou resign
All thy companions gay, and become mine?
 Wilt thou through woe and weal,
 Be my loved partner still,
 Share with me every ill,
  Nor e'er repine ?

Wilt thou, O lovely fair ! when I'm distress'd,
All my afflictions share, soothe them to rest ?
   Wilt thou, when comforts fail,
   When woe and want assail,
   With sympathising wail,
     Cling to this breast ?

Yes, yes, O dearest youth ! here I resign,
All else I prize on earth, thy fate to join ;
   Gladly I'll share thy woes,
   Soothe thee to calm repose,
   While heaven on me bestows
     Such love as thine.

Come then, Eliza dear, come to this breast,
Thou alone reignest here, kindest and best ;
   If wealth and rural peace,
   If love that ne'er shall cease,
   Can give thee ought like bliss,
     Thou shalt be bless'd.

               ALEX. RODGER.


## THE CAVALIER'S SONG.

A STEED ! a steed of matchless speed,
   A sword of metal keen !
All else to noble hearts is dross,
   All else on earth is mean,
The neighing of the war-horse proud,
   The rolling of the drum,
The clangour of the trumpets loud,
   Be sounds from heaven that come ;
And oh ! the thund'ring press of knights,
   When as their war-cries swell,
May toll from heaven an angel bright,
   Or rouse a fiend from hell.

Then mount, then mount, brave gallants all,
  And don your helms amain,
Death's couriers, Fame and Honour, call
  Us to the field again.
No shrewish tears shall fill our eye,
  When the sword-hilt's in our hand,
Heart-whole we'll part, and no whit sigh
  For the fairest of the land.
Let piping swain and craven wight,
  Thus weep and puling cry ;—
Our business is, like men to fight,
  And hero-like to die !

MOTHERWELL.

## YOUNG PADDY'S TUTOR.

SOME patriots howl o'er Paddie's wrongs,
  And raise such lamentation, O ;
Whilst others contrive with their speeches and songs,
  To complete her stultification, O.
Ould Father M'Flail, good honest man,
  Like a heavenly constellation, O,
Enlightens the Paddies as much as he can,
  With his system of education, O.

(*Spoken.*) "Come hither the whole varmint of ye, and let me see that ye're all present, and none ov ye absent. I see ye're all here, my honnies ; the more credit to you for the interest you take in your larnin'. But before commencin' the instruction of the day, let us attend to the comforts of the Academy. Phidre O'Gallach ! what sort of a turf is that ye brought with you this morning? Ye'll be after kaping it warm in your pocket, for shame, till ye come up to the school ;—did you ever expect that a handful like it could give a hap'worth of heat to comfort the Institution? Jim Mullen, now for you, my man : what sort of a way is that you've turn'd the corner of your catechism? don't abuse the literature of the country. Are ye at it already? paice childer—houl' your paice, I say, agin ; for I don't know whether my tongue is in my own mouth, or dancin' agin the teeth of all the childer in the Academy. Mike Linahan, there's no hearin', for you're roaring as if a score of ducks were houlding a holiday in your mouth ; them black-nosed pepper-boxes on Dublin Castle, with the brimstone breath comin' up their throats, couldn't hear themselves speakin' for you ! turn the dumb side of your tongue uppermost, or I'll glue it agin the ceilin' of your mouth ! Winny M'Coy, my little pot of honey ; there's not a sweeter mouth in ould Ireland, nor one that M'Flail would like to put knowledge and letters into, but there is no opening or pretinsion yet in your intellects ; the mighty big letters coming up from the bottom of your breast, would be splittin' your throat to ribbands, and opening another mouth below your illigant chin ; and there would be no raison for your takin' in sustenance and comforts there, my sweet potato blossom ; just trot away home on that purty little foot of your's, that couldn't hurt a hair on the head of a daisy, and come back agin to the instruction when the turf is puttin' on its clothes for summer. Now, children, go on with the instruction of the day. Looney M'Twolter, ye scoundrel, what's the name of that letter that's starin' you there in the face?" "Q, sur." "It's a lie, sir ! that's A ; didn't I tell you that a month ago? Sure you might see the two legs of it standing up there like the sticks at your grandmother's clay cabin door? O, Looney, Looney I you'll never make a clargy in the 'varsal world. And what's the name of the next letter that comes after the A? sure you haven't forgot it already ! What do you call the little gintleman, with the sting in his tail, and yellow jacket over his shoulders, that flies about the bogs and the ditches?" "Bee, sur." "That's the name of it, you blackguard ; many's the day you run after him when ye should have been following your edication. And what do you call the fellow of the B?" "That's the moon, sur." "Thunder and thump ! that's murderous ; who ever heard of a letter called the moon? What do I do when I look through my spectacles, ye rapscalliou, ye?" "Ye squint, sur." (*Beats him.*) "And what else?" "You see, sur." "Troth, I do that, and C is the very name ov it ; run away to your sate, an' turn the sharpest corner of your eye to your lesson."

And thus the worthy Father lays,
    Of knowledge the sure foundation, O,
The system every one should plase,
    For its all of his own creation, O.
The Arts and Sciences every one,
    From the very first emanation, O,

He explains to all as clear as the sun,
What a brilliant elucidation, O.

" Charley M'Flusky, come hither; but first of all take that fly out
of your mouth. What would you think now, if that little creature
contained in its tiny body the soul of your own ould grandmother?
but you don't understand transmugrification; never catch flies in the
school, sur. Denis Hourigan, now, tell me the name of that letter
I was explaining to you yesterday—the long one there, for all the
world like a May-pole? You've forgot, I see, that's sartain. What
was't your father gave to your mother last Saturday night, when he
came home?" "He gived her a black eye, sur." "And isn't I the
very name of the letter? And what's the name of the next but one
after the I? What does your mother open the door with?" "A
latch, please your worship." "Anything else?" "A key, sur."
"Sure, and K's the very name of it too. Well, and what's the name
of that round letter like the full moon, afore she turns herself into a
raping-hook agin, as our own Belfast prophets foretel? I wonder if
I can 'ring it out ov ye?" (*Pulls his ear.*) "O murder, murder!"
"That's it now; I'll take the O, and lave the murder to yourself.
Tell me now, before I dismiss you, the name of that one with the slop
over his head. Sure you know what mother takes to her breakfast
on Sunday morning?" "Rum, sur." "Oh ye little tell-tale! well
does I love it my own self too, as well as a duck does a dhurty day;
an' it were not for a dhrop or two of it, my ould throat would get
dhry with spaking—and my body a lump of dhry dust—ould Father
M'Flail, your tutor, would be blown about like the dust in the very
air you're breathin'. Does your mother never take anything else?"
"Tay, sur." "And T's the very word I want; so get away to your
seat, and pay more attention for the future. And now, Dennis
O'Neal, you are farther on with your larning; tell me how many
cases them Latins had amongst them." "Six, please your honour."
"Then fire away and let's hear their names." "There was the
Nomativ, and the Ginitiv, and the Jockativ." "Thunder and turf,
who ever heard of the Jockativ case; take that (*knocks him down*),
and remember that is the *Knockativ.* There is a lesson in jigo-
nometry for you, that your mother never contracted for. Larry
Hoolagan, spell Babelmandel, an' be hanged t'ye." "B-a-able-m-a-
mandle, Babelmandel." "That's the thing, my boy. Spell us Constantinople." "C-o-n-con-s-t-a-n-stantinople, Constantinople." "Do
you know the meanin' of that mighty word, now? That's the name
of the Grand Turk, sir, who commands the cratures with the three

tails. There's the benefit of navigation to you without ever puttin'
your foot on water.'

> Now boys and girls go home I say,
>   And see ye give over flirtation, O ;
> Nor dare any more the truant to play,
>   But get on with your idication, O.
> May English, Irish, Scotch, each one,
>   Soon make an amalgamation, O,
> With heart, and soul, and blood, and bone,
>   To confirm their liberation, O.

## WEARIE'S WELL.

> In a saft simmer gloamin',
>   In yon dowie dell,
> It was there we twa first met
>   By Wearie's cauld well.
> We sat on the brume bank
>   And look'd in the burn,
> But sidelang we look'd on
>   Ilk ither in turn.
>
> The corn-craik was chirming
>   His sad eerie cry,
> And the wee stars were dreaming
>   Their path through the sky :
> The burn babbled freely
>   Its love to ilk flower,
> But we heard and we saw nought
>   In that blessed hour.
>
> We heard and we saw nought
>   Above or around ;
> We felt that our love lived,
>   And loathed idle sound.
> I gazed on your sweet face
>   Till tears filled my e'e,
> And they drapt on your wee loof —
>   A warld's wealth to me.

Now the winter's snaw's fa'ing
  On bare holm and lea ;
And the cauld wind is strippin'
  Ilk leaf aff the tree.
But the snaw fa's not faster,
  Nor leaf disna part
Sae sune frae the bough, as
  Faith fades in your heart.

Ye've waled out anither
  Your bridegroom to be ;
But can his heart luve sae
  As mine luvit thee ?
Ye'll get biggings and mailings,
  And monie braw claes ;
But they a' winna buy back
  The peace o' past days.

Fareweel, and for ever,
  My first luve and last,
May thy joys be to come—
  Mine live in the past,
In sorrow and sadness,
  This hour fa's on me ;
But light, as thy luve, may
  It fleet over thee !

MOTHERWELL.

## MY HEID IS LIKE TO REND, WILLIE.

My heid is like to rend, Willie,
  My heart is like to break—
I'm wearin' aff my feet, Willie,
  I'm dyin' for your sake !
Oh lay your cheek to mine, Willie,
  Your hand on my briest-bane—
Oh say ye'll think on me, Willie,
  When I am deid and gane !

Its vain to comfort me, Willie,
　　Sair grief maun hae its will—
But let me rest upon your briest,
　　To sab and greet my fill.
Let me sit on your knee, Willie,
　　Let me shed by your hair,
And look into the face, Willie,
　　I never sall see mair !

I'm sittin' on your knee, Willie,
　　For the last time in my life—
A puir heart-broken thing, Willie,
　　A mither, yet nae wife.
Aye, press your hand upon my heart,
　　And press it mair and mair—
Or it will burst the silken twine,
　　Sae strang is its despair !

Oh wae's me for the hour, Willie,
　　When we thegither met—
Oh wae's me for the time, Willie,
　　That our first tryst was set !
Oh wae's me for the loanin' green
　　Where we were wont to gae—
And wae's me for the destinie,
　　That gart me luve thee sae !

Oh ! dinna mind my words, Willie,
　　I downa seek to blame—
But oh ! it's hard to live, Willie,
　　And dree a warld's shame !
Het tears are hailin' owre your cheek,
　　And hailin' owre your chin ;
Why weep ye sae for worthlessness,
　　For sorrow and for sin ?

I'm weary o' this warld, Willie,
　　And sick wi' a' I see—
I canna live as I ha'e lived,
　　Or be as I should be.

But fauld unto your heart, Willie,
　　The heart that still is thine—
And kiss ance mair the white, white cheek,
　　Ye said was red langsyne.

A stoun' gaes through my heid, Willie,
　　A sair stoun' through my heart—
Oh ! haud me up and let me kiss
　　Thy brow ere we twa pairt.
Anither, and anither yet !
　　How fast my life-strings break !
Fareweel ! fareweel ! through yon kirk-yard
　　Step lichtly for my sake !

The lav'rock in the lift, Willie,
　　That lilts far ower our heid,
Will sing the morn as merrilie
　　Abune the clay-cauld deid ;
And this green turf we're sittin' on,
　　Wi' dew-draps shimmerin' sheen,
Will hap the heart that luvit thee
　　As warld has seldom seen.

But oh ! remember me, Willie,
　　On land where'er ye be—
And oh ! think on the leal, leal heart,
　　That ne'er luvit ane but thee !
And oh ! think on the cauld, cauld mools,
　　That file my yellow hair—
That kiss the cheek and kiss the chin,
　　Ye never sall kiss mair !　MOTHERWELL.


## THE BLOOM HATH FLED THY CHEEK, MARY.

THE bloom hath fled thy cheek, Mary,
　　As spring's rath blossoms die.
And sadness hath o'ershadowed now
　　Thy once bright eye ;

But, look on me, the prints of grief
    Still deeper lie.
        Farewell !

Thy lips are pale and mute, Mary,
    Thy step is sad and slow,
The morn of gladnesss hath gone by
    Thou erst did know ;
I, too, am changed like thee, and weep
    For every woe.
        Farewell !

It seems as 'twere but yesterday
    We were the happiest twain,
When murmured sighs and joyous tears,
    Dropping like rain,
Discoursed my love, and told how loved
    I was again.
        Farewell !

'Twas not in cold and measured phrase
    We gave our passion name ;
Scorning such tedious eloquence,
    Our hearts' fond flame,
And long imprisoned feelings fast
    In deep sobs came.
        Farewell !

Would that our love had been the love
    That merest worldlings know,
When passion's draught to our doomed lips
    Turns utter woe,
And our poor dream of happiness
    Vanishes so !
        Farewell !

But in the wreck of all our hopes,
    There's yet some touch of bliss,

Since fate robs not our wretchedness
　　Of this last kiss :
Despair, and love, and madness, meet
　　In this, in this.
　　　　　Farewell !
　　　　　　　　　　MOTHERWELL.


## MAY MORN SONG.

THE grass is wet with shining dews,
　　Their silver bells hang on each tree,
While opening flower and bursting bud
　　Breathe incense forth unceasingly ;
The mavis pipes in greenwood shaw,
　　The throstle glads the spreading thorn,
And cheerily the blythesome lark
　　Salutes the rosy face of morn.
　　　　　'Tis early prime ;
　　　　　　And hark ! hark ! hark !
　　　　　His merry chime
　　　　　　Chirrups the lark :
　　Chirrup ! chirrup ! he heralds in
　　The jolly sun with matin hymn.

Come, come, my love ! and May-dews shake
　　In pailfuls from each drooping bough,
They'll give fresh lustre to the bloom
　　That breaks upon thy young cheek now.
O'er hill and dale, o'er waste and wood,
　　Aurora's smiles are streaming free ;
With earth it seems brave holiday,
　　In heaven it looks high jubilee.
　　　　　And it is right,
　　　　　　For mark, love, mark !
　　　　　How bathed in light
　　　　　　Chirrups the lark :
　　Chirrup ! chirrup ! he upward flies,
　　Like holy thoughts to cloudless skies.

They lack all heart who cannot feel
  The voice of heaven within them thrill,
In summer morn, when mounting high
  This merry minstrel sings his fill.
Now let us seek yon bosky dell
  Where brightest wild-flowers choose to be
And where its clear stream murmurs on,
  Meet type of our love's purity ;
      No witness there,
        And o'er us, hark !
      High in the air
        Chirrups the lark :
Chirrup ! chirrup ! away soars he,
Bearing to heaven my vows to thee !
               MOTHERWELL.

## HE IS GONE! HE IS GONE!

HE is gone ! he is gone !
  Like the leaf from the tree ;
Or the down that is blown
  By the wind o'er the lea.
He is fled, the light-hearted !
Yet a tear must have started
To his eye, when he parted
  From love-stricken me !

He is fled ! he is fled !
  Like a gallant so free,
Plumed cap on his head,
  And sharp sword by his knee ;
While his gay feathers fluttered,
Surely something he muttered,
He at least must have uttered
  A farewell to me !

He's away ! he's away
  To far lands o'er the sea—

And long is the day
　Ere home he can be ;
But where'er his steed prances,
Amid thronging lances,
Sure he'll think of the glances
　That love stole from me !

He is gone ! he is gone !
　Like the leaf from the tree ;
But his heart is of stone
　If it ne'er dream of me !
For I dream of him ever :
His buff-coat and beaver,
And long sword, oh, never
　Are absent from me !

MOTHERWELL.

## OH, WAE BE TO THE ORDERS.

OH, wae be to the orders that marched my luve awa',
And wae be to the cruel cause that gars my tears doun fa';
Oh, wae be to the bluidy wars in Hie Germanie,
For they hae ta'en my luve, and left a broken heart to me.

The drums beat in the mornin' afore the screich o' day,
And the wee, wee fifes piped loud and shrill, while yet
　　the morn was gray ;
The bonnie flags were a' unfurl'd, a gallant sight to see,
But waes me for my sodger lad that marched to Germanie.

Oh, lang, lang is the travel to the bonnie Pier o' Leith,
Oh, dreich it is to gang on foot wi' the snaw-drift in the
　　teeth !
And, oh, the cauld wind froze the tear that gather'd in
　　my e'e,
When I gade there to see my luve embark for Germanie !

I looked ower the braid blue sea, sae lang as could be seen
Ae wee bit sail upon the ship that my sodger lad was in ;
But the wind was blawin' sair and snell, and the ship
    sail'd speedilie,
And the waves and cruel wars hae twinn'd my winsome
    luve frae me.

I never think o' dancin', and I downa try to sing,
But a' the day I spier what news kind neibour bodies
    bring ;
I sometimes knit a stocking, if knittin' it may be,
Syne for every loop that I cast on, I am sure to let doun
    three.

My father says I'm in a pet, my mither jeers at me,
And bans me for a dautit wean, in dorts for aye to be ;
But little weet they o' the cause that drumles sae my e'e :
Oh, they hae nae winsome luve like mine in the wars o'
    Germanie !

MOTHERWELL.

## BRITAIN'S QUEEN, VICTORIA.

AIR—"Rob Roy Macgregor O."

BRIGHTEST gem of Britain's Isle !
Born to wear the British crown,
Millions basking in your smile,
Crowd around your noble throne,
Rending air with loud applause,
Swearing to defend your cause,
British rights and British laws,
    And Britain's Queen, Victoria.

Bravest Britons guard your crown !
Patriots, statesmen, honest men—
Tyrants, traitors, trample down !
Never more to rise again ;—

Let corruption wither'd parch !
Let reform and knowledge march !
Through perfection's glorious arch,
 Led by Queen Victoria !

Equal rights, and equal laws,
Let the people all enjoy,
Peace proclaim'd with loud huzzas !
Never more let war destroy ;—
Agriculture, lead the van ;
Commerce, free to ev'ry man ;
Religion pure, complete the plan,
 Glory to Victoria.

JOHN PATERSON.

## I MET TWA CRONIES.

I MET twa cronies late yestreen,
 Wham blythe I've aft been wi' ;
And ilka mind soon felt inclined
 To taste the barley-bree :
We sat sae late, and drank sae deep,
 That roarin' fou gat we :
And haith ! I found, when I gaed hame,
 My wife had ta'en the gee.

All lanely by the fire she sat,
 Her brows hung ower her e'e ;
And wistfu' hush'd she aye the bairn,
 Though sleeping on her knee—
I saw the storm was masking fast,
 That soon wad fa' on me ;
Sae quietly slipt I aff to bed,
 And left her in the gee.

Neist day her looks were sour and sad,
 And ne'er a word spak she ;

But aye the tear-drap gather'd big,
  And dimm'd her bonnie e'e :
Quo' I, "My dear, what's past let gang,
  And frown nae mair on me,
The like again I'll never do,
  Gin ye'll ne'er tak' the gee !"

When this she heard, her brows she raised,
  And down beside me sat ;
I kiss'd her, for her heart was fu',
  And, puir wee thing ! she grat :
Quo' she, "Gin ye'll but keep your word,
  And bide at hame wi' me—
Hae, there's my han', that, while I live,
  I'll never tak' the gee !"

Then let us ca', and pay our drap,
  And toddle while we doo ;
For gin we drink anither bowl
  We'll a' get roarin' fou :
My wifie's smile is aye sae kind,
  When blythe or pleased is she,
To anger her wad be a sin,
  Or gar her tak' the gee !


## MARRY FOR LOVE AND WORK FOR SILLER.

WHEN I and my Jenny thegither were tied,
  We had but sma' share o' the world between us ;
Yet lo'ed ither weel, and had youth on our side,
  And strength and guid health were abundantly gi'en us ;
I warsled and toiled through the *fair* and the *foul*,
  And she was right carefu' o' what I brought till her,
For aye we had mind o' the canny auld rule,
  "Marry for love, and work for siller."

Our bairns they cam' thick—we were thankfu' for that,
  For the *bit* and the *brattie* cam' aye alang wi' them ;

Our *pan* we exchanged for a guid *muckle pat*,
   And somehow or ither, we aye had to gi'e them.
Our laddies grew up, and they wrought wi' mysel',
   Ilk ane gat as buirdly and stout as a miller,
Our lasses they keepit us trig aye, and hale,
   And now we can count a bit trifle o' siller.

But I and my Jenny are baith wearin' down,
   And our lads and our lasses hae a' gotten married ;
Yet see, we can rank wi' the best i' the town,
   Though our noddles we never too paughtily carried.
And mark me—I've now got a braw *cockit hat*,
   And in our *civic building* am reckon'd a pillar ;
Is na THAT a bit honour for ane to get at,
   Wha married for love, and wha wrought for siller ?
                          ALEX. RODGER.


## IT'S NO THAT THOU'RT BONNIE.

IT'S no that thou'rt bonnie, it's no that thou'rt braw,
It's no that thy skin has the pureness o' snaw,
It's no that thy form is perfection itsel',
That mak's my heart feel what my tongue canna tell ;
But oh ! its the soul beaming out frae thine e'e,
That mak's thee sae dear and sae lovely to me.

It's pleasant to look on that mild blushing face,
Sae sweetly adorn'd wi' ilk feminine grace,
It's joyous to gaze on these tresses sae bright,
O'ershading a forehead sae smooth and sae white ;
But to dwell on the glances that dart frae thine e'e,
O Jeanie ! it's evendown rapture to me.

That form may be wasted by lingering decay,
The bloom of that cheek may be withered away,
Those gay gowden ringlets that yield sic delight,
By the cauld breath o' time may be changed into white ;

But the soul's fervid flashes that brighten thine e'e,
Are the offspring o' heaven, and never can dee.

Let me plough the rough ocean, nor e'er touch the shore,
Let me freeze on the coast of the bleak Labrador,
Let me pant 'neath the glare of a vertical sun,
Where no trees spread their branches, nor streams ever run;
Even there, my dear Jeanie, still happy I'd be,
If bless'd wi' the light o' thy heavenly e'e.

ALEX. RODGER.

## A LULLABY.

O SAFTLY sleep, my bonnie bairn!
  Rock'd on this breast o' mine;
The heart that beats sae sair within,
  Will not awaken thine.

Lie still, lie still, ye canker'd thoughts!
  That such late watches keep;
An' if ye break the mother's heart,
  Yet let the baby sleep.

Sleep on, sleep on, my ae, ae bairn!
  Nor look sae wae on me,
As if ye felt the bitter tear
  That blin's thy mither's e'e.

Dry up, dry up, ye saut, saut tears
  Lest on my bairn ye dreep;
An' break in silence, waefu' heart,
  An' let my baby sleep.

RITCHIE.

## THE DOCTORS.

BE honours which to Kings we give,
　To Doctors also paid ;
We're the King's *subjects* while we live,
　The Doctor's when we're dead.

Though when in health and thoughtless mood,
　We treat them oft with scoffing ;
Yet they, returning ill with good,
　Relieve us from our *coughing* (coffin).

At times they kill us, to be sure,
　In cases rather tickle ;
But when they've kill'd—they still can *cure*
　Their patients—in a *pickle*.

And when at last we needs must die,
　The Doctors cannot save
From death—they still most kindly try
　To *snatch us* from the *grave*.


## LADY'S POCKET ADONIS.

THERE was a lady lived at Leith,
　A lady very stylish, man,
And yet, in spite of all her teeth,
　She fell in love with an Irishman,
　　A nasty, ugly Irishman,
　　A wild tremendous Irishman,
A tearing, swearing, thumping, bumping, ramping, roaring
　　Irishman.

His face was no ways beautiful,
　For with small-pox 'twas scarr'd across ;
And the shoulders of the ugly dog
　Were almost double a yard across.

Oh the lump of an Irishman,
   The whisky-devouring Irishman—
The great he-rogue, with his wonderful brogue, the fight-
      ing, rioting Irishman.

One of his eyes was bottle-green,
   And the other eye was out, my dear ;
And the calves of his wicked-looking legs,
   Were more than two feet about, my dear.
   Oh the great big Irishman,
      The rattling, battling Irishman—
The stamping, ramping, swaggering, staggering, leather-
      ing swash of an Irishman.

He took so much of Lundy-foot,
   That he used to snort and snuffle, O ;
And in shape and size, the fellow's neck,
   Was as bad as the neck of a buffalo.
   Oh the horrible Irishman,
      The thundering, blundering Irishman,
The slashing, dashing, smashing, lashing, thrashing,
      hashing Irishman.

His name was a terrible name, indeed,
   Being Timothy Thady Mulligan ;
And whenever he emptied his tumbler of punch,
   He'd not rest till he filled it full again.
   The boozing, bruising Irishman,
      The 'toxicated Irishman—
The whisky, frisky, rummy, gummy, brandy, no dandy
      Irishman.

This was the lad the lady loved,
   Like all the girls of quality ;
And he broke the skulls of the men of Leith,
   Just by the way of jollity.
   Oh, the leathering Irishman,
      The barbarous, savage Irishman—
The hearts of the maids, and the gentlemen's heads, were
      bother'd, I'm sure, by this Irishman.
                                    DOCTOR MAGINN.

## A COOK'S LEGACY.

BLEAK now the winter blaws, thick flee the driftin' snaws,
    A' the warld looks cauld and blae ;
Birds wha used to sing, now wi' shiverin' wing,
    Dozen'd sit on the frosted spray ;
But though the wintry winds blaw keenly,
    What are the wintry winds to me,
When by the kitchen fire sae cleanly,
    My love is baking a pie for me !

Oh, when I think on her cheeks sae greasy,
    Oh, when I think on her shoulders fat,
Never a lass have I seen like Leezy,
    She makes my poor heart to go pitty-pat !
All the way home though never so dreary,
    It charms my heart to think of thee ;
How by the kitchen fire sae cheery,
    My love is baking a pie for me ;

Some yield their hearts to the charms of beauty,
    Doating with pleasure upon her smile,
But when they've caught their long-wish'd booty,
    'Twill neither make pat nor pan to boil ;
And wi' their beauty they aft catch a Tartar—
    Often it happens, as all may see ;
Then for beauty, I'll scorn to barter
    The maid that is baking a pie for me !

CARRICK.

## JUNE AND JANUARY.

### AIR—"*Willie was a Wanton Wag.*"

FROSTY-bearded warlock body,
    Wife to you I'll never be ;
Rather wad I wed the wuddie,
    Or a runkled maiden die ;

Gang your wa's, an' seek some ither—
    Ane that's weary o' her life,
For ye're liker Death's half-brither,
    Than a man that wants a wife.

What care I for a' your grandeur,
    Gear an' lands, and houses braw?
Sapless rung! the witch o' Endor
    Scarce wad ta'en you wi' them a'!
Troth, ye might hae hain'd your siller,
    That ye've spent on fripperies vain;
Dotard fool! to think a tailor
    E'er could mak' you young again!

When you gat your dandy stays on,
    Was't to mak' you trig an' sma';
Or for fear that ye might gyzen,
    And in staves asunder fa'?
Ye wad tak' me to your bosom,
    Buy me braws an' ilk thing nice!
Gude preserve's! I'd soon be frozen,
    Clasp'd by sic a sherd o' ice!

Hoot! haud aff—ye're quite ridic'lous
    Wi' your pow as white as snaw,
An' your drumstick-shanks sae feckless,
    Aping youth o' twenty-twa;
Wha could thole your senseless boasting,
    Squeaking voice, an' ghaistlike grin?
Doited driveller! cease your hoasting,
    Else gie ower your fulsome din.

Wha could sit an' hear a story,
    'Bout a bosom's burning pains,
Frae an auld "*Memento mori,*"
    Sand-glass, skull, an' twa cross banes?
But for fear my scorn should cool ye,
    Hark! I'll tell you what I'll do,
When December's wed to July,
    There's my *fit*, I'll then tak' you.

                      ALEX. RODGER.

## MY GUDEMAN.

AIR—"*Loch-Erroch Side.*"

MY gudeman says aye to me,
Says aye to me, says aye to me ;
My gudeman says aye to me,
    Come cuddle in my bosie !
Though wearin' auld, he's blyther still
Than mony a swankie youthfu' chiel,
And a' his aim's to see me weel,
    And keep me snug and cozie.

For though my cheeks, where roses grew,
Hae tint their lively glowing hue,
My Johnnie's just as kind and true
    As if I still were rosy.
Our weel-won gear he never drank,
He never lived aboon his rank,
Yet wi' a neebour blythe and frank,
    He could be as jocose aye.

We hae a hame, gude halesome cheer,
Contentment, peace, a conscience clear,
And rosy bairns, to us mair dear,
    Than treasures o' Potosi :
Their minds are formed in virtue's school,
Their fau'ts are check'd wi' temper cool,
For my gudeman mak's this his rule,
    To keep frae hasty blows, aye.

It ne'er was siller gart us wed,
Youth, health, and love, were a' we had,
Possess'd o' these, we toil'd fu' glad,
    To shun want's bitter throes, aye ;
We've had our cares, we've had our toils,
We've had our bits o' troubles whiles,
Yet, what o' that ? my Johnny's smiles
    Shed joy o'er a' our woes, aye.

Wi' mutual aid we've trudged through life,
A kind gudeman, a cheerfu' wife ;
And on we'll jog, unvexed by strife,
  Towards our journey's close, aye ;
And when we're stretch'd upon our bier,
Oh, may our souls, sae faithfu' here,
Together spring to yonder sphere,
  Where love's pure river flows, aye.[1]

ALEX. RODGER.

## O, PETER M'KAY.

*Ane sober advice to ane drucken Souter in Perth.*

AIR—"*Come under my Plaidie.*"

O, PETER M'KAY ! O, Peter M'Kay !
Gin ye'd do like the brutes, only drink when ye're dry,
Ye might gather cash yet, grow gawcy and gash yet,
And carry your noddle Perth-Provost-pow-high ;
But poor drucken deevil, ye're wed to the evil
Sae closely, that naething can sever the tie ;
Wi' boring, and boosing, and snoring, and snoozing,
Ye emulate *him* that inhabits—the sty.

O, Peter M'Kay ! O, Peter M'Kay !
I'm tauld that ye drink ilka browster wife dry ;—
When down ye get sitting, ye ne'er think o' flitting,
While cogie or caup can a dribble supply ;—
That waur than a jaw-box, your monstrous maw soaks
Whate'er is poured in till't, while "give" is the cry ;
And when a' is drunk up, ye *bundle* your *trunk* up,
And bid, like the *sloth*, the bare *timmer* good-bye.

O, Peter M'Kay ! O, Peter M'Kay !
Gang hame to your awls, and your lingals apply,
Ca' in self-respect, man, to keep you correct, man—
The task may be irksome—at ony rate try ;

---

[1] The first four lines form the chorus of a very old song.

But gin ye keep drinking, and dozing, and blinking,
Be-clouding your reason, God's light from on high,
Then Peter depend on't, ye'll soon make an end on't,
And close your career 'neath a cauld wintry sky.

ALEX. RODGER.

## MARY'S GANE.

O WAE'S my heart, now Mary's gane,
   An' we nae mair shall meet thegither,
To sit an' crack at gloamin' hour,
    By yon auld grey-stane amang the heather.
     Trysting-stane amang the heather,
     Trysting-stane amang the heather,
How bless'd were we at gloamin' hour,
    By yon auld grey-stane amang the heather.

Her faither's laird sae gair on gear,
   He set their mailin to anither,
Sae they've selt their kye, and ower the sea
    They've gane, and left their native heather.
     Left their native blooming heather,
     Left their native blooming heather,
They've selt their kye, and ower the sea
    They've gane, and left their native heather.

Her parting look bespake a heart,
   Whase rising grief she couldna smother,
As she waved a last fareweel to me
    An' Scotland's braes an' blooming heather ;
     Scotland's braes and blooming heather,
     Scotland's braes and blooming heather,
'Twas sair against the lassie's will,
    To lea' her native blooming heather.

A burning curse licht on the heads
   O' worthless lairds colleagued thegither,

To drive auld Scotland's hardy clans
  Frae their native glens and blooming heather.
    Native glens and blooming heather,
    Native glens and blooming heather,
To drive auld Scotland's hardy clans
  Frae their native glens and blooming heather.

I'll sell the cot my granny left,
  Its plenishing an' a' thegither,
An' I'll seek her out 'mang foreign wilds,
  Wha used to meet me amang the heather;
    Used to meet me amang the heather,
    Used to meet me amang the heather,
I'll seek her out 'mang foreign wilds,
  Wha used to meet me amang the heather.

CARRICK.

## OUR JOHN HIELANMAN.

I'VE sax eggs in the pan, gudeman,
I've sax eggs in the pan, gudeman;
I've ane for you, an' twa for me,
An' three for our John Hielanman.

Oh Johnny has a shapely leg,
Weel fitted for the philibeg;
While we've a hen to lay an egg,
  That egg's to our John Hielanman.
    I've sax eggs, etc.

Ye ken, gudeman, you're failing noo,
An' heavy wark ye canna do,
Ye neither thrash nor haud the plough
  Sae weel as our John Hielanman.
    I've sax eggs, etc.

The folk that work should always eat,
An' Johnny's wordy o' his meat.

For ne'er a job that's incomplete
    Is done by our John Hielanman.
        I've sax eggs, etc.

As yet, gudeman, I'm no to blame,
For I've maintain'd an honest fame ;
But just stap aff to your lang-hame,
    An' I'll wed our John Hielanman.
        I've sax eggs, etc.

CARRICK.

## THE HERRING-HEAD CLUB.

As we journey through life let us live by the way,
A famous remark which a sage once did say ;
We all now are met, spite of care the old scrub,
And we'll pass half an hour in the Herring-head club.
    Derry down, down, down, derry down.

Some good folks complain of the times being bad,
But the way to improve them is not to be sad ;
To laugh is no sin, if we raise no hubbub,
At least so we think at the Herring-head club.
    Derry down, etc.

King Fergus the First, who in Scotland did reign,
Was a merry old blade who did seldom complain :
No glasses had he, so he drank from a shell,
His nobles and he had a glorious spell.
    Derry down, etc.

One night being merry and full of much glee,
For with herrings and drink they were all on the spree—
This meeting, cried Fergus, it is now time to dub,
So, my drouthies, we'll call it the Herring-head club.
    Derry down, etc.

And now I command that ye keep the thing up,
Be sure once a month that on herrings ye sup,

And if ye forget it, my ghost shall ye drub,
And this was the rise of the Herring-head club.
    Derry down, etc.

Then drink to King William, and drink to the Queen,
May their pains be all past and their sorrows all seen;
May we all pass through life without jostle or rub,
And often come back to the Herring-head club.
    Derry down, etc.

## THE AULD SCOTTISH BRUGH.

AIR—"*John Anderson my Joe.*"

IN Scotland stands an ancient brugh, wi' some twal-
    hundred people,
A lang and narrow strip o' street, and ae high-shoulder'd
    steeple;
Ilk grocer i' the borough is a bailie, or has been,
But the Provost was perpetual, and drave the hail machine.

At twal o'clock, the Provost cam, and stood upo' the
    street,
And waggit to his right-hand man, i' the public house to
    meet;
The Bailie threw his apron by, and o'er their gill they sat,
And they managed a' the Toun's affairs in a bit quiet
    chat.

The Deacon, wi' a face half-wash'd, gaed consequential
    by—
But the Deacon, as a' body kent, had nae finger i' the pie.
The Deacon made the Provost's breeks, and a' his laddies'
    claes—
And the Provost, though the best o' friends, was yet the
    warst o' faes.

And oh ! the Provost was a man o' consequence and
    worth—
He managed weel, he strutted weel, yet had nae wit nor
    birth :
He led the Council in a string, and the member, ken't,
    I trow,
That, if he said the word, 'twas done, and there were
    votes enow.

And when the canvassin' cam' round, the member walk'd
    about,
And bughted i' the Provost's arm—they sought the
    Deacon's out ;
The bodies threw their nightcaps by, or wi' them cleaned
    a chair,
And the member sat i' the ben house, wi' a condescendin'
    air.

The gudewife stood aside, and beck'd and twirled her
    apron strings,
And wunner'd that the member deign'd to speak to them,
    puir things !
The Parliamentar roar'd, and talked, and syne kiss'd the
    gudewife—
And the wife declares the Deacon's vote is now as sure's
    his life.

The Bailie's wife, wi' a braw head, frae her window looks
    out,
And cried, "Preserve 's ! he's comin' now—what are ye
    a' about ?
Put down the wine, ye lazy jad !—the lassie's surely
    mad !"
And down she sits, to be surprised, upon her cosh bit
    pad.

The Bailie bustles in before—his very lugs are red—
The gudewife hears upo' the trance a Parliamentar's
    tread ?

He enters a' sooawvity, and chucks each chubby laddie,
And swears how ane is like to her, anither to its daddy.

And now the Provost walks him hame to dinner wi'himsel',
And the member tak's his seat atween the leddie and
    Miss Bell—
And the leddie cracks o' Dr. John, and syne o' Captain
    Sandy,
Wha, by his Honour's influence, to India got so handy.

But, waes my heart ! the auncient town has now gane
    down the hill,
And vested rights o' families are stolen by Russell's Bill—
And vulgar weaving touns, I trow, like Glasgow and
    Dundee,
Maun steal the honours frae our brughs o' high antiquity ?

## MISTER PETER PATERSON.

### Or, a Bailie in his Cups.

MISTER Peter Paterson,
Ye will find that late or soon,
If ye dinna change your tune,
    Ye will most dearly rue.
Mister Peter Paterson,
Mister Peter Paterson,
Mister Peter Paterson,
    I see you're gayan' fu'.

You're a Bailie now, ye ken,
Then drink wi' nane but sober men,
Nor sit in ony dirty den
    Wi' ony vulgar crew.
For I maun tell it to your face,
That it's a sin and a disgrace
For you to sit in sic a place,
    And drink till ye get fu'.
So, Mister Peter Paterson, etc.

Mistress Peter Paterson,
Ye aye tak' the gate ower soon,
To snool your pet an' keep him down,
   Before ye ken what's true :
Believe me, I was nae sic gates,
But dining wi' the magistrates,
An' some o' them gaed *ower the sklates*,
   As weel's your dainty dow.

So, Mistress Peter Paterson,
Mistress Peter Paterson,
Mistress Peter Paterson,
   I'm no sae vera fu'.
Provost Brodie he was there,
But yet they gart me tak' the chair,
Guidsake, Kate, had ye been there,
   You'd keckled weel, I true.

Deacon Roset when he saw't,
He left the room he was sae chawt,
And on his tail we ne'er coost saut,
   The hail nicht lang I true.
So, Mistress Peter Paterson,
Mistress Peter Paterson,
Mistress Peter Paterson,
   I'm no sae vera fu'.

(*Bailie hiccuping and laughing as he proceeds*).—" I'm no sae vera fu', Mrs. Paterson, and its vera ill-done o' you to say sae ; besides, it's no a proper expression to use to a man filling a civil as weel as an official capacity, and who has got a cocket hat on his head, and a goud chain about his neck—ha, ha, lass, ca' ye that naething ?—lang looked-for's come at last—I've got the cocket hat noo—you did na ken what I was about these twa-three days. Little thought ye o' the braw tow I had on my rock—ha, ha, lass, catch a cat sleeping wi' a mouse in her lug ! I've been on the hunt these twa days, and I've catched cocky at last. But noo, Mrs. Paterson, since you're a Bailie's wife, I maun gi'e you a word o' advice :— Never say the Bailie cam' hame fu'.' O woman ! woman ! what wad the Provost's wife think o' you? she's the prudent woman ! she never says the Provost cam' hame fu',—na, na, the Provost cam hame 'a *leetle elevated*,' that's her prudent expression, worthy woman that she is; so dinna forget, Mrs. Paterson, but just say, whan ye speak about me and the town's affairs, that 'the Bailie cam' hame a *leetle elevated*.' But what d'ye think we're gaun to be about the morn? Ha, ha, lass, we're to be great folks the morn— the morn's the Lord's day, ye ken, Mrs. Paterson, and me and the magistrates are gaun to hae a grand *paraad* to the kirk, and we're to hae the town-officers afore us, wi' their hats aff and their halberts in their han's; ay, woman, they're to be a' afore us, guid-be-thanket! they're to be *afore us*, I've been sair eneugh fashed i' my day wi' them *gaun after me*. Mony a time the buffers took me *afore* the Bailie; but praise be blessed! I've got them *afore the Bailie now*; time about's fair play, ye ken, Mrs. Paterson. Now, Mrs. Paterson, there's just ae favour I want o' you the night, Mrs. Paterson, and ye maunna deny me. You needna laugh, Mrs. Paterson, I'm a wee new-fangled about my cocket hat; ye ken, I had a lang and a sair strussel to get it; now, I acknowledge I'm a *leetle elevated* the night, as the Provost's wife says, and I canna think to part wi't, woman. Now, what I want o' you, Mrs. Paterson, is just to let—let —let me sleep wi' my cocket hat on the night—I just want to lie in *state* for ae nicht; and ye ken, Mrs. Paterson, you would be so agreeably astonished when ye waukened in the morning, and found yoursel lying beside a Bailie, a *real Bailie*, woman! wi' his three-cornered night-cap and a' his paraphernalia on. Now, Mrs. Paterson, you'll oblige me the night, like a dear, and I'll tell you the morn about a town's job that I'm to get that'll do me muckle good and you *little ill*. Thou's get the best silk gown to be had within the four quarter's o' this or ony ither town in Scotland. What d'ye think o' that, Mrs. Paterson?"

> There's mony a job about a toun
> To gar a Bailie's pat play brown,
> But on ae job I'll keep my thumb
>   Ye'll hear't some ither day.
> So, Mistress Peter Paterson,
> Mistress Peter Paterson.
> So, Mistress Peter Paterson,
>   I'm no sae vera fu'.            CARRICK.

## "LO'E ME LITTLE, AND LO'E ME LANG."

Awa' wi' your wheezing, your coaxing, and teasing,
  Your hugging and squeezing, I beg you'll let be ;
Your praising sae fulsome, too sweet to be wholesome,
  Can never gang down wi' a lassie like me ;
Nae mair than a woman, nae higher than human,
  To Sylphs and to Seraphs I dinna belang ;
Then if ye wad gain me, the way to attain me,
  Is " Lo'e me little, and lo'e me lang."

Wi' some silly gawkie, your fleeching sae pawkie,
  Like sweet dozing draughts, will glide cannily down ;
Hence, seek some vain hizzy, and doze her till dizzy,
  She'll quickly consent a' your wishes to crown ;
But pester na me wi't, my heart canna 'gree wi't,
  I'm sick o' your cuckoo's unvarying sang,
Cease, therefore, your canting, your rhyming and ranting,
  But " Lo'e me little, and lo'e me lang."

The love that lowes strongest, say, lasts it the longest ?
  The fires that bleeze brightest burn soonest awa' ;
Then keep your flame steady—a moderate red aye,
  Or else ye may yet hae a cauld coal to blaw ;
And quat your romantics, your airs, and your antics,
  Tak' truth's honest track, and you'll seldom gae wrang ;
Then win me, and welcome, let weal or let ill come,
  I'll " Lo'e you little, but lo'e you lang."

                              ALEXANDER RODGER.


## THE AULD SCHOOL.

### A NEW SANG TO A NEW TUNE.

Is there ony that kens nae my auld uncle Watty,
Wi' 's buckled knee breekums an' three cockit hattie ?
Is there ony that kens nae my auld auntie Matty,

Wi' 'r wee black silk cloak, and her red collar'd cattie?
        O, auld uncle Watty,
        An' auld auntie Matty,
Ye may gang whare ye like, but their match winna see.

They've a weel plenished house, an' a weel stockit pantry,
Kegs o' gin in their press, kegs o' ale on their gantree;
An' the lean parish poor, an' the fat county gentry,
Ne'er find sic a bien couthy hame in the kintry.
        O, auld uncle Watty,
        An' auld auntie Matty,
Ye're dear unto a', but ye're dearer to me.

They've saved a' they hae, tho' they never were greedy,
Gang to their house hungry, they're sure aye to feed ye,
Gang to their house tatter'd, they're sure aye to cleed ye,
O, wha 'll fill their place to the puir an' the needy?
        O, auld uncle Watty,
        An' auld aunty Matty,
Ye're kind unto a', but ye're kinder to me.

I mind nae o' mither, I mind nae o' faither,
Yet ne'er ken't the ha'eing or wanting o' either,
For the puir orphan sprout, that was left here to wither,
Gat uncle for faither, and aunty for mither.
        O, auld uncle Watty,
        An' auld aunty Matty,
Few orphans ha'e uncle and aunty like me.

An' didna my bosom beat fondly an' fou,
When up like an aik 'neath their nursing I grew;
While a tear in their e'e, or a clud on their brow,
Was aye sure to pierce my fond heartie right through.
        O, auld uncle Watty,
        An' auld aunty Matty,
Ye're faither, an' mither, an' a' thing to me.

But luve play'd a plisky, that maist rave asunder
Three hearts that ye'll no find the like in a hunder;

I married wee Mary, to a' body's wonder,
An' maistly had paid for my het-headed blunder;
   For auld uncle Watty,
   An' auld aunty Matty,
Vow'd they wad ne'er own either Mary or me.

But Mary's kind heart, aye sae couthy an' slee,
Soon won the auld bodies as she had done me;
When our callant cam' hame, to the kirk wi't cam' she—
Ca'd it Watty—the auld folks sat bleer't in the e'e.
   An' auld uncle Watty,
   An' auld aunty Matty,
Cam' nursin' the wean hame 'tween Mary an' me.

An' wow but the callant grows buirdly an' strang,
There's nae Carritch question, nor auld Scottish sang,
But the loun screeds ye aff in the true lowland twang,
I doubtna he'll beat his ain faither or lang;
   For auld uncle Watty,
   An' auld aunty Matty,
Are learnin' the callant as aince they did me.

Gae bring me the pinks o' your famed infant schools,
Whase wee sauls are laden wi' newfangled rules,
Gif wee Watty dinna mak' a' o' them fools,
I'll e'en gie ye leave to lay me in the mools:
   An' auld uncle Watty,
   An' auld aunty Matty,
May throw down their buiks an' gae booby for me.
       JAMES BALLANTINE.


## MY COUSIN JEAN.

Tune—"*When she cam' ben she bobbit.*"

### CHORUS.

My Cousin Jean—my cousin Jean,
A wild little hempie was my cousin Jean;

For gentle or semple she ne'er cared a preen,
Yet the toast o' our parish is my cousin Jean.

I mind her right weel whan the cricket was young,
She'd a stap like the roe an' a glibly gaun tongue,
An' a' the schule callants she skelpit them clean,
Sae supple the neives gat o' my cousin Jean.

Whar mischief was brewin', or devilry wrought,
A lum set a-low, or a teugh battle fought,
At the head of the foray was sure to be seen,
The wild wavin' ringlets o' my cousin Jean.

O, rade ye to market, or rade ye to fair,
Ye were sure to fa' in wi' my daft cousin there;
Yet the puir, an' the feckless, aye gat a gude frien',
An' a plack frae the pouches o' my cousin Jean.

She helpit the tinklers their dour mules to load,
She follow'd them miles on their moorland road,
Syne frighted the bairns wi' their stories at e'en;
Weel kent were their cantrips to my cousin Jean.

But our auld Mess John had a Lunnun bred son,
Wha lang had an e'e after Jean and her fun,
An' he begg'd but an hour frae his father at e'en,
To convert the wild spirit o' my cousin Jean.

I wat a sweet convert the stripling soon made,
But gif a' wi' his preachin', troth's no to be said,
For precious to him were the dark glancin' e'en,
Whilk laugh'd 'neath the arch'd brows o' my cousin Jean.

Young Jean took to reading o' queer prented buiks,
An' wander'd at midnight 'mang hay-ricks and stooks—
Whilst the college-bred birkie right aften was seen,
Pointing out heaven's wonders to my cousin Jean.

Nae doubt the hale parish was spited to see,
Sic a dance in her gait, sic a sang in her e'e,

An' ilk auld wifie wager'd her life to a preen,
She would soon get a down-come—my young cousin Jean.

Dumfounder'd were a' the hale parish, I trow,
When they saw the next week i' the minister's pew,
At the young laird's right han', they could scarce trust their
    e'en—
A modest young bride sat my young cousin Jean.

Now crabbit auld wisdom should ne'er slight a tree,
Though when it is young it may waver a wee,
In its prime it may flourish the fair forest queen,
For sae was the upshot o' my cousin Jean.

ALEX. MacLAGGAN.

## THE PEASANT'S FIRESIDE.

AIR—"For lack o' gowd."

How happy lives the peasant, by his ain fireside,
Wha weel employs the present, by his ain fireside,
Wi' his wifie blythe and free, and his bairnie on her knee,
Smiling fu' o' sportive glee, by his ain fireside.
Nae cares o' State disturb him, by his ain fireside,
Nae foolish fashions curb him, by his ain fireside,
In his elbow chair reclined, he can freely speak his mind,
To his bosom-mate sae kind, by his ain fireside.

When his bonny bairns increase, around his ain fireside,
That health, content, and peace, surround his ain fireside,
A' day he gladly toils, and at night delighted smiles,
At their harmless pranks and wiles, around his ain fireside.
And while they grow apace, about his ain fireside,
In beauty, strength, and grace, about his ain fireside,
Wi' virtuous precepts kind, by a sage example join'd,
He informs ilk youthfu' mind about his ain fireside.

When the shivering orphan poor, draws near his ain fireside,
And seeks the friendly door, that guards his ain fireside,

She's welcomed to a seat, bidden warm her little feet,
While she's kindly made to eat, by his ain fireside.
When youthfu' vigour fails him, by his ain fireside,
And hoary age assails him, by his ain fireside,
With joy he back surveys, all his scenes of bygone days,
As he trod in wisdom's ways, by his ain fireside.

And when grim death draws near him, by his ain fireside,
What cause has he to fear him, by his ain fireside,
With a bosom-cheering hope, he takes heaven for his prop,
Then calmly down does drop, by his ain fireside.
O may that lot be ours, by our ain fireside,
Then gladly fly the hours, by our ain fireside,
May virtue guard our path, till we draw our latest breath,
Then we'll smile and welcome death, by our ain fireside.

ALEX. RODGER.

## TAK' IT MAN, TAK' IT.

TUNE—"*Brose and Butter.*"

WHEN I was a miller in Fife,
　Losh ! I thought that the sound o' the happer,
Said tak' hame a wee flow to your wife,
　To help to be brose to your supper.
Then my conscience was narrow and pure,
　But someway by random it rackit ;
For I lifted twa neivefu' or mair,
　While the happer said—tak' it man, tak' it.
　　Hey for the mill and the kill,
　　　The garland and geer for my cogie,
　　Hey for the whisky or yill,
　　　That washes the dust ower my craigie.

Altho' it's been lang in repute,
　For rogues to mak' rich by deceiving ;
Yet I see that it disna weel suit
　Honest men to begin to the thieving.

For my heart it gaed dunt upon dunt,
  Od ! I thought ilka dunt it would crack it ;
Sae I flang frae my neive what was in't,—
  Still the happer said—tak' it man, tak' it.
           Hey for the mill, etc.

A man that's been bred to the plough,
  Might be deaved wi' its clamorous clapper ;
Yet there's few but would suffer the sough,
  After kenning what's said by the happer.
I whiles thought it scoff'd me to scorn,
  Saying shame ; is your conscience no chackit ?
But when I grew dry for a horn,—
  It changed aye to—tak' it man, tak' it.
           Hey for the mill, etc.

The smugglers whiles cam' wi' their pocks,
  'Cause they kent that I liked a bicker ;
Sae I barter'd whiles wi' the gowks,
  Gied them grain for a soup o' their liquor.
I had lang been accustom'd to drink,
  And aye when I purposed to quat it,—
That thing wi' its clapperty clink,—
  Said aye to me—tak' it man, tak' it.
           Hey for the mill, etc.

Now, miller and a' as I am,
  This far I can see through the matter ;
There's men mair notorious to fame,
  Mair greedy than me for the muter.
For 'twad seem that the hale race o' men,
  Or wi' safety the half we may mak' it,
Had some speaking happer within,
  That said to them—tak' it man, tak' it.
           Hey for the mill, etc.
              DAVID WEBSTER.

## RONALD MACGIECH.[1]

AIR—"*Hills o' Glenorchy.*"

O RONALD MACGIECH was a kenspeckle loon,
Had cash in ilk pocket, and feres in ilk town ;
He was idle and thro'ither, and drucken an' a',
His face it was round, and his back was aye braw.
He ate o' the daintiest, drank o' the best,
At sma' cost to him, as the neighbourhood wist ;
He troubled the change-folk baith often and dreigh—
Yet wha was sae welcome as Ronald Macgiech ?

Tho' landlord and maid wad fain answer'd his bell,
The landlady ever served Ronald hersel' ;
She'd sit to taste wi' him, though ever sae thrang,
An' see him a' right, though a' else should gae wrang.
An' rise when he liket at e'en to gae 'wa',
He ne'er got a hint for his lawing ava ;
Baith merchants and customers boost stand abeigh,
No ane wad she look at but Ronald Macgiech.

Sae lichtly, nae lad in the hale kintra side,
Could dance you a hornpipe, or set to a bride :
At fairs, in the reel-house he'd caper and spreigh,
Till the rantle-tree rattled wi' Ronald Macgiech.
Though o' him the men were a' rede and unfain,
The lasses aye leuch when they met him again :
To a' ither wooers though saucy and skeigh,
They were aye unco cosh-like wi' Ronald Macgiech.

[1] Ronald Macgiech—with other aliases—who paid the forfeit of his crimes in front of the Glasgow Jail, along with an associate in crime—Robert M'Kinlay, alias Rough Rab, in 1819. Ronald was a veteran in his profession, and thoroughly understood all the Outs and Ins of burglary. He had attained the moral hardihood—which only a course of crime can induce—to turn into humorous burlesque the exit from the scaffold—by remarking, "That it was sair on the e'e-sicht." When his hosiery had been the worse for wear, he used to say that it "saved him trouble, for he could draw them on by whatever end he catched first."

Whate'er was awn him he was aye sure to get,
But ne'er could remember to pay his ain debt ;
The luckiest wight too he was in the land,
For ithers aft lost things, but Ronald aye fand.
At last he did something—no ane could tell what,
The Wiggies[1] were down on him, nae guid sign that ;
He died in his shoon, about twa stories heich,
'Twas sair on the e'esicht of Ronald Macgiech.

THOMAS DICK.

## I'LL TEND THY BOWER, MY BONNIE MAY.

I'LL tend thy bower, my bonnie May,
　In spring-time o' the year,
When saft'ning winds begin to woo
　The primrose to appear—
When daffodils begin to dance,
　And streams again flow free—
An' little birds are heard to pipe
　On the sprouting forest tree.

I'll tend thy bower, my bonnie May,
　When summer days are lang—
When Nature's heart is big wi' joy,
　Her voice laden wi' sang—
When shepherds pipe on sunny braes,
　And flocks roam at their will,
An' auld an' young in cot an' ha',
　O' pleasure drink their fill.

I'll tend thy bower, my bonnie May,
　When autumn's yellow fields—
That wave like seas o' gowd—before
　The glancin' sickle yields ;
When ilka bough is bent wi' fruit—
　A glorious sight to see !—

1 Lords of Justiciary.

And showers o' leaves, red, rustling, sweep
Out ower the withering lea.

I'll tend thy bower, my bonnie May,
  When thro' the naked trees,
Cauld, shivering on the bare hill side,
  Sweeps wild the frosty breeze ;
When tempests roar, an' billows rise,
  Till Nature quakes wi' fear—
And on the land, and on the sea,
  Wild winter rules the year.

WILLIAM FERGUSON.

## THE MERMAYDEN.

*Set to Music by R. A. Smith.*

" THE nicht is mirk, and the wind blaws schill,
  And the white faem weets my bree,
And my mind misgies me, gay mayden,
  That the land we sall never see."
Then up and spak the mermayden,
  And she spak blythe and free,
" I never said to my bonnie brydegroom
  That on land we should weddit be.

" Oh, I never said that ane erthlie priest
  Our bridal blessing should gie ;
And I never said that a landwart bower
  Should hald my love and me."
" And whare is that priest, my bonnie mayden,
  If ane erthlie wicht is na he ?"
" Oh the wind will sough, and the sea will rain
  When weddit we twa sall be."

" And whare is that bower, my bonnie mayden,
  If on land it should na be ?"
" Oh my blythe bower is low," said the mermayden,
  " In the bonnie green hows o' the sea.

My gay bower is biggit o' the gude ships' keels,
    And the banes o' the drown'd at sea ;
The fish are the deer that fill my parks,
    And the water waste my drurie.

" And my bower is sklaitit wi' the big blue wave,
    And paved wi' the yellow sand ;
And in my chalmers grow bonnie white flowers
    That never grew on land.
And have ye e'er seen, my bonnie brydegroom,
    A leman on earth that wad gie
Aiker for aiker o' the red plough'd land,
    As I'll gie to thee o' the sea ?

" The mune will rise in half ane hour,
    And the wee bricht starns will shine,
Then we'll sink to my bowir 'neath the wan water,
    Full fifty fathoms and nine."—
A wild, wild skreich gied the fey bridegroom,
    And a loud, loud lauch the bryde ;
For the mune rose up, and the twa sank down,
    Under the silver'd tide.
                WILLIAM MOTHERWELL.

## WHETHER OR NO.

*Set to Music by John Turnbull.*

'MANG a' the braw lads that come hither to woo me,
    There's only but ane I wad fain mak' my joe ;
And though I seem shy, yet sae dear is he to me,
    I scarce can forgie mysel' when I say "No."
My sister she sneers 'cause he hasna the penny,
    And cries, "ye maun reap, my lass, just as ye sow,'"
My brither he bans, but it's a' ane to Jenny,
    She'll just tak' the lad she likes—whether or no.

My father he cries, "Tak' the laird o' Kinlogie,
    For he has baith mailins and gowd to bestow ;"

My mither cries neist, "Tak' the heir o' Glenbogie,"
  But can I please baith o' them?—weel I wat no !
And since 'tis mysel' maun be gainer or loser—
  Maun drink o' life's bicker, be't weal or be't woe,
I deem it but fair I should be my ain chooser ;—
  To love will I lippen, then—whether or no.

Cauld Prudence may count on his gowd and his acres,
  And think them the sum o' a' blessings below,
But tell me, can wealth bring content to its makers?
  The care-wrinkled face o' the miser says "No !"
But oh when pure love meets a love corresponding,
  Such bliss it imparts as the world cannot know ;
It lightens life's load, keeps the heart from desponding,
  Let Fate smile or scowl, it smiles—whether or no !
                                   ALEX. RODGER.


## THE WIDOW'S EXCUSE.

AIR—"*O saw ye the Lass wi' the bonnie blue een.*"

"O LEEZIE M'CUTCHEON, I canna but say,
Your grief hasna lasted a year and a day ;
The crape aff your bonnet already ye've ta'en ;
Nae wonner that men ca' us fickle and fain.
Ye sich't and ye sabbit, that nicht Johnnie dee't,
I thought my ain heart wad hae broken to see't ;
But noo ye're as canty and brisk as a bee ;
Oh ! the frailty o' women I wonner to see :

  The frailty o' women, I wonner to see,
  The frailty o' women, I wonner to see ;
  Ye kiss'd his cauld gab wi' the tear in your e'e ;
  Oh, the frailty o' women I wonner to see.

"When Johnnie was living, oh little he wist,
That the sound o' the mools as they fell on his kist,
While yet like a knell, ringing loud in your lug,
By anither man's side ye'd be sleeping sae snug.

O Leezie, my lady, ye've surely been fain,
For an unco-like man to your arms ye have ta'en ;
John M'Cutcheon was buirdly, but this ane, I trow,
The e'e o' your needle ye might draw him through :

O, the e'e o' your needle ye might draw him through,
His nose it is shirpit, his lip it is blue,
Oh Leezie, ye've surely to wale on had few,
Ye've looted and lifted but little, I trow."

"Now, Janet, wi' jibing and jeering hae dune,
Though it's true that anither now fills Johnnie's shoon,
He was lang in sair trouble, and Robin, ye ken,
Was a handy bit body, and lived butt and ben.
He was unco obliging, and cam' at my wag,
Whan wi' grief and fatigue I was liken to fag ;
'Deed, John couldna want him—for aften I've seen
His e'e glisten wi' gladness whan Robin cam' in.

Then, how can ye wonner I gi'ed him my haun' !
Oh, how can ye wonner I gi'ed him my haun',
When I needed his help, he was aye at commaun' ;
Then how can ye wonner I gi'ed him my haun' ?

"At length when John dee't, and was laid in the clay,
My haun' it was bare, and my heart it was wae ;
I had na a steek, that was black, to put on,
For wark I had plenty wi' guiding o' John ;
Now Robin was thrifty, and ought that he wan
He took care o't, and aye had twa notes at commaun',
And he lent me as muckle as coft a black goon,
Sae hoo can ye wonner he's wearing John's shoon ?

Then hoo can ye wonner he's wearing John's shoon ?
My heart-strings wi' sorrow were a' out o' tune ;
A man that has worth and twa notes at commaun',
Can sune get a woman to tak him in haun'."

WILLIAM FINLAY.

## AULD JOHN NICOL.

Air—"*John Nicol.*"

I sing of an auld forbear o' my ain,
    Tweedledum twadledum twenty-one ;
A man wha for fun was never out-done,
    And his name it was auld John Nicol o' Quhain.

Auld John Nicol was born—he said,
    Tweedledum, etc. ;
Of man or of maid's no weel kent—sin he's dead,
    Sae droll was the birth o' John Nicol o' Quhain.

Auld John Nicol he lo'ed his glass,
    Tweedledum, etc. ;
And auld John Nicol he lo'ed a lass,
    And he courted her tocher—the lands o' Balquhain.

Auld John Nicol he made her his wife,
    Tweedledum, etc. ;
And the feast was the funniest feast o' his life,
    And the best o' the farce he was laird o' Balquhain.

The lady was fifty, his age was twal' mair,
    Tweedledum, etc. ;
She was bow-hough'd and humph-back'd, twined like a
        stair,
    "But her riggs are fell straucht," quo' John Nicol o'
        Quhain.

By some chance or ither auld John got a son,
    Tweedledum, etc. ;
He was laid in the cupboard for fear that the win',
    Wad hae blawn out the hopes o' the house o' Balquhain.

The lady was canker'd and eident her tongue,
    Tweedledum, etc. ;
She scrimpit his cog—thrash'd his back wi' a rung,
    And dousen'd for lang auld John Nicol o' Quhain.

Ae day cam a ca'er wi' mony lang grane,
 Tweedledum, etc. ;
"Oh ! death "—quo' the laird, " come stap your wa's ben,
 Ye'se be welcome to tak Mrs. Nicol o' Quhain."

Auld John was a joker the rest o' his life,
 Tweedledum, etc. ;
And his ae blythest joke was the yirdin' his wife,
 For it left him the laird o' the lands o' Balquhain.
PATRICK BUCHAN.

## I HAD A HAT, I HAD NAE MAIR.

AIR—"*I had a horse, I had nae mair.*"

I HAD a hat, I had nae mair,
 I gat it frae the hatter ;
My hat was smash'd, my skull laid bare,
 Ae night when on the batter ;
And sae I thocht me on a plan,
 Whereby to mend the matter—
Just turn at ance a sober man,
 And tak to drinking water.

My plan I quickly put in force,
 Yea, stuck till't most sincerely,
And now I drive my gig and horse,
 And hae an income yearly.
But, had I still kept boozing on,
 Twa'd been anither matter,
My credit, cash, and claes had gone,
 In tatter after tatter.

My wife, perhaps, a worthless pest,
 My weans half-starved and duddy ;
And I, mysel', at very best,
 Gaun wi' an auld coal cuddie ;

Wi' scarce a stick in a' the house,
  Or spoon, or bowl, or platter,
Or milk, or meal, to feed a mouse,
  Or blanket save a tatter.

Now, Gude be praised, I've peace o' mind,
  Clear head and health o' body,
A thrifty wifie, cosh and kind,
  And bairnies plump and ruddy.
Hence, I'd advise ilk weirdless wight,
  Wha likes the gill-stoup's clatter,
To try my plan this very night,
  And tak' to drinking water.

ALEX. RODGER.

## PAT MULLIGAN'S COURTSHIP.

'TIS our duty to love both our father and mother,
Give up talking nonsense, and all sorts of bother,
But greater by far is the duty to smother
      Our love, when beginning to ail :

O dear ! dear ! what can the matter be !
Och botheration now, what can the matter be,
Thunder and turf ! why what can the matter be ?
      How, Cupid, my poor heart doth flail !

" Och, Judy, but you have kilt me now, I can nather ate, sup, sleep, nor drink, for thinking ov ye, ye've made a hole in my heart like a bung-hole, for which I hope you will live to repint and be forgiven. Bad cess to me ! if the people ar'nt beginnin' to think that I am the livin' atomy, aich of us, both saw at Donnybrook Fair, an' if my flesh, an' bones, an' blood, dhrop off me longer, they'll be in earth's keeping before my own eyes. Living, you must be mine, and if I die, I shall lay my death agin ye every night till I bring you to your senses, you murthering jewel !"

Then I search'd all around for a sweetheart less cruel,
In the hope she would make me forget my first jewel ;

This only was adding fresh fire to the fuel,
And making more trouble and wail.

" It is all over with you now, Paddy, says I ; so before the breath
laves yer body, you had better consult your own clargy, Father
Murphy, and get a mouthful of ghostly consolation to die with.
Father, says I to him, I am going to die." "Then you're a great
big fool," says he, "what puts that into your head, my son?"
"Judy has kilt me," says I, "and it's of no use livin' any longer."
"Paddy, my son," says he, "you ought to know that this world on
which you are placed, is just like a potful of praties—ye are all sent
here to jumble, and tumble, and bubble, and roar ; and, the man
that remains longest in the pot of affliction without his skin breakin'
intirely—that man, you may dipind on't, is the true potato."
"Arrah Father," says I, "it's not that at all, it's Judy."

Then dear ! dear ! what can the matter be !
Och botheration now, what can the matter be,
Pewter and pots ! why what can the matter be ?
Cupid, my poor heart doth flail.

So finding no peace, I determined to marry,
Get Judy's consent, and no longer to tarry,
'Tis the road all must go, though a few will miscarry,
As onward through life they do sail.

"Judy," says I, "will you have me iver, and always, and amin?"
"Well Pat, an' suppose I were, should I be any the worse for't?
Troth an' myself often wondered that you were niver axin me."
" Is't your own self that I'm hearin' spakin'—beauty an' blessing on
every tether linth o' ye, Judy?" "It's not in the natur of woman to
refuse ye, Pat Mulligan," says she. "Then it's done in the closing
of an eye-cover," says I ; "and next Sunday Father Murphy took
us afore him, and repated the last bindin' words, that we should be
one in sowl, body, an' nature, seed, breed, an' giniration for ever,
and I never ripinted ; and I would advise all love-sick swains, just
to ax their sweethearts, and maybe they'll answer like my own Judy,
it's not in the natur' of woman to refuse ye."

Well ! well ! now nought can the matter be,
Honey, and sugar now, nought can the matter be,
Pigs and paraties since nought can the matter be,
Paddy no longer need wail.

## THOU ZEPHYR, AS THOU FLITT'ST AWAY.

THOU zephyr, as thou flitt'st away,
    Wafting thy perfume o'er the grove,
If in thy course thou chance to stray
    Along the cheek of her I love ;
Oh ! tell her that thou art a sigh,
    Breathed from a fond and humble heart,
By fate debarred from hopes so high,
    But do not tell from whom thou art !

Thou streamlet murmuring sweetly o'er,
    The pebbles in thy rocky bed,
If ever near thy lonely shore,
    Her wandering foot should chance to tread ;
Oh ! whisper softly in her ear,
    That with thy pure transparent wave,
There mingles many a bitter tear,
    But do not tell the eye that gave !

                E. PINKERTON.


## THEY COME ! THE MERRY SUMMER MONTHS.

THEY come ! the merry summer months of Beauty, Song,
    and Flowers ;
They come ! the gladsome months that bring thick leafiness
    to bowers ;
Up, up, my heart ! and walk abroad, fling cark and care
    aside,
Seek silent hills, or rest thyself where peaceful waters glide ;
Or, underneath the shadow vast of patriarchal tree,
Scan through its leaves the cloudless sky in rapt tranquil-
    lity.

The grass is soft, its velvet touch is grateful to the hand,
And like the kiss of maiden love, the breeze is sweet and
    bland ;

The daisy and the buttercup are nodding courteously,
It stirs their blood, with kindest love, to bless and welcome
    thee :
And mark how with thine own thin locks—they now are
    silvery grey—
That blissful breeze is wantoning, and whispering " Be
    gay ! "

There is no cloud that sails along the ocean of yon sky,
But hath its own winged mariners to give it melody :
Thou see'st their glittering fans outspread all gleaming like
    red gold,
And hark ! with shrill pipe musical, their merry course
    they hold.
Heaven bless them ! all these little ones, who far above this ·
    earth,
Can make a scoff of its mean joys, and vent a nobler mirth.

But soft ! mine ear upcaught a sound, from yonder wood it
    came ;
The spirit of the dim green glade did breathe his own glad
    name ;—
Yes, it is he ! the hermit bird, that apart from all his kind,
Slow spells his beads monotonous to the soft western wind ;
Cuckoo ! Cuckoo ! he sings again—his notes are void of art,
But simplest strains do soonest sound the deep founts of the
    heart !

It is a rare and gracious boon ! for thought-crazed wight
    like me,
To smell again these summer flowers beneath this summer
    tree !
To suck once more in every breath their little souls away,
And feed my fancy with fond dreams of youth's bright sum-
    mer day,
When rushing forth like untamed colt, the reckless truant
    boy,
Wander'd through green woods all day long, a mighty heart
    of joy.

I'm sadder now, I have had cause ; but oh ! I'm proud to
   think
That each pure joy-fount loved of yore, I yet delight to
   drink ;—
Leaf, blossom, blade, hill, valley, stream, the calm un-
   clouded sky,
Still mingle music with my dreams, as in the days gone by.
When summer's loveliness and light fall round me dark and
   cold,
I'll bear indeed life's heaviest curse—a heart that hath
   waxed old !

MOTHERWELL.

## OCH ! WHILE I LIVE, I'LL NE'ER FORGET.

OCH ! while I live, I'll ne'er forget
   The troubles of that day.
When bound unto this distant land,
   Our ship got under weigh.
My friends I left at Belfast town,
   My love at Carrick shore,
And I gave to poor old Ireland
   My blessing o'er and o'er.

Och ! well I knew, as off we sail'd,
   What my hard fate would be ;
For, gazing on my country's hills,
   They seem'd to fly from me.
I watch'd them, as they wore away,
   Until my eyes grew sore
And I felt that I was doom'd to walk
   The shamrock sod no more !

They say I'm now in Freedom's land,
   Where all men masters be ;
But were I in my winding-sheet,
   There's none to care for me !

I must, to eat the stranger's bread,
 Abide the stranger's scorn,
Who taunts me with thy dear-loved name,
 Sweet isle, where I was born !

Och ! where—och ! where's the careless heart
 I once could call my own ?
It bade a long farewell to me
 The day I left Tyrone.
Not all the wealth, by hardship won
 Beyond the western main,
Thy pleasures, my own absent home !
 Can bring to me again !
     WILLIAM KENNEDY.


## THE PEERLESS ROSE OF KENT.

WHEN beauty, youth, and innocence,
 In one fair form are blent,
And that fair form our vestal Queen,
 The Peerless ROSE of KENT,
Say, where's the Briton's heart so cold—
 The Briton's soul so dead,
As not to pour out ardent prayer
 For blessings on her head !

This is the day, the joyous day,—
 That sees our lady crown'd,
Hence, may not one disloyal heart,
 In Albion's Isles be found ;
But may she find in every breast
 An undisputed throne,
And o'er a gallant people reign,
 Whose hearts are all her own.

For ne'er did woman's hand more fair
 The regal sceptre hold,

And ne'er did brow more spotless wear
   The coronal of gold ;
And ne'er beneath the purple robe
   Did purer bosom beat ;
So ne'er may truer lieges kneel
   A lovelier Queen to greet.

May every blessing from above,
   On Kent's fair Rose descend,
While wisdom, dignity, and grace,
   On all her steps attend.
Still may she wear fair Virtue's bloom,
   Throughout a happy reign,
And long be hail'd the "Queen of Isles"—
   Fair Mistress of the Main ![1]
                ALEXANDER RODGER.


## THE SONG OF THE SLAVE.

O ENGLAND ! dear home of the lovely and true
   Loved land of the brave and the free,
Though distant—though wayward—the path I pursue,
   My thoughts shall ne'er wander from thee.
      Deep in my heart's core,
      Rests the print of thy shore,
   From a die whose impression fades never ;
      And the motto impress'd,
      By this die, on my breast,
Is "England, dear England, for ever,"
May blessings rest on thee for ever !

As Queen, she sits throned with her sceptre of light,
   Aloft on the white-crested wave ;
While billows surround her, as guards of her right
   To an island where breathes not a slave.

[1] This song was written on the Coronation of Queen Victoria, 28th June 1838.

And her sceptre of light
Shall through regions of night,
Shed a radiance like darts from day's quiver,
Till the unfetter'd slaves,
To the Queen of the Waves,
Shout "Freedom and England for ever,"
May blessings rest on thee for ever !

How often hath Fame, with his trumpet's loud blast,
Praised the crimes of mock-heroes in war,
Whose joy was to revel o'er nations laid waste,
And drag the fallen foe at their car?
But a new law, from heaven,
Hath by England been given
To Fame—and from which she'll ne'er sever,—
" No hero but he
Who saves and sets free,"
Saith England, free England, for ever.
May blessings rest on thee for ever !

J. D. CARRICK.

## BAULD BRAXY TAM,

### A WEEL KENNED CHIEL IN CARNWATH MUIR.

TUNE—" *The Campbells are coming.*

BAULD BRAXY TAM, he lives far in the West,
Whaur the dreary Lang Whang heaves its brown heather
crest ;
He's bauld as a lion, tho' calm as a lamb—
Rede ye nae rouse him, our bauld Braxy Tam.
The strang stalwart loon wons upon the hill tap
In a peat-biggit shieling wi' thin theekit hap—
Yet he ne'er wants a braxy, nor gude reestit ham,
And snell is the stamack o' bauld Braxy Tam.

See how his straught form, 'midst the storm flecker'd lift,
Stalks athwart the bleak muir, thro' the dark wreaths o'
    drift
  While the wowff o' the colley or bleat o' the ram
  Are beacons o' light, to guide bauld Braxy Tam.
When April comes in aye sae sleety and chill,
And mony young lammie lies dead on the hill,
  Though miss'd by its owner, and left by its dam,
  It's gude gusty gear to our bauld Braxy Tam.

Tho' some o' us think he gets mair than eneugh—
That he finds them himsel', whilk he cast in the heugh,
  The bauldest amang us maun keep a sough calm—
  He's a lang luggit deevil, our bauld Braxy Tam.
He ne'er parts wi' master, nor master wi' him—
When the headsman luiks sulky, the herdsman luiks grim.
  Syne they souther a' up wi' a flyte and a dram,
  For Tam's like the master, the master like Tam.

Thro' a' our braid muirlands sae stunted an' brown,
There's nane fear'd nor lo'ed like the hellicat loun ;
  Our fair freckled maidens feel mony love dwaum,
  When milking the ewes o' our bauld Braxy Tam ;
For the wild roving rogue has the gled in his e'e,
Twa three-neukit e'ebrees, aye louping wi' glee,
  Wi' a black bushy beard, and a liquory gam—
  O wha wad be kittled by bauld Braxy Tam !

At the lown ingle cheek, in the lang winter night,
Tam's welcomed wi' pleasure aye mingled wi' fright ;
  Queer sangs, and ghaist stories, a' thro' ither cram,
  In the big roomy noddle o' bauld Braxy Tam.
Then the weans cour in neuks frae the fancy-raised ghaist,
And ilk lad faulds his arms round his ain lassie's waist ;
  The auld folks gae bed, in an ill-natured sham,
  But the young gape till midnight round bauld Braxy Tam.

They wad fain hae him married, his courage to cowe,
For he's fickle's the clouds, tho' he's het as the lowe,

He courts a' the lasses without e'er a qualm,
Yet for nane by anither cares bauld Braxy Tam.
But a puir auld sheep-farmer cam' here to the muir,
Wi' a daughter as fair as her faither is puir ;
    She's pure as the dew-drap, an' sweet as the balm,
    And she's won the stout heart o' our bauld Braxy Tam.
JAMES BALLANTINE.

## THE SMIDDIE.

*AIR—" The days o' langsyne."*

YE'LL mount your bit naggie an' ride your wa's doun,
'Bout a mile and a half frae the neist borough toun,
There wons an auld blacksmith, wi' Janet his wife,
And a queerer auld cock ye ne'er met i' your life,
    As this cronie o' mine, this cronie o' mine ;
    O ! be sure that ye ca' on this cronie o' mine.

Ye'll fin' 'im as I do, a trust-worthy chiel,
Weel temper'd wi' wit frae his head to his heel,
Wi' a saul in his body auld Nick ne'er could clout,
And a spark in his throat, whilk is ill to drown out.
    This cronie o' mine, this cronie o' mine,
    For a deil o' a drouth has this cronie o' mine.

His smiddie ye'll ken by the twa trough stanes
At the auld door cheeks, an' the black batter'd panes—
By the three iron cleeks whilk he straik in the wa',
To tye up wild yads when heigh customers ca'.
    Oh this cronie o' mine, this cronie o' mine,
    Sure the hail countrie kens him, this cronie o' mine.

Up agen the auld gable 'tis like you may view,
A tramless cart, or a couterless plough,
An' auld teethless harrow, a brechem ring rent,
Wi' mae broken gear, whilk are meant to be ment
    By this cronie o' mine, this cronie o' mine ;
    He's a right handy craftsman, this cronie o' mine.

There's an auld broken sign-board looks to the hie road,
Whilk tells ilka rider whar his naig may be shod,
There's twa or three wordies that ye'll hae to spell,
But ye needna find fault for he wrote it himsel';
    This cronie o' mine, this cronie o' mine,
    He's an aul' farran carl, this cronie o' mine.

When ye fin' his auld smiddie, ye'll like, there's nae doubt,
To see the inside o't as well as the out ;
Then stap ye in bauldly, altho' he be thrang,
Gif the pint-stoup but clatter, ye'll ken him ere lang,
    This cronie o' mine, this cronie o' mine,
    Baith wit, fun, and fire, has this cronie o' mine.

Twa or three chiels frae the town-end are sure to be
    there—
There's the bauld-headed butcher, wha taks aye the chair,
'Mang the queerest auld fallows ae way and anither,
That e'er in this world were clubbit thegither,
    A' cronies o' mine, a' cronies o' mine,
    They'll a' mak ye welcome, these cronies o' mine.

There's Dominie Davie, sae glib o' the mou ;
But it's like ye will fin' the auld carl blin' fou ;
Wi' the wee barber bodie, an' his wig fu' o' news,
Wha wad shave ony chap a' the week for a booze ;
    A' cronies o' mine, a' cronies o' mine,
    They'll a' mak ye welcome, these cronies o' mine.

There's our auld Toun-Clerk, wha has taen to the pack,
Whilk is naething in bulk to the humph on his back ;
His knees are sae bow't, his splay feet sae thrawn,
Troth it's no easy tellin' the road whilk they're gaun,
    Tho' a cronie o' mine, a bauld cronie o' mine,
    They'll a' mak ye welcome, these cronies o' mine.

There's Robin the ploughman, wha's cramm'd fu' o' fun,
Wee gamekeeper Davie, wi' bag, dog, and gun,

And the miller, wha blythly the pipes can play on,
So your sure to fa' in wi' the "Miller o' Drone,"
    A' cronies o' mine, a' cronies o' mine,
    They'll a' mak ye welcome, these cronies o' mine.

Then wi' thumpin' o' hammers, and tinklin' o' tangs,
Wi' auld fashion'd stories wrought into queer sangs,
Wi' this soun', and that, ye'll ablins be deaved—
And tak' care o' your breeks that they dinna get sieved
    Wi' this cronie o' mine, this cronie o' mine,
    For an arm o' might has this cronie o' mine.

Then the Vulcan his greybeard is aye sure to draw,
Frae a black sooty hole whilk ye'll see i' the wa',
And lang or it's empty, frien', I meikle doubt,
Gif the tae chap kens weel what the tither's about,
    Wi' this cronie o' mine, this cronie o' mine—
    O ! be sure that ye ca' on this cronie o' mine.

Come now my gude frien' gie's a shake o' your haun',
The night's wearin' thro', and ye maun be gaun,
The callan will bring down your naig in a blink,
But before that ye mount again let us drink
    This cronie o' mine, this cronie o' mine,
    Here's lang life and pith to this cronie o' mine.
              ALEXANDER MacLAGGAN.

## SOME PASSAGES

### FROM THE PRIVATE LIFE OF LANG KATE DALRYMPLE,

#### A CELEBRATED BALLAD SINGER.

TUNE—" *Whistle, and I'll come to ye, my lad.*"

O KATIE's worth gowpens o' gowd to me,
O Katie's worth gowpens o' gowd to me,
Gang favour, gang fortune, I carena a flee,
My Katie's worth gowpens o' gowd to me.

She's nippit, decrepit—she's crabbit and wee,
Looks twa ways at ance wi' a grey greedy glee,
But she turns round on me wi' the tail of her e'e,
An' ilk glance has the glamour o' sunshine to me.
　　O Katie's worth, etc.

I'm couring and cauldrife, I'm lang and I'm lean,
Hae a leg like a lath, an' an arm like a preen,
Hae a face like a knife, an' a head like a bean,
Yet I'm comely and dear in my kind Katie's e'en.
　　O Katie's worth, etc.

We live man and wife, by nae priest ever tied,
We are bound by love's fetters, nae bondage beside ;
We were made, Kate an' me, to be ilk ither's pride,
Nane else covets me, nor yet fancies my bride.
　　O Katie's worth, etc.

O why should a blackcoat tie me to my joe,
Sic bands may bring weal, but they sometimes bring woe ;
Gin ye're no match'd aboon, ye'll ne'er souther below,
Far better shake hands on't, syne bundle and go.
　　O Katie's worth, etc.

I ance was a wabster, and sair did bewail
That bonny wee Katie should sup water kail,
She windit my pirns, I was fond, she was frail,
So to fend for our weanies, I took to the trail.
　　O Katie's worth, etc.

Syne I learnt a bit sang that spak kindly o' Kate,
Her name had a music that rang in my pate,
An' I sang't wi' sic birr thro' the streets air and late,
That a' body bought it wha cam' in my gate.
　　O Katie's worth, etc.

When weans cry lang Katie, I e'en let them cry,
When fou fools wad fash me, I jouk an' gae bye,
When lasses come flirtin, I coax them fu' sly,
Sae there's nane comes my way, but my ballant they buy.
　　O Katie's worth, etc.

Guid-natured contentment is aye sure to please,
I souther a' jars wi't, a' life's wheels I grease ;
Like the sweet sighing sough o' the saft summer breeze,
Is a well scrapit tongue, tho' its laden wi' lees.
 O Katie's worth, etc.

Then wha wad e'er fash wi' a loon that's sae slee,
Wha shouthers life's rubs wi' a heart fu' o' glee,
Ye'll ne'er break my heart, nor yet bluther my e'e,
Sae lang's ye leave Katie to cuddle wi' me.
 Then my Katie's worth, etc.

JAMES BALLANTINE.

## THE EVIL E'E.

AN evil e'e hath look't on thee,
 My puir wee thing, at last,
The licht has left thy glance o' glee,
 Thy frame is fading fast.
Wha's friens—wha's faes in this cauld warld
 Is e'en richt ill to learn,
But an evil e'e hath look'd on thee,
 My bonnie—bonnie bairn.

Your tender buik I happit warm,
 Wi' a' a mither's care,
I thought nae human heart could harm
 A thing sae guid an' fair.
An' ye got aye my blessing when
 I toil'd, your bread to earn,
But an evil e'e hath look't on thee
 My bonnie—bonnie bairn.

The bloom upon thy bonnie face,
 The sunlicht o' thy smiles,
How glad they make ilk eerie place,
 How short the langsome miles ;

For sin' I left my minnie's cot
　Beside the brig o' Earn,
O ! ours has been a chequer'd lot,
　My bonnie—bonnie bairn.

I can forgie my mither's pride,
　Though driven frae my hame,
I can forgie my sister's spite—
　Her heart maun bear its blame.
I can forgie my brither's hard
　And haughty heart o' airn,
But not the e'e that withers thee,
　My bonnie—bonnie bairn.

I ken that deep in ae black breast
　Lies hate to thee and me ;
I ken wha bribed the crew that press'd
　Thy father to the sea.
But hush !—he'll soon be back again,
　Wi' faithfu' heart I learn,
To drive frae thee the evil e'e,
　My bonnie—bonnie bairn.

ALEXR. MacLAGGAN.

## OUR AIN GUDE TOWN.

### SCOTTISH BALLAD.

AIR—" *The young May moon.*"

O LEEZE me now on our ain gude Town !
　I wat there's few like our ain gude Town ;
On the crown o' the land, may be mony mair grand,
　But there's nae ane sae dear as our ain gude Town.

There's lads fu' rare in our ain gude Town,
　And lasses fu' fair in our ain gude Town :
The light o' their e'e is a fountain o' glee,
　And it flows to the heart in our ain gude Town.
　　O leeze me now, etc.

O dearly we loe thee, our ain gude Town,
  And meikle we owe thee, our ain gude Town ;
The friendship, the love, we were fated to prove,
  Were happiest aye in our ain gude Town.
    O leeze me now, etc.

Then here's to the health o' our ain gude Town,
  The wisdom and wealth o' our ain gude Town ;
May plenty and peace, ilka blessing increase,
  And sweet freedom aye halo our ain gude Town !
    O leeze me now, etc.

THOS. DICK.

## THE KAIL BROSE OF AULD SCOTLAND.[1]

WHEN our ancient forefathers agreed wi' the laird
For a spot o' good ground for to be a kail-yard,
It was to the brose that they had the regard ;
  O ! the kail brose of auld Scotland ;
  And O ! for the Scottish kail brose.

[1] This song has been reprinted in our collection as being an exact copy from the original MS.—which we have seen in the hands of Mr. Peter Buchan, the indefatigable ballad collector. The author was Alex. Watson, merchant tailor in Aberdeen, who was at one time Deacon of the Incorporated Trades, in the northern metropolis. The circumstance that first suggested the idea to the author, was a Scottish regiment recruiting in Aberdeen, playing in their processions the "Roast Beef of Old England" oftener than the patriotic Deacon thought consistent with true national spirit—thus, as he thought, holding his country in invidious contrast—and so, while the goose was hot, he struck off the "Kail Brose of Auld Scotland." We think it contains incontestible evidence that the worthy Deacon knew that there were other sorts of padding that would relieve the acute angles in the framework of man besides roast beef. The reader will observe that there are two or three stanzas in the original not printed in the current version ; and the third stanza but the last, "Now State," etc., was never before given. This song was written during the period of the American war, 1781, and the guardians of the Press in those days were so nervous, they feared, if published, it might be construed into sedition.

When Fergus, the first of our kings, I suppose,
At the head of his nobles had vanquish'd his foes,
Before they began they had dined upon brose.
    O ! the kail brose, etc.

Then our sodgers were drest in their kilts and short hose,
With bonnet and belt, which their dress did compose,
With a bag of oatmeal on their back to make brose.
    O ! the kail brose, etc.

In our free early ages a Scotsman could dine
Without English roast beef, or famous French wine,
Kail brose, if weel made, he always thought fine.
    O ! the kail brose, etc.

At our annual election of bailies or mayor,
Nae kickshaws of puddings or tarts were seen there,
A dish of kail brose was the favourite fare.
    O ! the kail brose, etc.

It has been our favourite dish all along,
It our ladies makes beauties, our gentlemen strong—
When moderately used, it our life does prolong.
    O ! the kail brose, etc.

While thus we can live, we dread no kind of foes—
Should any invade us, we'll twist up their nose,
And soon make them feel the true virtue of brose.
    O ! the kail brose, etc.

Now State politicians new taxes propose,
Involving our country in numberless woes,
What a blessing it is ! there's yet nane upon brose !
    O ! the kail brose, etc.

But aye since the thistle was joined to the rose,
And Englishmen no more accounted our foes,
We have lost a great part of our stomach for brose.
    O ! the kail brose, etc.

But each true-hearted Scotsman, by nature jocose,
Can cheerfully dine on a dishful of brose,
And the grace be a wish to get plenty of those.
O ! the kail brose of auld Scotland,
And O for the Scottish kail brose !


## LASS, GIN YE WAD LO'E ME.

" LASS, gin ye wad lo'e me,
  Lass, gin ye wad lo'e me,
Ye'se be ladye o' my ha',
  Lass, gin ye wad lo'e me.
A canty butt, a cosie ben,
  Weel plenished ye may true me ;
A brisk, a blythe, a kind gudeman—
  Lass, gin ye wad lo'e me !"

" Walth, there's little doubt ye hae,
  An' bidin' bein an' easy ;
But brisk an' blythe ye canna be,
  An' you sae auld and crazy.
Wad marriage mak you young again ?
  Wad woman's love renew you ?—
Awa', ye silly doitet man,
  I canna, winna lo'e you."

" Witless hizzie, e'en's ye like,
  The ne'er a doit I'm carin' ;
But men maun be the first to speak,
  An' wanters maun be speirin'.
Yet, lassie, I hae lo'ed you lang,
  And noo I'm come to woo you—
I'm no sae auld as clashes gang,
  I think you'd better lo'e me !"

" Doitet bodie !—auld or young,
  Ye needna langer tarry,

Gin ane be loutin' ower a rung,
 He's no for me to marry.
Gae hame and ance bethink yoursel'
 How ye wad come to woo me—
And mind me i' your latter-will,
 Bodie, gin ye lo'e me !"

ALEX. LAING.

## TA PRAISE O' OUSKIE.

*AIR—" Neil Gow's farewell to whisky."*

TA praise o' ouskie, she will kive,
An' wish ta klass aye in her neive ;
She tisna thought that she could live
 Without a wee trap ouskie, O.

For ouskie is ta thing, my lad,
Will cheer ta heart whene'er she's sad ;
To trive bad thoughts awa' like mad,
 Hoogh ! there's naething like kood ouskie, O.

Oh ! ouskie's koot, an' ouskie's cran,
Ta pestest physick efer fan ;
She wishes she had in her han',
 A kreat pig shar o' ouskie, O.

Ta Lallan loon will trank at rum,
An' shin tat frae ta Tutchman come ;
An' pranty—Fieugh ! tey're a' put scum,
 No worth a sneesh like ouskie, O.

Ta shentles they will trank at wine,
Till faces like ta moon will shine ;
Put what's ta thing can prighten mine ?—
 Poogh ! shust a wee trap ouskie, O.

Ta ladies they will klour and plink,
Whene'er tey'll saw't a man in trink ;

Put py temsel tey'll never wink,
　　At four pig tram ò' ouskie, O.

An' some will trank a trashy yill,
Wi' porter some their pellies fill ;
For Loch Ard fu', a sinkle shill
　　She wadna gie o' ouskie, O.

Some lads wi' temprant rules akree,
An' trench their kite wi' slooshy tea ;
She's try't tat too, but nought for me—
　　Is like a wee trap ouskie, O.

What kars her roar, and tance, and sing?
What kars her loup ta highlan' fling?
What kars her leuk as pault's ta king?
　　Put shust a wee trap ouskie, O.

Whene'er she's towie, fex, and wae,
Whane'er ta cauld her nose maks plac,
What cheers her heart py night an' tay?
　　Hoogh ! shust a wee trap ouskie, O.

ALEX. FISHER.

## SINCE FATE HAS DECREED IT.

AIR—"*A' body's like to get married but me.*"

SINCE Fate has decreed it—then e'en let her gang,
I'll comfort mysel' wi' a canty bit sang :
Yes ; I'll sing like a lintie and laugh at it a',
Though the auld donnart dotard has wiled her awa'.
O wae worth that siller ! what mischief it breeds,
Dame Fortune's pet weans, how it pampers and feeds ;
It has made them baith ane whom auld Nature meant twa,
And has torn frae my arms, my dear lassie awa'.

The neighbours will clatter about the affair,
But e'en let them talk—that's the least o' my care,
For the sugh will blaw by in a fortnight or twa,
But ne'er can restore to me her that's awa'.
Come cheer up my heart !—yet, what need'st thou be
     wae ?
There are thousands behint her, sae e'en let her gae ;
Yes ; thousands, as bonnie, as good, and as braw—
Then why should'st thou grieve for her, now she's awa'?

But ah ! hapless lassie, my heart's wae for thee,
To think what a comfortless life thou maun dree ;
How cheerless to sit in a rich splendid ha'
'Midst desolate grandeur, when love is awa'.
And thou, her auld mither, ah ! what wilt thou say,
When thou seest thy poor lassie, heart-broken and wae ;
Ah ! what will avail then, her cledding sae braw,
When it covers a bosom that's riven in twa?

ALEX. RODGER.

## DOWN THE WATER.

AIR—"The Jorum."

Quo' Jean to me the tither morn, while munching at our
    toast, sir,
" Dear me, gudeman, ye're unco worn—ye're looking like
    a ghost, sir—
Ye're thin and wan—yer colour's gane—I trow ye are nae
    fatter—
In troth ye'll needs subtract a day, and journey down the
    water.

I'm sure 'twill do us meikle gude—a waucht o' cauler air,
    sir,
A cauler douk—a cauler breeze—and cauler fish and fare,
    sir ;

Besides, ye ken, I'm far frae weel—and sae is Jane our
    daughter,
Sae trouth, gudeman, ye'll needs consent to journey down
    the water.

There's Will, and Bob, and George, and Ned, are hardly
    cured the measles ;
And Jess, and May, and Jean, and I—our skins are din
    as weazles ;
Besides, ye ken, its just the thing—and see there's Mrs.
    Clatter,
And ilka creature ought genteel—for weeks been down
    the water."

" Weel, weel, gudewife, sin' e'en 'tis sae, and naething less
    will please ye,
We'll see and set about it straucht—but losh it's no that
    easy ;
For things are looking slack, and cash—is no a plenty
    matter—
Ye'll needs douk twa-three times a-day—and fuddle lots
    o' water."

I true the packing soon began—odds and ends galore,
    sirs—
Wi' Mackintoshes—pots and pans—and cordials a store,
    sirs ;
Syne bundling a' aboard—the boat maist aff ere we wan
    at her—
Her tether-tow maist stapp'd my breath and journey down
    the water.

Hardly frae the Broomielaw, wife and weans a' sea-sick,
Ane bocking here, anither there—their stomachs under
    physic ;
And then the landing—rumbling—tumbling—swearin'
    like a hatter,
And then to crown the job—mysel' maist drowned into
    the water.

Rescued frae fear o' sudden death—we gather consolation,
And, joyous hope, our trouble's o'er, within our new
location ;
An' now to see us pack'd and cramm'd like ony Yankee
squatter,
Nae less than five in ilka bed—that's high life down the
water.

A grumbling night o'erpast—the morn, we grumbling
don our jackets,
In haste to seize our promised jaunt—the rain pours
down in buckets ;
Neist day's the same—the neist—the neist—we hear its
ceaseless patter,
And sulky through the window glow'r—that's pleasure
down the water.

At last ae sunny day is sent to cheer each drooping
spirit,
In madden'd joy we hail the morn—for a' are downricht
weari't ;
But mark ye how sic pleasure ends—our auldest, favourite
daughter,
Ran aff galanting, nane kent whaur—wi' some chiel down
the water.

Wi' her restored—we journey back—in direfu' wrath and
shame, sirs,
And vowing that we ne'er again shall jaunt sae far frae
hame, sirs ;
Or if we do, by sooth and troth—I'se no be sic a fauter,
As move like Patriarchs of old—in families down the
water.

PATRICK BUCHAN.

## IT WAS NOT FOR THE DIAMOND RING.

*Set to Music by John Clow, Esq.*

IT was not for the diamond ring upon your lily hand,—
It was not for your noble name,—it was not for your
    land,—
I saw no gem, no lordly name, no broad domain with thee,
The day you stole my trusting heart and peace of mind
    from me.

You came—I knew not whence you came—we met—
    'twas in the dance—
There was honey in each word of yours, and glamour in
    each glance ;
Though many were around me then, I nothing saw but him
Before whose brow of starry sheen fresh-fallen snow were
    dim.

You're gone !—it was a weary night we parted at the burn;
You swore by all the stars above, that you would soon
    return ;
That you would soon return, light love ! and I your bride
    should be,
But backward will the burnie roll, ere you come back to
    me !

They say, that soon a smiling dame of lineage like to
    thine,
Will take thee by the fickle hand, thy falsehood placed
    in mine ;
The music and the rose-red wine to greet her will appear—
For wedding-song, a sigh I'll have—for bridal-pledge a
    tear.

O would that thou hadst passed me by, in coldness or
    in pride !
Nor wrought this deadly wrong to her, who on thy truth
    relied ;

The hunter's to the greenwood gone, his spear is in its rest,
But he'll not wound the trusting dove, that shelters in his
    breast.

WILLIAM KENNEDY.

## THE FLITTIN' O' THE COW.

AIR—"*Tak' your auld Cloak about ye.*"

IN summer when the fields were green,
    An' heather bells bloom'd ower the lea,
An' hawthorns lent their leafy screen,
    A fragrant bield for bird an' bee ;
Our Hawkie in the clover field
    Was chewin' her cud wi' gratefu' mou'
An' our gudewife, wi' eident hand,
    Had just been out to flit the cow.

O, our gudeman's a leal gudeman,
    But nane maun daur to say him na ;
There's nae a laird in a' the lan'
    Wi' higher hand mainteens the law.
Though he be poor he's unco proud,
    An' aye maun be obey'd at hame ;
An' there, when he's in angry mood,
    Wha conters him may rue the same.

"Gae flit the cow !" says our gudeman—
    Wi' ready tongue the dame replies,
"Gudeman, it is already dune"—
    "Gae flit the cow !" again he cries.
"My will ye'll do wi' hand an' heart,
    If ye're a wife baith kind an' true ;
Obedience is the woman's part—
    Make haste, gudewife, an' flit the cow."

"Gudeman, ye're surely clean gane gyte,
    The cow's already flittit been ;

To see you fume an' hear you flyte,
  I ferlie meikle what ye mean.
What need to gang an' do again
  The thing that I hae dune e'en now?
What idle tantrum's this ye've ta'en?"
  "I say, gudewife, gae flit the cow!"

"Gudeman, when we were lad an' lass,
  Your tongue was like a honey kaim;
An' aye ye vowed ye'd ne'er prove fause,
  But kythe like ony lamb at hame:
But now ye look sae dark an' doure,
  Wi' angry e'e an' crabbit mou',
Ye gar me aften rue the hour"——
  "I say, gudewife, gae flit the cow!"

Syne he began to loup an' ban,
  When out the wife flew in a huff—
"Come back! come back!" cries our gudeman—
  "Come back! obedience is enough!!
My sovereign will ye maun obey,
  When my commands are laid on you;
Obedient baith by night an' day,
  An' ready aye to '*flit the cow*!'"[1]

ALEX. SMART.

## JOSEPH TUCK.[2]

I'M Joseph Tuck, the tailor's son,
  A poor but honest blade, sirs,
And for these five-and-twenty years,
  A roving life I've led, sirs;

[1] We cannot but think that our friend, Mr. Smart, has represented the "Head of the House" as carrying authority with rather a high hand.

[2] We have inserted this song in our miscellany, though it has been in almost every collection of Comic Songs published within the last quarter of a century. The author's name was never before given—it is an early effusion of one of our contributors—Mr. William Finlay, Paisley.

But as I mean to settle here,—
    I'se tell you what my trade is,—
I'm barber, blacksmith, parish clerk,
    Man-midwife to the ladies.
        Bow, wow, wow, ri tum te edi.

I learn the bloods the way to box,—
    I show them how to fence, sirs,—
I teach the girls the way to coax,
    And also how to dance, sirs.
I'm skilled in every Highland reel,
    Strathspey, and Irish jig, sirs,—
And I can shave a parson's beard,
    And curl a lady's wig, sirs.
        Bow, wow, wow, etc.

My shop is stock'd with London toys,—
    Guns, wooden swords, and dolls, sirs,
Red herrings, treacle, blacking balls,—
    Sweet gingerbread and coals, sirs.
I sell all sorts of ladies' ware,—
    Rings, parasols, and muffs, sirs,
I also deal in sausages,
    And other garden stuffs, sirs.
        Bow, wow, wow, etc.

I keep all kinds of liquors, too,—
    Rum, brandy, ale, and porter,
I light the lamps the whole year through,
    Or take them by the quarter.
I dress all kinds of leather, too,
    And linens, fine or coarse, sirs,
I keep a school for singing psalms,
    And tools for shoeing horse, sirs.
        Bow, wow, wow, etc.

All kinds of sweetmeats, too, I sell,—
    Soap, sugar, salt, and spice, sirs,

Potatoes, spunks, and periwigs,—
    And traps for catching mice, sirs,
Ching's patent lozenges I sell,—
    And Godfrey's cordial roots, sirs,
I also both can make and mend
    All kinds of shoes and boots, sirs.
          Bow, wow, wow, etc.

I also have on hand for sale,
    All sorts of weaving ware, sirs,
Wheel-barrows, picks, and pouckin' pins,
    And cheeses made in Ayr, sirs.
All kinds of cobbler's tools I keep,
    Umbrellas, brogues, and awls, sirs,
Flay'd pigeons, speldings, bacon, hams.
    And imitation shawls, sirs,
          Bow, wow, wow, etc.

Thus I have given you in full,
    A statement of my ware, sirs,
My rings and ruffs—my dolls and muffs—
    My leather and my hair, sirs,
But not to wear your patience out,
    I here will make a stop, sirs,
And only hope you'll take the hint,
    And purchase at my shop, sirs.
          Bow, wow, wow, ri tum te edie.


## THE WIDOW'S WONDERS.

"O, LEEZIE, but I'm wae for you, nae wonder that ye
    mane,
Whaur will we fin' the like o' him that noo is dead and
    gane ?
The picture o' guid nature, aye sae hearty and sae kin',
Nae wonder when ye think on him your wits ye're like
    to tine."

" O, Janet, Janet, say nae mair about him, honest man,
I canna weel forget him, though I do the best I can ;
He was a kin', kin' man to me, and when I see the
    wreck
O' a' my peace and happiness, my heart is like to break.

I was an orphan lassie left, and hadna mony freens,
And, Janet lass, I mind it weel when I was in my teens,
I didna think without a man that I my life would dree,
But aft I wonder't to mysel' wha's lassie I would be.

At Lanrick fair I met wi' Pate, and few were like him
    then,
He had an unco takin' way—he was the wale o' men,
And on that day, when he and I, did hauns thegither
    join—
I wonder't if there was on yirth a happier lot than mine.

But wark grew scarce, and markets dear, and trouble on
    us cam',
And Pate turn'd ill that vera day that I lay in o' Tam,
I guided Pate, and mony a nicht as by his bed I sat,
I wonder't hoo we could come through, an' burstit out
    and grat.

Tam wither't like a sickly flower that frae its stalk does
    fa',
And in a twalmonth after that, puir Pate was ta'en awa ;
And as I laid him in his kist, and closed his glazed e'e,
I wonder't if the yirth contain'd a lanelier thing than me.

Noo I'm a waeful widow left, a' nicht I sich and grane,
And aften in my musin' moods when sitting here my lane,
There's ae thing, I'll confess to you, 'bout whilk I'm sair
    perplext,—
I aften wonder, Janet, now—wha's lassie I'll be next.

WILLIAM FINLAY.

## THE EWE MILKER'S SONG.

OH ! what is peace?
'Tis the bleat of the lamb as it plays on the mountain ;
'Tis the sound of the stream as it falls from the fountain ;
'Tis the soft evening breeze as it stirs among the trees,
And wakes the voice of melody to soothe and to please.
Oh ! this is peace.

Oh ! what is fair ?
'Tis the dew-laden primrose that droops her fair form ;
'Tis the harebell that glistens, tho' dashed with the storm ;
'Tis Cynthia's pale car ; 'tis the mild evening star,
That spies the fond lovers, and gladdens from far.
Oh ! this is fair.

But what is love ?
'Tis the cry of the cushat as it coos in the dale ;
'Tis the voice of my Colin as he sings in the vale :
'Tis the thick beating sigh : 'tis the fair melting eye,
That moistens with fondness when Colin is nigh.
Oh ! this is love.

WILLIAM NICHOL.


## COME AFF WI' YOUR BONNETS, HUZZA ! HUZZA !¹

COME aff wi' your bonnets, huzza ! huzza !
The Provost is comin', huzza ! huzza !
The bailies an' beddles, wi' hammers an' treddles,
An' lingles, an' barrels, an' a', an' a'.

¹ "*Come aff wi' your bonnets.*"—This song was written on the occasion of his Majesty's visit to Scotland in 1822, when the then civic dignitaries paid their loyal and dutiful respects to their Sovereign. A short time before this, a certain Chief Magistrate of Glasgow had called a public meeting of the inhabitants a little against the grain. When he came to the meeting, he found the

Gif in Embro' our dwelling ye saw, ye saw,
Wi' our ain provost's name on the ca', the ca',
An' a' that accords, ye wad tak' us for Lords,
An' let them wha win, just laugh awa, awa.
    Come aff wi' your bonnets, etc.

Town-Hall full of people. On his coming in, no notice was immediately taken of him, the people keeping on their hats. Taking fire,
at what he conceived a slight put upon him, he began a lecture upon
the proprieties, telling them they ought to take off their hats to the
Provost ; hence there came among some a saying of, "Aff hats to
the Provost," to which the first line of the song alludes.

"*The bailies and beddles.*"—The Church beadles were taken to
Edinburgh on the occasion, as livery servants.

"*Wi' hammers, and treddles, and lingles, and barrels.*"—These
various implements of trade are emblematical of certain individuals
in the Magistracy, there being then among our civic rulers, a smith,
a weaver, a shoemaker, and a cooper.

"*Gif in Embro' our dwelling ye saw,*" etc.—Those who wish to
see an account of the splendour of this dwelling, may consult a
pamphlet entitled *The King's visit to Edinburgh, as far as the
Magistrates and Town Council of Glasgow were concerned*, published in Glasgow, 1822, and said to be from the pen of an LL.D.
In it, among other things, we learn that the dwelling in question,
was at No. 66 Queen Street, Edinburgh; that it contained ample
accommodation, there being no less than stabling for eighteen horses ;
and that the Provost of Glasgow, "our ain Provost's name," was
engraven on a brass plate on the door.

"*We'll hing up our signs in a raw.*"—The signs of Glasgow were
at one time an object of no little pride to the citizens. Symptoms
of a change in this respect, however, begin now to manifest themselves. Certain mercantile, and even manufacturing concerns in
Glasgow, who would very lately have sported their signs, content
themselves now with a small notice in black and gold at the side of
the close or entry, as " Bogle Mirlees, first floor ;" and some of a still
more uppish cast, have no less than a front door like a dwelling-house
to their place of business, with a brass-plate by no means so large
as was "our ain Provost's name on the ca'," but smaller, and smell-
ing much more of gentility. Whether this feeling of disparagement
respecting our signs, has spread to the provinces or not, we cannot
tell ; but we know, that as late as the year 1821, the signs were
objects of great worship and regard to the country visitors of our

We'll hing up our signs, in a raw, a raw,
Mak' flunkies o' saulies sae braw, sae braw ;
Wi' gowd an' wi' green, how we'll dazzle folk's e'en,
An' let Glasgow aye flourish awa, awa.
  Come aff wi' your bonnets, etc.

good City. It is matter of history, that the attractions of our many great and gilded signs, proved a sore hindrance to the right discipline and effective order of the country troops, called in to quell the Radical rising of that year. No sooner did the gallant yeomen enter our streets, than their eyes, to the neglect of everything else, were irresistibly caught by the mass of gilded literature so abundantly spread over our walls ; and when, after the toils of the day, these brave men were dismissed, bands of them were seen wandering everywhere, diligently reading the signs. It was proposed to the commander of these troops (but whether carried into actual effect or not, the writer of this cannot tell), that in order at once to gratify their taste for reading, and to prevent them from wandering about in staring groups, to the defiance of all ease and convenience in passing the streets and pavements, each captain should convene his troop at a convenient place in the morning, and read for their amusement and information, two or three pages of the Glasgow Directory. And let those who are to come after us, consider well before they mock at our signs, when they are told, that when our Magistrates, and those of the surrounding towns, went to meet the King at Edinburgh, they erected booths by the highway, in which they arranged themselves to welcome him as he passed, and that over every booth there was an inscription or sign. The inscription on the Glasgow sign was, "Let Glasgow Flourish ;" the one next it, and in a line with it, "We come to welcome our King ;" on which the writer of the pamphlet already mentioned, remarks—"These two inscriptions being in a row, read together wonderfully well." Hence, "We'll hing up our signs in a raw."

"*Mak' flunkies o' saulies sae braw.*"—The beadles, whom we have already remarked, were made waiting-men to the bailies, are also, for the most part, saulies, or serving-men at funerals."

"*Wi' gowd an' wi' green.*"—The livery in which these beadles were dressed, was green and gold, and very showy. The beadles, moreover, were, for the most part well-made, well-fed, rosy fellows, and became their liveries well. One of these, Warrander Begerney, was uncommonly buirdly. He is said to have made the remark, "that the King and he looked best in a' their processions ;—an' nae

When to Majesty down we maun fa', maun fa',
Ilk bailie sae gaucie an' braw, an' braw,
We canna weel guess how great George can do less,
Than to mak' bits o' Knichts o' us a', us a'.

Come aff wi' your bonnets, huzza ! huzza !
The Provost is comin', huzza ! huzza !
The bailies an' beddles, wi' hammers an' treddles,
An' lingles, an' barrels, an' a', an' a'.


## BESSY'S WOOING.

Tune—" *The hills o' Glenorchy.*"

O GUESS ye wha's gane a becking an' bowing,
Guess ye wha's gane a billing an' cooing,
Guess ye wha's gane a coaxing and wooing,
　　To bonny young Bessy the flower o' the glen.

Auld Souter Rabby, that dresses sae brawly ;
Auld Barber Watty, sae smirky an' waly ;
Auld Elder Johnnie, sae meek an' sae haly—
　　Hae a' gane a-wooing to Bess o' the Glen.

Fat Deacon Sandy the heigh Council nabby ;
Wee Tailor Davie, sae glibby an' gabby ;
Dominie Joseph, sae thread-bare an' shabby—
　　Hae a' gane a-wooing to Bess o' the Glen.

wonner, for as to processions, the King an' me are best used to
them."

" *Let Glasgow aye flourish awa.*"—" Let Glasgow Flourish," the
well-known motto of the Glasgow Arms. Six coaches well painted
and furbished up for the occasion, by a certain *ci-devant* Deacon-
Convener, had the arms and motto emblazoned in large upon their
pannels. Twelve copies of the arms and motto, therefore, appeared
to "dazzle folk's e'en," wherever the civic procession moved. A
thirteenth copy of the motto appeared on the sign over the booth.
How could the writer omit " Let Glasgow aye flourish awa ?"

Big Mason Andrew, sae heavily fisted ;
Jock Gude-for-naething, wha three times had listed ;
Lang Miller Geordie, wi' meal a' bedusted—
    Hae a' gane a-wooing to Bess o' the Glen.

Gleed Cooper Cuddy, a' girded fu' tightly,
Red-nosed Sawyer Will, wi' his beak shining brightly ;
The tree-leggit Pensioner, marching fu' lightly—
    Hae a' gane a-wooing to Bess o' the Glen.

They're sighing and sabbing, they're vowing an' swearing;
They're challenging, duelling, boxing, an' tearing ;
While Bess, pawky jaud, is aye smirking an' jeering—
    There ne'er was a gillflirt like Bess o' the Glen.

But a young Highland drover cam' here wi' some cattle ;
Gat fou, an' swore Gaelic—gat fierce, an' gae battle ;
An' a' the hale pack did he lustily rattle—
    Hech ! was nae that fun to young Bess o' the Glen ?

His braid manly shouthers, caught Bessy's black eye ;
Her heart gae a stound, an' her breast gae a sigh ;
An' now the bauld Drover's gien ower driving kye—
    For troth he's baith Laird o' young Bess an' the Glen.
                JAMES BALLANTINE.

## BETSY BAWN.

TUNE—" *Blythe, blythe are we.*"

I LITTLE reck't that restless love
    Wad ere disturb my peace again :
I little reck't my heart would prove,
    A victim 'neath his galling chain.
I've bribed him o'er and o'er again,
    And mony a plack, I ween, hae drawn ;
But a' in vain, I pine in pain
For crookit-backit Betsy Bawn.

You've heard o' cheeks o' rosy hue—
    O' breath sweet as the bud's perfume ;
Ye've heard o' e'en whilk dang the dew
    For brightness, on the lily's bloom ;
Ye've heard o' waist sae jimp and sma'—
    Whilk ye nae doubt would like to span ;
Far other charms my fancy warms—
    Red goud's my terms wi' Betsy Bawn.

Right sad's the weary wanderer's fate,
    When round him roars the tempest's din,
When howling mastiff at ilk gate,
    Keeps a' without, and a' within.
I wot ! a harder fate they dree,
    Wha' maun at drouthy distancè stan'
Wi' langin' e'e, yet daurna pree
    The barley-bree o' Betsy Bawn.

Sweet love, ye work us meikle ill—
    Far mair than we daur sing or say ;
And weel ye ken had I my will,
    An hour wi' me ye doughtna stay.
Yet for the sake o' auld langsyne,
    I'll yet forgie ye—there's my han',
Gif wi' ane dart, ye pierce her heart—
    The flinty part o' Betsy Bawn.

Daft Beauty swears her e'en's like deil's ;
    Her humphy back is sax times bow't ;
Her wither'd limbs like twa auld eels—
    Are roun' and roun' ilk ither row't.
Let love be cross'd wi' spit and host,
    A parchment skin, a horny han',
Her purse is clad, sae I maun wed—
    And eke maun bed wi' Betsy Bawn.
                ALEX. MacLaggan.

## THE SEA! THE SEA!

### A PARODY. [1]

THE Sea! the Sea! Oh me! oh me!
The pail—be quick! I quail—I'm sick,—
  I'm sick as I can be;
I cannot sit, I cannot stand;
I prithee, steward, lend a hand;
  To my cabin I'll go,—to my berth will I hie,
  And like a cradled infant lie.
I'm on the Sea—I'm on the Sea!
I am where I would never be;
  With the smoke above, and the steam below,
  And sickness wheresoe'er I go;
If a storm should come no matter, I wot;
To the bottom I'd go—as soon as not.

I love, oh! how I love to ride
In a neat post chaise, with a couple of bays,
  And a pretty girl by my side:
But, oh! to swing amidst fire and foam,
And be steam'd like a mealy potato at home:
  And to feel that no soul cares more for your wo,
  Than the paddles that clatter as onward they go,
The ocean's wave I ne'er moved o'er,
But I loved my donkey more and more,
  And homeward flew to her bony back,
  Like a truant boy or a sandman's sack;
And a mother she was, and is, to me;
For I was—an ass—to go to sea!

The fields were green, and blue the morn,
And still as a mouse the little house
  Where I—where I was born;
And my father whistled, my mother smiled,
While my donkey bray'd in accents mild:

[1] This parody on Barry Cornwall's song of "The Sea," we have taken, with permission, from Fraser's Magazine.

Nor ever was heard such an outcry of joy
As welcomed to life the beautiful boy.
I have lived, since then, in calm and strife,
With my peaceable donkey and termagant wife!
    With a spur for the one, and a whip for the other ;
    Yet ne'er have wish'd to change with another :
And a proverb of old will apply to me—
" Who is born to be hang'd will not die in the sea ! "


### THE SAILOR'S REST.

WHY search the deep
For those who sleep
Beneath its heaving billow?
    Is that blue sea
    Now raging free
A more ignoble pillow,
    Than their's who die
    On shore—and lie
Where the green turf is spread?
    Away ! away !
    Let the Sleeper lay—
His—is a noble bed !—


There let him rest
His weary breast,
Upon the lonely wave,
    Whose glittering crest
    The sunny west
Hath made a golden grave.
    Upon the sea
    He will not be
The banquet of the worm ;
    But food for things
    With snow-white wings
That sport amid the storm.

He was not one
Who looked upon
The consecrated grave—
As better spot
Wherein to rot
Than on the deep sea wave.
His lot was cast
To brave the blast
Through life—and now laid low,
Methinks his rest
Would be unblest
Where the tempest cannot blow.

O ! let his tomb
Be where his home
Was ever in his life—
Amid the wrath
Of Ocean's path,
And the wild surge's strife.
The winds will be
Sweet melody
Unto his spirit near :
For their's was long
The only song
The Sailor cared to hear.

JOHN CROSS BUCHANAN.


## THE HAPPY MEETING.

AIR—" *Guardian Angels.*"

HAVE you hail'd the glowing morning,
    When the sun first gilds the plain ?
Or the genial spring returning,
    After winter's dreary reign ?
    Then conceive, to me how dear
    When my Anna—faithful, fair,
    After years of lonely pain,
Bless'd my fond eyes—my arms again.

Every charm more finely heighten'd,
　Fix'd my raptured, wondering eyes !
Every grace divinely brighten'd,
　Held my soul in sweet surprise ;
　O ! I could have gazed my last,
　On her bosom heaving fast—
　Met her eyes benignly bright,
With ever-growing new delight.

Who'd not bear a separation
　Thus again to fondly meet, ·
And to find no alteration,
　Save the heart's more ardent beat ?
Thus, the same soft hand to grasp,
Thus the same fair form to clasp,
Thus the same warm lips to kiss—
O, say, can Heaven give more than this ?
　　　　　　　　ALEXANDER RODGER.


## O THINK IT NOT STRANGE.

O THINK it not strange that my soul is shaken,
　By every note of thy simple song ;
These tears, like a summoning spell, awaken
　The shades of feelings that slumber'd long.
There's a hawthorn tree, near a low-roof'd dwelling ;
　A meadow green, and a river clear ;
A bird, that its summer-eve tale is telling ;
　And a form unforgotten—they all are here.

They are here, with dark recollections laden,
　From a sylvan scene o'er the weary sea ;
They speak of the time when I parted that maiden,
　By the spreading boughs of the hawthorn tree.
We sever'd in wrath—to her low-roof'd dwelling,
　She turn'd with a step which betray'd her pain—
She knew not the love that was fast dispelling
　The gloom of his pride, who was her's in vain.

We met never more—and her faith was plighted,
  To one who could not her value know ;
The curse that still clings to affections blighted,
  Tinctured her life's cup with deepest wo.
And these are the thoughts which thy tones awaken,
  The shades of feelings that slumber'd long—
Then think it not strange, that my soul is shaken
  By every note of that simple song.

W. KENNEDY.

## COME TO THE BANKS OF CLYDE.

AIR—"*March to the battle field.*"

COME to the Banks of Clyde,
  Where health and joy invite us ;
Spring, now, in virgin pride,
  There waiteth to delight us :
  Enrobed in green, she smiles serene—
    Each eye enraptured views her ;
  A brighter dye o'erspreads her sky,
    And every creature woos her.
Come to the Banks of Clyde,
  Where health and joy invite us ;
Spring, now, in virgin pride,
  There waiteth to delight us.

Mark ! how the verdant lea,
  With daisies she is strewing ;
Hark ! now, on every tree,
  The birds their mates are wooing :
  Love wakes the notes that swell their throats,
    Love makes their plumage brighter ;
  Old Father Clyde, in all his pride,
    Ne'er witness'd bosoms lighter ;

Mark ! how the verdant lea,
  With daisies she is strewing ;
Hark ! how, on every tree,
  The birds their mates are wooing.

ALEX. RODGER.

## WHAT THE BODY WANTED WI' ME.

A CARL cam' to our town,
  Whan little we war thinkin',
Wi' a rung out ower his riggin',
  Like a pedlar cam' he linkin'.
As he hanker'd at the ha' door,
  Sic pauky blinks he gae me,—
That I wonder'd in my mind,
  What the body wanted wi' me.

He said he was a lairdie,
  O' riggs and roughness plenty,
His stack-yard, and his stable stow'd
  Wi' corn and couts fu' dainty ;
And for a "serie something,"
  Had he wauchled wast to see me—
Still I wonder'd in my mind,
  What the body wanted wi' me.

He took me by the hand so shy,
  And fain wad stoun a prievin,
But I started like a stunkart quey,
  To see him sae behavin' :
"Be kind," quo he, "my lassie leel,
  Nor be sae fain to flee me ;"
Syne I hanker'd in my mind,
  What the body wanted wi' me.

I bade the cadgie carl devawl,
  And aye his aim was speerin' ;

" I'll tarry nane to tell," quoth he,
  " The ettle o' my eeran :
I'm coothly come your luve to win—
  Frae dool and doubting free me ;"
And sighing said—" the bridal bed"
  Was what he wanted wi' me.

When youth and beauty were my boast,
  I then had lovers plenty,
But sair I've rued my scorn sinsyne,
  When offers turn'd but scanty ;
I laid a laithfu' loof in his—
  But fain the fool was o' me,
Death left me lady of his lan',
  Before a towmond wi' me.

Now back comes beauty wi' a bang—
  For walth the wrinkle covers ;
As ance mysel', my siller now,
  Has charms, and choice o' lovers ;
But let them gang the gate they cam,
  Their flattering winna fee me ;
I'll hugg my hoard, an' beet my banes,
  Wi' what they're wanting wi' me.

                           G. MacIndoe.


## JOCK, RAB, AND TAM ;

### OR, NATURAL REQUISITES FOR THE LEARNED PROFESSIONS.

" Oh what'll we do wi' Jock, gudeman ?
  It's like he'll ne'er do weel—
He's aye at the head of a' mischief,
  And just as cunnin's the Deil."
" Ah ! hech ! he'll yet be a man, gudewife,
  O' whilk we'll baith be proud—
We'll gie the callan a while o' the schule,
  An' he'll be a lawyer gude !"

" An' what'll we do wi' Rab, gudeman—
    An' how will he win his bread ?
To plow and saw, to shear and maw,
    He hasna hands nor head ! "
" Ah ! hech ! he'll yet be a man, gudewife,
    O' whilk we'll baith be proud—
We'll gie the callan a while o' the schule,
    An' he'll be a doctor gude ! "

" But what'll we do wi' Tam, gudeman,
    It dings me maist of a'!
A gapin', glourin', witless coof,
    He's gude for nocht ava' ! "
Ah ! hech ! he'll yet be a man, gudewife,
    O' whilk we'll baith be proud—
We'll gie the callan a while o' the schule,
    An' he'll be a minister gude ! "

ALEX. LAING.

## THE LAKE IS AT REST.

AIR—" Angels whisper. "

THE lake is at rest, love,
    The sun's on its breast, love ;
How bright is its water, how pleasant to see !
    Its verdant banks showing
    The richest flow'rs blowing—
A picture of bliss, and an emblem of thee :

    Then oh ! fairest maiden,
    When earth is array'd in
The beauties of heaven, o'er mountain and lea ;
    Let me still delight in
    The glories that brighten,
For they are, dear Anna, sweet emblems of thee.

But, Anna ! why redden ?
I would not, fair maiden,
My tongue could pronounce what might tend to betray.
    The traitor ; the demon
    Who could deceive woman,
His soul's all unfit for the glories of day.

    Believe me then, fairest,
    To me thou art dearest ;
And tho' I in raptures view lake, stream, and tree—
    With flow'r-blooming mountains,
    And crystalline fountains,
I view them, fair maid, but as emblems of thee.


## STREET ORATORY.

Air—"*Bartholomew Fair.*"

'Tis a most amusing sight,
    For a philosophic wight,
Through the streets of the city to stroll—
    And mark the variation
    Of this mighty population,
As the great tide onward doth roll.

    What a bustle, what a noise,
    What variety of cries,
Every one tries another to out-bawl ;
    You would think the Tower of Babel
    Had again let loose its rabble,
Such a clatter ne'er was heard since the Fall ?

    What a comical compound,
    And diversity of sound,
From the motley group doth arise,
    From your salt and whit'ning venders,
    Fiddle scrapers, organ grinders,
And your sellers of yard-long shoe ties !

See yonder crowd collected,
Every one with ears erected
Around the far-famed Jamie Blue ;[1]

[1] Jamie Blue, *alias* Blue Thumbs, *alias* P.D., so nick-named from the circumstance of his having vended button blue as indigo, and pepper dust—as best black Jamaica pepper. The real name, however, of this Goose-dub Cicero, was James M'Indoe, and the parish of Killearn, county of Stirling, has a right to claim him as one of her sons, as well as the classical George Buchanan. For many years our orator was a dealer in hardwares, and carried his shop on his shoulders to country fairs, taking the houses and villages on his way to these marts of cattle, corn, and the etceteras of husbandry. The edge of his acquisitive disposition was rather too keenly set, and he made no scruple to make the most of his customers, as opportunity afforded. For some misdemeanour committed during his peregrinations, he was sent to board and berth in the Royal Navy, which sentence, however, he soon found means to contravene, by making his escape. Whether a patriotic spirit burned within the pepper dealer, with cayenne intensity, or an eye after the Government grant of enlistment money, we pretend not to say, though we incline to adopt the latter as the influencing motive ; but the man of button-blue, soon after, threw over his shoulders the scarlet uniform of his Majesty's 71st, or Glasgow Regiment. To obviate the necessity of desertion, he contrived to commit some crime for which he was discharged by tuck of drum, as an accompaniment to the Rogue's March. Our hero, after this, for some time went round the country vending leeches, dropping chains, and, for at least twenty-five years, he made shift to live by editing and vending street Gazettes. We have ourselves heard Jamie remark on the variety of occupation and life that he had led : "he now kent a' the teeth in the wheel." Though of a robust build by nature, the dissolute life which he had led, shattered the walls of the clayey tenement, and he was compelled to seek an asylum in the Glasgow Town's Hospital, where he resided for nearly the last two years of his life. When the cheering April sun of 1836 made its appearance, after the tempestuous weather that had preceded, James begged to get out to take pot luck with the world again ; remarking, "that he would just do like the Robin, come back to them again in winter." James fulfilled his promise, and died in the Hospital, 24th January 1837. During the time of his sojourn in that establishment, he conducted himself with great propriety, and appeared to feel his moral sores as he drew nigh to the precincts of the narrow house.

The affair, depend upon't
Of the which he gives account,
Is full, and particular, and true !

MEZZO TENORE.

" Here you have a full and particular account of the execution of
that poor unfortunate man, Saunders Widdie, for robbing the butter
and potatoe market at Buchty Brae, on the seventeenth day of
November last.

" You have an account of his behaviour during the awful period of
his confinement—after the fatal judgment was pronounced, till the
moment he ascended the scáffold for execution.

" He was attended in his devotions, by the Rev. Mr. Samuel
Pouch-the-penny, incumbent of that parish, but melancholy to relate,
so little effect had the admonitions of the pious clergyman on the
unfortunate culprit, that he carried with him to the fatal drop a
pund o' butter in ae hand, an' a potatoe in the other—ay, an' he
threw the potatoe wi' sic a birr, that it knockit doun an auld wiffie
at the fit o' the gallows."

Blind Aleck next appears,[1]
Whose head for many years,
A hot-bed of poesie has been :
With his violin in hand,
He now takes up his stand,
And thus his harangue doth begin :—

AIR—" John Anderson my Joe."

" I'm the author of every word I sing,
And that you may very well see ;
The music alone excepted,
But just of the poetree."

" Ladies and gentlemen !—Any of you that has a friend in the army
—just give me their Christian name, and the regiment to which they
are attached, and I'll make you a song as fast as my tongue can re-
peat it." (<i>From the crowd</i>)—" Well, Aleck, try your powers on the
Glasgow Volunteers, Colonels Hunter and Geddes, and Major Paterson." (<i>Symphony</i>)—fierce dash or two of the bow.

---

[1] See Note, page 133.

RECITATIVE—STACATTO.

" For they're the men I do declare,
   I mean the Royal Lanarkshire Volunteers.

AIR—" *O'er Bogie.*"

" The first comes Colonel Hunter,
    In a kilt see he goes,
Every inch is a man
    From the top to the toes :—

He is the loyal Editor,
    Of the Herald news-pa-per—
And no man at the punch bowl,
    The punch can better stir.

Like the fiery god of war,
    Colonel Geddes does advance,
On a black horse, that belonged
    To the murdered King of France.

And then comes Major Paterson,
    You'll say he's rather slim ;
But 'twill take a clever ball,
    For to hit the like of him.

(*Violin.*)  Tee ramp di damp, tee ramp di damp,
    Tee ramp di damp ti dee ;
Tee diddledam fiddledam riddledam,
    Liddledam, tiddledam fiddle-de-dee."

Thus ends Blind Aleck's song,
And from the list'ning throng,
A burst of applause is heard :
And the charitable section,
Of the crowd make a collection,
For the comfort of the poor blind bard.

So the comedy goes on,
And the characters each one,
Have their parts made exactly to fit.

But who, ye powers of mirth,
From the canvas next steps forth ?
'Tis Hawkie[1]—the orator and wit.

[1] We suppose the name Hawkie was bestowed on our Trongate
Demosthenes, on account of his manner of articulating ; a hawking
up-throat-sawing tone, as if there were a war in the windpipe, and
the antagonist forces very nearly balanced :—were our orator, instead of rattling pebbles in his mouth, to modulate the tone, to try
the friction of a bottle-brush in the passage, it were more likely to
do good.   This character must be known to most of our readers ; his
real name is William Cameron :—He was born near Bannockburn.
An accident befel him while an infant, that rendered a crutch necessary from the first step in life, onwards ; and this circumstance was
attended with another unhappy effect : the parents, instead of putting him under wholesome discipline, and restraining his somewhat
impetuous temper, petted and indulged the boy ; so that when he
got into his teens, no check they could impose would control him :
taking the curb between his teeth, he bade complete defiance to the
reigns of parental authority.   Cameron received an education more
liberal than people in the situation of his father usually bestow on
their children, partly to compensate for the defect in his limb, and
also, as he promised to be a boy of spirit, and above average talent.
He was apprenticed to a tailor, but would not, lame as he was, content himself to squat with the cross-legged fraternity, but made off
with a gang of strolling players, with whom he remained a considerable time.   This moral wreck may be seen, almost every night, in
one or other of our principal streets, surrounded by a mob,
haranguing them on the topics of the day.   Hawkie's readiness in
repartee is truly astonishing—and woe betide any of our whiskered-
cigar-smokers who attempt to break a lance with him ! the coarse
sarcasm with which he assails them is as easily borne as a ladleful
of boiling pitch poured down the back.   Hawkie is a very extensive
Manufacturer of Facts ; with a most copious vocabulary, the warp
and woof of his Munchausen fabrics, are of wonderful consistency.
He is far superior in point of natural talent to what Jamie Blue was,
even in his best days, between whom and Hawkie there existed a
most jealous rivalry.   Jamie put in his claim as greatly Hawkie's
superior in the Dialogue, indorsed with "It's aboon his fit."   Hawkie,
on the other hand, cut his rival as with a butcher's saw, telling him
that he knew nothing of the language, that he addressed the public
in, "Come out to the street, and be a listener, and I'll let you hear
the Scottish language in its pith and purity ; ye ken as muckle about

CROAKING BARITONE (*Anglice*—Barrowtone) OF VOICE.

"A-hey! bide a wee, bodies, and dinna hurry awa hame, till ye hear what I hae gotten to tell ye; do you think that I cam' out at this time o' nicht to cry to the stane wa's ·o' the Brig'-gate for naething, or for onything else than for the public guid?—wearing my constitution down to rags, like the claes on my carcase, without even seeking a pension frae her Majesty; though mony a poor beggar wi' a star o'er his breast, has gotten ane for far less."

(*Voice from the crowd*)—"Hawkie, ye should hae been sent to parliament, to croak there like some ither parliamentary puddocks till yer throat were cleared." (*Reply*)—"Tak' aff your hat when ye speak to a gentleman—it's no the fashion in this kintra to put hats on cabbage stocks—a haggis would loup its lane for fricht afore ye—ye'll be a king whare a horn-spoon is the emblem of authority!" (*Resumes*)—"Here ye hae the history of a notorious beggar, the full and particular account of his birth and parentage—at least on the mither's side.

"This heir to the wallets was born in the byre of a kintra farmer, an' just in the crib afore the kye, and was welcomed to the world by the nose of honest Hawkie." (*From the crowd*)—"Was this a sister of yours, Hawkie?" (*Answer*)—"Whatna kail yard cam' ye out o'? that's your brither aside ye, is't? you're a seemly pair, as the cow said to her cloots." (*Continues*)—"It ne'er could be precisely ascertained the hour o' this beggar's birth, though the parish records hae been riddled to get at the fact. I maun also tell ye, for I dinna like to impose on my customers, that there is great doubt about the day o' the month, an' even about the month itsel'; but that he was

---

it, as grumphy does about grammar." These feuds are now at rest. It fell to Hawkie as the survivor, to speak of his opponent, when removed from collision in their respective callings, in the lines concluding this somewhat lengthy note. To the credit of professional jealousy must we attribute their severity:

> Oh! Clootie, if to thy het hame,
>   His hapless soul has happed;
> Tak' care o' a' your whisky casks,
>   Or faith they'll soon be tapped.

> Chain! chain! bin' fast, the drunken cove,
>   For, Clootie, ye've nae notion
> Of Jamie's maw, gin he's let loose,
>   His drouth would drain an ocean.

born hasna been disputed, though it might hae been, if we hadna an account o' his life and death, to convince the gainsayers. As to whether he was a seven months' bairn, or a nine months' bairn—the houdie has gi'en nae ither deliverance, than that he was his father's bairn, and what her profession required her to do; but the public voice is strongly inclined to favour the opinion that he cam' hame at full time, as he arrived sooner at the years o' discretion than usual; an' if ye dinna ken the period when a beggar's bairn comes to his estate duly qualified I'll tell you—it's when he ceases to distinguish between ither folk's property and his ain." (*From the crowd*)—"What a poor stock ye maun hae; ye hae been yelling about that beggar, till the story is as bare as your ain elbows." (*Retort*)—"Hech, man, but you're witty—when ye set out on the tramp, dinna come to me for a certificate, for I really cou'dna recommend ye; ye havena brains for a beggar, and our funds are no in a condition to gi'e ony pensions the now." (*Continued*)—"Ye hae an account o' the education which he received riding across the meal pock; and the lair that he learnt aff the loofs o' his mither, which was a' the school craft he e'er received: but sic a proficient did he himsel' grow in loof lair, that, like a' weel trained bairns, he tried his hands on the haffits of his auld mither in turn, and gied her sic thunderin' lessons, that she gied up her breath and business in begging, at the same time, to her hopeful son and successor." (*Voice from the crowd*)—"Ye should hae keepit a school amang beggars, and micht hae ta'en your stilt for the taws." (*Retort*)—"Oh, man, I would like ither materials to work wi' than the like o' you; it's ill to bring out what's no in; a leech would as soon tak' blood out o' my stilt, as bring ony mair out o' you than the spoon put in." (*Resumes*) —"Ye hae an account of his progress in life, after he began business on his ain account, and what a skilful tradesman he turn'd out—he could 'lay on the cadge'[1] better than ony walleteer that e'er coost a pock o'er his shouther.

"Ye hae an account o' his last illness and death—for beggars die as weel as ither folk, though seldom through a surfeit; ye hae also a copy of his last Will and Testament, bequeathing his fortune to be drunk at his dredgy—the best action he ever did in his life, and which mak's his memory a standing toast at a' beggars' carousals— whan they hae onything to drink it wi'; and really, you'll allow me to remark, if we had twa or three mae public-spirited beggars in our day that would do the like, the trade might yet be preserved in the country—for it has been threatening to leave us in baith Scotland

---

[1] Skilful address in begging.—*Dict. of Buckish Slang.*

and England, in consequence of the opening up of the trade wi' Ireland, and the prices hae been broken ever since ; we hae a' this to contend wi' to preserve the pocks frae perishing, for the sake o' our children." (*Voice from the crowd*)—" Och, Willie, is it your own self that I'm hearin' this morning? and how did ye get home last night, after drinking till the daylight wakened ye? troth ye did not know your own crutch from a cow's tail." (*Retort*)—" Oh, man, Paddie, it's naething new to me to be drunk, but it's a great rarity to you—no for want o' will, but the bawbees. What way cam' ye here, Paddie? for ye had naething to pay for your passage ; and your claes are no worth the thread and buttons that haud them the-gither ;—gin I had a crown for every road that your trotters could get into your trowsers by, it would be a fortune to me. 'Take me over,' said you, to your ould croak-in-the-bog ;—' I wish I had my body across agin, out of this starvation could country, for there's nothing but earth and stones for a poor man to feed on ; and in my own country, I'll have the potatoe for the lifting.' Hech, man,—but the police keeps ye in order—and ye thought when ye cam' o'er, to live by lifting? man ! aff wi' ye to your bogs—there's nae place like hame for ye, as the Deil said when he found himsel' in the Court o' Session.

" Ye hae an account o' this beggar's burial, and his dredgy." (*Boy's voice from the crowd*)—" Was ye there, Hawkie? surely, if the stilt could haud ye up !" " Och, sirs, are ye out already—you're afore your time—you should hae staid a wee langer in the nest till ye had gotten the feathers on ye, and then ye would hae been a goose worth the looking at." (*Continues*)—" Sic a dredgy as this beggar had wad mak' our Lords o' Session lick their lips to hear tell o'—thae gentry come down among us like as mony pouther-monkeys —with their heads dipped in flour pocks, to gie them the appearance o' what neither the school or experience in the world could teach them ;—gin hangie would gie them a dip through his trap-door, and ding the dust aff their wigs—there's no a beggar frae John O'Groat's to the Mull o' Galloway, that wadna gie his stilts to help to mak' a bonfire on the occasion.

" Ye hae the order o' the procession at the burial—it's the rank in the profession that entitles to tak' precedence at a beggar's burial—ye never hear tell o' blood relations claiming their right to be nearest the beggar's banes ; we'll be thinking the warld is on its last legs, and like to throw aff its wallets too, when sic an event occurs."

(*Interrupted*)—" Your stilt would, nae doubt, be stumpin' at the head o' them a'." (*Reply*)—" Stan' aside, lads, I'm just wantin' to see if he has cloots on his trotters, for horns are sae common, now-a-days, amang the gentry o' the blood, whar we should look for an example, that they hae ceased to distinguish the class that nature intended them for." (*Goes on*)—"First in order was Tinklers, the beggars' cavalry, wha being in constant consultation with the gentry of the lang lugs, hae some pretensions to wisdom; next Swindlers, wha mak' the best bargains they can wi' their customers, without pretendin' to hae ony authority for doin't—no like our black coats, wha can only get authority on ae side, to gang to a scene of mair extensive usefulness, whar the preaching pays better—our brethren of the pock a' follow this example; they never stay lang whar there's naething either to get or to tak',—but I'm forgetting mysel'; at their heels was Pickpockets, wha just tak' the hangman's helter wi' them, and gang the length o' their tether—for hangie aye keeps the hank in his ain hand. Next, Chain-drappers—the jewellers in the camp, wha are ready to sell cheap, or half the profits wi' everybody they meet, and wha are like mony o' our public instructors—aye get mair than they gie—then Prick-the-loops, wha are sae familiar wi' the hangman's loop that they've turned the idea into business, and set up wi' their garter—which they can easily spare, as they hae seldom ony stockings to tie on wi't : by this simple expedient they mak' large profits on sma' capital. Next, Chartered-beggars or Blue-gowns—wha get a license frae the authorities to cheat and lie over the whole country. Next, the hale clanjamfrey o' Vagrants— for they're a' but beggars' bairns the best o' them—Randies, Thieves, Big-beggars and Wee-beggars, Bane-gatherers and Rowley-powleys —Criers o' Hanging speeches—wha, generally, should hae been the subject o' their ain story—some wi' weans, but a' wi' wallets, broken backs, half arms, and nae arms : some only wi' half an e'e—ithers wi' mair e'en than nature gied them—and that is an e'e after every-thing that they can mak' their ain; snub-noses, cock-noses, slit-noses, and half-noses; Roman noses, lang noses—some o' them like a chuckie-stane, ithers like a jarganell pear ; hawk-noses and goose-noses ; and, mind ye, I dinna find fault with the last kind, for nature does naething in vain, and put it there to suit the head ; but what-ever the size and description o' the neb, they could a' tak' their pick, for the hale concern, man and mither's son, had mouths, and whar teeth were wanting, the defect was mair than made up by desperate willin' gums.

"Some were lame, though their limbs were like ither folks ; there are mae stilts made than lame folk, for I maun tell ye some gang a-begging and forget their stilts, and hae to gang back for them afore they can come ony speed ; ithers had nae legs to be lame wi' ; a few like mysel' had only ae guid ane, like the goose in a frosty morning, but made up the loss by the beggar's locomotive, a stilt, which a poor goose canna handle wi' advantage.

"The rear o' this pock procession was closed by bands o' sweeps, wha are ready for a' handlings, whar there's onything to do for the teeth; an' they hae the advantage o' us, for they're aye in Court-dress, and like honest Colly, dinna need to change their claes.

"In the hame-coming there was a scramble, wha should be soonest at the feast, and a quarrel, an' you'll maybe be surprised that there was but ae quarrel, but I maun tell you, that they were a' engaged in't, an' maist o' them kentna what they were getting their croons cloored for, but just to be neighbour-like. The cracking o' stilts, the yelly-hooings o' wives and weans, and the clatter o' tinkler's wives, wad hae ca'm'd the sea in the Bay of Biscay—do ye ken the distance at which a beggar fights his duel?—it's just stilt-length, or nearer, if his enemy is no sae weel armed as himsel'.

"Ye hae a return o' the killed and wounded—four Blind Fiddlers with their noses broken—four Tinkler's wives with their tongues split, and if they had keepit them within their teeth, as a' wives' tongues should be, they would have been safe—there's nae souder or salve that can cure an ill tongue—five Croons crackit on the Outside —sixteen torn Lugs—four-and-twenty Noses laid down—four Left Hands with the thumb bitten aff—ten Mouths made mill doors o'— four dizen Stilts wanting the shouther-piece—twenty made down for the use of the family—in ither words, broken in twa; an' they're usefu', for we have a' sizes o' beggars. After a' this, the grand dredgy; but I havena time to tell you about it the night; but ye see what handlings beggars would hae if the public would be liberal.

"Buy this book: if ye hae nae bawbees I'll len' ye, for I'm no caring about siller. I hae perish'd the pack already, an' I am gaun to tak' my Stilt the morn's morning, and let the Creditors tak' what they can get."

> This is the end of all,
> High and low, great and small;
> This finishes the poor vain show,
> And the King, with all his pride,
> In his life-time deified—
> With the beggar is at last laid low.

## MINISTER TAM !

OH ! ken ye his reverence, Minister Tam ?
Oh ! ken ye his reverence, Minister Tam ?
Wi' a head like a hog, an' a look like a ram—
An' these are the marks o' Minister Tam.

Oh ! Minister Tam's mistaen his trade—
The parish beadle he should hae been made ;
The kintra clash i' the manse to tell,
To summon the Session, an' ring the bell !

He's gotten a kirk, but he's preach'd it toom ;
He ca's, examines, but nane will come ;
His elder bodies they daurna speak—
He's makin' an' breakin' them ilka week !

There's aye some will-o'-the-wisp in his pow,
That keeps the country side in a lowe ;
There'll never be peace, an' that ye'll hear tell
Till he hang as heigh as the parish bell.

ALEX. LAING.


## BRIGHTLY IS THE STREAMLET FLOWING.

AIR—"*Merrily every bosom boundeth.*"

BRIGHTLY is the streamlet flowing,
  Brightly oh ! brightly oh !
To its mother ocean going
  Brightly oh ! brightly oh !

O'er its current, rapid, dancing,
Stately oaks their arms advancing,
Are the lovely scene enhancing
  Brightly oh ! brightly oh !

Haste, then, streamlet to the ocean
  Sweetly oh ! sweetly oh !
Kiss thy mother in devotion
  Sweetly oh ! sweetly oh !

But no ray comes to illumine
My poor heart in grief consuming,
Tho' the flow'ry banks be blooming
  Sweetly oh ! sweetly oh !

But what sun illumes the bushes
  Radiant oh ! radiant oh !
'Tis Matilda's glowing blushes
  Radiant oh ! radiant oh !

Run then, streamlet, run, and never
From thy mother ocean sever ;
Oh ! Matilda's mine for ever,
  Radiant oh ! radiant oh !


## THE AULD BEGGAR MAN.

TUNE—"*The Hills o' Glenorchy.*"

THE auld cripple beggar cam' jumpin', jumpin',
Hech, how the bodie was stumpin', stumpin',
His wee wooden leggie was thumpin', thumpin',
  Saw ye e'er sic a queer auld man ?

An' aye he hirchelled, an' hoastit, hoastit,
Aye he stampit his foot an' he boastit,
Ilka woman an' maid he accostit,
  Saw ye e'er sic a hirplin crouse auld man ?

The auld wives cam' in scores frae the clachan,
The young wives cam' rinnin' a' gigglin' an' laughin',
The bairnies cam' toddlin' a' jinkin' an' daffin',
  An' pooket the tails o' the queer auld man.

Out cam' the young widows a' blinkin' fou meekly,
Out cam' the young lasses a' smirkin' fou sweetly,
Out cam' the auld maidens a' bobbin' discreetly,
  An' gat a bit smack frae the queer auld man.

Out cam' the big blacksmith a' smeekit an' duddy,
Out cam' the fat butcher a' greezy an' bluidy,
Out cam' the auld cartwright, the wee drunken bodie,
  An' swore they wad slaughter the queer auld man.

Out cam' the lang weaver wi' his biggest shuttle,
Out cam' the short snab wi' his sharp cutty whittle,
Out cam' the young herd wi' a big tatty beetle,
  An' swore they wad batter the queer auld man.

The beggar he cuist aff his wee wooden peg,
An' he show'd them a brawny sturdy leg,
I wat but the carle was strappin' an' gleg,
  Saw ye e'er sic a brisk auld man ?

He thumpit the blacksmith hame to his wife,
He dumpit the butcher, who ran for his life,
He chased the wee wright wi' the butcher's sharp knife,
  Saw ye e'er sic a brave auld man ?

He puff'd on the weaver, he ran to his loom,
He shankit the snab hame to cobble his shoon,
He skelpit the herd on his bog-reed to croon,
  Saw ye e'er sic a strong auld man ?

The wives o' the town they a' gather'd about him,
An' loudly an' blithely the bairnies did shout him,
They hooted the loons wha had threaten'd to clout him,
  Kenn'd ye e'er sic a lucky auld man ?
       JAMES BALLANTINE.

## COME, A SONG—A GLAD SONG.

COME a song—a glad song, when each heart with delight,
Like fix'd stars are beaming around us to-night,
When our faith is so steady, our friendship so strong,
Oh ! who would not join in a soul-stirring song ?

Sing on, happy hearts ! if your praises should be
Breathed forth for the land of the brave and the free,
Let the proud echoes swell Scotland's mountains among,
They're the altars of freedom ! the highlands of song !

Sing on, happy hearts ! and if love be the theme,
Then breathe in glad music the bliss of the dream,
For the ladies, God bless them ! who seldom are wrong,
Say " love's sweetest breath is a soul-melting song."

Sing on, merry hearts ! and if auld mother wit,
Be the prize you would aim at, the mark you would hit,
Go bathe your glad souls in the blood of the vine,
Till your hearts overflow with the lays o' langsyne.

Song—song was the joy of our boyhood's glad time ;
Song—song still shall cheer the proud home of our prime,
And when bent with old age, we go hirpling along,
We'll beat time with our crutch to a merry old song.

Then a song—a glad song, when each heart with delight,
Like fix'd stars are beaming around us to-night,
When our faith is so steady, our friendship so strong,
Oh ! who would not join in a soul-stirring song ?

ALEX. MACLAGGAN.

## SIMON BRODIE.

HEARD ye e'er o' our gudeman,
　The gaucy laird o' braid Dunwodie;
The wale o' cocks at cap or can,
　Honest, canty Simon Brodie :
　　Auld farran canty bodie,
　　　Winsome, pranksome, gleesome bodie,
　　The crack o' a' the kintra side,
　　　Is auld canty Simon Brodie.

Simon he's a strappin' chiel,
　For looks wad mell wi' ony bodie,
In height an ell but an' a span,
　An' twice as braid is Simon Brodie :
　　Troth he is a canty bodie,
　　　An auld farran canty bodie,
　　An' tho' his pow's baith thin and grey,
　　　Ye'd hardly match me Simon Brodie.

Simon Brodie had ane wife,
　I wat she was baith proud and bonny,
He took the dishclout frae the bink,
　And preen't it till her cockernony !
　　Wasna she a thrifty bodie,
　　　The braw, braw lady o' Dunwodie,
　　In claes sae fine to dress and dine,
　　　Wi' sic a laird as Simon Brodie.

An' Simon had a branded cow,
　He tint his cow and couldna find her,
He sought her a' the lee lang day,
　But the cow cam' hame wi' her tail ahind her.
　　Yet think na him a doited body,
　　　Think na him a davert body,
　　He has walth o' warld's gear,
　　　Mak's men respect auld Simon Brodie.

## THE DEACON'S DAY.[1]

AIR—"*Kebbockstane Weddin'*."

O RISE man, Robin, an' rin your wa's,
    The sun in the lift is bleezing brightly,
Put on the best o' your Sunday braws,
    And your gravat tie round your thrapple tichtly :
Then whip on your castor, and haste to the muster,
    The Trades i' the Green hae this hour been convenin',
And our wits we maun use, a good Deacon to choose ;
    'Tis a day " big with fate," at your post then be leanin'.

Now Robin has risen, and aff he has gane,
    To meet wi' the leaders o' ilk Corporation—
And awa they parade wi' their banners display'd—
    There has ne'er been it's like sin' the Queen's Corona-
        tion :
There were Tinklers and Tailors—and Wabsters and
        Nailers,
    And Barbers and Blacksmiths, and Gardeners sae
        gaudy ;
A' life to the heels, and as guid-looking chiels
    As e'er cam' to light by the help o' a howdie.

"Gentlemen,—We hae this day met for the purpose of electing a
head to our Master Court.  It is true that new-fangled notions hae
ta'en possession o' men's minds since the date o' our charter, and
mair particularly since the date o' our late Magna Charta—the
Reform Bill ; but will ony man possessed o' his seven senses argufy
me into the belief, that the Incorporation of Wrights, that I hae,
during the currency o' the last twalmonth, been the head o'—or
rather, I may say, the centre upon which a' its hinges turned—has
not been productive of substantious and manifest advantage to the
public in general, and to the craft in particular.  Noo, Gentlemen,
to keep to the square o' my speech—rough and knotty though it be,

---

[1] The Deacon Convener in Glasgow is head of the Incorporated
Trades, and presides over the meetings of these chartered crafts—
he is also entitled, *ex-officio*, to a seat in the City Council.

and micht be a' the better o' a strip frae a jack plane—I like to be
special in a' my specialities, and to keep to the dove-tail o' the
matter—I, therefore, before proceeding to the election, have to request that you will allow me to say a word or twa touching the
matter in hand. Although I am yet the tongue o' the trump, it
would, nevertheless, and notwithstanding, be unwise, as well as
ill-bred, to tak' up much o' your time at the present moment, seeing
how much we have before us this day, independent of what we have
to o'ertak', and tak'-o'er, too—the better tak' o' the twa—before bed-
time ; therefore, I will be exceedingly brief, for I'm beginning to
fear that ye'll think me a boring-bit ; to use the words of my frien',
the late Deacon Convener, I will be 'very whuppy in the matter o'
my speech.' Weel, Gentlemen, we have all heard o' my friend and
brother in the management o' his ain corporation—Geordy Wriggles,
present Deacon of the Incorporation of Weavers. Our man is nae
man of mere thrums, or a piece of veneer manufacture—put the
wummle through him, ye wad find the same piece outside and in—
nane o' your fley-the-doos, but a man o' means and measures, and
who will dress up and keep in thorough repair, a' the building about
our Corporation—Wha seconds Deacon Wriggles?" "Me, Deacon,"
answers Deacon Snipe the Tailor. "Weel, lads, I see my friend is
carried unamous (at least I'm unamous) by a great majority.—Cheer
the Deacon till the kebars shake."

A shout of applause which rent the air,
  Was heard at the grand Master Deacon's election
And awa to his dwelling they now repair,
  That his friends may rejoice in the happy selection.
His comely guidwiffie sprang out in a jiffie,
  And stood at the door in her best every steek on ;
Joy danced in her e'en as she welcomed them in
  To dine, and to drink to the health o' the Deacon.

The dinner was tasty, their appetites guid—
  For tradesmen hae stomachs as weel as their betters,
And they syned doun the sappy, substantial food,
  Wi' a capfu' o' yill, and a glass o' strong waters ;
Then up raise the auld Deacon, a subject to speak on,
  For which he lamented his powers were not fitting ;
But he scarted his lug, gied his wig a bit rug,
  And thus, after hoasting, broke forth to the meeting—

"After what I hae this day spoken in anither place, there's nae occasion again to put the bit through the same bore, or to run the plane o'er a dressed plank, sae I'll gie ye Deacon Convener Wriggles' good health, no forgetting wife and sproots—they'll be a' trees belyve—and may every guid attend him and them ; and may he aye be able to keep a guid polish on the face o' our Corporation affairs, and leave them without a screw loose to his successor.—Umbrells [1] to Deacon Wriggles."

The health was drunk aff wi' three times three ;
 And the roar and the ruffing a' fairly subsided—
The young Deacon blush'd, and sat fidging a wee,
 For he saw that a speech couldna weel be avoided.
He scarcely, we reckon, for gospel was takin',
 A' that the auld Deacon had said on his merit ;
But like a' men in place, he received it with grace,
 Then raise up to his feet, and address'd them in spirit.

"Really, freens, it's out o' the power o' speech or language, whether in print or out o't, to tell ye the feelings o' my heart.—Did ever a bairn o' Willie Wriggles' think to come to such preferment—really if I could speak, there's plenty o' room for scope, but my heart is tumbling the wullcat, and I canna trust the tongue in my ain head. I doubt that I'll no be able to ca' a pirnfu' o' waft into the wab o' my discourse on this occasion, but hae to gather up the ends afore I begin ; but ultimately in the end, and in the middle o' the meantime, my gratitude and respect for ye a' will never hae done, for the lasting, permanent, and never-ending honor ye hae conferred on me this day. I expect to learn my duty as I get mair into the marrow o' our Corporation matters—you'll no expect me to be perfited in ae day. My father used to say to me, ' Geordy, my man, keep aye a canny hand—just get on by degrees gradually,' whilk I hae aye tried to do ; for when I took langer steps than the length o' my limbs would allow, I aye spelder'd mysel, and cam' down to my knees, and lost my time and my standing—forbye being laught at : I ca' canny, and never draw back my shuttle till it is clear o' the selvidge—and this preserves my wab o' life free o' cluds and scobs, a'ways even. I would advise ane an' a' o' ye to do the like, and then the fabric o' your wark in the ways o' the world will be a pattern for ithers ; and when your shaft is at the beam-head, you may cut your wab by the

---

[1] Toast drunk off and glasses inverted.

thrum-keel, wi' credit to yoursel'. I hae now gotten to the hill-tap o' my ambition ; and to think o' me being advanced to be Deacon o' Deacons, is an honour that's reserved for but few. It hasna cost me a great strussel either, sic preferment—but this may be fleeching mysel', but I canna help it—ye a' ken it's true ; nae doubt the watering-can[1] has been gaun about, an' been gayan often filled sin' I set my e'e on the Deacon's chair, but I hae stood my water and corn brawly. (*Noise in the street.*) Dear me, freens, what's that I hear ? The very weans on the street crying—gude day to you, Deacon." "No, no, Deacon, it's Hawkie crying a hanging speech, or maybe his cure for ill wives." "Is that a'? Weel, lads, that wad be better than Solomon's Balm—for wise as he was, he couldna help himsel' when he got his wab misbet—I was saying, wasn't I, that I had stood my corn and water? aye lay in your corn first, and ye'll be the better able to stand a tap dressing—do like the Kilbarchan calves, drink wi' a rip i' your mouth. Mony a time, and often, hae I gaen, or was taen hame, wi' as mony great thochts in my head, working like a crock fu' o' sour dressing, as would sair ony o' our town's ministers to work wi' for a towmond ; but when I lifted my e'e neist morning, the warp o' my ideas had lost the fees ;—I couldna mak' onything o' them ; but had onybody been able to put it through a right ravel, they wad hae benefited mankind an' been the very best stroke ever drawn through a reed. Noo, ultimately in the end—as I am on my last pirn—I may just relate to you for your encourage-ment, frae what a sma' beginning I hae come to this pinnacle o' honour and prosperity, as ye see this day, so that nane o' ye may be discouraged, although ye begin wi' a wab o' ill yarn ; and it's possible you may get up the ladder o' preferment—yea, e'en to the last step, gin ye put on your feet steadily, and aye put the richt ane first ; this thing and that may gie ye a jundie, but keep a firm grip wi' baith hands o' the ladder rails, and your e'e fixed on the tap, and nae fear. Weel, after I was done wi' my 'prenticeship—and mony a time my stomach thocht my wizen was sneckit during that time—for what wi' gauze parritch, and muslin kail—ae barley-pile a hale dressing frae the ither, and dancing curcuddie in the pot a-boil—I thocht mony a time my heart wad ne'er been able to send a shot mair through the shed ; but I got through, and then tried a bit shop in the Kirk-raw, wi' the house in the ben end, and a bit a garter o' garden ahint ; sae on I wrocht as my father advised, by degrees gradually, and made a fendin' o't, and bettered my condition ; and by and bye, I says to my laird—man, could ye no put back the yard dykes a bore, and gie

---

[1] Gill-stoup.

me mair elbow room, for I could yerk my shuttle in at the ae side, and catch't at the ither without stressing mysel'; that's the very words I said to him, but he laughed me aff frae ae Martinmas till anither, till at last—for the bit property was only his in name—a burden o' debt that lay on its back, brack down the shouthers o' the laird, and landed it on mine—whilk I could easily bear, for mair has been added till't since, and the shouthers hae stood it a'. Noo ye see what can be done; keep Providence aye on ae side o' ye, and a consistent life on the ither—and you'll work your last thrum into the very heddles wi' comfort to yoursel', and leave an example to the youngsters wha are just beginning to put their feet on the treddles."

At length in his chair the Deacon sat down,
   And the sweat for a wee frae his haffits he dichtet;
The glass and the song, and the joke gaed roun'
   Till ilka ane's wit by his neighbour's was lichted:
Sic laughin' and daffin', and roarin' and ruffin'—
   Care couldna a hole see to stap his cauld ·beak in;
And when they broke up, the glorious group
   Gaed hobblin' hame—hiccupin'—Health to the Deacon.


## THE BRITISH HERO.

Up with our native banner high! and plant it deep and
   strong!
And o'er the empire let its folds in glory float along;
For a thousand years have come and gone, and a thousand
   years shall go,
Ere tyrant force, or traitor wile, shall lay that banner low!

And come, my friends, your goblets fill, till the wine o'er-
   swell the brim,
And pledge me in a willing cup of gratitude to him,
Who, when the bravest shrank appall'd, that banner lifted
   high,
Till, where'er he stepp'd, it waved above a field of victory!

Whose arm was like the thunderbolt to do whate'er his
   mind—
Swift as the lightning-flash, had once imagined and combined;

Whose soul no timid doubts could stay, nor coward fears
　　could quell,
Not calmer in the festive hall than 'mid the battle's yell !

Who shall forget, that felt the joy, when every morning's
　　sun,
Was hail'd with rattling guns, to tell another field was
　　won ;
When, after years of doubt and gloom, one universal roar
Proclaim'd through Europe's gladden'd realms that the
　　tyrant ruled no more ?

Then here's to him, the foremost man of all this mortal
　　world,
Who down to dust the ruthless foe of earth and mankind
　　hurl'd !
Long may he live to wield and grace the baton of command,
That marshall'd kings and nobles once in his unconquer'd
　　hand !

And never in a worthier grasp the leading-staff was worn—
For ever honour'd be his name to ages yet unborn ;
And be it still the proudest boast, when a thousand years
　　are gone,
To be a native of the land that rear'd a WELLINGTON.

E. PINKERTON.


## TA OFFISH IN TA MORNING.[1]

### TUNE—" *Johnnie Cope.*"

IIER nainsel' come frae ta hielan' hill,
Ta ponny town o' Glascow till,
But o' Glascow she's koten her pelly fill,
　　She'll no forget tis twa tree mornin'.

---

[1] This graphic piece of Celtic humour was written by one of our
contributors, and has obtained great local popularity. We have reprinted it in our collection, the current version being very incorrect.

She'll met Shony Crant her coosin's son,
An' Tuncan, an' Toukal, an' Tonal Cunn,
An' twa tree more—an' she had sic fun,
    But she'll turn't oot a saut saut mornin'.

Sae Shony Crant, a shill she'll hae
O' ta fera cootest usquapae,
An' she'll pochtet a shill, ay an' twa tree mae,
    An' she'll trank till ta fera neist mornin'.

She'll sat, an' she'll trank, an' she'll roar an' she'll sang,
An' aye for ta shill ta pell she'll rang,
An' she'll maet sic a tin t'at a man she'll prang,
    An' she'll say't—"Co home tis mornin'."

Ta man she'll had on ta kreat pig coat,
An' in her han' a rung she'll cot,
An' a purnin' cruzie, an' she'll say't you sot
    She'll maun go to ta Offish tis mornin'.

She'll say't to ta man—"*De an diaoul shin duitse?*"[1]
An' ta man she'll say't—"Pe quiet as ta mouse,
Or nelse o'er her nottle she'll come fu' crouse,
    An' she'll put ta Offish in you in ta mornin'."

Ta man she'll dunt on ta stane her stick,
An' t'an she'll pe sheuk her rick-tick-tick,
An' t'an she'll pe catchet her by ta neck,
    An trawn her to ta Offish in ta mornin'.

Ta mornin' come she'll be procht pefore
Ta shentlemans praw, an' her pones all sore,
An' ta shentlemans say't, "You tog, what for
    You'll maet sic a tin in tis mornin'?"

She'll teukit aff her ponnet and she'll maet her a poo,
An' she'll say't, "Please her Crace she cot hersel' fou,
But shust let her co and she'll never to
    Ta like no more in ta mornin'.

[1] Pronounced—De an diaul shean toose. *Anglice*—What the Devil's that to you?

But t'an she'll haet to ta shentlemans praw
Ta *Sheordie* frae out o' her sporan traw,
An' she'll roart out loot—" De an diaoul a ha ĕ gra ? [1]
  Oh hone O ri 'tis mornin' ! "

O t'an she'll pe sait ta shentlemans, " she'll no unterstoot
What fore she'll pe here like ta lallan prute,
But she'll maet her cause either pad or coot,
  For she'll teuk you to ta law tis mornin'."

Ta shentlemans say't, " Respect ta coort,
Or nelse my koot lat you'll suffer for't,
Shust taur to spoket another wort,
  An' she'll send her to ta Fiscal in ta mornin'."

Oich ! she didna knew what to do afa,
For she nefer found herself so sma',
An' klat she was right to kot awa,
  Frae oot o' ta offish in ta mornin'.

Oh ! tat she war to ta Hielans pack,
Whar ne'er ta pailie's tere to crack,
An' whar she wad gotten ta sorro' a plack,
  Frae n'oot o' her sporan in ta mornin'.

An' tat there was there her coosin's son,
An' Tuncan, an' Tookal, and Tonal Cunn,
An' twa tree more, she wad haet sic fun,
  And no be plaiget wi' pailies in ta mornin'.
ALEX. FISHER.

## ROLL, FAIR CLUTHA.

### AIR—"*Rule Britannia.*"

WHEN Nature first, with mighty hand,
  Traced Clyde's fair windings to the main,
'Twas then the Genii of the land,
  Assembled round, and sung this strain :

---

[1] Pronounced—Tee an diaul a how craa. *Anglice*—What the
devil do you say ?

" Roll, fair Clutha, fair Clutha to the sea,
And be thy banks for ever free."

For on thy banks in future times,
   A brave and virtuous race shall rise,
Strangers to those unmanly crimes,
   That taint the tribes of warmer skies.
    " Roll," etc.

And stately towns and cities fair,
   Thy lovely shores shall decorate ;
With seats of science, to prepare
   Thy sons for all that's good and great.
    " Roll," etc.

And on thy pure translucent breast,
   Shall numerous fleets majestic ride ;
Destined to south, north, east, and west,
   To waft thy treasures far and wide.
    " Roll," etc.

And up thy gently sloping sides,
   Shall woods o'er woods in grandeur tower ;
Meet haunts for lovers and their brides,
   To woo in many a sylvan bower.
    " Roll," etc.

And early on each summer morn,
   Thy youth shall bathe their limbs in thee ;
Thence to their various toils return
   With increased vigour, health, and glee.
    " Roll," etc.

And still on summer evenings fair,
   Shall groups of happy pairs be seen,
With hearts as light as birds of air,
   A-straying o'er thy margin green.
    " Roll," etc.

And oft the Bard by thee will stray,
   When Luna's lamp illumes the sky,

Musing on some heart-melting lay,
  Which fond hope tells him ne'er shall die.
    " Roll, fair Clutha, fair Clutha to the sea,
    And be thy banks for ever free."
                    ALEX. RODGER.


## THE HOWDIE.[1]

TUNE—"*Jenny Nettles.*"

AIBLINS ye'll ken Jeanie Glen,
  Jeanie Glen, Jeanie Glen ;
Gif no, it's little loss—d'ye ken ?—
  She's an auld drucken howdie !
O wow but she's a rantin' queen—
Her like was never heard nor seen
O wow but she's a rantin' queen,
  The auld drucken howdie.

I gat her unto my wife Bet,
  My wife Bet, my wife Bet—
I vow that morn I'll ne'er forget,
  The auld drucken howdie :
The ne'er a fit she'd leave her hame,
Till twa het pints were in her wame ;
The ne'er a fit she'd leave her hame,
  The auld drucken howdie.

I brought her 'hint me on the meer,
  On the meer, on the meer—
She maist brack Bess's back I swear—
  The auld drucken howdie ;
A wallet wore she round her waist,
Would haud a bow o' meal amaist—

---

[1] This portrait is drawn by William Ferguson, journeyman plumber in Edinburgh, and is but too true a picture of these country petticoat practitioners, who, with possets, caudle-cups, and panado, really turn the house upside down. If the colouring is strong, the subject admits not of delicate tints.

The pouch that hung about her waist ;
The auld drucken howdie.

Mutches wore she, nine or ten,
  Nine or ten, nine or ten,
Shapet like a clockin' hen,
  The auld drucken howdie :
In her breast a sneeshin' mull,
I wadna like to hae't to fill—
Her siller-tappit sneeshin' mull—
  The auld drucken howdie.

My trouth she kept the house asteer,
  House asteer, house asteer ;
Sic a dust, the guid be here !—-
  The auld drucken howdie :
Auld an' young she drave about,
Wi' rowing pin, or auld dishclout ;
Auld an' young she drave about,
  The auld drucken howdie.

Aye she sought the tither dram,
  Tither dram, tither dram—
An' flate like fury till it cam',
  The auld drucken howdie.
She turn'd the hale house upside down,
Swagg'ring like a drunk dragoon,
She turn'd the hale house upside down,
  The auld drucken howdie.

Ne'er a preen she cared for Bet,
  Cared for Bet, cared for Bet—
Roar, she might, like rivers met,
  The auld drucken howdie.
When the wean was brought to licht,
I wat she was a dais'd like sicht,
When the wean was brought to licht,
  The auld drucken howdie.

She could neither stand nor gang,
　　Stand nor gang, stand nor gang—
Yet up she got a caidgy sang,
　　The auld drucken howdie.
The sweat was hailin' ower her brow,
　　An' she was dancin' fiddler fou,
The sweat like sleet, fa'in frae her brow,
　　The auld drucken howdie.

She gat the wee thing on her knee,
　　On her knee, on her knee—
An' roar'd like wud, to mask the tea !
　　The auld drucken howdie.
Neist she cut the cheese in twa,
Trouth she was neither slack nor slaw,
At whangin' o' the cheese in twa,
　　The auld drucken howdie.

Seven cups o' tea an' toast,
　　Tea an' toast, tea an' toast,
Her wally wizen glibly cross'd,
　　The auld drucken howdie.
" She'll ne'er be done," cried little Jock,
" The cheese we'll in the aumry lock,
She'll ne'er be done," roar'd little Jock,
　　" The auld drucken howdie."

Aye the tither whang she took,
　　Whang she took, whang she took,
'Twad sair'd a sober chiel' an' ook,
　　The auld drucken howdie.
" She'll eat us up," quo' Bet my wife !
" That pang gaed thro' me like a knife,
She'll eat us up," quo' Bet my wife,
　　" The auld drucken howdie."

" Tell her that the bottle's toom !
　　Bottle's toom, bottle's toom,

She'll drink else till the day o' doom !
　　The auld drucken howdie."
" The deil be in your maw," quo' I,
" I'm sure ye're neither boss nor dry ;
The deil be in your maw," quo' I,
　　" Ye auld drucken howdie."

She swore I was a nither't loun,
　　Nither't loun, nither't loun,
Said, she'd clour my cuckold crown,
　　The auld drucken howdie.
At last she spak' o' gaun awa',
O' what joy it gied us a' !
When'er she spak' o' gaun awa',
　　The auld drucken howdie.

A hale hour sat she langer still,
　　Langer still, langer still,
Her tongue gaun like a waukin' mill,
　　The auld drucken howdie.
At length she took her hood an' cloak,
Syne to see how she did rock,
When she got on her hood an' cloak,
　　The auld drucken howdie.

Says she, " Gudeman, I'll soon ca' back,
　　Soon ca' back, soon ca' back"—
I look't right queer, but naething spak—
　　The auld drucken howdie.
I gar'd the callant yoke the cart,
An' set her on't wi' a' my heart,
Right glad was I wi' her to part,
　　The auld drucken howdie.

## MEARNS MUIR MAGGY,

### A MEARNS MUIR TRADITION.

In a wild track o' country, the lang Mearns Muir,
Whaur the sky is sae bleak, and the soil is sae puir,
Whaur the rain fa's in floods, an' the wind gurls chill,
And as the *Flood* left it, sae Nature stands still—
    There deep in a dell, down below a steep craggy,
    There liv'd an auld wifie, ca'd Mearns Muir Maggy.

She was wylie wi' wit, she was laden wi' lair,
Could charm awa' sorrow, or fley awa' care—
Could smooth down sick pillows, wi' sic soothing skill,
That nae weanie grew sick, nor nae wifie fell ill,
    But the *Head* o' the *House* had to mount his best naggy,
    An' bring hame ahint him auld Mearns Muir Maggy.

Ae night when the muir was half deluged wi' rain,
An' the cauld gowlin blast swept athwart the wild plain,
A lonely black female, sair laden wi' pain,
Cam' into Meg's cot, an' gae birth to a wean,
    Ere the morn she was gane, an' had left a gowd baggie
    Wi' the bairn to be nursed by auld Mearns Muir Maggy.

Years pass'd, and the callant grew up to a man,
An' the clashing still gather'd, the rumour still ran,
That the loun was nae canny, that Meg an' his faither,
Whoever he was, were acquaintit wi' ither,
    An' some wha wad fain haen her burnt for a haggie,
    Ca'd *Auld Nick* the lover o' Mearns Muir Maggy.

But scandal still quail'd 'neath her mild beaming eye,
The Kirk never miss'd her in wat day or in dry,
An' the strong burly black, as if bound by a charm,
Cam' aye kindly leading auld Meg in his arm,
    Tho' mony a braw lassie wad sald her last raggie,
    To hae clung to the arm that led Mearns Muir Maggy.

But auld Maggy died, and the Black left alane,
Roam'd like a wild spirit ower mountain an' plain,
Bright freedom, his charter, true courage his targe,
Daur ca' him a poacher, he'd scowl at the charge,
    Till warm wi' his wand'ring he shot a proud staggie,
    That belong'd to the landlord o' Mearns Muir Maggy.

The lord, a rich nabob, had come frae afar,
'Twas said he had fought in the wild Indian war,
An' come hame fortune laden, frae these sunny climes,
Whaur fortunes like his aft are purchased wi' crimes,
    For grasping an' greedy, heart stinted an' scraggy,
    Was the judge o' the orphan o' Mearns Muir Maggy.

The judge e'ed the poacher, the poacher the judge,
As if they bore ither some lang gather'd grudge ;
The pannel a miniature tore from his neck !—
'Twas the judge fondly pressing a sweet female black !
    The old sinner shook as if seized with an ague—
    His son was the black rear'd by Mearns Muir Maggy.

An' whaur was there e'er sic a baron of old ?
As the Black Knight of Mearns Muir, burly an' bold ?
There's mony brave nobles hae sprung frae his reins,
That hae held braider sway o'er auld Scotland's domains,
    But nae friend was mair manly, nae foemen mair jaggy,
    Than the comely black foundling o' Mearns Muir Maggy.
                 JAMES BALLANTINE.

## HIGHLAND COURTSHIP.

" OICH will you had ta tartan plaids ?
    Or will you had ta ring, mattam !
Or—will you had a kiss frae me—
    An' tat's a petters ting, mattam ?"

(REPLY—PIANO OF VOICE.)

"Oh haud awa! bide awa!
    Haud awa frae me, Donald;
I'll neither kiss, nor hae a ring—
    Nae tartan plaid for me, Donald."

"Oich tear—ay—what's noo?

O see you not her praw new hose—
    Her fleckit plaid, plue green, mattam,
Ta twa praw hose—an' prawer spiog,
    An' ta shouther-pelt 'peen a', mattam."
        "O haud awa! bide awa—
            Haud awa frae me, Donald;
        Your shouther-knots, and trinkabouts,
            Hae nae great charm for me, Donald."

"No! it's a terrible potheration—eh—no!

Her can pe shaw ta petter houghs,
    Tan him tat wear ta crown mattam—
Nainsel' hae pistol an' claymore,
    Wad fley ta Lallan loon, mattam."
        "No haud awa—bide awa,
            Haud awa frae me, Donald;
        Gae hame and hap your Highlan' houghs,
            An' fash nae mair wi' me, Donald."

"Ay, laty, is tat ta way you'll spoke—put—yes maybe for all tat

Hersel' hae a short coat—pi pocht
    No trail my feet at rin, mattam,
A cuttie-sark o' goot harn-sheet,
    My mither he'll pe spin, mattam."
        "Just haud awa—bide awa— .
            Haud awa frae me, Donald;
        Awa and cleed your measled shanks,
            An' screen them 'boon the knee, Donald.'

"Oich after all, surely and moreover—my tear,

You'll ne'er pe pitten wrocht a turn,
    At ony kin' o' spin, mattam;

Noch—shug your laeno[1] in a skull
   An' tidal Highland sing, mattam.

Noo heard you tat ?"

   "Just haud awa—bide awa,
      Haud awa frae me, Donald ;
   Our jugging skulls, an' Highlan' reels—
      They'll soun' but harsh wi' me, Donald."

" It's a perfect pestoration—hoo—never surely—after all I'll spoke.

An' in ta mornings whan you'll rise,
   You'll got fresh whey for tea, mattam—
Ream an' cheese, as much you please !
   Far cheaper nor pohea, mattam.

Noo, I'm sure !—ah—yes "—

   " Haud awa—bide awa—
      Bide awa frae me, Donald ;
   I wadna quit my morning's tea—
      Your whey could ne'er agree, Donald."

" Weel—weel—weel—I'll thocht that's all—put—

Haper-gaelic ye'se pe learn !—
   Tat's ta pretty speak, mattam ;
You'll got a cheese and putter-milk—
   Come wi' me gin ye like, mattam.

Oh, yes—I'll saw your face noo."

   " Na—haud awa—bide awa—
      Haud awa frae me, Donald ;
   Your gaelic sang, and Highland cheer,
      Will ill gang down wi' me, Donald."

"Never more yet—oich !—oich !—it's an awfu' this.

I'll got for you a sillar prooch—
   Pe piggar as ta meen, mattam ;

   [1] *Laeno*—child.

Yes! you'll ride in curroch 'stead o' coach—
Tan wow but you'll pe fine, mattam!

Tat's ta thing noo, my ponniest dautie—you'll not say no—no
more for ever—oh, yes"—

" But—haud awa—bide awa—
Haud awa frae me, Donald;
For a' your Highland rarities,
You're no a match for me, Donald."

" What ! tat's ta way tat you'll be kin'!
Praw pretty man like me, mattam!
Sae lang's claymore hung py my pelt,
I'll never marry thee, mattam.

A shentleman to be disdain !"

" Oh come awa—come awa—
Come awa wi' me, Donald—
I wadna lea' my Highlandman !
Frae lallands set me free, Donald."

" Tat's my doo—noo always for ever and never."


## BANKRUPT AND CREDITORS.

HAE ye heard o' Will Sibbald—my trouth there were few,
That had less in their pouch, or had mair in their pow;
A master for lang he had faithfully sair'd,
Till he thocht as he ae nicht sat straiking his beard:
"Through wat and through dry a' my life I hae drudged,
And to work late and early I never have grudged;
I've been a man's slave since my name I could spell—
What think ye though noo I should work for mysel'?"

So he took a bit shop, and sell't gingebread and snaps,
Spunks, treacle, and brumstane, and laif-bread and baps;
But a' wad na do—at his wares nane wad look,
So a wide gaucy shop in the main street he took:

Ilk day like a gin-horse he eidently wrocht—
Makin' siller like sclate stanes, as a' body thocht,
Till ae day wi' a dunt that astonish'd the town,
The great Willie Sibbald—the barrow laid down.

O' his freens and acquaintance a meeting was ca'd,
An' a lang face sly Willie put on to the squad ;
" My gude worthy freens," he then said wi' a grane,
I have naething to show you—for books I keep nane ;
My father ne'er learnt me to write my ain name,
An' my master, I'm sure I maun say't to his shame,
Ne'er made up the defect, sirs—but keepit me ticht,
'Tween the trams o' a barrow frae morning till nicht."

The freens then on Willie began to leuk queer,
And ane that sat next him then said wi' a sneer—
" Man, Will, I'm dumfouner't—ye wrocht air an' late—
Something gude might be surely brought frae your estate ;"
" Estate, man," quo' Willie—" I'se tell ye, my freen,
Ilk maik through my fingers has noo slippit clean—
And for an estate, I can solemnly swear,
Gif I had had that, faith I wudna be here."

'Mang Willie's rare talents, an' these were not few,
By the virtue of which mankind's noses he drew,
He could sing like a mavis—and ane o' his freens,
Wha to Willie's guid fortune had furnish'd the means,
On his creditors' list he just stood at the tap,
So he looks in Will's face, and says he—" My auld chap,
The best way I ken ye'll get out o' this fang,
Instead o' oor siller—just gie's a bit sang."

### THE DIVIDEND.

" ALACK ! what will come o' me noo, I hae been stricken sair,
I never drank like ither men, nor fed on costly fare—
I wrocht aye till 'twas late at e'en, raise wi' the morning dawn,
And yet ye see the barrow-trams hae drappit frae my haun'.

" Ye've socht a wee bit sang frae me, but brawly ye may see
I'm no, whatever some may think, in ony singing key ;
But your promise o' a free discharge I trust ye winna shift,
For 'twerna wi' the hope o' that, my lip I couldna lift.

" I wonner what gart folk suppose that I could siller mak'—
They ne'er saw ony signs o't on my belly or my back ;
My waistcoat aye was o' the plush—my coat o' coarsest drab—
I keepit nae establishment—nae servants, horse, nor cab.

" Ye talk o' putting me in jail, but trouth ye needna fash,
Ye'll only lose your temper, and, what's waur—ye'll lose your cash ;
For neither house nor ha' hae I—nor grun', nor guids, nor gear,
Or, as I said before to ye—ye wudna seen me here.

" I thocht when auld I wad have had a gude rough bane to pike,
And nocht to do but streek me on the lea side o' the dike ;
But I ha'e disappointed been—my boat has gane to staves,
And left me bare and helpless to the mercy o' the waves."

WM. FINLAY.

## THOU CAULD GLOOMY FEBERWAR.[1]

THOU cauld gloomy Feberwar,
 Oh ! gin thou wert awa' !
I'm wae to hear thy soughin' winds,
 I'm wae to see thy snaw ;
For my bonnie braw young Hielandman,
 The lad I loe sae dear,
Has vowed to come and see me,
 In the spring o' the year.

A silken ban' he gae me,
 To bin' my gowden hair ;
A sillar brooch an' tartan plaid,
 A' for his sake to wear ;
And oh ! my heart was like to break,
 (For partin' sorrow's sair),

---

[1] The first verse of this song is a fragment of the late lamented
Tannahill—the supplement by Patrick Buchan, the oldest son of Mr.
Peter Buchan, with whom the reader is already familiar.

As he vow'd to come and see me,
   In the spring o' the year.

Aft, aft as gloamin' dims the sky,
   I wander out alane,
Where buds the bonny yellow whins,
   Around the trystin' stane :
'Twas there he press'd me to his heart,
   And kiss'd awa' the tear,
As he vow'd to come and see me,
   In the spring o' the year.

Ye gentle breezes saftly blaw,
   And cleed anew the wuds ;
Ye lav'rocks lilt your cheery sangs,
   Amang the fleecy cluds ;
Till Feberwar and a' his train,
   Affrichted disappear—
I'll hail wi' you the blythsome change,
   The spring-time o' the year.

## PUSH ROUN' THE BICKER.

YE, wha the carking cares of life,
Have aft times caused to claw your haffet,
Leave for a while the bustling strife,
And worldly men and matters laugh at :
Let fools debate 'bout kirk and state,
Their short lived day let patriots flicker ;
Let Outs and Ins kick ither's shins ;
Ne'er mind, my boys—push roun' the bicker.

A' things that glitter are not gowd,
Then push the stoup roun'—lads be hearty ;
Wha e'er had fortune at his nod,
Like that bauld birkie, Bonaparte ;
He tumbled kings—thae costly things,
Wha thocht they on their stools sat sicker ;
But his crown at last to the yirth was cast,
And the vision past—push roun' the bicker.

And wha could cope wi' Philip's son ?
The greatest hero that we read o',
How did he hound his armies on,
To conquer worlds he had nae need o'.
His beast he rade with thundering speed,
And aye his pace grew quick and quicker,
Till down he sat—poor fool, and grat—
His pipe was out—push roun' the bicker.

Then let us drive dull care adrift,
Life's day is short even at the langest ;
" The race is no aye to the swift,
Nor is the battle to the strangest !"
'Bout kirk and state let fools debate,
Their short-lived day let statesmen flicker ;
Let Outs and Ins kick ither's shins,
Ne'er fash your beards—push roun' the bicker.

WILLIAM FINLAY.

## JOHN GUN.

HE's a bauld beggarman, John Gun, John Gun,
  He's a bauld beggarman, John Gun ;
O far he has been an' muckle he's seen,
  An' mony an ill deed he's dune, John Gun,
  An' mony an ill deed he's dune.

He's been 'mang the French, John Gun, John Gun,
  He's been 'mang the French, John Gun ;
But sune he came hame—he made little o' them,
  They had vagrants enou' o' their ain, John Gun,
  They had vagrants enou' o' their ain.

The fouks a' fear John Gun, John Gun,
  The fouks a' fear John Gun ;
When he comes in, ye'll hear nae din,
  But our breath gaun thick out an' in, John Gun—
  But our breath gaun thick out and in.

An' how does he fend? John Gun, John Gun,
  An' how does he fend? John Gun—
He fends unco weel, he gets milk, he gets meal—
  But no for his guid but his ill, John Gun—
  But no for his guid but his ill.

ALEX. LAING.

## THE PIRATE'S SERENADE.

My boat's by the tower, my bark's in the bay,
And both must be gone ere the dawn of the day;
The moon's in her shroud, but to guide thee afar,
On the deck of the Daring's a love-lighted star;
Then wake, lady! wake! I am waiting for thee,
And this night, or never, my bride thou shalt be!

Forgive my rough mood; unaccustom'd to sue,
I woo not, perchance, as your land-lovers woo;
My voice has been tuned to the notes of the gun,
That startle the deep, when the combat's begun;
And heavy and hard is the grasp of a hand
Whose glove has been ever the guard of a brand.

Yet think not of these, but, this moment, be mine,
And the plume of the proudest shall cower to thine;
A hundred shall serve thee, the best of the brave,
And the chief of a thousand will kneel as thy slave;
Thou shalt rule as a queen, and thy empire shall last
Till the red flag, by inches, is torn from the mast.

O islands there are, on the face of the deep,
Where the leaves never fade, where the skies never weep;
And there, if thou wilt, shall our love-bower be,
When we quit, for the greenwood, our home on the sea;
And there shalt thou sing of the deeds that were done,
When we braved the last blast, and the last battle won.

Then haste, lady, haste! for the fair breezes blow,
And my ocean-bird poises her pinions of snow;
Now fast to the lattice these silken ropes twine,
They are meet for such feet and such fingers as thine;
The signal, my mates—ho! hurra for the sea!
This night, and for ever, my bride thou shalt be.

WM. KENNEDY.

## MEG MEIKLEJOHN.

YE kentna Meg Meiklejohn, midwife in Mauchlin?
She was the widow of lilti-cock Lauchlan;
He was a body gaed rockin' and rowin'—
His ae leg was stracht—its neibour a bow in't.

Maggy was boussie frae croon to the causey,
Lauchie was gizen'd 's an auld girnal bassie;
And as for their features, folk said it that kent them,
If nature meant sour anes, she needna repent them.

Of the stark aquavitæ they baith lo'ed a drappie,
And when capernutie then aye unco happy;
Of a' in the parish this pair was the bauldest,
As burns brattle loudest when water's the shaulest.

Whiles Lauchie wad spurn at the whisky like poison,
But after he preed it, wad drucken an ocean;
Maggy, too, had a fell tippling gate o't,
An' aye took a drappie whene'er she could get it.

Lauchie had looms, but was lag at the weaving;
His fingers and thumbs though, were active in thieving;
Lauchie had looms that but few could hae wrought on,
For Lauchie had schemes that but few wad hae thought on.

Lauchie had secrets weel worthy the keeping,
For Lauchie made siller while ithers were sleeping;
Lauchie a second sight surely had gi'en him,
An' saw things wi' less light than ithers could see them.

But Lauchie did dee, and was welcomely yirdet,
The folks said his conscience was unco ill girdet ;
When it took a rackin, it beat a' description,
His oily gaun tongue, too, was fu' o' deception.

Now Lauchie's awa, and the bodies in Mauchlin,
Wish Meg in her kist, an' as deep sheugh'd as Lauchlan ;
But Lauchie for cunning surpass'd a' his fellows,
He died just in time for escaping the gallows.

DAVID WEBSTER.

## THE TREE OF LIBERTY.[1]

*Tune—" Up an' waur them a', Willie."*

HEARD ye o' The Tree o' France ?
I watna what's the name o't—
Aroun' it a' the Patriots dance,
Weel Europe kens the fame o't :
It stands whare ance the Bastile stood,
A prison built by kings, man,
Where superstition's hellish brood
Kept France in leading-strings, man.

Upon this Tree there grows sic fruit,
Its virtues a' can tell, man ;
It raises man aboon the brute,
It mak's him ken himsel', man.

[1] This song is said to be a production of the Ayrshire Ploughman,
and although it is not equal in concentrated power and vigour to some
of his avowed poems, it must be admitted to be a piece of no ordinary merit, and a most successful imitation of his manner. We have
submitted it to a gentleman of the highest respectability, to whose
opinion Burns paid great deference, and to whom he was in the habit
of showing his compositions, and he had never heard the Poet allude
to "The Tree of Liberty." Burns, too, who outlived the stormiest
period of the French Revolution, would doubtless have qualified
many of the expressions, had he given them, after having seen some
of the effects of that dreadful political hurricane which deluged that
unhappy country with blood.

Gif ance the peasant taste a bite,
　He's greater than a lord, man ;
An' wi' the beggar shares a mite
　O' a' he can afford, man.

This fruit is worth a' Afric's wealth,
　To comfort us 'twas sent, man,
To gie the sweetest blush o' health,
　An' mak us a' content, man :
It clears the e'en, it cheers the heart,
　Mak's high an' low guid friens, man ;
An' he wha acts the traitor's part,
　It to perdition sends, man.

My blessings aye attend the chiel
　Wha pitied Gallia's slaves, man,
An' staw'd a branch, spite o' the De'il,
　Frae yont the Western waves, man.
Fair virtue water'd it wi' care,
　An' now she sees, wi' pride, man,
How weel it buds an' blossoms there,
　Its branches spreading wide, man.

But vicious folk aye hate to see
　The works o' virtue thrive, man,
The courtly vermin bann'd the Tree,
　An' grat to see't alive, man.
King Louie thocht to cut it down,
　When it was unco sma', man ;
For it the watchman crack'd his crown,
　Cut aff his head an' a', man ! ! !

A wicked crew syne on a time,
　Did tak' a solemn aith, man,
It ne'er should flourish in its prime—
　I wat they pledged their faith, man ;
Awa' they gaed, wi' mock parade,
　Like beagles huntin' game, man ;
But sune grew weary o' the trade,
　An' wish'd they'd been at hame, man.

For freedom standing by the Tree,
    Her sons did loudly ca', man ;
She sung a sang o' Liberty,
    Which pleas'd them ane an' a', man.
By her inspir'd, the new-born race
    Sune drew the avengin' steel, man,
The hirelings ran—her foes gi'ed chase,
    An' bang'd the despots weel, man.

Let Britain boast her hardy oak,
    Her poplar, an' her pine, man,
Auld Britain ance could crack her joke,
    An' o'er her neibours shine, man ;
But seek the forest round an' round,
    An' soon 'twill be agreed, man,
That sic a tree cannot be found
    'Tween Lon'on an' the Tweed, man.

Without this Tree, alake ! this life
    Is but a vale o' woe, man
A scene o' sorrows, mix'd wi' strife,
    Nae real joys we know, man.
We labour sune, we labour late,
    To feed the titled knave, man,
An' a' the comfort we're to get,
    Is—that ayont the grave, man !

Wi' plenty o' sic Trees, I trow,
    The warld wad live in peace, man ;
The sword wad help to mak' a plough,
    The din o' war wad cease, man.
Like brethren in a common cause,
    We'd on each ither smile, man,
An' equal rights an' equal laws,
    Wad gladden every isle, man.

Wae worth the loon wha wadna eat
    Sic halesome, dainty cheer, man—
I'd gie the shoon frae aff my feet
    To taste sic fruit, I swear, man.

Syne let us pray, auld England may
　　Sune plant this far-famed Tree, man ;
An' blythe we'll sing, and hail the day
　　That gave us Liberty, man.


## KITTY O'CARROL.

O TALK not of battles and wars,
　　Where nations and monarchs will quarrel ;
Of Venus, and Cupid, and Mars,
　　I'm for Kitty O'Carrol !
Kitty's the joy of my soul,
　　She has made my poor heart to surrender :
That heart, once as sound as a coal,
　　Is now almost burnt to a cinder.

Och ! my darlin', every eye in your head is mild and lovely, and
every thing lookin' out of them that's good and natural in the world.
Ah ! my jewel, but every morsel of your purty body, hands and feet,
body and shoulders, mouth and nose, all illigance itself intirely.  Oh !
you creature of all creatures aneath the stars and the moon, not for-
gettin' the great sun himself ! I'm sure the very daisy that you
tread upon will lift its head and look after ye, cryin', " My dew-drop,
when shall I have another kiss of your purty toes?"

O when I get up in the morn,
　　Her image is standin' 'fore me,
Murder, but I am forlorn—
　　Kitty, I live to adore ye !
Morning, or evening, or noon,
　　Eatin' or drinkin', or sleepin',
Mine you will surely be soon,
　　Or else I will kill me wid weepin'.

Love has been compared to a giddiness ; faith ! I think it is rather
like law, or a rat-trap ; when once you get into it, there's no getting
out agin ; or the great bog of Allen, the farther in the deeper.  Surely
she must relent some time ; there is nothing in this world like perse-
verance, as the cat said when she scratched her way into the milk-

house. Och, what is really to become of me—it is better to die at
once than be kilt intirely, from mornin' till night ; och, sure and my
body is lavin' my bones altogether. My clothes are beginnin' to
wonder what has become of me—and they'll be after seekin' some
other carcase to cover themselves wid—ar'n't they roarin' " murder "
at every corner of my bones? I'm good for nothing now but stanin'
amongst the praties whan they're comin' forward to be useful to the
mouth, and cryin' to them black-nosed thieves, " Be after takin' your
body away gin the feathers will carry you, Master Horny-beak, and
lave the blessings to the people that have some naturality in them,
for it will be better for me to be stuck up among the swate pratie
blossoms, and purtectin' the fruit, than runnin' about like a walkin'
bone-fire among the bogs."

Oh Kitty I live but for you,
    For you, love, I daily am dyin',
My heart you have bor'd through an' through,
    And kilt me with groaning and cryin'.
Consint now, and say you'll be mine,
    For I know you are full of good nature,
To me you are all but divine,
    You murtherin', coaxin' young crature !


## 'TWAS MORN.

AIR—" *Within a mile of Edinburgh Town.*"

TWAS morn—and the lambs on the green hillocks played,
    The laverock sang sweetly on high,
The dew-draps bespangled ilk green spiky blade,
    And the woods rang wi' music and joy ;
        When young Patie down the vale
        Met fair Kitty wi' her pail,
        He clasp'd her hand and blythely speered,
            " Dear lassie, where to now ?"
        " A wee bit down the glen," quo' she,
            " To milk our bruckit cow."

"O Kitty! I've lo'ed you this towmond an' mair,
  And wha lo'es na you canna see,
There's nane on our plains half sae lovely and fair,
  No ;—nane half sae lovely to me :
    Will you come, dear lass, at e'en,
    Up the burnie's bank sae green ?
    And there beneath the beechen shade,
      You'll meet a lover true."
    " Na, na," she cried, " I canna come
      At e'en to meet wi' you.

" My mither will flyte and my father will ban,
  Gin here meikle langer I stay,
Come cease wi' your wheezin', and let gae my han',
  It's daft like at this time o' day."
    " Dearest lassie, ere ye gang,
    Tell me shall we meet ere lang ?
    Come say't and seal't wi' ae sweet smack
      O' that enticing mou' ; "
    " Haud aff," she cried, " nor think that I
      Was made for sport to you."

" Then fareweel, proud lassie, for since ye're sae shy,
  Nae langer I'll press you to bide ;
E'en show aff your airs, toss your head and look high,
  Your beauty demands a' your pride ;
    I may find some ither where,
    Ane mair kind, although less fair."
    He turned to gang—she laughing cried,
      " Stop, lad, I've ta'en the rue,
    Come back and set the tryst wi' me,
      And I will meet wi' you."

ALEX. RODGER.

## BEACON SONG.

THERE'S fire on the mountains, brave knights of the north,
    Mount, mount your fleet steeds and away ;
There's fire on the mountains, mount knights of the north,
    For our beacons blaze bright as the day.
        Haste away, haste away.

Let your war-flags wave wild on the blast of the night,
    To the notes of the bold bugle-horn ;
Though your steeds may get warm in your fiery advance,
    They'll grow cool in the dews of the morn.
        Haste away, haste away.

Hot foot comes the foe from his home in the south,
    To ravage our dear native land ;
Haste away, haste away, brave knights of the north,
    And meet him with buckler and brand.
        Haste away, haste away.

From litter, from loch-side, from corry and glen,
    The mountain-men come to your aid,
With broadsword and axe newly ground for the fray,
    And all in their tartans arrayed.
        Haste away, haste away.

Haste away, haste away, brave knights of the north,
    There's glory, there's fame to be won ;
Berwick law, Berwick law, is your mustering ground,
    Oh ! shame if the conflict's begun.
        Haste away, haste away.

The foe you now meet, you have oft met before,
    And oft driven him back with dismay ;
Though his spear-heads, in thousands, gleam bright to
    our fires,
    Clap spurs to your steeds and away.
        Away, haste away.
                J. D. CARRICK.

## FIRST LOVE.[1]

THOU think'st that nought hath had the power
　This heart to softness move ;
Thou'rt wrong—no knight more faithfully
　Ere wore his lady's glove,
Than I within my breast have borne
　A first, an only love.

Her form—I cannot paint her form—
　In life I was but young,
Even when I last knelt at her feet,
　And on her accents hung.
I would not swear her beautiful—
　Yet such she must have been,—
And in my dreams of paradise
　She mingles in each scene.

This present time, in crowded halls,
　Surrounded by the gay,
I follow, in forgetfulness,
　Her image far away ;
And if I list a touching voice
　Or sweet face gaze upon,
'Tis but to fill my memory
　With that beloved one.

For days—for months—devotedly
　I've lingered by her side,
The only place I coveted
　Of all the world so wide ;
And in the exile of an hour,
　I consolation found,

---

[1] We have, with the author's kind permission, taken this exquisite
ballad from " Fitful Fancies," by William Kennedy, from which we
have already extracted so liberally. It is, perhaps, the most finished
piece published in modern times—whether as respects the intensity
of feeling, or the classical elegance of expression.

Where her most frequent wanderings
   Had marked it holy ground.

It was not that in her I saw
   Affection's sovereign maid,
In beauty and young innocence
   Bewitchingly arrayed ;
'Twas more—far more ;—I felt, as if
   Existence went and came,
Even when the meanest hind who served
   Her father breathed her name.

I longed to say a thousand things,
   I longed, yet dared not speak,
Half-hoped, half-feared, that she might read
   My thoughts upon my cheek.
Then, if unconsciously she smiled,
   My sight turned faint and thick,
Until with very happiness,
   My reeling heart grew sick.

O days of youth ! O days of youth !
   To have these scenes return,
The pride of all my riper years
   How gladly would I spurn !
That form—the soul of my boy life—
   Departed, and none came,
In after-time, with half the charm
   Which cleaves unto her name.

Nor vanished she, as one who shares
   The stain of human birth,
But, like an angel's shade that falls
   In light upon the earth ;
That falls in light, and blesses all
   Who in its radiance lie,
But leaves them to the deeper gloom
   Whene'er it passes by.

## RHYMING RAB THE RANTER.[1]

WHEN Scotia's pipe had tint her tune,
  Lang reestin' in the reek, man,
And pipers were sae faithless grown,
  They scarce could gar her squeak, man ;
A doughty chiel cam' down the hill,
  Ca'd Rhymin' Rab the Ranter—
But pipers a' their chafts might claw,
  When he blew up the chanter.

He blew sae sweet, he blew sae shrill,
  He blew sae loud and lang, man,
Baith hill and dale can tell the tale,
  They ne'er gat sic a sang, man ;

[1] This song was produced on the Anniversary of the Kilbarchan Burns' Club.

It may not be known, generally, that Kilbarchan was the birth-place of Habbie Simson, rival to Rab the Ranter. There is a tradition that Habbie, who could not bear a rival, was fairly beat by Rab in a trial of their musical powers, and that, determining to be avenged, he put his hand to his sword, and aimed a most dreadful blow at his successful rival, turning away his head at the same time to avoid seeing the deadly gash that his weapon had inflicted. Taking the direction of Blackstone Moss, he bogged himself for three days in one of the hags. The stomach, ever selfish, and not caring about the sympathies of the neck, put in her irresistible alternative, " Better be hanged than starved ;" so the combative piper returned to a friend's house, who was anxious about him, and could not account for his absence. Habbie, relating the detail of the murder, claimed his protection against the fangs of justice. " Gae wa', ye daft gouk ! my certie, Rab's baith meat and claith like ; I saw him this verra day, and there didna appear to me the scart o' a preen about his face." Habbie, though relieved from fear, would not have cared though his rival's drone had been for ever silenced. On examining the scabbard of his sword, he found the blade sleeping quietly and bloodless ; the hilt having come away in the haste and fury of the enraged piper.

A statue of Habbie graces a niche in the Kilbarchan church steeple, blowing with as much expression as rudely chiselled freestone can give ; at least two bagfuls of spare wind in his inflated cheeks.

Fame heard the soun' a' Scotland roun',
　　By sooth he didna saunter,
Like fire and flame flew fast the name,
　　O' Rhymin' Rab the Ranter.

From John o'Groats to 'cross the Tweed,
　　And round the English border,
Was heard the rant o' Rabbie's reed,
　　Sae weel 'twas kept in order.
To shepherd knowes where shamrock grows,
　　Wi' sic a stound he sent her,
Auld Erin's drone her hood put on,
　　To shun the Scottish chanter.

Our lasses linket to the lilt,
　　The lads they lap and caper'd,
The carlins coost their crummies tilt,
　　Sae vauntingly they vapour'd,
Auld gutchers gray streek't up their clay,
　　To club the merry canter ;
Whilst wood and glen prolong'd the strain,
　　O' Rhymin' Rab the Ranter.

But Scotia weel may wail her skaith,
　　And break her drones an' a', man,
For death has marr'd her piper's breath,
　　Nae langer can he blaw, man ;
She e'en may sit her down and sigh,
　　And wi' a greet content her,
She'll ne'er again on hill or plain,
　　Meet Rhymin' Rab the Ranter.

Here's health to Scotland and her lair,
　　Her heighs and hows sae scraggie ;
Her doughty sons and dochters a',
　　Her haggis and her coggie.

And when the wee drap's in her e'e,
  To 'fend her frae mishanter,
Her toast triumphant still shall be
  Here's Rhymin' Rab the Ranter.

G. MACINDOE.


## FRIENDS AROUND THE TABLE SET.

AIR—"*Scots wha hae wi' Wallace bled.*"

FRIENDS around the table set,
Blythe am I to see you met ;
See that your ills ye a' forget,
    And sing your sang wi' glee.

Nae doubt but ye have a' some grief,
For ae night wont ye tak' relief,
For ae short night your sails unreef,
    And take the tide sae free.

Wha would sit in sullen gloom,
For sic a ane we hae nae room,
Wi' gude peat-reek your brain perfume,
    And let us merry be.

Wha never grumbles, stan' or fa',
However fortune rows the ba',
But aye weel pleased his cork can draw,
    That's the man for me.

Then tak' your tumbler while its warm,
A wee drap drink can do nae harm,
It cheers the heart, and nerves the arm—
    At least it's so wi' me.

Man's life is but a wee bit span,
And is it no the wisest plan,
To be as happy as we can,
    And aye contented be ?

D. S.

## THE TINKLER'S SONG.

Air—"*Allan-a-Dale.*"

O WHO are so hearty, so happy and free,
Or who for the proud care so little as we?
No tyrants control us, no slaves we command,
Like free passage-birds we traverse sea and land;
And still to the comfort of all we attend,
By singing out "caldrons or kettles to mend."

Each climate—each soil, is to us still the same,
No fix'd local spot for our country we claim;
Yon lordly domain, with its castles and towers,
We care not a pin for—the world it is ours;
Superiors we know not—on none we depend,
While our business is caldrons or kettles to mend.

The law says we're vagrants—the law tells a lie,
The green earth's our dwelling, our roof the blue sky,
Then tho', through the earth, for employment we roam,
How can we be vagrants, who ne'er are from home?
Our neighbours are mankind, whom oft we befriend,
While trudging about, pots or kettles to mend.

No rents, tithes, nor taxes, we're called on to pay,
We take up our lodgings wherever we may,
If people are kind, we show kindness to them,
If people are churlish, why we are the same;
But those who are friendly fare best in the end,
While their pots, bellows, caldrons, or kettles we mend.

Not even the parson, the squire, nor my lord,
A daintier supper than we can afford,
For nature profusely each blessing doth grant,
Then why should her children be ever in want?—
Let them share with each other whate'er she may send,
Like us—while we've caldrons or kettles to mend.

Then fill to the stranger a cup of the best,
And when he is wearied conduct him to rest,
For the poor lonely wanderer, homeless and bare,
Should ever the wanderers' sympathy share ;
Now we've one consolation—whate'er be our end,
While the world remains wicked—*we* daily do *mend*.

ALEX. RODGER.

## COW KATE.

### AN ANNANDALE STORY.

*Seeking a Tune.*

THERE's a green velvet hollow, amang Moffat hills,
Ca'd the Deevil's Beef Pot, where in three little rills
The Tweed, Clyde, an' Annan, sweet babbling arise
Amang bald mountain-tops, that brave cauld gowlin skies ;
There nature—wild nature—reigns glorious an' great,
An' there by the Annan dwells bonnie Cow Kate.

Cow Kate was brought up by a rich Border Laird,
Wha'd mony braid acres o' Annan's best sward,
Nae workin', nor daffin', her mettle could tire,
For the lassie wrought hard in the fields an' the byre,
An' simmer an' winter, an' early an' late,
Aye up to the oxters was bonnie Cow Kate.

She grew like a tree, and she bloom'd like a flower,
Wi' her growth there cam' grace, wi' her beauty cam' power,
An' she tripped up the hill, an' she strade down the glen,
Envied by the lasses, adored by the men ;
Yet the farmers were shy, an' the herdsmen were blate,
An' nane cam' a-wooing to bonnie Cow Kate.

There's changes in a' thing, e'en fortune will change,
An' faces look fond, that were wont to look strange,
An' hunders o' wooers baith stalwart an' braw,
Cam' round her when death took the auld laird awa',

An' the clatter gaed round he had left his estate
To his ae strappin' daughter, our bonnie Cow Kate.

Kate kilted her high, an' she stood in the byre,
Sent her wooers to Annan to drown out their fire,
Ca'd her sheep to the tryst, an' her kye to the fair,
Ne'er ae better drover or herdsman was there,
An' mony a jockie was fain to retreat,
Wi' his wit for his winning, frae bonnie Cow Kate.

The shyest are catch'd, when they're catch'd wi' a start,
The head may be cool, but waes me for the heart,
Even Katie fand out, 'mid a mirk wreath o' snaw
That a herdsman had stoun a' her heart's peace awa',
Wrapt warm in his bosom, he bare hame elate,
An' had for his valour our bonnie Cow Kate.

JAMES BALLANTINE.

## HURRAH FOR THE THISTLE.

*Music by Mr. Turnbull, Glasgow.*

HURRAH for the Thistle!—the brave Scottish Thistle,
The evergreen Thistle of Scotland for me ;
A fig for the flowers, in your lady-built bowers ;
The strong bearded—weel guarded, Thistle for me.

'Tis the flower the proud eagle greets in its flight,
When he shadows the stars with the wings of his might ;
'Tis the flower that laughs at the storm as it blows,
For the greater the tempest, the greener it grows.
Hurrah for the Thistle.

Round the love-lighted hames o' our ain native land,
On the bonneted brow—on the hilt of the brand—
On the face of the shield, 'mid the shouts of the free,
May the Thistle be seen, whare the Thistle should be.
Hurrah for the Thistle.

Hale hearts we hae yet to bleed in its cause,
Bold harps we hae yet to sound its applause,
How then can it fade, when sic chiels an' sic cheer,
And sae mony braw sprouts o' the Thistle are here.

Then hurrah for the Thistle !—the brave Scottish
    Thistle,
The evergreen Thistle of Scotland for me ;
A fig for the flowers, in your lady-built bowers,
The strong bearded—weel guarded, Thistle for me.
                      ALEX. MacLAGGAN.

## WHA DAUR MEDDLE WI' ME?

ROUGH, sturdy, beardy, fire-crown'd king,
Thou jaggy, kittly, gleg wee thing,
Wha dares to brave the piercing sting
           O' Scotia's thistle ?
Soon scamper aff, hap stap an' fling,
           Wi' couring fustle.

'Midst scenes o' weir, in days o' yore,
When the grund swat wi' life's red gore,
And Scotia's land frae shore to shore
           Groan'd sair wi' waes,
Thy form dim seen, 'midst battle's roar,
           Aft scared her faes.

When Wallace, sturdy patriot wight,
His trusty broad sword glancing bright,
Gar'd Southron reivers scour like fright
           Frae Scotland's braes,
Thou snelly shot thy horns o' might,
           An' brogged their taes.

When Bruce at Bannockburn's red field
Made Edward's doughty army yield,

An' Southrons down in thousands reeled,
                    Stark, stiff an' dour,
The vera weans did thistles wield,
                    An' fought like stour.


Since then no foe hath dared to tread
Upon thy guarded, crimson head,
But proudly from thy mountain bed
                    Thy head thou rear'st.
By flowing springs of freedom fed,
                    No blast thou fear'st.


Thy native land is free as air,
Her sons are bold, her daughters fair,
Bright soul'd, warm hearted, fond to share
                    The social smile,
Pure love, true friendship, glorious pair
                    Adorn the soil.


Rear high thy head, thou symbol dear,
Sae meek in peace, sae bauld in weir,
Mine e'e dimm'd wi' a full proud tear,
                    I bow before thee,
An' while life's pulse beats warm, I swear
                    Still to adore thee.
                        JAMES BALLANTINE.


## THE BUIKIN' O' ROBIN AND MIRREN.

TUNE—"*Brose and Butter.*"

GAE bring me my rokeley o' grey,
   My mutch and red ribbons sae dainty,
And haste ye, lass, fling on your claes,
   Auld Rab's to be buiked to aunty.
Ae gloamin' last ouk he cam' wast,
   To speer for my auld lucky daddie,

Tho' sair wi' the hoast he was fash'd,
  Ae blink o' auld aunt made him waddie.
    Sae mak' yoursel' braw, braw,
      And busk yoursel' tidy and canty,
    Guid luck may as yet be your fa',
      Sin' Rab's to be buiked to aunty.

The body cam' hirplin' ben,
  Tho' warstlin' wi' eild, he was canty,
And he o'erly just speer'd for the men,
  But he cadgily cracket wi' aunty.
Or e'er he had sitten a blink,
  He sang and he ranted fu' cheery,
And auld aunty's heart he gar'd clink,
  Wi' " Mirren, will ye be my deary?
    For I'm neither sae auld, auld,
      Nor am I sae gruesome or uggin,
    I've a score o' guid nowt i' the fauld,
      And a lang neck'd purse o' a moggin."

At this Mirren's heart gae a crack,
  Like the thud o' a waukin' mill beetle,
And she thocht, but she ne'er a word spak,
  " Weel, I'd e'en be contented wi' little."
For Mirren, tho' threescore and ane,
  Had never had " will ye," speer'd at her,
So she laid a fond loof in his han',
  And quo' Robin " that settles the matter."
    Sae busk ye, lass, braw, braw,
      Busk and let's aff, for I'se warran',
    We'se hae daffin' and laughin' an' a',
      At the buikin' o' Robin and Mirren.
                    PATRICK BUCHAN.

## MY AIN COUNTRIE.

TUNE—"*The Brier Bush.*"

How are ye a' at hame,
 In my ain countrie?
Are your kind hearts aye the same,
 In my ain countrie?
Are ye a' as fu' o' glee,
As witty, frank, and free,
As kind's ye used to be?
 In my ain countrie.

Oh! a coggie I will fill
 To my ain countrie!
Ay, and toom it wi' gude will
 To my ain countrie!
Here's to a' the folk I ken,
'Mang the lasses and the men,
In ilk canty " but " an' " ben,"
 O' my ain countrie!

Heaven watch thou ever o'er
 My ain countrie!
Let tyrants never more
 Rule my ain countrie!
May her heroes dear to thee—
The bauld hearts and the free—
Be ready aye to dee,
 For their ain countrie!

May a blessin' licht on a'
 In my ain countrie!
Baith the grit folk an' the sma'
 In our ain countrie!
On whatever sod I kneel—
Heaven knows I ever feel—
For the honour and the weal
 O' my ain countrie!

ALEX. MACLAGGAN.

## THE HIGHLAND MAID.

TUNE—"*42d March.*"

AGAIN the lav'rock seeks the sky,
    And warbles, dimly seen,
And summer views wi' sunny joy,
    Her gow'ny robe o' green.
But ah ! the summer's blythe return
    In flowery pride array'd,
Nae mair can cheer the heart forlorn,
    Or charm the Highland maid.

My true love fell by Charlie's side,
    Wi' mony a clansman dear,
A gallant youth, ah ! wae betide ,
    The cruel Southron's spear.
His bonnet blue is fallen now,
    And bloody is the plaid,
That aften on the mountain's brow
    Has wrapp'd his Highland maid.

My father's shieling on the hill,
    Is cheerless now and sad ;
The passing breezes whisper still,
    " You've lost your Highland lad."
Upon Culloden's fatal heath
    He spak' o' me, they said,
And faulter'd wi' his dying breath,
    " Adieu ! my Highland maid."

The weary night for rest I seek,
    The langsome day I mourn,
The smile upon my wither'd cheek
    Ah ! never can return.
But soon beneath the sod I'll lie,
    In yonder lowly glade,
Where haply ilka passer by
    Shall mourn the Highland maid.

## SIR BENJAMIN BUFFSTRAP.[1]

AIR—"*Black Jock.*"

HAVE you ever heard of Sir Benjamin Buffstrap, the Broad,
That knight of the razor so outre and odd—
　　The barbarous barber of Barrowfield bar?
Sure a sharper short shaver has seldom been seen,
With his buffstrap so black and his blades all so keen,
And his suds in his soap-box as white as the snow—
How closely the crop of the chin he can mow!
　　The barbarous barber at Barrowfield bar.

Though a barbarous barber Sir Benjamin be,
Yet, like his neighbour shaver, no Savage[2] is he,
　　The barbarous barber at Barrowfield bar:
For all his barbarities tend but to smooth
The wrinkles of age down to dimples of youth,
While the blood of his victims he studiously spares,
And only cuts off stiff rebellious hairs—
　　The barbarous barber of Barrowfield bar.

This barbarous barber's a wonderful wight,
For his breadth is exactly the length of his height!—
　　The barbarous barber of Barrowfield bar;
And his broad bluffy face is so pregnant with glee,
And his wild wit comes flashing so fearless and free,
That to see and to hear him, I'm certain would make
A whole congregation of Quakers' sides ache—
　　The barbarous barber at Barrowfield bar.

[1] This clever little, facetious, bustling personage, is a particular friend of the author; is considered a great accession to every social party—and is as ready at repartee as the celebrated Jemmy Wright. He still resides at Barrowfield bar, Bridgeton—is barber, toll-man, spirit-dealer, farmer of ladle-dues, draff and sand contractor, punster, and poet. The term barbarous, has only an alliterative application; the worthy polisher of chins is as smooth and agreeable in his manners as the edge of his own blades.

[2] Savage is the name of a neighbour strap.

'Tis said, too, that he can disguise so the truth,
As to give to old age the resemblance of youth—
 The barbarous barber at Barrowfield bar ;
Can make the dark countenance lively and fair,
And give the bald pate an exub'rance of hair ;
Nay, more—by the help of his combs and his curls,
Can transform mouldy maids into gay giddy girls—
 The barbarous barber at Barrowfield bar.

Long may this sharp shaver successfully shave
The chin of the just man—the cheek of the knave—
But while light sweeps his hand o'er the honest man's chin,
Ne'er causing wry faces, nor scratching the skin,
May the cheek of the villain severely be stung
By the rough rugged razor, or keen cutting tongue,
 Of the barbarous barber at Barrowfield bar.

ALEX. RODGER.

## THE BLACK SHEEP.[1]

*Air—" John Anderson my jo."*

Oh John, what can be keeping you—how lang, man, will
 ye bide,
Ye surely hae mista'en your road, and dauner't into Clyde ;
Here, weary by the ingle side, a lanely wife I sit—
I'm sure that's Twa that's chappit noo, and nae word o'
 ye yet.

Of our John's reformation I lang hae tint a' houp,
He never thinks o' rising while a drap there's in the stoup :
Wi' gaunting and wi' gaping, my puir head's like to split—
I hear his voice upon the stair—and surely that's his fit.

(*John soliloquising on the stair*). "That's no our stair—no the
ane that I gang up to my nest on—I think it's coming down to meet

---

[1] This piece of exquisite humour is a contribution of the late John
D. Carrick, to the second series of the Laird of Logan, and we have
thought that it is not out of its element in this collection.

me—and it's gaun round about too—there's no twa stanes in't like
ane anither—some o' them wad haud twa feet, and ithers a sparrow
couldna get fittin' on. Weel, gin I were at the head o't, and on the
inside o' my ain door, I'll raise a skellihewit wi' Janet, it will I—
because, gin I dinna do't wi' her, she'll do't wi' me—an' a man should
be aye master in his ain house, right or wrang; it's a' the same
whether the parritch is ready or no—on the fire or af't—cauld or het,
I maun be het ;—if she's pouterin' at the fire, and keeping it in for
me, I'll tell her she had nae business staying up—she might hae been
aneath the blankets, for she would pouter a while, afore the fire
could len' ony light for me to come hame wi' ;—and if she be in her
bed, I'll mak' her lugs stoun' wi' her carelessness about her half
marrow—that he might hae been robbed or murdered for ony care
she had o' him, but lying there snoring like a dog in a tod's hole.
But there she is—I hear her,—can I really be angry wi' her?—Yes ;
I maun be angry at something."—(*Chaps*). (*Inquires*)—"Wha's
that?" "Open the door, and ye'll see—it's ill to ken folk through a
twa-inch plank." "I would like to ken wha it is, before I open my
door to onybody." "Weel, Janet, you're perfectly right—there's
naething like being cautious." "Is't you, John, after a'? siccan a
night as I hae spent, thinking a' the ills on earth had happened to
you ; whar hae ye been, John?" "Oh, Janet, dinna be in sic a
hurry." "In a hurry, John, near three o'clock in the morning!"
"Janet, it's the first time since you and I cam thegither, that I hae
seen you wasting onything !" "Me wasting, John !—the only thing
I'm wasting is mysel." "Na, Janet, that's no what I mean ; what's
the use o' burning twa crusies to let ae body see—an' ye might hae
lighted half a dizen an' they a' couldna let me see to come hame ?"
"John, John, you're seeing wi' mae een than your Maker gied ye this
night—your een are just gaun thegither." "I'm no a hair fley'd for
that, my doo, Janet, as lang's my nose is atween them." "Ou ay,
John, but ye hav'na tell't me whar ye hae been till this time in the
morning?" "Did ye ever hear sic a high wind as is blawin' frae
the lift this night? the cluds will be blawn a' to rags—there'll no be
a hale corner left in them to haud a shower in, afore the mornin'—
no a gas-lamp blinkin' in the Trongate ; gin ye get up wi' the ducks
in the mornin', Janet, you'll see the Green scattered ower wi' the
kye's horns, for they couldna keep their roots in siccan a win'—an'
ye'll get them for the gathering." "Ay, John, it's a high wind, but
for onything that I hear, it's blawin' nae higher than your ain head ;
whar was ye?" "Dear me, did I no tell ye, Janet? I'll hae forgotten
then ; I might hae tell't ye—I'm sure I was nae ill gate—that's a
lang an' no vera tenty stair o' ours to come up ; I maist missed my

fit this night coming up it mair than ance—we'll hae to flit next term,
I doubt : ye maun gang and look after anither ane the morn, an I'll
gang wi' ye—twa heads are better than ane, quo' the wife, gaun wi'
her dog to the market." "Come, come, John, nane o' your palavers,
ye needna think to draw the blade ower an auld body's e'e ; the stair,
John, atweel's nane o' the best, but the stair that would suit you best
this night is ane wi' nae steps in't ;—but whar was ye ? and wha was
ye wi' ?" "Janet, ye hae little pity for me ; if I should crack ane o'
my pins (limbs) ye maybe think, because I'm a shaver o' corks, that
I can easily mak' a new ane—but, Janet, fu' o' curiosity too !
woman, it's a dangerous thing to be ower inquisitive—ye mind what
the mither o' us a' got by't ; besides, 'Gied,' as honest Rabbie
Burns says, 'the infant world a shug, maist ruined a'—oh, but it is
a pithy word that *shug !* there's no a part o' speech in the English
tongue like it." "Whaur was ye, John, *whaur !* I doubt ye hae
been in ill company, this night—ye never put me aff this way before ;
will ye no tell me, John ?" "Weel, weel, Janet, dinna be sae toutit
about it—I was awa' at a burial." "At a burial, John !—what
burial could there be at this hour? It could be nae decent body,
I'm sure, that had to be huddled awa' at sic an untimeous time o'
nicht." "'Deed, Janet, you're richt there ; she was a very trouble-
some kind o' body, and raised muckle discord amang families ; we
were a' saying, she's weel awa' if she bide." "But wha is she ?"
"Just our auld frien' ANNIE, and she never cam' about the house
but *ill weather* was sure to follow ; now, I think ye may guess.'
"Ay, puir body !—has she win awa' at length, puir creature? Annie !
Annie !—oh aye, but whan I mind—there's mae Annies than ane—
was it Annie Spittle ?" "Oh no, it wasna her, poor body !" "Was
it Annie Dinwiddie ?" "No ; that woman's *din* is enough to drive
ony man to the *wuddie.*" "Weel, John, I ken nae mae o' the
name ; but I see you're just trying, as usual, to mak' game o' me.
Waes me ! it's a hard thing to be keepit sae lang out o' my bed to
be made a fou man's fool."

Says John, "no ane that ye hae nam'd 's the lassie that
   I mean—
Ae Annie yet, my dearest doo, ye hae forgotten clean ;
We buried ANI-MOSITY—an trouth I thought it fit,
That whan we had her in the yird, a skinfu' I should get."

## OUR FAIR YOUNG QUEEN.

AIR—"*Caledonia.*"

O ! SCOTLAND's hills are bonny hills,
    A' clad wi' heather bells,
And music warbles in the rills
    Which sport adown the dells ;
And there be glens in fair Scotland
    Where foe hath never been,
And wild and free we'll keep them yet
        For our young Queen !

O ! wad she cross the Tweed some day,
    Our Scottish glens to view,
Our fairy lakes and streamlets grey,
    Lone isles and mountains blue.
And see auld Scotland's goodly bands,
    Wi' belt and buckle sheen,
In proud array come forth to greet
        Their fair young Queen !

For Scotland has her yeomen leal,
    And sturdy loons they be,
That whirl, like willow wands, their steel,
    When marshall'd on the lea.
And should a foe invade our soil,
    No braver band, I ween,
Would fight beneath the banners broad
        Of our young Queen !

And Scotland has her clansmen brave,
    Who bear the targe and brand ;
Who'd spend their dearest blood to save
    Their own romantic land.
And they would leave their hills of mist,
    And glens of lovely green,
To form a living bulwark round
        Their fair young Queen !

And Scotland has her lovely ones,
    A beauteous train are they ;
But much she mourns her tuneful sons,
    Her bards and minstrels grey.
For they who wak'd her sweetest lyres,
    Sleep 'neath the turf so green,
We've few to sing the welcome now
            Of our young Queen !

We've heard of merry England's scenes,
    And trusty souls are there ;
And Erin boasts her green domains,
    Rich woods, and prospects fair.
But Scotland boasts her stormy hills,
    Where freemen aye have been,    .
O come and let us doat on thee,
            Our fair young Queen !

*James Murray*

## OUR BRAW UNCLE.

*Set to Music by Peter M'Leod, Esq.*

My auld uncle Willie cam' doun here frae Lunnon,
    An' wow, but he was a braw man ;
An' a' my puir cousins around him cam rinnin',
    Frae mony a lang mile awa', man.
My uncle was rich, my uncle was proud—
He spak' o' his gear, and he bragg'd o' his gowd ;
An' whate'er he hinted, the puir bodies vow'd
    They wad mak' it their love an' their law, man.

He stay'd wi' them a' for a week time about,
    Feastin', an fuddlin', an' a', man,

Till their pantries and patience he baith riddled out,
    An' they thocht he was ne'er gaun awa', man.
And neither he was ; he had naething to do,
He had made a' their fortunes and settled them too ;
Though they ne'er saw a boddle they'd naething to say,
    For they thocht they wad soon hae it a', man.

But when our braw uncle had stay'd here a year,
    I trow but he wasna a sma' man,
Their tables cam' down to their auld hamilt cheer,
    An' he gat himsel' book'd to gae wa', man.
Yet e'er the coach started, the hale o' his kin
Cam' to the coach-door, maistly chokin' him in,
And they prest on him presents o' a' they could fin',
    An' he vow'd he had *done* for them a', man.

And sae did he too ; for he never cam' back,
    My sang ! but he wasna a raw man,
To feast for a year without paying a plack,
    An' gang wi' sic presents awa', man.
An' aften he bragg'd how he cheated the greed
O' his grey gruppy kinsmen be-north o' the Tweed,
The best o't, when auld uncle Willie was dead,
    He left them—*just naething ava, man.*

*James Ballantine*

## WILLIE WINKIE.[1]

*A Nursery Rhyme.*

WEE WILLIE WINKIE rins through the toon,
Up stairs an' doon stairs in his nicht-gown,
Tirlin' at the window, crying at the lock,
" Are the weans in their bed, for it's now ten o'clock ?"

[1] The Scottish Nursery Morpheus.

" Hey, Willie Winkie, are ye comin' ben?
The cat's singin' grey thrums to the sleepin' hen,
The dog's speldert on the floor and disna gie a cheep,
But here's a waukrife laddie, that *wunna fa' asleep.*"

Onything but sleep, you rogue, glow'rin' like the moon,
Rattlin' in an airn jug wi' an airn spoon,
Rumblin', tumblin' roon about, crawin' like a cock,
Skirlin' like a kenna-what, waukenin' sleepin' folk.

" Hey, Willie Winkie, the wean's in a creel,
Wamblin' aff a bodie's knee like a verra eel,
Ruggin' at the cat's lug and ravelin' a' her thrums—
Hey, Willie Winkie—see, there he comes."

Wearit is the mither that has a stoorie wean,
A wee, stumpie, stousie, that canna rin his lane,
That has a battle aye wi' sleep afore he'll close an e'e—
But a kiss frae aff his rosy lips gies strength anew to me.

*William Miller*

## THE E'ENING DRAPPIE.

AIR—"*When the kye come hame.*"

WHILE drinkers revel in excess, let tenty folk abstain,
The spendthrift meet the knave's caress, the miser hoard
　　his gain,
We scorn excess in ilka form, and keep the line between,
Aye steerin' clear o' calm and storm, when ower a glass
　　at e'en.

Wi' it the auld heart canty grows, the waefu' cease to
　　mourn,
Within ilk breast a feeling lows, that heats but disna burn.

VOL. I.　　　　　　　　　　　　　　　Y

The niggard's hand it opens wide, and makes the simple
keen,
A magic change that winna hide, springs frae a glass at
e'en.

When nith'rin cares begin to bite, and life's gay spring
runs dull.
Afore sic showers o' life and light, they tide it fresh and
full.
Ilk clud frae aff the mind it blaws, and leaves the soul
serene,
An' ilka frosty feeling thaws outower a glass at e'en.

The tale that's told o' ithers' wo comes wi' a sharper thrill,
And melts and moulds wi' kindly glow, ilk passion to its
will,
Our very feelings, thaw'd wi' it, to virtue's side will lean,
It waukens pity, sharpens wit, a canny glass at e'en.

The stane that plumbs the sleeping pool, an eddy frae it
springs,
Till owre the surface nought is found but wavy wimplin'
rings,
And so the stagnant, selfish heart, where feeling ne'er
was seen,
Wi' kindness circles and expands, when ower a glass at
e'en.

When round the fire we tak' our sup, ilk feelin' brighter
beams,
The ills o' life a' bundled up, leave nought but pleasant
dreams,
Ilk object bears a warmer tint, afore that wasna seen,
Ane likes the world and a' that's in't, when ower a glass
at e'en.

*M. A. Foster*

## THE ROYAL UNION.

THERE'S joy in the Lowlands and Highlands,
There's joy in the hut and the ha';
The pride o' auld Britain's fair islands,
Is woo'd and wedded an' a' :
She's got the dear lad o' her choosing—
A lad that's baith gallant and braw ;
And lang may the knot be a-loosing
That firmly has buckled the twa.
     Woo'd an' wedded an' a',
     Buckled an' bedded an' a',
     The loveliest lassie in Britain
     Is woo'd an' wedded an' a'.

May heaven's all-bountiful Giver
Shower down His best gifts on the twa ;
May love round their couch ever hover,
Their hearts close and closer to draw.
May never misfortune o'ertake them,
Nor blast o' adversity blaw ;
But every new morning awake them
To pleasures unsullied as snaw.
     Woo'd an' wedded an' a', etc.

Then here's to our Queen an' her Marrow,
May happiness aye be their fa',
May discord and sickness and sorrow
Be banish'd for ever their ha'.
So, fy let us coup aff our bicker,
And toast meikle joy to the twa,
And may they, till life's latest flicker,
Together in harmony draw.
     Woo'd an' wedded an' a', etc.

*Alex␣ Rodger*

## THE AULD GUDEWIFE AN' HER FOUR GUDE KYE.

*Air*—"*Cutty-spoon an' tree-ladle.*"

THE auld gudewife gaed out at e'en,
An' ower the craft her leefu' lane,
An' sought her kye and cried them hame,
An' ca'd them ilka ane by name.
Come hame, ye jauds! the byre is clean,
Your lair is made o' the breckans green,
An' the yellow clover fills your sta';
Come hame, ye jauds!—come here awa'.
　　　Come hame, etc.

What hauds the house i' saip an' saut,
What buys the houps to brew the maut,
An' mony a needfu' thing forbye?
Atweel its just my four gude kye.
Better kye there's nae i' the braes,
Brownie for butter, Brandie for cheese,
Hawkie for milk, Hornie for whey;
I wat fu' weel I'm proud o' my kye.
　　　Better kye, etc.

*Alex Laing*

## OH! AND NO.

"MARY, Mary, long have I
Heaved for thee the weary sigh."
　　　"Oh!" said she,
"Canst thou not some kindness show
Him that doteth on thee so?"
　　　"No!" said she.

"Hast thou not, upon my breast,
Love as warm as mine confessed ?"
          "Oh !" said she.
"I charge thee, then, if thou art true,
Do as love would have thee do."
          "No !" said she.

"By that cheek, whose living red
Shames the tint o'er rose-leaves shed !"
          "Oh !" said she,
"Let that cheek, I charge thee, know
Love's deeper, richer, warmer, glow !"
          "No !" said she.

"By thine eye, whose dazzling blue
Dulls the light of heaven's own hue !"
          "Oh !" said she,
"Let, I charge thee, love inspire
That holy eye with subtler fire !"
          "No !" said she.

"Still one plea remains at least,
Might not we go seek the priest ?"
          "Oh !" said she,
"If I asked you there to fly,
Could you still my suit deny ?"—
          "No !" said she.

*E. Buchanan Hall*

## DRINKING SONG.

AIR—"*Fake away.*"

SEE, see that each glass, and each jug be full,
          Each jug be full !
We must have a strong, and a powerful pull,
                    Drink away !

And I'll tell you to-night, if you all agree,
A bit of my mind in a melodie,
        Then drink away, boys, drink away!
        Steadily, readily, drink away!


I know there are fools in this world who sneer,
        In this world who sneer,
At our merry songs, and our hearty cheer,
        Drink away!
But wine is good, is wise Solomon's say,
To fill up the cracks in our thirsty clay,
        Then drink away, boys, drink away!
        Cheerily, merrily, drink away!


See, see that ye fill, boys! for time and tide,
        For time and tide,
The old sages say, will on no man bide,
        Drink away!
But what care we how the tides may go,
When the rivers of wine beside us flow!
        Then drink away, boys, drink away!
        Steadily, readily, drink away!


I wish that the wise in their solemn schools,
        In their solemn schools,
Would mix with their mournful, some merry rules,
        Drink away!
And if wisdom, old lady, won't dry her tears,
We must pack her off with our roaring cheers;
        Then drink away, boys, drink away!
        Cheerily, merrily, drink away!


See, see that you fill, boys! come now a toast!
        Come now a toast!
Here's a health to the lass each lad loves most!
        Drink away!

And thick be the thorns on his life's highway,
Who would a sweet lass, or a friend betray !
      Then drink away, boys, drink away!
      Steadily, readily, drink away !

*A. MacLeggan*

## DRINKIN' BODY.

AIR—"*Dainty Davie.*"

O ! MONY ills we ken thee bie,
    Drinkin' body, blinkin' body ;
And fearfu' ills I wat they be,
    Auld drinkin', blinkin' body.
O mony ills we ken thee bie,
    Thy tremblin' han' and sunken e'e,
The sad effects o' barley-bree,
    Poor drinkin', blinkin' body.

Thou's scarce a dud upon thy back,
    Reckless body, feckless body !
Whilk ance was clad right bein, alack !
    Auld reckless, feckless body !
Thou's scarce a dud upon thy back,
    Just like a house without its thack,
And yet thou'lt fuddle ilka plack,
    Poor reckless, feckless body.

Thou boasted ance thy lands to plough,
    Tauntin' body, vauntin' body ;
Thy sax guid yads as ever drew,
    Auld tauntin', vauntin' body ;

Thou boasted ance thy lands to plough ;
  A butt, a ben, and aumry fu',
But whar the mischief are they now ?
  Poor tauntin', vauntin' body.

Now, thou's neither milk nor meal,
  Senseless body, menseless body,
Butter'd cake, nor kebbuc heel,
  Auld senseless, menseless body.
Now thou's neither milk nor meal,
  Weel stock'd byre, nor cozy beil ;
Thou's dancin' daily to the deil !
  Poor menseless, senseless body.

Gif sober housewife say thou's wrang,
  Tatter'd body, batter'd body,
When 'gainst her winnock thou com'st bang,
  Auld tatter'd, batter'd body.
Gif sober housewife say thou's wrang,
  Thou bids her for a witch gae hang,
'Syne dings her wi' a roguish sang,
  Poor tatter'd, batter'd body.

For gudesake mend while yet thou can,
  Witless body, fitless body ;
Forsake thy drouthy, clouty clan,
  Auld witless, fitless, body.
For gudesake mend, if yet thou can ;
  'Tis human nature's wisest plan,
To sink the brute and raise the man !
  Poor witless, fitless body.

*A. MacLeggan.*

## MAY, SWEET MAY.

O ! MAY, dear May,
A thousand welcomes, May !
At sight of thee my spirit springs
Aloft, as it were borne on wings !
Nor care nor toil,
I reck the while
I'm baskin' in thy glorious smile,
Upon thy bosom, May.

O ! May, dear May,
Fond, flowery bosom'd May !
Thy briery-scented breath again
Plays round my cheek, as fresh as when
Upon the green,
From morn till e'en,
With dallyings of love between,
I danced with thee, young May.

O ! May, dear May,
Blithe, song-inspiring May !
Thy joyful presence setteth free
The slumb'ring founts of melody.
And young and old,
The dull, the cold,
Their summer songs and hearts unfold,
To greet thy coming, May.

O ! May, dear May,
Sport, laughter-loving May !
Hie we to thy woodbine bowers,
Nor idly spend the fleeting hours,
For soon, too soon !
The waning moon
Will bring thy buxom sister, June,
And banish thee, sweet May.

O ! May, dear May,
　　Ripe, rosy-lippèd May,
'Tho' brief the while thou ling'rest here,
I'll woo thee all the coming year ;
　　For she, sweet life !
　　My promis'd wife,
With every charm of nature rife,
Thine image is, my May.

O ! May, dear May,
　　Mine own lov'd natal May,
Thy blessèd light it was which first
Upon mine infant eyelids burst ;
　　And when they close,
　　With all my woes,
And I am laid to long repose,
Light thou my grave, loved May.

*W Fergusson*

## THE DAINTY BIT PLAN.

AIR—"*Brose and Butter.*"

OUR May had an e'e to a man,
　　Nae less than the newly-placed Preacher ;
And we plotted a dainty bit plan
　　For trapping our spiritual teacher.
O, we were sly, sly ! O, we were sly and sleekit !
But ne'er say a herring is dry until it be reestit and reekit.

We treated young Mr. M'Gock,
　　We plied him wi' tea and wi' toddy ;
And we praised every word that he spoke,

Till we put him maist out o' the body.
    O, we were sly, sly ! etc.

And then we grew a' unco guid—
    Made lang faces aye in due season ;
When to feed us wi' spiritual fuid,
    Young Mr. M'Gock took occasion.
      O, we were sly, sly ! etc.

Frae the kirk we were never awa',
    Except when frae hame he was helping ;
And then May, and often us a',
    Gaed far and near after him skelping.
      O, we were sly, sly ! etc.

We said aye, which our neighbours thought droll,
    That to hear him gang through wi' a sermon,
Was, though a wee dry on the whole,
    As refreshing as dews on Mount Hermon.
      O, we were sly, sly ! etc.

But to come to the heart o' the nit—
    The dainty bit plan that we plotted
Was to get a subscription afit,
    And a *watch* to the minister voted.
      O, we were sly, sly ! etc.

The young women folk o' the kirk,
    By turns lent a hand in collecting ;
But May took the feck o' the wark,
    And the trouble the rest o' directing.
      O, we were sly, sly ! etc.

A gran' watch was gotten belyve,
    And May, wi' sma' prigging, consentit
To be ane o' a party o' five
    To gang to the Manse and present it.
      O, we were sly, sly ! etc.

We a' gied a word o' advice
 To May in a deep consultation,
To hae something to say unco nice,
 And to speak for the hale deputation.
  O, we were sly, sly ! etc.

Taking present and speech baith in hand,
 May delivered a bonny palaver,
To let Mr. M'Gock understand
 How zealous she was in his favour.
  O, we were sly, sly ! etc.

She said that the gift was to prove
 That his female friends valued him highly,
But it couldna express a' their love ;
 And she glintit her e'e at him slyly.
  O, we were sly, sly ! etc.

He put the gold watch in his fab,
 And proudly he said he would wear it ;
And, after some flattering gab,
 Tauld May he was gaun to be marryit.
O, we were sly, sly ! O, we were sly and sleekit !
But Mr. M'Gock was nae gowk wi' our dainty bit plan
 to be cleekit.

May cam' hame wi' her heart at her mouth,
 And became frae that hour a Dissenter ;
And now she's renewing her youth,
 Wi' some hopes o' the Burgher precentor.
O, but she's sly, sly ! O, but she's sly and sleekit !
And cleverly opens ae door as soon as anither ane's steekit.

## TA KRAN HIGHLAN' PAGPIPE.

You'll may spoke o' ta fittle, you'll may prag o' ta flute,
Ay an' clafer o' pynas, pass trums, clairnet an' lute,
Put ta far pestest music you'll may heard, or will fan,
Is ta kreat Hielan' pagpipe, ta kran Hielan' pagpipe, ta
    prite o' ta lan'.

O ! tere is no one can knew all her feelin', her thought,
Whan ta soon o' ta piproch, will langsyne to her prought,
An' her mint whirl rount apout wi' ta pleasure once fan,
Whan she hears ta kreat pagpipe, ta kran, etc.

A teefishal lee is tolt apout Orpus, poor shiel,
Who went awa' toon to peg her wife pack frae ta teil,
Tey'll tolt tat she sharm'd Satan wi' a lute in her han',
No such thing, 'twas ta pagpipe, ta kran Hielan', etc.

It is lang since ako, tey'll spoke o' music ta got,
(Apollo tey ca' her) put she'll thocht fery ott
Tat tey'll paint her, so ponny, wi' a lyre in her han',
When tey'll knew 'twas the pagpipe, etc.

Fan ta Greek wi' him's pibrochs sharmed Allister Mhor,
And made him's heart merry—and made him's heart sore,
Made him greet like a childrens, and swore like a man,
Was't his lyre ?—'twas ta pagpipe, etc.

Whan ta clans all pe kather't, an' all reaty for fought,
To ta soon o' ta fittle, woult tey march, tid you'll thought ?
No, not a foot woult tey went, not a claymore pe trawn,
Till tey heard ta kreat pagpipe, ta kran, etc.

Whan ta funeral is passin' slow, slow through ta klen,
Ta hearts all soft wi' ouskie, what prings tears from ta men?
Tis ta Coronach's loot wail soonin', solemn an' kran,
From ta kreat Hielan' pagpipe, ta kran Hielan', etc.

Whan ta wattin' teuks place, O ! what shoy, frolic, an' fun,
An' ta peoples all meetit, an' ta proose has peen run,

'Tere's no music for tancin', has yet efer peen fan,
Like ta kreat Hielan' pagpipe, ta kran Hielan', etc.

O, tat she hat worts to tolt all her lofe an' telight
She has in ta pagpipe, twoult teuk long, long years to
  write ;
Put she'll shust teuk a trap pefore her task she'll pegan ;
So here's to ta pagpipe, ta kran Hielan' pagpipe, ta prite o'
  ta lan'.

*Allen Fisher*

## THE LONELY DWELLIN'.

O ! I ha'e seen the wild flowers blaw
 On gentle Spring's returnin',
O ! I ha'e seen the sere leaves fa',
 And Nature clad in mournin' ;
But even then, my heart was light,
 I knew nor care nor sorrow ;
For Fancy painted a' things bright,
 And hope smiled on the morrow.

Now, waes my heart ! the flowers may blaw,
 The fleeting seasons vary ;
I only mark the leaves that fa'
 Around the grave o' Mary !
The moaning winds of Winter rise,
 And on the ear come swellin' ;
While crisp and cauld the cranreuch lies
 Upon her lonely dwellin'.

*Charles Gray.*

## AS I WEND THROUGH THE WILD WOOD.

THE gloamin' is gloomin', the daylight awa',
Adown the lang loanin' the owsen come slaw,
Lowne sings the mavis on yonder auld tree,
And the lark leaves the clud for its nest on the lea ;
    As I wend through the wild wood, the dark wood, sae
      eerie,
    As I wend through the lang wood to meet thee, my
      dearie.

The auld crazy mill seems to deepen its din,
While louder the burnie rairs o'er the wee linn,
And the howl of the mastiff, sae lang and sae drear,
'Maist dauntens my heart as it fa's on my ear.
    As I wend, etc.

Nae moon climbs the dull lift, sae bare and sae blue,
Whare ae little starnie looks glimmerin' through ;
And the saft westlin' breeze as it passes me by,
Lifts the locks frae my brow wi' a pitifu' sigh.
    As I wend, etc.

Ilk wee bird has faulded its wing for the night,
And the howlet belyve, frae yon auld turret's height,
Whare it dozes its lane, will be hootin' awa'
To the wanderin' sterns as they rise and they fa'.
    Then haste through the wild wood, the dark wood
      sae eerie,
    Haste, haste through the lang wood to meet me, my
      dearie.

*W Fergusson*

## THE BOROUGH BAILIE.

To our borough my lord in his chariot rolled,
And his flunkies were gleaming in purple and gold ;
And the smile on his face, and the glance of his e'e
Seemed as fair to my sight as the flowers on the lea.

Like bees round their hives when the summer is green,
The councillors all round the tavern were seen ;
Like bees when the leaves of the forest are strewn,
That party by midnight were all overthrown.

For the steam of the alcohol rose to their brains,
And the window-frames shook with their bacchanal strains,
And in bumpers they drank to his lordship's success,
Till they dropp'd on the carpet like pears on the grass.

And there lay the butcher in holiday pride,
Not a cowl on his head, nor a steel by his side,
And the *sugh* of the sleeper waxed noisier still,
Though the shoemaker bawled for a *finishing* gill.

And there lay the tailor dejected and wan,
A shrivelled abortion,—a fraction of man ;—
And the room is all silent, the carpet all wet ;
The tumblers demolished, the tables upset.

And the matrons were angry and loud in their wail,
That their doves had imbibed so much whisky and ale ;
But a compliment kindly and decently shored,[1]
And they melted in smiles at the glance of my lord !

---

[1] Offered.

## THE TOWN PIPER'S LAY.

*Air—" Will ye gang to the ewe-bughts, Marion? "*

NAINSEL frae ta hills wad pe flittin',
    An' come to a toon on ta coast :
An' as it was proper an' fittin',
    She soon got a shentleman's post.
Her cousin ta laird o' Petgrunsel
    A letter did send in a crack ;
An' syne frae ta provos' an' council
    She got a *toon*-coat on her back !

She disna pe drink in ta mornin',
    Except it be trams ane or twa ;
An' when ta lord provos' gies warnin'
    She aye studes his henchman fu' pra'.
She disna pe drink in ta e'enin',
    Unless it pe four or five cann ;
An' if she pehaves where she's peen in,
    She'll soon pe ta provos' pest man.

She marches ilk week to ta preachin'
    An' shoulders her halbert like daft ;
An' aye while ta minister's teachin',
    She sleeps in ta magistrate's laft.
But though she's o' shentle connection,
    She scorns for to prag or to plaw ;
Weel may ye deshest your refection !
    Goot nicht, Sirs, an' shoy wi' ye a' !

*David Vedder.*

## LAUCHIE FRASER'S PROMOTIONS.

*Air—" Johnny Cope."*

NAINSEL she was porn 'mang ta Hielan' hills,
'Mang ta goats, an' ta sheeps, an' ta whiskee stills,
An' ta brochan, an' brogues, an' ta snuishin' mills,
      Oich ! she was ta ponnie land she was porn in ;
For a' ta lads there will be shentlemans porn,
An' will wear *skean-dhu* an' ta praw snuishin'-horn,
An' ta fine tartan trews her praw houghs to adorn,
      An' mak' her look fu' spruce in ta mornin'.

Noo, ta shentlemans will no like to wroughtin' at a',
But she'll sit py ta *grieshach* her haffets to claw ;
An' pe birsle her shanks, till they're red as ta haw,
      An' a' fu' o' measles ilka mornin'.
But her nainsel at last to ta Lalans cam' doon,
An' will got her a place mang ta *mhor* Glaschow toon ;
Whar she's noo *prush-ta-poot*, an' pe *polish-ta-shoon*,
      An' pe shentleman s *flunkie* in ta mornin'.

But at last she will turn very full o' ta *proud*,
An' she'll hold up her heads, an' she'll spoke very loud,
An' she'll look wi' disdains 'pon ta low tirty crowd,
      Tat will hing 'pout ta doors ilka mornin'.
Noo, her nainsel is go to have one merry ball,
Whar she'll dance *Killum Callum*, hoogh ta best o' them all,
For ta ponniest dancer she'll pe in ta hall,
      Ay, either 'mang ta evenin' or mornin'.

Ither lads will have lassies, hersel will have *no*,
It pe far too expense wi' ta *lassie* to go ;
So, she'll shust dance hersel', her fine *preedings* to show,
      Tat she learn 'mang ta place she was porn in.
Then ta lads will cry "Lauchie, where from did you'll cam',
Tat you'll not give ta lassie ta dance an' ta dram ?"
But te're a' *trouster mosachs*, every one shust ta sam',
      They wad spulzie all her sporran ere ta mornin'.

Noo, she's thochtin' she'll yet turn a praw *waiter's pell*,
When she wear ta fine pump an' pe dress very well;
An' py Sheorge ! ere she'll stop, she'll pe maister herself,
  In spite o' a' their taunts an' their scornin'.
Syne wha like ta great Maister Fraser will pe,
When she'll hing up ta sign o' the " Golden Cross Key,"
An' will sit in her parlour her orders to gie
  To her waiters an' her boots in ta mornin' ?

*Alex<sup></sup> Rodger*

## RHYMING RAB O' OUR TOUN.

DOUN by, near our smiddy, there lives a queer boddie,
 As couthie an' canty's the simmer day's lang ;
An' auld funny story sets him in his glory,
 For aft he knocks 't into some pithy bit sang.
Tho' aye ha'flins modest, his cracks are the oddest
 That ever were heard thro' the hale kintry roun',
Aye tauld aff sae freely, sae pauky an' sleely,
 He's far an' near kent, Rhyming Rab o' our toun.

Tho' deep read in pages o' auld langsyne sages,
 As meikle's micht maist turn the pows o' us a'.
Sent soon to the shuttle, his schule-craft's but little,
 Yet auld mither Nature him kindness did shaw ;
Wi' first glint o' morning he's up, slumber scorning,
 Enraptur'd to hail ilk melodious soun',
Whar clear wimplin' burnie trots slow on its journey,
 Ye're sure then to see Rhyming Rab o' our toun.

When e'en but a younker, he'd cowr in a bunker
 Wi' 's beuk, daft gaffawers to mixna amang,
It pleas'd him far better than gowk's sillie clatter,
 The deeds o' our gutchers in auld Scottish sang.

When e'enin's clud's fa'en', and cauld win's are blawin',
  His fireside 's the shelter o' ilk beggar loun,
Wi' kimmer or carle he'd share his last farle,
  A warm-hearted chiel's Rhyming Rab o' our toun.

He's free o' deceivry, the basest o' knavery,
  An 's blythe aye the face o' a cronnie to see ;
Wi' him the lang mouter, mysel', an' the souter,
  Hae aften forgather'd an' had a bit spree ;
There's naething we crack o' but he has the knack o',
  When we ower the stoup an' the cauppie sit doun,
Tho' chiels we've had clever, the equal we never
  Had yet o' this bauld Rhyming Rab o' our toun.

There's nae Gothic chaumer, whar deils their black glaumer
  Hae niffert wi' auld wives langsyne, late at e'en ;
Nae cave, crag, nor cairnie, by time-blasted thornie,
  Ower Scotland's braid borders that he hasna seen.
But this Monday comin' we meet at the gloamin',
  In wee Andro Sibbal's, our sorrows to droun,
Sae gin, my auld hearty, ye're ane o' the party,
  Ye'll baith see an' hear Rhyming Rab o' our toun.

*Robert Clark*

## SWEET MAY ! SWEET MAY !

Air—"*Miss Graham of Inchbraickie.*"

SWEET May ! sweet May ! revives again
  The buds and blossoms of the year ;
And, clad anew, each hill and plain
  In emerald green appear.
How bright the view from yonder bank,
  Of primroses and daisies fair,

Where high o'erhead the joyous lark
　　Makes vocal all the air ;
And round and round the spangled mead
　　The bounding lambkins frisk and play,
And little rills, like living light,
　　Gleam in the sunny ray.

But what were nature's fairest scenes,
　　Though graced with all her gayest flowers,
Unless we loved, unless we felt,
　　One fond, fond heart, were ours !
Then come, my own dear Mary, come,
　　My all on earth I prize most dear ;
And in yon blooming hawthorn shade,
　　The glowing landscape near,
I'll tell to thee my hopes and fears,
　　And all my heart to thee confess,
And if thou giv'st me love for love,
　　I'll own no higher bliss.

## OUR PUIR COUSIN.

*To an original Air, by Peter M'Leod, Esq.*

My young cousin Peggy cam' doun frae Dunkeld,
　　Wi' nae word o' lawlants ava, man,
But her blue speakin' een a' her kind meaning tald,
　　An' her brow shone as white as the snaw, man ;
She cam' here to shear, and she stay'd here to spin,
She wrought wi' the fraumit, an' liv'd wi' her kin,
She laid naething out, but she laid muckle in,
　　An' she livit upon naething ava, man.

An' wow but the lassie was pawky an' slee,
　　For she smiled an' she smirkit till a', man,
Growing a' bodies' bodie, baith muckle an' wee,
　　An' our folk wadna let her awa', man,
For when there was trouble or death in the house,
She tended the sick-bed as quiet as a mouse,
An' wrought three folks' wark aye sae canny an' douce,
　　Ye wad thought she did naething ava, man.


She grew rich in beauty, she grew rich in gear,
　　She learnt to speak lawlants an' a', man ;
Her wit it was keen, and her head it was clear,
　　My sang, she was match for us a', man ;
She was trysted to suppers, and invitit to teas,
Gat gude wappin' presents, an' braw slappin' fees,
An' e'en my ain billies sae kittle to please,
　　She tickled the hearts o' them a', man.


But the sweet Highland lassie, sae gentle and meek,
　　Refused them for gude an' for a', man,
Aye gaun to the auld Highlan' kirk ilka week,
　　While the minister aft gae a ca', man ;
O his was the fervour, and her's was the grace,
　　They whisper'd sweet Gaelic, he gazed in her face,
Like light, true love travels at nae laggard pace—
　　She's the star o' his heart an' his ha', man.

_James Ballentine_

## THE BORRISTOUN.

*Written to an unpublished Gaelic Melody.*

'Twas on a cauld an' rainy day,
   When coming ower the hills o' Dee,
I met a lassie young an' gay,
   Wi' rosy cheeks an' lily bree ;
An' laith that sic a flow'r should bloom,
   Without the bield o' bush or tree ;
I said, My lassie, will ye come
   An' dwell in Borristoun wi' me ?

O wha may think to stay the hand
   That turns the page o' destinie ?
The broken ship has come to land,
   The stately bark has sunk at sea.
But fain to woo, and free to wed,
   I'll bless the doom I hae to dree
That ettled her, my Highland maid,
   To dwell in Borristoun wi' me !

*Alex Laing*

## PETTICOAT WOOING.

Air—"*Braes of Bogie.*"

Ye'll come to the wooin', dear laddie,
   Ye'll come to the wooin' at e'en ;
An' gin ye can win my auld daddie,
   We'se sune mak' a bridal, I ween.
'Tis true we hae baith a beginnin',
   Tho' nane o' his siller we see ;
But the gudewill is aye worth the winnin'
   Whan there's mair than guide wishes to gie.

Your *luve* you may hang i' the widdie—
  Your *sighs* you may stick to the wa' ;
They'll do wi' the dochter, my laddie,
  But no wi' the daddie at a' ;
Ye'll crack awa' doucely an' cannie,
  Of markets, of farmin', and flocks ;
Ye'll ruse up the days o' your grannie,
  Auld fashions, an' auld-fashion'd folks.

An' whan ye maun wish him guide-e'enin',
  I winna be far out o' view,
I'll come frae my dairy or spinnin',
  An' gang out the loanin' wi' you ;
An' gin the auld bodie's nae gloomin',
  Gin nane o' his tauntin' he flings,
Niest Friday ye'll ca' i' the gloamin',
  An' overly speak about things.

But gin ye see like a storm brewin',
  Ye'll to your auld stories again ;
An' we'll tak' anither week's wooin',
  An' try him mair cannily then.
I've heard my ain mither declarin',
  An' wha could hae kend him sae weel ?
My father wad lead wi' a bairn,
  But wadna be ca'd for the de'il.

*Alex Laing*

## THE KISS AHINT THE DOOR.

O MEIKLE bliss is in a kiss,
  Whyles mair than in a score,
But wae betak' the stouin' smack
  I took ahint the door.

"O laddie, whisht ! for sic a fright
  I ne'er was in afore,
Fu' brawly did my mither hear
  The kiss ahint the door.
The wa's are thick, ye needna fear,
  But gin they jeer and mock,
I'll swear it was a startit cork,
  Or wyte the rusty lock."
        O meikle, etc.

We stappit ben, while Maggie's face
  Was like a lowin' coal,
An', as for me, I could hae crept
  Into a mouse's hole :
The mither look'd, safe's how she look'd !
  Thae mithers are a bore,
An' gleg as ony cat to hear
  A kiss ahint the door.
        O meikle, etc.

The douce gudeman, tho' he was there,
  As weel micht been in Rome,
For by the fire he fuff'd his pipe,
  An' never fashed his thoom.
But tittrin' in a corner stood
  The gawky sisters four,
A winter's nicht for me they micht
  Hae stood ahint the door.
        O meikle, etc.

"How daur ye tak' sic freedoms here ?"
  The bauld gudewife began ;
Wi' that a foursome yell gat up,
  I to my heels an' ran ;
A besom whiskit by my lug,
  An' dishclouts half-a-score,
Catch me again, tho' fidgin' fain,
  At kissing 'hint the door.
        O meikle, etc.
            T. C. LATTO.

## WHEN THE BUTTERFLY.

WHEN the butterfly swung on the rose's fair breast,
    And zephyrs would steal from the sky,
When each bird had for pleasure forsaken the nest,
    Fair Rosa in anguish would sigh ;
Yet ev'n she was lovely as e'er was the thought
    Of innocence smiling in sleep ;
And happy—till love in her bosom had sought
    A birth-place, and left her to weep.

When the halls of old Sarnia echoed the song,
    And the dance and the music were there ;
When pleasure and revelry reign'd in the throng,
    Fair Rosa would sigh in despair ;
Yet once would her presence give bliss to the spot
    Where the hours did in revelry fly ;
Yet soon were her name and her presence forgot,
    And alone she unheeded would sigh.

The roses of health and of beauty soon fled,
    Youth's noon was benighted with care ;
Old Sarnia's sepulchre yawned for the dead,
    The priest with his missal stood there ;
And peaceful and lone in the dark house she sleeps,
    Where love enters not to annoy,
And nought save the wind o'er the dismal spot weeps ;
    But Rosa will waken in joy.

## THERE'S A THRILL OF EMOTION.

*Music by Peter M'Leod, Esq.*

THERE'S a thrill of emotion, half painful half sweet,
When the object of untold affection we meet,
But the pleasure remains, though the pang is as brief
As the touch and recoil of the sensitive leaf.

There's a thrill of distress, between anger and dread,
When a frown o'er the fair face of beauty is spread ;
But she smiles—and away the disturber, is borne,
Like sunbeams dispelling the vapours of morn.

There's a thrill of endearment, all raptures above,
When the pure lip imprints the first fond kiss of love !
Which, like songs of our childhood, to memory clings ;
The longest, the last, of terrestrial things.

E. CONOLLY.

## SCOTLAND'S GUID AULD CHANNEL STANE.[1]

AIR—"*Highland Harry.*"

OF a' the games that e'er I saw,
　Man, callant, laddie, birkie, wean,
The bravest far aboon them a',
　Was aye the witching Channel Stane !

O for the Channel Stane !
The fell gude game, the Channel Stane !
There's no a game amang them a',
Can match auld Scotand's Channel Stane !

I've played at quoiting i' my day,
　And maybe I may do't again,
But still unto mysel' I'd say,
　O this is no the Channel Stane !
　　　　O for, etc.

I've been at bridals unca glad ;
　In courting lassies wondrous fain ;
But what was a' the fun I've had,
　Comparit wi' the Channel Stane !
　　　　O for, etc.

[1] Another name for the Curling Stone.

Were I a sprite in yonder sky,
   Never to come back again,
I'd sweep the mune an' starlits by,
   And beat them at the Channel Stane.
        O for, etc.

We'd boom across the Milky Way,
   One tee should be the Northern Wain,
Another bright Orion's ray,
   A comet for a Channel Stane!
        O for, etc.

*James Mogg*

## THE POETS, WHAT FOOLS THEY'RE TO DEAVE US.

AIR—"*Fy, let us a' to the Bridal.*"

THE poets, what fools they're to deave us,
   How ilka ane's lassie's sae fine;
The first ane's an angel, and, save us!
   The neist ane you meet wi's divine;
An' then there's a lang-nebbit sonnet,
   Be't Katie, or Janet, or Jean;
An' the moon or some far awa' planet 's
   Compared to the blink o' her een.

The earth an' the sea they've ransackit
   For figures to set aff their charms,
An' no a wee flower but's attackit
   By poets, like bumbees in swarms.
What signifies now a' this clatter
   By chiels that the truth winna tell?
Wad it no be settlin' the matter
   To say—Lass, ye're just like yoursel'?

An' then there's nae end to the evil,
    For they are no deaf to the din,
That, like me, ony puir luckless deevil
    Daur scarce look the gate they are in !
But e'en let them be wi' their scornin',
    There's a lassie whase name I could tell,
Her smile is as sweet as the mornin',
    But whisht !. I am ravin' mysel'.

But he that o' ravin' 's convickit,
    When a bonnie sweet lass he thinks on,
May he ne'er get anither strait jacket
    Than that buckled on by Mess John !
An' he wha, though cautious an' canny,
    The charms o' the fair never saw,
Though wise as king SOLOMON's grannie,
    I swear is the daftest of a'.

*Rob Gilfillan*

## THE LOSS OF THE ROEBUCK.

How oft by the lamp of the pale waning moon,
Would Kitty steal out from the eye of the town ;
On the beach as she stood, when the wild waves would roll,
Her eye shed a torrent just fresh from the soul ;
And, as o'er the ocean the billows would stray,
Her sighs follow after as moaning as they.

I saw, as the ship to the harbour drew near,
Hope redden her cheek, then it blanch'd with chill fear ;

She wished to inquire of the whispering crew,
If they'd spoke with the Roebuck, or ought of her knew;
For long in conjecture her fate had been tost,
Nor knew we for certain the Roebuck was lost.

I pitied her feelings, and saw what she'd ask,
(For Innocence ever looks through a thin mask),
I stepp'd to Jack Oakum, his sad head he shook,
And cast on sweet Kitty a side-glancing look :
" The Roebuck has founder'd—the crew are no more—
Nor again shall Jack Bowling be welcom'd on shore !"

Sweet Kitty, suspecting, laid hold of my arm :
" O tell me," she cried, " for my soul's in alarm;
Is she lost ?"   I said nothing ; while Jack gave a sigh,
Then down dropp'd the curtain that hung o'er her eye ;
Fleeting life, for a moment, seem'd willing to stay,
Just flutter'd, and then fled for ever away.

So droops the pale lily, surcharg'd with the shower,
Sunk down as with sorrow, so dies the sweet flower ;
No sunbeam returning, nor spring ever gay,
Can give back the soft breath once wafted away ;
The eye-star when set, never rises again,
Nor pilots one vessel more over the main !<sup>1</sup>

*S. Blamire*

<sup>1</sup> From a volume of Poems and Songs by Miss Susanna Blamire,
with a Memoir and some account of her writings, by Mr. Patrick
Maxwell, Edinburgh.   Miss Blamire was a native of Cumberland ;
she was born at Thackwood, in the parish of Sowerby, in 1747, and
died in Carlisle in 1795.   She has long been favourably known as
the author of "What ails this heart o' mine," "The Nabob's
Return," "The Chelsea Pensioners," and lately has been proved

## MATTHEW M'FARLANE.

### THE KILBARCHAN RECRUIT.

*Air—" Kenmure's on an' awa' " etc.*

WHARE cam' the guineas frae, Matthew, my dear?
I trow thou had nane till the sodgers cam' here;
If they be the king's, or the sergeant's, my son,
Gi'e them back, for thou never maun carry the gun.

Could thou e'er think to gang o'er the braid sea,
To lea'e the loan-head, the auld bigging, and me;
The smith and the smiddy, thy loom, and the lass
That stands at the gavle and laughs when ye pass?

Mind, Matthew! for thou likes thy belly fu' weel,
There is naething abroad like our hearty aitmeal,
Nor guid sheep-head-kail, for nae outlandish woman
Has the gumption to ken that they need sic a scummin'.

In thy lug tho' that wild Highland sergeant may blaw,
And talk o' the ferlies he's seen far awa',
And the pleasures and ease o' a sodgering life,
Believe me, it's naething but labour and strife!

If thy fit should but slip in the midst o' the drilling,
The ranking and rawing, and marching and wheeling,
The sergeant would cry, " Shoot the stammering loon!"
  or else,
" Tie the scoonerel up to the halberds, ye scoonerels!"

And when our king George to the wars wad be prancing,
Wi' the crown on his head, and his sceptre a' glancing,
Wi' chariots, and horsemen, and cornels, a host o' them,
And Sergeant M'Tavish as proud as the best o' them;

to have written that exquisite Scottish lyric, "An' ye shall walk in silk attire." Her songs amount to between thirty and forty, many of them of surpassing beauty; and her poems bear the impress of a highly gifted poetical mind.

My son, and the rest o' the puir single men would be
Trudging behint them wi' their legs twining wearily :
Laden like camels, and cringing like colly dogs,
Till the Frenchman in swarms wad come bizzin' about
   their lugs.

Then to meet Bonaparté rampaging and red
To the verra e'en holes wi' the spilling o' bluid !
O, maybe the fiend in his talons wad claught thee !
And rive thee to sprawls without speering whase aught
   thee !

Thou maunna wear claes o' red, Matthew M'Farlane !
Nor ringe wi' twa sticks on a sheep's-skin my darlin' !
Nor cadge wi' a knapsack frae Dan to Beersheba, nor
Dee like thy father at wearifu' Baltimore !

Bide still in Kilbarchan ! and wha kens but thou
May be some day an elder, and keep a bit cow,
And ha'e for thy wife the braw throughither lass
That stands at the gavle and laughs when ye pass.

But if thou man sodger, and vex thy puir mither,
It's ae comfort to me, should I ne'er ha'e anither,
Whaever may shoot thee, their prey when they mak' o'
   thee,
Will e'en get a gude linen sark on the back o' thee.

WM. CROSS.

## THE CURLERS' GARLAND.

CURLERS, gae hame to your spades, or your ploughs,
   To your beuks, to your planes, or your thummills ;
Curlers, gae hame, or the ice ye'll fa' thro';
   Hame, swith ! to your elshins, or wummills.

The curlin's ower, for the thow is come ;
   On Mistilaw the snaw is meltin',

His hetherie haffets kythe black in the win',
   And the rain has begun a peltin'.

A lang fareweel to greens and beef,
   To yill, to whisky, and bakes :
Fu' o' cracks is the ice, but we'll smuir our dule
   By gorblin' up parritch and cakes.

We'll nae mair think o' the slithery rink,
   Nor the merry soun' " Tee high,"
Nor " Inwick here," nor " Break an egg there,"
   Nor " He's far ower stark, soop him bye."

We maunna think o' the slithery rink,
   Nor of hurras a volley ;
The ice is dauchie, nae fun can we get,
   For ilka stane lies a collie ;

Nor roar " Besoms up, he's a capital shot ;"
   " Now Jock, lie here, I say ;"
" He's weel laid on, soop him up, soop him up ;"
   " Now guard him, and won is the day."

But we trow when winter comes again,
   Wi' a' its frosts an' snaws,
We'll on the ice ance mair forgether,
   Before life's gloamin' close.

—Curlers, gae hame to your spades or your ploughs,
   To your pens, to your spules, or your thummills ;
Curlers, gae hame, or the ice ye'll fa' through—
   Tak' your ellwands, your elshins, or wummills.

When writing these verses the author had in his eye Castlesemple
Loch in Renfrewshire, a famous place for curling. Mistilaw is a conspicuous hill in the neighbourhood.

## HALKERTON'S CALF.

Tune—"*The Corby and Pyet.*"

An ill-deedy limmer is Halkerton's cow,
An' ower mony marrows has Halkerton's cow ;
But the auldest greybeard sin' he kent a pickstaff,
Ne'er heard o' a marrow to Halkerton's calf.
                    Ne'er heard, etc.


Whan the kailyard is out o' its best cabbage stock,
An' the hairst-rig is short o' a thrave or a stouk,
An' the stack has been eased o' the canny drawn sheaf,
The mark o' the cloven foot tells o' the thief.
                    The mark, etc.


He's doure i' the uptack, the deil canna teach,
This wonderfu' calf has the rare gift o' speech ;
Has scripture by heart, as the gowk has its lied,
An' fechts wi' his tongue for a kirk an' a creed.
                    An' fechts, etc.


At alehouse an' smiddy he rairs an' he cracks,
'Bout doctrines, an' duties, an' statutes, and acts ;
At blythemeat, an' dredgy, yulefeast, an' infare,
He's ready aff-hand wi' a grace or a prayer.
                    He's ready, etc.

*Alex Laing*

## WHEN AUTUMN HAS LAID HER SICKLE BY.

*Music by P. M'Leod, Esq.*

WHEN Autumn has laid her sickle by,
And the stacks are theekit to haud them dry;
And the sapless leaves come down frae the trees,
And dance about in the fitfu' breeze;
And the robin again sits burd-alane,
And sings his sang on the auld peat stane,
When come is the hour of gloamin' grey,
Oh! sweet is to me the minstrel's lay.

When Winter is driving his cloud on the gale,
And spairgin' about his snaw and his hail,
And the door is steekit against the blast,
And the winnocks wi' wedges are firm and fast,
And the ribs are rypet, the cannel alight,
And the fire on the hearth is bleezin' bright,
And the bicker is reamin' wi' pithy brown ale;
Oh! dear is to me a sang or a tale!

Then I tove awa' by the ingle-side,
And tell o' the blasts I was wont to bide,
When the nights were lang, and the sea ran high,
And the moon hid her face in the depths of the sky,
And the mast was strained, and the canvas rent,
By some demon on message of mischief sent;
O! I bliss my stars that at hame I can bide,
For dear, dear to me is my ain ingle-side!

*Charles Gray.*

## THE SOCIAL CUP.

AIR—"*Andro and his cutty gun.*"

BLYTHE, blythe, and merry are we,
   Blythe are we, ane and a';
Aften hae we cantie been,
   But sic a nicht we never saw!

The gloamin' saw us a' sit down,
   And meikle mirth has been our fa';
Then let the sang and toast gae roun'
   'Till chanticleer begins to craw!
Blythe, blythe, and merry are we,
   Pick and wale o' merry men;
What care we tho' the cock may craw,
   We're masters o' the tappit-hen!

The auld kirk bell has chappit twal,
   Wha cares tho' she had chappit twa!
We're licht o' heart and winna part,
   Tho' time and tide may rin awa'!
Blythe, blythe, and merry are we,
   Hearts that care can never ding;
Then let time pass—we'll steal his glass,
   And pu' a feather frae his wing!

Now is the witchin' time o' nicht,
   When ghaists, they say, are to be seen;
And fays dance to the glow-worm's licht
   Wi' fairies in their gowns of green.
Blythe, blythe, and merry are we,
   Ghaists may tak' their midnight stroll,
Witches ride on brooms astride,
   While we sit by the witchin' bowl!

Tut! never speir how wears the morn,
   The moon's still blinkin' i' the sky,
And, gif like her we fill our horn,
   I dinna doubt we'll drink it dry!

Blythe, blythe, and merry are we,
  Blythe, out-ower the barley bree ;
And let me tell, the moon hersel'
  Aft dips her toom horn i' the sea.

Then fill us up a social cup,
  And never mind the dapple dawn ;
Just sit a while, the sun may smile
  And licht us a' across the lawn !
Blythe, blythe, and merry are we ;
  See ! the sun is keekin' ben ;
Gie Time his glass—for months may pass
  Ere we hae sic a nicht again !

*Charles Gray.*

## SIMMER DAYS ARE COME AGAIN.

AIR—"*Cameron's got his wife again.*"

THE simmer days are come again,
The rosy simmer's come again,
The sun blinks blythe on hill and plain,
The simmer days are come again.

A gowany mantle cleeds the green,
The blossom on the tree is seen,
And Willie saw a bat yestreen ;
I'm sure the simmer's come again.
            The simmer days, etc.

The hazle bushes bend nae mair
Beneath the lades that crushed them sair,
And Tweed rows past her waters fair,
The cheerfu' simmer's come again.
            The simmer days, etc.

The glens are green that looked sae ill,
The blast that shored our lambs to kill,
The wind has gliff'd it ower the hill,
And gladsome simmer's come again.
          The simmer days, etc.

Ye little birdies, ane and a',
Aloud your tunefu' whistles blaw ;
The wind's gane round, and fled's the snaw,
And lightsome simmer's come again.
          The simmer days, etc.

Now, simmer, ye maun use us weel,
Wi' shower and sunblink at its heel ;
We're unco glad ye're come, atweel,
Ye're doubly welcome back again.
       Then welcome simmer back again, etc.

For Spring, ye see, ne'er minds us now,
To nurse the lambs, or tend the plough.
There's nane to tak' our pairt but you,
And wow ! we're glad ye're back again !
    Then welcome simmer back again,
    Rosy simmer back again,
    The wuds sall ring wi' mony a strain,
    To welcome simmer back again.

*James Murray*

## MOULDYBRUGH.

I KENT a wee toon, and a queer toon it was,
 Auld Mouldybrugh, that was its name ;
A dreary dull village, wi' battered grey wa's,
 Where onything new never came ;
Just twa or three houses, a' dismal and black,
 And twa or three shoppies sae sma' ;
A market, where whiles the folk gathered to crack,
 And drive a bit bargain or twa.

Besides an auld jail, wi' the court-house hard by,
 A cross, and a mossy stane well ;
A kirk and a steeple, that dinlit the sky
 Wi' a clinkin' auld timmer-tongued bell.
While the brown battered tower on the hoary hill tap,
 That frowned ower the silly auld toon,
Tald o' its auld pith, for a bold baron chap
 Had biggit it ne'er to come doun.

The hills lay in silence behind the auld toon,
 A bleak heathery moor lay before ;
There we sported oursels in the days that are flown,
 And dearly we loved the grey moor.
Ah ! thou wert an Eden—yea, truly a land
 Of milk and of honey to me ;
Where we herded the kye, a happy young band,
 And harried the bike of the bee.

So quiet was the toon, and so douce were the folk,
 They lived in a kind o' a dream ;
But at last they were roused wi' a desperate shock,
 By that vapourin' article steam.
For wha wad hae thocht it ?   A railway was made
 Across the lang heather sae dreary ;
The canny auld toonsfolks grew perfectly wud,
 An' a' thing was turned tapsalteery.

Auld Mouldybrugh fairly was rowed aff its feet,
   And naething gat leave to stand still ;
They pulled doun the houses, and widened the street,
   And biggit a muckle brick mill.
And droves o' new comers, that naebody kent,
   Were workin', they kentna at what ;
The bodies were just in a perfect ferment,
   And didna ken what to be at.

Sic smashin' and chappin' was a' round about,
   Sic clankin', sic rattlin', an' din ;
Wi' rocks blaun like thunder frae quarries without,
   And smiddies an' reeshlin' within ;
And wheelbarrows drivin' a' hours of the day,
   Wi' Eerishmen swearin' like Turks ;
And horses were fechtin' wi' cartfu's o' clay,
   And plaister and stanes for the works.

Soon a' kinds o' traders cam' flockin' in shoals,
   The railway brocht wonders to pass ;
Colliers cam howkin' to sair us wi' coals,
   And gas-bodies cam' to make gas ;
And butchers sae greasy, wi' sheep, beef, and pigs,
   And schoolmasters cam' for the teachin' ;
And doctors wi' doses, and barbers wi' wigs,
   And kirks were ereckit for preachin'.

But dearer to me is the auld biggit toon,
   Wi' its cottages hoary and grey,
Where naething is altered, and naething dung doon,
   Except by the hand of decay.
And O ! for the bodies sae simple and plain,
   Aye faithfu', and kindly, and true ;
And O ! for the days that we'll ne'er see again,
   When they dreamt na of onything new !

                            B. II.

## THE PRIDEFU' TAID.

Air—"*Nancy's to the greenwood gane.*"

Wow me! for sic a pridefu' taid
    Our Tibbie's grown, the hizzie ;
She cuts sic capers wi' her head,
    'Twad ding a bodie dizzie.
D'ye think it's her braw clouts o' claes
    That mak's her look sae saucy ?
Her bannet's but a bunch o' straes,
    Does she ken that ? vain lassie !

A cauldrife silken tippet's neist
    Aboon her shoulders wavin' ;
A lang white ribbon, round her waist,
    Hangs like a crookit shavin' !
What tho' her slender sides shine braw
    Wi' dashin' duds o' muslin,
Her share o' mither wit's but sma',
    As yon new cleckit goslin'.

On Sunday, see her trip to kirk
    Wi' rhymin' Rab, auld Nan's son ;
Neist day, she's aff wi' this gay spark,
    To some grand ball o' dancin'.
Sae Tibbie means to let her life
    Dance down the paths o' pleasure,
An' thinks, nae doubt, soon for his wife,
    The chield will gladly seize her.

But thoughtless Tib, my bonnie doo,
    I'm fley'd ye'll be mistaken ;
For promise never yet prov'd true
    Frae chiels wha gang a rakin'.

The days o' peace your breast now feels,
  Will change to months o' mournin';
Frae ane wha kens sic flighty chiels,
  Dear Tibbie, tak' a warnin'!

*Robt Carmichael*

## THE HAPPY PAIR.

AIR—"*Johnnie M'Gill.*"

Low down in a valley fu' snugly and braw,
  There liv'd a blythe bodie o' saxty an' twa;
Nae wranglin' to deave him, nor sorrow to grieve him,
  He aye was contented an' happy wi' a'.

On his ain snug bit craftie, delighted fu' aft he
  Belabour'd frae mornin' to e'enin' awa';
Sae cheery an' dainty, he sang like a lintie,
  Till gloamin', when darkness began for to fa'.

For Bessie his wifie, to comfort his life aye,
  Wad cleed him fu' cozie, in time o' the snaw;
And tho' she was fifty, sae tidy and thrifty,
  She aye made her hallan to shine like a ha'.

Near han' was a weddin', the bodies war bidden,
  An' there they were buskit, fu' cleanly and braw;
But fu' o' rejoicin' they thocht na o' risin',
  Until that the daylight began for to daw.

Their auld favourite doggie, a wee sleekit rogie,
  Had toddled ahint them, when they gaed awa',
For aye he was timefu' to get a gude wamefu',
  Altho' that he hadna ae tusk in his jaw.

Sae strong was the whisky, the carlie grew frisky,
  For seldom he'd toom'd sic a drap in his maw;

But while he was cheerfu', his Bessie was fearfu'
  That ony mishanter her Johnnie should fa'.

The drinkin' o' toddy, it made the auld bodie ·
  The white o' his e'en, like the parson, to shaw;
Wi' arms high uplifted, he roar'd an' he rifted,
  "I'm up in the happy place—Bess, come awa'!"

## FAREWELL TO SCOTIA.

FAREWEEL to ilk hill whaur the red heather grows,
To ilk bonnie green glen whaur the mountain stream rows,
To the rock that re-echoes the torrent's wild din,
To the graves o' my sires, and the hearths o' my kin.

Fareweel to ilk strath an' the lav'rock's sweet sang,
For trifles grow dear whan we've kenn'd them sae lang;
Round the wanderer's heart a bright halo they shed,
A dream o' the past, whan a' others hae fled.

The young hearts may kythe, tho' they're forced far away,
But its dool to the spirit whan haffets are grey;
The saplin' transplanted may flourish a tree
Whaur the hardy auld aik wad but wither and dee.

They tell me I gang whaur the tropic suns shine
Ower landscapes as lovely and fragrant as thine;
For the objects sae dear that the heart had entwined,
Turn eerisome hame-thoughts, and sicken the mind.

No, my spirit shall stray whaur the red heather grows!
In the bonnie green glen whaur the mountain stream rows;

'Neath the rock that re-echoes the torrent's wild din,
'Mang the graves o' my sires, round the hearths o' my kin.

*M. A. Foster*

## THE WIDOW MALONE.[1]

DID ye hear of the Widow Malone,
                    Ohone !
Who lived in the town of Athlone
                    Alone ?
Oh ! she melted the hearts
Of the swains in them parts,
So lovely the Widow Malone,
                    Ohone !
So lovely the Widow Malone.

Of lovers she had a full score,
                    Or more ;
And fortunes they all had galore
                    In store ;
From the minister down
To the clerk of the crown,
All were courting the Widow Malone,
                    Ohone !
All were courting the Widow Malone.

But so modest was Mrs. Malone,
                    'Twas known
No one ever could see her alone,
                    Ohone !
Let them ogle and sigh,
They could ne'er catch her eye,

[1] We acknowledge most gratefully our obligations to the Publishers of " CHARLES O'MALLEY, the Irish Dragoon," for permission to extract from that work this most exquisite Irish ballad, by Dr. Charles Lever, the author.

So bashful the Widow Malone,
　　　　　Ohone ;
So bashful the Widow Malone.

'Till one Mister O'Brien from Clare,
　　　　　How quare !
It's little for blushing they care
　　　　　Down there,
Put his arm round her waist,
Gave ten kisses at laste,
" Oh !" says he, " you're my Molly Malone,
　　　　　My own ;
" Oh !" says he, " you're my Molly Malone."

And the Widow they all thought so shy,
　　　　　My eye !
Ne'er thought of a simper or sigh,
　　　　　For why ?
But " Lucius," says she,
" Since you've made now so free,
You may marry your Mary Malone,
　　　　　Ohone !
You may marry your Mary Malone."

There's a moral contained in my song,
　　　　　Not wrong ;
And one comfort it's not very long,
　　　　　But strong :
If for widows you die,
Larn to *kiss, not* to *sigh ;*
For they're all like sweet Mistress Malone,
　　　　　Ohone !
Oh ! they're all like sweet Mistress Malone.

## RANDY NANNY.

I SING ye o' a wife
  Wha carried a' our water ;
Cause o' muckle strife
  Was her clashin' clatter.
Ilka wee bit fau't
  A' the warld kenned o't ;
Gin ye gat ye're mau't,
  Ye ne'er heard the end o't.
    Aye clashin', clashin',
      Nanny was nae canny ;
    Wives plashin', washin',
      Matched nae Water Nanny.

Nanny had a man,
  A drunken market caddy ;
Connaught cocked-nose Dan,
  A swearin', tearin' Paddy.
Sic a knuckled han',
  Sic an arm o' vigour ;
Nan might scold an' ban,
  But brawly could he swigg her.
    Aye smashin', smashin',
      Danny was nae canny ;
    Few could stand a thrashin'
      Frae stieve-fisted Danny.

They lived up a stair
  Down in the Laigh Calton ;
Siccan shines were there,
  Siccan noisy peltin' ;
Danny with his rung
  Steekin' ilka wizen ;
Nanny wi' her tongue,
  Nineteen to the dizen.

Aye clashin', crashin',
  Trouth it was nae canny ;
Ony fashin', fashin',
  Danny and his Nanny.

Bodies round about
  Couldna thole nor bide them ;
Fairly flitted out,
  Nane were left beside them ;
Their bink was a' their ain,
  Nane could meddle wi' them,—
Neighbour lairds were fain
  A' the land to lea' them.
    Some gae hashin', smashin',
      Makin' siller canny,
    Wha gat rich by clashin' ?
      Danny an' his Nanny.

They'd a bonnie lassie,
  Tonguey as her mither ;
Yet as game and gaucie
  As her fightin' faither.
O ! her waist was sma',
  O ! her cheeks were rosy,
Wi' a shower o' snaw,
  Flaiket ower her bozy.
    Sun rays brightly flashin'
      Ower the waters bonny,
    Glanced nae like the lashin',
      Sparklin' een o' Anny.

Sight ye never saw,
  Like the Laird and Leddy,
Wi' their dochter braw,
  An' themselves sae tidy ;
Wi' their armies crost,
  On their ain stair muntit ;
Gin ye daured to hoast,
  How their pipies luntit.

Wooers e'er sae dashin',
  Durst nae ca' on Anny,
Dauntit wi' the clashin'
  O' her mither Nanny.

Beauty blooming fair
  Aye sets hearts a bleezing;
Lovers' wits are rare,
  Lovers' tongues are wheezing.
Barred out at the door,
  A slee loon scaled the skylight,
An' drappit on the floor,
  Afore the auld folks' eyesight.
    In a flaming passion,
      Maul'd by faither Danny,
    Aff to lead the fashion,
      Scamper'd bonny Anny.

*James Ballantine*

## MARY MACNEIL.

AIR—"*Mrs. Kinloch of Kinloch.*"

THE last gleam o' sunset in ocean was sinkin',
  Ower mountain an' meadowland glintin' fareweel;
An' thousands o' stars in the heavens were blinkin',
  As bright as the een o' sweet Mary Macneil.
A' glowin' wi' gladness she lean'd on her lover,
  Her een tellin' secrets she thought to conceal;
And fondly they wander'd whaur nane might discover
  The tryst o' young Ronald an' Mary Macneil.

O! Mary was modest, an' pure as the lily
  That dew-draps o' mornin' in fragrance reveal;
Nae fresh bloomin' flow'ret in hill or in valley
  Could rival the beauty of Mary Macneil.

She mov'd, and the graces play'd sportive around her,
    She smil'd, and the hearts o' the cauldest wad thrill ;
She sang, an' the mavis cam' listenin' in wonder,
    To claim a sweet sister in Mary Macneil.

But ae bitter blast on its fair promise blawin',
    Frae spring a' its beauty an' blossoms will steal ;
An' ae sudden blight on the gentle heart fa'in',
    Inflicts the deep wound naething earthly can heal.
The simmer saw Ronald on glory's path hiein'—
    The autumn, his corse on the red battle-fiel' ;
The winter, the maiden found heart-broken, dyin' ;
    An' spring spread the green turf ower Mary Macneil !
                    E. CONOLLY.


## WE SAT BENEATH THE TRYSTIN' TREE.

WE sat beneath the trystin' tree,'
    The bonnie dear auld trystin' tree,
Whaur Harry tauld in early youth,
    His tender tale o' love to me ;
An' walth o' wedded happiness
    Has been our blessed lot sinsyne,
Tho' foreign lands, lang twenty years,
    Hae been my Harry's hame an' mine.
Wi' gratfu' glow at ilka heart,
    An' joyfu' tears in ilka e'e,
We sat again, fond lovers still,
    Beneath the bonnie trystin' tree.

We gaz'd upon the trystin' tree,
    Its branches spreading far an' wide,
An' thocht upon the bonnie bairns
    That bless'd our blythe bit ingle-side ;
The strappin' youth wi' martial mien,
    The maiden mild wi' gowden hair,
They pictur'd what oursels had been,
    Whan first we fondly trysted there ;

Wi' gratfu' glow at ilka heart,
　　An' joyfu' tears in ilka e'e,
We blest the hour that e'er we met
　　Beneath the dear auld trystin' tree !

E. CONOLLY.


## THE MIDNIGHT WIND.

MOURNFULLY ! oh, mournfully
　　This midnight wind doth sigh,
Like some sweet plaintive melody
　　Of ages long gone by :
It speaks a tale of other years—
　　Of hopes that bloomed to die—
Of sunny smiles that set in tears,
　　And loves that mouldering lie !

Mournfully ! oh, mournfully
　　This midnight wind doth moan ;
It stirs some chord of memory
　　In each dull heavy tone :
The voices of the much-loved dead
　　Seem floating thereupon—
All, all my fond heart cherishèd
　　Ere death had made it lone.

Mournfully ! oh, mournfully
　　This midnight wind doth swell,
With its quaint pensive minstrelsy,
　　Hope's passionate farewell
To the dreamy joys of early years,
　　Ere yet grief's canker fell
On the heart's bloom—ay ! well may tears
　　Start at that parting knell !

*William Motherwell*

## THOU KNOW'ST IT NOT, LOVE.

THOU know'st it not, love, when light looks are around
 thee,
 When Music awakens its liveliest tone,
When Pleasure, in chains of enchantment, hath bound
 thee,
 Thou knowest not how truly this heart is thine own.
It is not while all are about thee in gladness,
 While shining in light from thy young spirit's shrine,
But in moments devoted to silence and sadness,
 That thou'lt e'er know the value of feelings like mine.

Should grief touch thy cheek, or misfortune o'ertake thee,
 How soon would thy mates of the summer away!
They first of the whole fickle flock to forsake thee,
 Who flatter'd thee most when thy bosom was gay.
What though I seem cold while their incense is burning,
 In depths of my soul I have cherish'd a flame,
To cheer the loved one, should the night-time of mourning,
 E'er send its far shadows to darken her name.

Then leave the vain crowd,—though my cottage is lonely,
 Gay halls, without hearts, are far lonelier still;
And say thou'lt be mine, Mary, always and only,
 And I'll be thy shelter, whate'er be thine ill.
As the fond mother clings to her fair little blossom,
 The closer, when blight hath appeared on its bloom,
So thou, love, the dearer shalt be to this bosom,
 The deeper thy sorrow, the darker thy doom.

*Will. Kennedy*

## MY AULD UNCLE JOHN.

I SING not of prince, nor of prelate, nor peer,
Who the titles and trappings of vanity wear;
I sing of no hero whose fame has been spread
O'er the earth, for the quantum of BLOOD he hath shed;
But of one, who life's path with humility trod,
The friend of mankind, and at peace with his God;
Who indeed died to " Fame and to Fortune unknown,"
But who lives in my heart's core—my auld Uncle John.

His manners were simple, yet manly and firm—
IIis friendship was generous, and constant, and warm;
To Jew and to Gentile alike he was kind,
For the trammels of party ne'er narrow'd his mind:
IIis heart, like his haun', was aye open and free,
And tho' he at times had but little to gie,
Yet even that little with grace was bestow'n,
For it cam' frae the heart o' my auld Uncle John.

O weel do I mind, tho' I then was but young,
When he cam' on a visit, how blythely I sprung
To meet the auld man, who with visage so meek
Would a kiss of affection imprint on my cheek;
Then I'd place him his chair—take his staff, and his hat—
Then climb up on his knee, whaur delighted I sat;
For never was monarch sae proud on his throne,
As I on the KNEE o' my auld Uncle John.

When at school, to his snug room with pleasure I'd hie,
And often I've seen the fire flash from his eye—
And a flush o' delight his pale cheek overspread,
When a passage from Shakspeare or Milton I read. .
For me the best authors he'd kindly select,
He then to their beauties my eye would direct,
Or the faults to which sometimes great genius is prone—
So correct was the taste o' my auld Uncle John.

'Twas said, when a stripling, his feelings had been
Storm-blighted and rent by a false-hearted quean ;
But this sour'd not his temper, for maidens would bloom
More brightly and fresh, when among them he'd come.
They would cluster around him, like flow'rs round the oak,
To weep at his love-tale, or laugh at his joke ;
For his stories were told in a style and a tone
That aye put them in raptures wi' auld Uncle John.

To all he was pleasing—to auld and to young—
To the rich and the poor, to the weak and the strong ;
He laugh'd with the gay—moralis'd with the grave—
The wise man he honour'd—the fool he forgave.
Religion with him was no transient qualm,
'Twas not hearing a sermon, or singing a psalm,
Or a holiday-robe for a season put on,
'Twas the everyday garb o' my auld Uncle John.

His country he lov'd, for her glory he sigh'd,
Her struggles of yore for her rights were his pride ;
He lov'd her clear streams, and her green flow'ry fells—
Her mists and her mountains, her dens and her dells.
Yes, the land of his fathers—his birth-place he lov'd !
Her science, her wit, and her worth he approv'd ;
But men of each kindred, and colour, and zone,
As brethren were held by my auld Uncle John.

His last sickness I tended ; and when he was dead,
To the grave, in deep sorrow, I carried his head ;
The spot is not mark'd by inscription or bust—
No child nor lone widow weeps over his dust ;
But oft when the star of eve brightly doth burn,
From the bustle and noise of this world I turn ;
And forget, for a while, both its smile and its frown,
O'er the green turf which covers my auld Uncle John.

*Wm Finlay*

## THOUGH BACCHUS MAY BOAST.[1]

THOUGH Bacchus may boast of his care-killing bowl,
　And folly in thought-drowning revels delight,
Such worship, alas ! has no charms for the soul,
　When softer devotions the senses invite.
To the arrow of fate, or the canker of care,
　His potions oblivious a balm may bestow ;
But to fancy that feeds on the charms of the fair,
　The death of reflection's the birth of all woe !

What soul that's possessed of a dream so divine
　With riot would bid the sweet vision be gone ?
For the tear that bedews sensibility's shrine
　Is a drop of more worth than all Bacchus's ton !
The tender excess which enamours the heart,
　To few is imparted—to millions denied ;
The finer the feelings, the keener the smart,'
　And fools jest at that for which sages have died.

Each change and excess has through life been my doom,
　And well can I speak of its joy and its strife ;
The bottle affords us a glimpse through the gloom,
　But love's the true sunshine that gladdens our life !
Then come, rosy Venus, and spread o'er my sight
　The magic illusions which ravish the soul,
Awake in my heart the soft dream of delight,
　And drop from thy myrtle one leaf in my bowl ?

Then deep will I drink of the nectar divine,
　Nor soon, jolly god, from thy banquet remove ;
Each throb of my heart shall accord with the wine
　That's mellow'd by friendship and sweeten'd by love !

---

[1] This song has been several times in print, but not with Miss
Blamire's name appended, nor with the last stanza.　We give it
from the original MS. in the hands of Mr. Maxwell.

And now, my gay comrades, the myrtle and vine
  Shall united their blessings the choicest impart ;
Let reason, not riot, the garland entwine—
  The result must be pleasure and peace to the heart.

*S. Blamire*

## THE WARY CHIEL.

THEY wad gi'e me a wife yestreen,
  Without my will—against my will ;
They ettled wi' a winsome queen
  To trap a wary chiel like me.
Had I been a silly fool,
  Fast wad I been on the brier,
For free and pawky was the lass,
  And witnesses she had to swear.
Deep and cunning was their plan
  To beguile me—to beguile me ;
Guid be praised ! a single man
  I am yet, and aye will be.

It's no a joke to marry folk
  Wha want na wives—wha want na wives ;
There's mair nor me that canna dree
  The saftest tether a' their lives.
I heard them laugh when I ran aff
  An' left them a'—the bride an' a' :
But deil may care ; I well can spare
  To gie them mair than ae guffaw.
Let them laugh and let them jeer,
  I am easy—I am easy—
Never shall a woman wear
  Breeks o' mine, for a' their jaw.

I ance was ower the lugs in love,
  When daft and young—when daft and young,
But how I played the turtle-dove
  Shall ne'er be sung—shall ne'er be sung.
And though I'm safe, and draw my breath
  Wi' freedom now—wi' freedom now,
I fear I may some luckless day
  Still tine my precious liberty.
A' yestreen I dreamt some lass,
  Unco bonnie—sinfu' bonnie,
Stievely held me round the ha'se,
  And roughly kiss'd and towzled me.

                              GEORGE JAAP.


## AULD ELSPA'S SOLILOQUY.

THERE'S twa moons the nicht,
  Quoth the auld wife to hersel',
As she toddled hame fu' cantie,
  Wi' her stomach like a stell !

There's twa moons the nicht,
  An' watery do they glower,
As their wicks were burnin' darkly,
  An' the oil was rinin' ower !

An' they're aye spark, sparkin',
  As my ain auld cruizie did,
When it blinket by the ingle,
  When the rain drapt on its lid.

O ! but I'm unco late the nicht,
  An' on the cauld hearthstane
Puir Tammie will be croonin',
  Wae an' weary a' his lane.

An' the wee but spunk o' fire I left
  By this time's black and cauld,—

I'll ne'er stay out sae late again,
　For I'm growin' frail an' auld.

I never like to see twa moons,
　They speak o' storm and rain,
An' aye, as sure's neist morning comes,
　My auld head's rack'd wi' pain !

*Andrew Park*

## MY AULD BREEKS.

Air—"*The Cornclips.*"

My mither men't my auld breeks,
　An' wow ! but they were duddy,
And sent me to get Mally shod
　At Robin Tamson's smiddy ;
The smiddy stands beside the burn
　That wimples through the clachan,
I never yet gae by the door,
　But aye I fa' a laughin'.

For Robin was a walthy carle,
　An' had ae bonnie dochter,
Yet ne'er wad let her tak' a man,
　Tho' mony lads had sought her ;
But what think ye o' my exploit ?
　The time our mare was shoeing,
I slippit up beside the lass,
　And briskly fell a wooing.

An' aye she e'ed my auld breeks,
　The time that we sat crackin',
Quo' I, my lass, ne'er mind the *clouts*,
　I've new anes for the makin' ;

But gin ye'll just come hame wi' me,
   An' lea' the carle, your father,
Ye'se get my breeks to keep in trim,
   Mysel' an' a' thegither.

'Deed lad, quo' she, your offer's fair,
   I really think I'll tak' it,
Sae, gang awa', get out the mare,
   We'll baith slip on the back o't ;
For gin I wait my father's time,
   I'll wait till I be fifty ;
But na !—I'll marry in my prime,
   An' mak' a wife most thrifty.

Wow ! Robin was an angry man,
   At tynin' o' his dochter :
Thro' a' the kintra side he ran,
   An' far an' near he sought her ;
But when he cam' to our fire-end,
   An' fand us baith thegither,
Quo' I, gudeman, I've ta'en your bairn,
   An' ye may tak' my mither.

Auld Robin girn'd an' shook his pow,
   Guid sooth ! quo' he, you're merry,
But I'll just tak' ye at your word,
   An' end this hurry-burry ;
So Robin an' our auld wife
   Agreed to creep thegither ;
Now, I hae Robin Tamson's pet,
   An' Robin has my mither.

*Alexr Rodger*

## "THE DREAM OF LIFE'S YOUNG DAY."

ONCE more Eliza, let me look upon thy smiling face,
For there I with the "joy of grief" thy mother's
    feature's trace ;
Her sparkling eye, her winning smile, and sweet bewitch-
    ing air—
Her raven locks which clustering hung upon her bosom
    fair.

It is the same enchanting smile, and eye of joyous mirth,
Which beamed so bright with life and light in her who
    gave thee birth ;
And strongly do they bring to mind life's gladsome happy
    day,
When first I felt within my heart love's pulse begin to play.

My years were few—my heart was pure ; for vice and
    folly wore
A hideous and disgusting front, in those green days of
    yore.
Destructive dissipation then, with her deceitful train,
Had not, with their attractive glare, confus'd and turn'd
    my brain.

Ah ! well can I recall to mind how quick my heart would
    beat,
To see her in the house of prayer, so meekly take her
    seat ;
And when our voices mingled sweet in music's solemn
    strains,
My youthful blood tumultuously rush'd tingling through
    my veins.

It must have been of happiness a more than mortal dream,
It must have been of heavenly light a bright unbroken
    beam :

A draught of pure unmingl'd bliss ; for to my wither'd
heart
It doth, e'en now, a thrilling glow of ecstasy impart.

She now hath gone where sorrow's gloom the brow doth
never shade—
Where on the cheek the rosy bloom of youth doth never
fade ;
And I've been left to struggle here, till now my locks are
grey,
Yet still I love to think upon this " dream of life's young
day."

*Wm Finlay*

## "O CHARLIE IS MY DARLING."[1]

### (A NEW VERSION.)

*O Charlie is my darling,*
*My darling, my darling ;*
*O Charlie is my darling,*
*The young Chevalier.*

WHEN first his standard caught the eye,
His pibroch met the ear,
Our hearts were light, our hopes were high,
For the young Chevalier.

Then plaided chiefs cam' frae afar,
Wi' hearts without a fear ;
They nobly drew the sword for war,
An' the young Chevalier.

[1] This, and the songs that precede, are from a volume entitled
" Lays and Lyrics," lately issued at Edinburgh, by Capt. Charles
Gray, R.M.

But they wha trust to fortune's smile,
  Hae meikle cause to fear ;
She blinketh blythe but to beguile
  The young Chevalier.

O dark Culloden—fatal field
  Fell source o' mony a tear ;
There Albyn tint her sword and shield,
  And the young Chevalier.

Now Scotland's " flowers are wede away,"
  Her forest trees are sere ;
Her royal oak is gane for aye,
  The young Chevalier !

*Charles Gray.*

## THE GOSSIPS.

Air—"*Laird o' Cockpen.*"

Losh ! sit down, Mrs. Clavers, and bide ye a wee,
I'll put on the kettle and mask a drap tea ;
The gudeman's at the fair, 'twill be nicht or he's back,
Sae just sit ye down noo, and gie's a' your crack.
Ah ! woman, I'll tell ye what I heard yestreen,
Somebody was some way they shouldna hae been ;
It's no that I'm jalousin' ocht that is ill,
But we aye ken our ain ken, and sae we'll ken still.

'Twas just i' the gloamin' as our kimmer Nell,
Wi' her stoups and her girr, was gaun down to the well ;
She heard sic a rustle the bushes amang,
And syne sic a whistle sae clear, laigh, and lang ;
She thocht 'twas the kelpie come up frae the loch,
But she fand her mistak', and was thankfu' enouch ;

It's no that I'm jalousin' ocht that is ill,
But we aye ken our ain ken, and sae we'll ken still.

A shepherd-like chiel junket round by the dyke,
She kenn'd wha it was by the yamph o' his tyke;
Syne through the laird's winnock he just gied a keek,
And the door gied a jee, syne did cannily steek :
There she saw some ane, dress'd in a braw satin gown,
Gang oxterin' awa' wi' her faither's herd loon ;
It's no that I'm jalousin' ocht that is ill,
But we aye ken our ain ken, and sae we'll ken still.

His lang-nebbit words and his wonderfu' lare
Gar'd his honour the laird and the dominie stare ;
But, losh ! how they'll glow'r at the wisdom o' Jock,
When somebody lets the cat out o' the pock ;
My certes ! the leddy has surely gane gyte,
But if onything happens we'll ken wha to wyte ;
It's no that we're jalousin' ocht that is ill,
But we aye ken our ain ken, and sae we'll ken still.

*Alex. A. Ritchie*

## THE ADMONITION.

Oh ! that fouk wad weel consider,
What it is to tyne a name.—MACNIELL.

" HECH ! lasses, ye're lichtsome—it's braw to be
    young,"
Quo' the eldren gudewife, wi' her ailments sair dung ;
" Ye're thrang at your crack about maybees an' men—
Ye're thinkin', nae doubt, about hames o' your ain ;
An' why should ye no—I was ance young mysel',
An' sae weel's I've been married my neighbours can tell !

"In jokin' an' jamphin' there's nae ony crime,
Yet youth is a trying, a dangerous time;
Tho' now ye're as happy as happy can be,
Yet trouble may come i' the glint of an e'e.
When roses wad seem to be spread i' your path,
Ye may look for the briars to be lurking aneath;
But do weel and dree weel, there's nae meikle fear,
The lot's unco hard the leal heart canna bear.

"I've liv'd i' the warld baith maiden an' wife,
An' mony's the change I hae' seen i' my life—
Tho' some may na think it, it mak's na to me,
There's few for the better or likely to be.
When I was as young as the youngest o' you,
The men were mair faithfu', the women mair true;
There was na the folly an' ill-fashion'd ways,
Amang the young fouk that we see now-a-days.

"Yet, lasses, believe me, I'm happy wi' you,
Ye're thochtfu' an' prudent as mony, I trow;
Though like's an ill mark, it's a pleasure to me,
When I look to ithers, your conduct to see;
I canna say flichter'd an' foolish ye've been—
I canna say failin's an' fau'ts ye hae nane—
The best has them baith, as ye've aften heard tell,
They rade unco sicker that never ance fell.
Sae mind your ain weakness, be wary an' wise;
Let age an' experience your conduct advise;
And tho' it is said, youth an' eild never 'gree,
There's nae fear o' flytin' atween you an' me.

"It maybe there's some, tho' I'm sure, nane o' you,
Wad think wi' sic things I hae little to do—
Wad think that behaviour was naething to me,
Gin servants were tentie—were worth meat an' fee.
Wae's me! is there ony to think sae inclin'd,
They ken na the duties I've daily to mind;

While I ha'e the fremmit my hallan within—
My bannock to brack, an' my errand to rin ;
The present, the future, their gude an' their gain,
I'm bound to look ower as gin they were my ain ;
To see to their conduct afield an' at hame,
To be, as it were, like a mither to them !

　　" Ye mind the auld proverb, auld fouk were na blate—
' Misfortune's mair owing to folly than fate '—
Sae, lasses, for ance, ye maun lend me your ear,
Frae me an' my counsel ye've naething to fear.
Look weel to the ford ere ye try to wade thro',
It's just atween tyning an' winning wi' you ;
Ye've wooers about ye as mony's ye may—
Ye've hopes an' ye've wishes as a' women ha'e ;
Ye're young, and the lads, it wad seem, think ye fair ;
But sma's your experience, I rede ye—BEWARE.
A woman's gude name is a treasure—a mine,
But ance be imprudent, an' ance let it tyne,
Her lost reputation she canna regain—
*Tak' care* o' yoursel's, an' *beware* o' the men !"

*Alex Laing*

## MY AULD LUCKY DAD.

My auld lucky dad was a queer couthie carl,
　　He lo'ed a droll story, and cog o' guid yill ;
O' siller he gather'd a won'erfu' harl,
　　By the brisk eident clack o' his merry-gaun mill.

He wasna a chicken, tho' blythsome and vaunty,
　　For thrice thretty winters had whiten'd his pow ;
But the body was aye unco cheery and canty,
　　And his big moggin knot set my heart in a low.

At the close o' the day, when his labour was ended,
　He dandled me kindly fu' aft on his knee ;
Thro' childhood and danger me fed and defended,
　And lang was a gude lucky daddy to me.

But death cam' athort him, and sairly forfoughten,
　He hurkl'd down quietly—prepared for to dee ;
And left a' the bawbees he aye had a thocht on,
　The mill, and his lang-neckit moggin to me.

A cottar hard by had a bonnie young dochter,
　Sae winsome and winning, she made my heart fain ;
Her heart and her hand she gae when I socht her,
　Syne blushing, consented—she soon was my ain.

Noo, Maggy and I are baith cozy and happy,
　Wi' bairnies around us, in innocent glee ;
Sae I'll aye be joyfu', and tak' out my drappy,
　That I too an auld lucky daddy may die.

My neighbours they ca' me the little cot lairdie :
　Bless'd peace and contentment aye dwall round our
　　hearth,
And a clear siller burn wimpling thro' our bit yairdie,
　Alang wi' the flowers, mak' a heaven upon earth.

While the loud roaring winds thud against our het hallan,
　My wifie sits spinning, and lilts a bit sang ;
Nae trouble nor sorrow is kent in the dwallin'—
　Nae nicht in December to us seems ower lang.

And when hoary age crowns my pow, still contented,
　I'll lead the same life that my forbear had led,
That, when laid in the yird, I may lang be lamented
　By kind-hearted oys, as a guid lucky dad.

*D. S. Buchan*

## MY AIN JESSIE.

THE primrose loves the sunny brae,
To meet the kiss o' wanton May ;
The mavis loves green leafy tree,
An' there makes sweetest melodie ;
The lammie loves its mither's teats,
An' joyfu' by her side it bleats ;
For heather-bells the wild bee roves—
A' Nature's creatures hae their loves,
   An' surely I hae mine, Jessie.

Thou little kens, my bonnie lass !
Thou hast me brought to sic a pass ;
Thy e'e sae saftly dark an' bright,
Like early simmer's day an' night ;
Its mildness and its sunny blink
Hae charm'd me sae, I canna think
O' aught in earth, or sky, but thee,
An' life has but ae joy to me—
   That is in lovin' thee, Jessie.

Last Sunday, in your faither's *dais*,
I saw thy bloomin' May-morn face ;
An' as I aften staw a look,
I 'maist forgot the holy book ;
Nor reck't I what the preacher preach'd,
My thoughts, the while, were sae bewitch'd !
An' aye I thought when thy bright e'e
Wad turn wi' lovin' look to me,
   For a' my worship's there, Jessie.

But short time syne I held in scorn,
An' laugh'd at chiels whom love did burn ;
I said it is a silly thought
That on a bonnie face could doat !

But now the laugh is turn'd on me—
The truth o' love is in thine e'e ;
An' gin its light to me wad kythe,
I something mair wad be than blythe,—
      For in its smile is heaven, Jessie.

*John Struay*

## THE PANG O' LOVE.

*Set to Music by Mr. M'Leod.*

THE pang o' LOVE is ill to dree—
  Hech wow ! the biding o't—
'Twas like to prove the death o' me,
  I strove sae lang at hiding o't.

When first I saw the wicked thing,
  I wistna it meant ill to me :
I straiked its bonny head and wing,
  And took the bratchet on my knee ;
I kiss'd it ance, I kiss'd it twice,
  Sae kind was I in guiding o't,
When, whisk !—it shot me in a trice,
  And left me to the biding o't.

    An' hey me ! how me !
      Hech wow ! the biding o't !
    For ony ill I've had to dree
      Was naething to the biding o't.

The doctors pondered lang and sair,
  To rid me o' the stanging o't ;
And skeely wives a year and mair,
  They warstled hard at banging o't.

But doctors' drugs did fient a haet—
  Ilk wifie quat the guiding o't—
They turned, and left me to my fate,
  Wi' naething for't but biding o't.

    An' hey me! how me!
      Hech wow! the biding o't!
    For ony ill I've had to dree
      Was naething to the biding o't.

When freends had a' done what they dought,
  Right sair bumbazed my state to see,
A bonny lass some comfort brought—
  I'll mind her till the day I dee;
I tauld her a' my waefu' case,
  And how I'd stri'en at hiding o't,
And, blessings on her bonny face!
  She saved me frae the biding o't.

    An' hey me! how me!
      Hech wow! the biding o't!
    For a' the ills I've had to dree
      Were trifles to the biding o't.

*James Murray*

## THE LAST LAIRD O' THE AULD MINT.[1]

AULD Willie Nairn, the last Laird o' the Mint,
Had an auld farrant pow, an' auld farrant thoughts in't;

[1] The Old Mint of Scotland, in which this eccentric philanthropist and antiquarian resided, is situated in South Gray's Close, and forms one of the most remarkable curiosities to the visitor of the Scottish metropolis.

There ne'er was before sic a bodie in print,
As auld Willie Nairn, the last Laird o' the Mint :
   So list and ye'll find ye hae muckle to learn,
   An' ye'll still be but childer to auld Willie Nairn.

Auld Nanse, an auld maid, kept his house clean an' happy,
For the bodie was tidy, though fond o' a drappy ;
An' aye when the Laird charged the siller-taed cappy,
That on great occasions made caaers aye nappy.
   While the bicker gaed round, Nanny aye got a sharin'—
   There are few sic-like masters as auld Willie Nairn.

He'd twa muckle tabbies, ane black and ane white,
That purred by his side, at the fire, ilka night,
And gazed in the embers wi' sage-like delight,
While he ne'er took a meal, but they baith gat a bite :
   For baith beast an' bodie aye gat their full sairin'—
   He could ne'er feed alane, couthy auld Willie Nairn.

He had mony auld queer things, frae queer places
     brought—
He had rusty auld swords, whilk Ferrara had wrought—
He had axes, wi' whilk Bruce an' Wallace had fought—
An' auld Roman bauchles, wi' auld baubees bought ;
   For aye in the Cowgate, for auld nick-nacks stairin',
   Day after day, daundered auld, sage Willie Nairn.

There are gross gadding gluttons, and pimping wine-bibbers,
That are fed for their scandal, and called pleasant fibbers ;
But the only thanks Willie gae them for their labours,
Were, " We cam' nae here to speak ill o' our neighbours."
   O ! truth wad be bolder, an' falsehood less darin',
   Gin ilk ane wad treat them like auld Willie Nairn.

His snaw-flaiket locks, an' his lang pouthered queue,
Commanded assent to ilk word frae his mou' ;
Though a leer in his e'e, an' a lurk in his brow,
Made ye ferlie, gin he thought his ain stories true ;
   But he minded o' Charlie when he'd been a bairn,
   An' wha, but Bob Chambers, could thraw Willie Nairn?

Gin ye speered him anent ony auld hoary house,
He cocked his head heigh, an' he set his staff crouse,
Syne gazed through his specks, till his heart-springs brak'
    loose,
Then 'mid tears in saft whispers, wad scarce wauk a mouse ;
    He told ye some tale o't, wad mak' your heart yearn,
    To hear mair auld stories frae auld Willie Nairn.

E'en wee snarling dogs gae a kind yowffin' bark,
As he daundered down closes, baith ourie and dark ;
For he kenn'd ilka door stane and auld warld mark,
An' even amid darkness his love lit a spark :
    For mony sad scene that wad melted cauld airn,
    Was relieved by the kind heart o' auld Willie Nairn.

The laddies ran to him to redd ilka quarrel,
An' he southered a' up wi' a snap or a farl ;
While vice that had daured to stain virtue's pure laurel,
Shrunk cowed frae the glance o' the stalwart auld carl :
    Wi' the weak he was wae, wi' the strong he was stern—
    For dear, dear was virtue to auld Willie Nairn.

To spend his last shilling auld Willie had vowed ;—
But ae stormy night, in a coarse rauchan rowed,
At his door a wee wean skirled lusty an' loud,
An' the Laird left him heir to his lands an' his gowd !
    Some are fond o' a name, some are fond o' a cairn,
    But auld Will was fonder o' young Willie Nairn.

O ! we'll ne'er see his like again, now he's awa !
There are hunders mair rich, there are thousands mair
    braw,
But he gae a' his gifts, an' they whiles werena sma',
Wi' a grace made them lightly on puir shouthers fa' :
    An' he gae in the dark, when nae rude e'e was glarin'—
    There was deep hidden pathos in auld Willie Nairn.

*James Ballantine*

## I WILL THINK OF THEE, MY LOVE.

I WILL think of thee, my love,
  When, on dewy pinions borne,
The lark is singing far above,
  Near the eyelids of the morn.
When the wild flowers, gemm'd with dew,
  Breathe their fragrance on the air,
And, again, in light renew
  Their forms, like thee, so fair.

I will think of thee, my love,
  At noon when all is still,
Save the warblers of the grove,
  Or the tinkling of the rill;
When the Zephyr's balmy breeze
  Sighs a pleasing melody;
Then, beneath the spreading trees,
  All my thoughts shall be of thee.

I will think of thee, my love,
  At evening's closing hour,
When my willing footsteps rove
  Around yon ruin'd tower.
When the moonbeam, streaming bright,
  Silvers meadow-land and tree,
And the stars have paled their light—
  Then, my love, I'll think of thee.

I will think of thee, my love,
  At morning, noon, and night,
And everything I see, my love,
  My fancy shall delight.
In flowers I'll view thy lovely face;
  Thy voice—the lark's sweet song
Shall whisper love; and thus I'll trace
  Thine image all day long.

*Thomas C. Gray*

## O, MARY, WHEN YOU THINK OF ME.[1]

O, MARY, when you think of me,
  Let pity hae its share, love ;
Tho' others mock my misery,
    Do you in mercy spare, love,
      My heart, O Mary, own'd but thee,
      And sought for thine so fervently !
      The saddest tear e'er wet my e'e,
      Ye ken *wha* brocht it there, love.

O, lookna wi' that witching look,
  That wiled my peace awa', love !
An' dinna let me hear you sigh,
    It tears my heart in twa, love !
      Resume the frown ye wont to wear !
      Nor shed the unavailing tear !
      The hour of doom is drawing near,
      An' welcome be its ca', love !

How could ye hide a thought sae kind,
  Beneath sae cauld a brow, love ?
The broken heart it winna bind
    Wi' gowden bandage, now, love.
      No, Mary !   Mark yon reckless shower !
      It hung aloof in scorching hour,
      An' helps na now the feckless flower
      That sinks beneath its flow, love.

*William Thom*

----

[1] This touching piece is from the pen of a hand-loom weaver at Inverury, an occupation anything but favourable to the cultivation, even the very existence of poetic feeling.  Mr. Thom will, we trust, ere long give to the world more substantial evidence of his talents, and which we have heard is in contemplation.—ED.

## A HIGHLAND GARLAND.

### IN TWO PARTS.

*(A biographical sketch of Duncan M'Rory.)*

#### PART FIRST.

His honour the laird, in pursuit of an heiress,
Has squander'd his money in London an' Paris,
His creditors gloom, while the black-legs are laughin' :
The gauger's the mightiest man i' the clachan !

Our worthy incumbent is wrinkled an' auld,
An' whiles tak's a drappie to haud out the cauld ;
Syne wraps himself round in his auld tartan rachan :
The gauger's the mightiest man i' the clachan !

The dominie toils like a slave a' the week,
An', although he's a dungeon o' Latin and Greek,
He hasna three stivers to clink in his spleuchan :
The gauger's the mightiest man i' the clachan !

The doctor's a gentleman learned and braw,
But his outlay is great, an' his income is sma' ;
Disease is unkent i' the parish o' Strachan :
The gauger's the wealthiest man i' the clachan !

Auld Johnnie M'Nab was a bien bonnet-laird,
Sax acres he had, wi' a house an' a yard ;
But now he's a dyvor, wi' birlin' an' wauchin' :
The gauger's the mightiest man i' the clachan !

The weel-scented barber, wha mell'd wi' the gentry,
The walking gazette for the half o' the kintra—
*His* jokes hae grown stale, for they ne'er excite laughin' :
The gauger's the wittiest man i' the clachan !

The drouthy auld smith, wi' his jest an' his jeer,
Has shrunk into nought since the gauger cam' here ;
The lang-gabbit tailor's as mute as a maukin :
The gauger's the stang o' the trump i' the clachan !

On Sunday the gauger's sae trig an' sae dashin',
The model, the pink, an' the mirror, o' fashion ;
He cleeks wi' the minister's daughter, I trow,
An' they smirk i' the laft in a green-cushion'd pew !

At meetings, whenever the Bailie is preses,
He tak's his opinion in difficult cases ;
The grey-headed elders invariably greet him ;
An' brewster-wives curtsey whenever they meet him !

The bedral, wha howffs up the best in the land,
Aye cracks to the gauger wi bonnet in hand ;
Tho' cold, wi' his asthma, is sair to be dreaded,
He *will*, in his presence, continue bare-headed.

At dredgies an' weddings he's sure to be there,
An' either is *in*, or sits *next* to the chair ;
At roups an' househeatin's, presides at the toddy,
An' drives hame at night i' the factor's auld noddy.

At Yule, when the daft-days are fairly set in,
A ploy without him wadna be worth a pin ;
He opens ilk ball wi' the toast o' the parish,
An' trips like Narcissus, sae gaudy and garish.

An' when he's defunct, and is laid in the yerd,
His banes maunna mix wi' the mere vulgar herd
In the common kirkyard, but be carried in style,
An' buried deep, deep, in the choir, or the aisle.

## PART SECOND.

### BEING, WHA WAS HE THINK YOU?

CRITIC—"Pray, who is this rare one? The author's to
blame—
Not to tell us long since of his lineage and name."
AUTHOR—"A truce with your strictures—don't ravel
my story;
If I *must* tell his name, it is Duncan M'Rory.


"An' as for his ancestors—Sirs, by your leave,
There were GRANTS in the garden with Adam and Eve;
Now, Duncan held this an apocryphal bore,
But he traced up his fathers to Malcolm Canmore!


"An' they had been warriors, an' chieftains, an' lairds,
An' they had been reivers, an' robbers, an' cairds;
They had filled every grade from a chief to a vassal;
But MAC had been Borrisdale's *ain* dunniwassel.


"The chief an' M'Rory had hunted together,
They had dined i' the Ha' house an' lunched on the
heather;
M'Rory had shaved him an' pouthered his wig—
My certie! nae wonder M'Rory was big!


"When Borrisdale sported his jests after dinner,
M'Rory guffaw'd like a laughing 'hyena*r*',
An' thunder'd applause, and was ready to 'swear,
'Such peautiful shestin' she neffer tit hear.'


"When Borrisdale raised a young regiment called 'local,'
An' pibrochs an' fifes made the mountains seem vocal,
M'Rory was aye at his post i' the raw,
An' was captain, an' sergeant, an' corplar, an' a'.

"An' he drill'd the recruits wi' his braw yellow stick,
Wi' the flat o' his soord he gae mony a lick :
An' in dressin' the ranks he had never been chidden ;
An' he dined wi' the cornal whene'er he was bidden.

"On his patron's estate he was principal actor,
Gamekeeper an' forester, bailie an' factor,
An' mony a poacher he pu'd by the lugs,
An' mony a hempie he set i' the jougs !

"But Borrisdale gaed to the land o' the leal,
An' his *country* was bought by a nabob frae Keel ;
So M'Rory's a gauger sae trig an' sae garish,
The mightiest man i' the clachan or parish !"

## A BAILIE'S MORNING ADVENTURE.

THE sun clam up outower the Neilston braes,[1]
   And frae his e'ebrows scuff'd the mornin' dew ;
And warnin' dargsmen to put on their claes,
   Began to speil alang the lift sae blue.

He sheuk his sides, and sent a feckfu' yeild,
   An' rais'd the simmer lunts[2] frae loch an' linn ;
The wunnocks skinkl't in the heartsome beild,
   And ilka dew-drap shone a little sin.

[1] Neilston Braes—Rising ground in the parish of that name, to the south of Paisley and Glasgow.
[2] Simmer-lunts—Exhalations rising from the ground in warm weather.

The funneit tod cam' forth to beik himsel' ;
    The birds melodious chirpit in the shaw ;
Sae braw a mornin' gae a bodeword fell,
    That some wanchance was no that far awa'.

For deils and warlocks earthly things foreken,
    And wyse their fause end by a pawky quirk—
Sae aft they harbinger the weird o' men,
    An' wind a bricht pirn for a cast richt mirk.

As rose the sun afore the sax-hour bell,
    Sae rose the Bailie, and stravaigit out ;
Guess ye the Bailie, whose exploit I tell,
    In five-feet verses jinglin' time about.

Nae feck o' care was in the Bailie's head ;
    He thocht nae mair nor common bodies think ;
Sae witches draw us stownlins to our deid,
    And wyse us smilin' to the very brink.

He daunert on, ne'er thinkin' whar-awa' ;
    He walkit stately—bailies douna rin ;—
Till, wi' a start he thocht he halflins saw
    Some fearsome bogle wavelin' in the sin.

He cried, but naething answered to his ca' :
    His steps he airtit to the bogle's stance ;
But aye the bogle lap a bit awa' ;
    He only wan whar it had kyth'd to dance.

Awhile he glowr'd ; hech, what an eerie sicht !
    A bushy shaw grew thick wi' dulesome yew ;
Sure sic a spat was made to scaur the licht,
    And hide unearthly deeds frae mortal view.

How lang he stood, dementit, glowrin' there ;
    Whether he saw a wraith, or gruesome cow ;
How near he swarf'd, how started up his hair,
    Are secrets still deep buried in his pow.

What words he spak', we'll aiblins ne'er find out ;
　But some fell charm he surely mann'd to mutter ;—
For at the very bit he turn'd about,
　And doddit hame to eat his rows and butter.

*And. Crawfurd*

## I'LL LIVE A SINGLE LIFE.

Some foolish ladies will have men,
　Whatever these should be,
And fancy they are getting old,
　When scarcely twenty-three :
They never once reflect upon
　The trials of a wife ;
For me, I'll pay my lovers off,
　And live a single life !

I cannot think of Mr. Figg ;—
　I do not like the name ;
And as for Mr. Tikeler,
　Why that is much the same !
And Mr. *Goold* has grown so *poor*,
　He could not keep a wife,
And Mr. *Honey* looks so *sour*—
　I'll live a single life !

I see some ladies who were once
　The gay belles of the town,
Though but a short year married,
　All changed in face and gown.
And Mr. *Gentle* rudely *scolds*
　His little loving wife ;
And Mr. *Lowe* has grown so *cold*—
　I'll live a single life !

There's Mr. *Home* is always *out*
  Till twelve o'clock at night ;
And Mr. *Smart* is *dull* and *black*,
  Since married to Miss *White*.
And Mr. *Wright* has all gone *wrong*,
  And beats his loving wife ;—
I would not have such men, I trow—
  I'll live a single life !

Miss *Evans* looks so very *odd*,
  Since wed to Mr. Strang :
Miss *Little* looks so very *broad*
  Beside her Mr. *Lang*.
Miss *Hartley* looks so *heartless* now,
  Since Mr. *Wishart's* wife ;
Miss *Rose* has turn'd so *lily*-pale—
  I'll live a single life !

There's Mr. *Foot* has begg'd me oft
  To give him my fair *hand :*
And Mr. *Crabbe* has sought me too,
  And so has Mr. *Bland ;*
And Mr. *Young* and Mr. *Auld*
  Have asked me for their wife ;
But I've denied them every one—
  I'll live a single life !

So, ladies who are single yet
  Take heed to what I say ;
Nor cast your caps, and take the pet,
  As thoughtless maidens may :
Remember 'tis no common task
  To prove a prudent wife ;
For me, no one my hand need ask—
  I'll live a single life !

*Andrew Park*

## MARY DRAPER.[1]

AIR—"*Nancy Dawson.*"

DON'T talk to me of London dames,
Nor rave about your foreign flames,
That never lived,—except in drames,
   Nor shone, except on paper ;
I'll sing you 'bout a girl I knew,
Who lived in Ballywhacmacrew,
And, let me tell you, mighty few
   Could equal Mary Draper.

Her cheeks were red, her eyes were blue,
Her hair was brown, of deepest hue,
Her foot was small, and neat to view,
   Her waist was slight and taper ;
Her voice was music to your ear,
A lovely brogue, so rich and clear ;
Oh ! the like I ne'er again shall hear
   As from sweet Mary Draper.

She'd ride a wall, she'd drive a team,
Or with a fly she'd whip a stream,
Or maybe sing you "Rousseau's Dream,'
   For nothing could escape her :
I've seen her too—upon my word—
At sixty yards bring down her bird ;
Oh ! she charmed all the Forty-third ;
   Did lovely Mary Draper.

And at the spring assizes ball,
The junior bar would, one and all,
For all her fav'rite dances call,
   And Harry Deane would caper ;

[1] Taken, with permission, from Charles O'Malley, the Irish Dragoon.

Lord Clare would then forget his lore,
King's Counsel, voting law a bore,
Were proud to figure on the floor,
    For love of Mary Draper.

The parson, priest, sub-sheriff too,
Were all her slaves, and so would you,
If you had only but one view
    Of such a face and shape, or
Her pretty ankles—but, ohone !
It's only west of old Athlone
Such girls are found—and now they're gone—
    So here's to Mary Draper.

## I'VE AYE BEEN FOU' SIN' THE YEAR CAM' IN.

AIR—"*Laird o' Cockpen.*"

I'VE aye been fou' sin' the year cam' in,
I've aye been fou' sin' the year cam' in ;
It's what wi' the brandy, an' what wi' the gin,
I've aye been fou' sin' the year cam' in !

Our Yule friends they met, and a gay stoup we drank,
The bicker gaed round, an' the pint-stoup did clank :

But that was a naething, as shortly ye'll fin'—
I've aye been fou' sin' the year cam' in !

Our auld timmer clock, wi' thorl an' string,
Had scarce shawn the hour whilk the new year did bring,
When friends and acquaintance cam' tirl at the pin—
An' I've aye been fou' sin' the year cam' in !

My auld auntie Tibbie cam' ben for her cap,
Wi' scone in her hand, and cheese in her lap,
An' drank a gude New Year to kith an' to kin—
Sae I've aye been fou' sin' the year cam' in !

My strong brither Sandy cam' in frae the south—
There's some ken his mettle, but nane ken his drouth ;
I brought out the bottle, losh ! how he did grin !
I've aye been fou' sin' the year cam' in !

Wi' feastin' at night, an' wi' drinkin' at morn,
Wi' here tak' a caulker, and there tak' a horn,
I've gatten baith doited, and donner't and blin'—
For I've aye been fou' sin' the year cam' in !

I sent for the doctor, an' bade him sit down,
He felt at my hand, an' he straiket my crown ;
He order'd a bottle—but it turned out gin ;
Sae I've aye been fou' sin' the year cam' in !

The Sunday bell rang, an' I thought it as weel
To slip into the kirk, to steer clear o' the De'il ;
But the chiel at the plate fand a groat left behin'—
Sae I've aye been fou' sin' the year cam' in !

'Tis Candlemas time, an' the wee birds o' spring
Are chirming an' chirping as if they wad sing ;
While here I sit bousing—'tis really a sin !—
I've aye been fou' sin' the year cam' in !

The last breath o' winter is soughin' awa',
An' sune down the valley the primrose will blaw ;
A douce sober life I maun really begin,
For I've aye been fou' sin' the year cam' in !

## THE VOICE OF MERRIMENT.[1]

I HEARD the voice of merriment—
  Of man in his glad hour,—
And there the joyous bumper lent
  To mirth its maddening power :
And when I asked the reason why,
  They told me that the year
Was agèd, and about to die—
  Its end was drawing near.—

How strange a thing the human heart,
  To laugh at time's decay,
When every hour we see depart
  Is hurrying us away !
Away—from all the scenes that we
  Have loved so much, so well ;
To where ? ah ! whither do we flee—
  Whose is the tongue to tell ?

[1] The amiable and accomplished author of these lines, and " The Sailor's Rest," died of aneurism of the heart, in July 1839. Whilst

## MY BEAUTIFUL SHIP.

My beautiful ship! I love thee,
  As if thou wert living thing;
Not the ocean bird above thee,
  That speeds on its snow-white wing,
To its hungry brood at even,
  Hath a fonder, gladder breast,
Than mine, when I see thee driven
  By the wind that knoweth no rest!

When the silvery spray flies o'er thee,
  Like a shower of crystal gems,
And the wave divides before thee
  Wherever thy bold bow stems—
Oh! my heart reboundeth then,
  With a beat, which hath been rare,
Since the gay glad moments—when
  The blood of my youth gushed there.

These are joys the Landsman's soul
  Can never wot of, I wean,
No more than the buried mole
  Can tell of the earth that's green.
Oh! bear me, my ship, away,
  Away on the joyous wave!

he was seated with Mrs. Buchanan, witnessing the gambols of
their children, death suddenly entered the joyous circle, and be-
reft his family and the world of an ornament of literature, and an
accomplished gentleman; a premature grave closing over him at the
age of thirty-six.

In 1833 a volume of poetry, entitled "Edith," was issued anony-
mously from the Glasgow press, and although the author chose to
conceal his name, the reading portion of the world was not long in
tracing the authorship to the sequestered shades of Auchintoshan, in
Dumbartonshire, Mr. Buchanan's family seat, where he had so successfully courted the tuneful Nine.

I cannot abide earth's clay—
For it minds me of the grave.

Thou art to mine eyes the fairest
    Of all the fair things that be ;
Every joy of my life thou sharest,
    That bringest new life to me.
Shall my soul then cease to love thee,
    My beautiful sea-home ? Never !
As long as the sky's above me,
    Thou shalt be my Idol ever.

*John Crosse Buchanan*

## I'M LIVING YET.

THIS flesh has been wasted, this spirit been vext,
Till I've wish'd that my deeing day were the next ;
But trouble will flee, an' sorrow will flit,
Sae tent me, my lads—I'm living yet !

Ay, when days were dark, and the nights as grim,
When the heart was dowff, an' the e'e was dim,
At the tail o' the purse, at the end o' my wit,
It was time to quit—but I'm living yet !

Our pleasures are constantly gi'en to disease,
An' Hope, poor thing, aft gets dowie, and dies ;
While dyester Care, wi' his darkest litt,
Keeps dipping awa'—but I'm living yet !

A wee drap drink, an' a canty chiel,
Can laugh at the warl', an' defy the deil ;
Wi' a blink o' sense, an' a flaught o' wit,
O ! that's the gear keeps me living yet !

*Hew Ainslie*[1]

---

[1] Hew Ainslie, who recently died in America, was born in the parish of Dailly, Ayrshire, in 1792. His father removed to Edinburgh in 1809, and his son, the subject of this note, was employed as a copying clerk in the Register Office for some time.  He occasionally acted as amanuensis to the late Dugald Stewart, after that celebrated metaphysician and elegant writer had resigned the chair of Moral Philosophy in the Edinburgh University.  Ainslie wrote with great rapidity and elegance, but the fastidious taste of the critic frequently marred by nice corrections the flowing caligraphy of his recorder. Mr. Ainslie again returned to the Register Office, and soon after married his cousin, Janet Ainslie.  The mechanical drudgery of copying legal records sickened the poet, and he resolved on emigrating to America.  After one or two unsuccessful attempts to establish a business, he at last so far succeeded in realising for himself and his large family, if not wealth, a sufficient competency.  Mr. Ainslie is the author of several published pieces of great merit, a list of which may be seen in a publication issued in Edinburgh, entitled "The Contemporaries of Burns," a work wherein much local talent, hitherto unknown, has been brought to light.  He was also the author of a series of papers contributed to the Newcastle Magazine, which were considered worthy of being republished in a volume, and entitled "A pilgrimage to the Land of Burns," a name now used to designate the locality of Burns's nativity.  Mr. Ainslie went out alone to America, to find a resting-place for his family ere he should remove them from Scotland, and it was during this period of separation from all that was dear to him, and under a fit of sickness, that the labouring and scathed heart sought relief in the gush of affection, entitled "The Absent Father."

## MY LAST SANG TO KATE REID.

I'LL sing a sang to thee, Kate Reid,
  It may touch a lonesome string ;
I'll sing a sang to thee, Kate Reid,
  Be 't the last that e'er I sing, Kate Reid,
  Be 't the last that e'er I sing.

For I hae sung to thee, fair Kate,
  When the young spring, like thysel',
Kythed bonnilie on Roslin lea,
  In Gourton's flowery dell, Kate Reid, etc.

And simmer eves hae seen us, Kate,
  Thy genty hand in mine,
As, by our pleasant waterside,
  I mix'd my heart wi' thine, Kate Reid, etc.

And harvest moons hae lighted us,
  When in yon silent glen
Ye sat, my living idol, Kate—
  Did I not worship then, Kate Reid? etc.

Hymns frae my heart hae sung o' thee ;
  And trees by my auld hame,
That echoed to thy praises aft,
  Stand graven wi' thy name, Kate Reid, etc.

Thrice seven lang years hae past us, Kate,
  Since thae braw days gaed by ;
Anither land's around me, Kate,
  I see anither sky, Kate Reid, etc.

My simmer hour is gane, Kate Reid,
  The day begins to dow ;
The spark hath left this e'e, Kate Reid,
  The gloss hath left this brow, Kate Reid, etc.

Yet fresh as when I kiss'd thee last,
  Still unto me ye seem ;
Bright'ner o' mony a dreary day,
  Ye've sweeten'd mony a dream, Kate Reid, etc.

*Hew Ainslie*

## THE ABSENT FATHER.

THE friendly greeting of our kind,
  Or gentler woman's smiling,
May soothe a weary wand'rer's mind,
  Some lonely hours beguiling ;—

May charm the restless spirit still,
  The pang of grief allaying ;—
But, ah ! the soul it cannot fill,
  Or keep the heart from straying.

Oh ! how the fancy, when unbound,
  On wings of rapture swelling,
Will hurry to the holy ground
  Where loves and friends are dwelling.

My lonely and my widow'd wife,
  How oft to thee I wander !
And live again those hours of life,
  When mutual love was tender.

And now with sickness lowly laid,
  All scenes to sadness turning,
Where will I find a breast like thine,
  To lay the brow that's burning?

And how's 't with you, my little ones ?
  How have those cherubs thriven,
That made my hours of leisure light,
  That made my home like heaven ?

Does yet the rose array your cheeks,
  As when in grief I bless'd you ?
Or are your cherry lips as sweet,
  As when with tears I kiss'd you ?

Does yet your broken prattle tell—
  Can your young memories gather
A thought of him who loves you well ?—
  Your weary, wand'ring father.

Oh ! I've had wants and wishes too,
  This world has choked and chill'd ;
Yet bless me but again with you,
  And half my prayer 's fulfill'd.

*Hew Ainslie*

## WHY DO I SEEK THE GLOAMING HOUR?

WHY do I seek the gloaming hour,
  When others seek the day ?
Why wander 'neath the moon's pale light,
  And not the sun's bright ray ?
Why beats my heart as every blast
  Gaes whistling through the trees ?
Be still in pity, gentle wind,
  My Willie's on the seas.

And should an angry mood come o'er
  Thy balmy summer breath,

Remember her who courts thy smiles,
  Nor seek my sailor's death :
Think on a mother's burning tears,
  The wee things on her knee ;
Be still in pity, gentle wind,
  My Willie's on the sea.

For oh ! I fear the azure caves,
  Thine angry mood explores ;
And sorely dread the hidden rocks,
  And shelving iron shores.
Bespeak the love-sick moon's control,
  And bless with fav'ring breeze—
Blow soft and steady, gentle wind,
  My Willie's on the seas.

J. S.

## THE INDIAN COTTAGER'S SONG.

*Founded upon St. Pierre's tale of the Indian Cottage, and adapted
to a Hindostance air.*

*Arranged and harmonised by R. A. Smith.*

THO' exiled afar from the gay scenes of Delhi,
  Although my proud kindred no more shall I see,
I've found a sweet home in this thick-wooded valley,
  Beneath the cool shade of the green banyan tree ;
'Tis here my loved Paria [1] and I dwell together,
Though shunned by the world, truly blest in each other,
And thou, lovely boy ! lisping "father" and "mother,"
  Art more than the world to my Paria and me.

How dark seemed my fate, when we first met each other,
  My own fatal pile ready waiting for me ;

---

[1] "Paria," the most degraded among the Indian castes ; a Paria
is one whom none belonging to other castes will deign to recognise.

While incense I burned on the grave of my mother,
   And knew that myself the next victim [1] would be :
'Twas then that my Paria, as one sent from 'heaven,
To whom a commission of mercy is given,
Shed peace through this bosom, with deep anguish riven,
   To new life, to love, and to joy waking me.

He wooed me with flowers,[2] to express the affection
   Which sympathy woke in his bosom for me ;
My poor bleeding heart clung to him for protection ;
   I wept—while I vowed with my Paria to flee.
My mind, too, from darkness and ignorance freeing,
He taught to repose on that merciful Being,
The Author of Nature, all-wise and all-seeing,
   Whose arm still protecteth my Paria and me.

Now safely we dwell in this cot of our rearing,
   Contented, industrious, cheerful, and free ;
To each other still more endeared and endearing,
   While Heaven sheds its smiles on my Paria and me.
Our garden supplies us with fruits and with flowers,
The sun marks our time, and our birds sing the hours,
And thou, darling boy ! shooting forth thy young powers,
   Completest the bliss of my Paria and me.

*Alex Rodger*

---

[1] " The next victim." The person here is supposed to have been the widow of a young Hindoo, condemned by the barbarous laws of the Brahmins to be burned alive on the funeral pile of her husband.

[2] " He wooed me with flowers." The mode of courtship in many eastern countries, especially among the Hindoos.

## LAMENT FOR CAPTAIN PATON.[1]

TOUCH once more a sober measure,
    And let punch and tears be shed,
For a prince of good old fellows,
    That, alack aday! is dead;
For a prince of worthy fellows,
    And a pretty man also,
That has left the Saltmarket
    In sorrow, grief, and wo.
Oh! we ne'er shall see the like of Captain Paton no mo!


His waistcoat, coat, and breeches,
    Were all cut off the same web,
Of a beautiful snuff-colour,
    Or a modest genty drab;
The blue stripe in his stocking
    Round his neat slim leg did go,
And his ruffles of the cambric fine
    They were whiter than the snow.
Oh! we ne'er shall see the like of Captain Paton no mo!

---

[1] We have, with the kind permission of Messrs. Blackwood, taken
this Lament, written by Mr. Lockhart, from their Magazine, published in September 1819. We know of no piece of the serio-comic
to compare with it: it has, in fact, no rival. As a specimen of the
fine arts in verse, the portrait is complete—there is scarcely a touch
wanting to present the living man—a limber-built, whalebone-frame
standing in erect column, five feet eight, or so—tailoring decorations,
precise to a stitch, and adjusted on his person with the nicety of a
gold balance—in his gait erect as if the spine were a solid, instead of
a flexible column—and as little use made as possible of the foldings
at the knee.

Captain Archibald *Patoun* was a son of Dr. David Patoun, a
physician in Glasgow, who left to his son the tenement in which he
lived for many years preceding his decease, called "Patoun's Land,"
opposite the Old Exchange at the Cross. The broad pavement, or
"plainstones," as it was called, in front of the house, formed the

His hair was curled in order,
  At the rising of the sun,
In comely rows and buckles smart
  That about his ears did run ;
And before there was a toupée
  That some inches up did go,
And behind there was a long queue
  That did o'er his shoulders flow.
Oh ! we ne'er shall see the like of Captain Paton no mo !

And whenever we foregathered,
  He took off his wee three-cockit,
And he proffered you his snuff-box,
  Which he drew from his side-pocket ;
And on Burdett or Bonaparte,
  He would make a remark or so,
And then along the plainstones
  Like a provost he would go.
Oh ! we ne'er shall see the like of Captain Paton no mo !

In dirty days he picked well
  His footsteps with his rattan ;
Oh ! you ne'er could see the least speck
  On the shoes of Captain Paton ;

daily parade ground of the veteran.  The Captain held a commission
in a regiment that had been raised in Scotland for the Dutch service ;
and after he had left the tented field, lived with two maiden sisters,
and Nelly, the servant, who had, from long and faithful servitude,
become an indispensable in the family.  He was considered a very
skilful fencer, and excelled in small sword exercise, an accomplish-
ment he was rather proud of, and often handled his rattan as if it
had been the lethal instrument which he used to wield against the
foe.  The wags of the day got up a caricature of the Captain parry-
ing the horned thrusts of a belligerent bull in the Glasgow Green.
The Captain fell in that warfare from which there is no discharge on
the 30th July 1807, at the age of sixty-eight, and was interred in the
sepulchre of his father in the Cathedral, or High Church burying
grounds.  The ballad has, by a slight mistake, deposited his remains
in the Ram's-horn, now St. David's, churchyard.

And on entering the coffee-room
　　About *two*, all men did know,
They would see him with his Courier
　　In the middle of the row.
Oh ! we ne'er shall see the like of Captain Paton no mo !


Now and then upon a Sunday
　　He invited me to dine,
On a herring and a mutton chop
　　Which his maid dressed very fine ;
There was also a little Malmsey,
　　And a bottle of Bordeaux,
Which between me and the Captain
　　Passed nimbly to and fro.
Oh ! I ne'er shall take pot-luck with Captain Paton no mo !


Or if a bowl was mentioned,
　　The Captain he would ring,
And bid Nelly to the West-port,[1]
　　And a stoup of water bring ;
Then would he mix the genuine stuff,
　　As they made it long ago,
With limes that on his property
　　In Trinidad did grow.
Oh ! we ne'er shall taste the like of Captain Paton's
　　punch no mo !


And then all the time he would discourse,
　　So sensible and courteous ;
Perhaps talking of the last sermon
　　He had heard from Dr. Porteous,[2]
Or some little bit of scandal
　　About Mrs. So-and-so,

[1] A well, the water of which was excellently adapted for the compounding of cold punch, situated, in the days of the Captain, a little east of the Black Bull, Argyll Street.　　[2] A favourite preacher.

Which he scarce could credit, having heard
    The *con* but not the *pro.*
Oh ! we ne'er shall hear the like of Captain Paton no mo !

Or when the candles were brought forth,
    And the night was fairly setting in,
He would tell some fine old stories
    About Minden-field or Dettingen—
How he fought with a French major,
    And despatched him at a blow,
While his blood ran out like water
    On the soft grass below.
Oh ! we ne'er shall hear the like of Captain Paton no mo !

But at last the Captain sickened,
    And grew worse from day to day,
And all missed him in the coffee-room,
    From which now he stayed away ;
On Sabbaths, too, the Wee Kirk [1]
    Made a melancholy show,
All for wanting of the presence
    ` Of our venerable beau.
Oh ! we ne'er shall see the like of Captain Paton no mo !

And in spite of all that Cleghorn
    And Corkindale could do, [2]
It was plain, from twenty symptoms,
    That death was in his view ;
. So the Captain made his test'ment,
    And submitted to his foe,
And we laid him by the Rams-horn-kirk [3]—
    'Tis the way we all must go.
Oh ! we ne'er shall see the like of Captain Paton no mo !

Join all in chorus, jolly boys,
    And let punch and tears be shed,

---

[1] Now the Tron Church.     [2] Eminent Physicians.
[3] Now St. David's Church.

For this prince of good old fellows,
　　That, alack a day ! is dead ;
For this prince of worth fellows,
　　And a pretty man also,
That has left the Saltmarket
　　In sorrow, grief, and wo !
For it ne'er shall see the like of Captain Paton no mo !

*[signature]*

---

### THE FA' O' THE YEAR.

AFORE the Lammas' tide
　　Had dun'd the birken-tree,
In a' our water-side
　　Nae wife was blest like me ;
A kind gudeman, and twa
　　Sweet bairns were round me here ;
But they're a' ta'en awa'
　　Sin' the fa' o' the year.

Sair trouble cam' our gate,
　　An' made me, when it cam',
A bird without a mate,
　　A ewe without a lamb.
Our hay was yet to maw,
　　And our corn was to shear,
When they a' dwined awa'
　　In the fa' o' the year.

I downa look afield,
　　For aye I trow I see
The form that was a bield
　　To my wee bairns and me ;

But wind, and weet, and snaw,
  They never mair can fear,
Sin' they a' got the ca'
  In the fa' o' the year.

Aft on the hill at e'ens
  I see him 'mang the ferns,
The lover o' my teens,
  The faither o' my bairns ;
For there his plaid I saw
  As gloamin' aye drew near—
But my a's now awa'
  Sin' the fa' o' the year.

Our bonny rigs theirsel'
  Reca' my waes to mind,
Our puir dumb beasties tell
  O' a' that I hae tyned ;
For wha our wheat will saw,
  And wha our sheep will shear,
Sin' my a' gaed awa'
  In the fa' o' the year ?

My hearth is growing cauld,
  And will be caulder still ;
And sair, sair in the fauld
  Will be the winter's chill ;
For peats were yet to ca'—
  Our sheep were yet to smear,
When my a' dwined awa'
  In the fa' o' the year.

I ettle whiles to spin,
  But wee, wee patterin' feet
Come rinnin' out and in,
  And then I just maun greet :
I ken it's fancy a'
  And faster rows the tear,

That my a' dwined awa'
  In the fa' o' the year.

Be kind, O Heav'n abune !
  To ane sae wae and lane,
And tak' her hamewards sune,
  In pity o' her mane,
Lang ere the March winds blaw,
  May she, far far frae here,
Meet them a' that's awa'
  Sin' the fa' o' the year

*Thomas Smibert*

## SHE COMES IN A DREAM OF THE NIGHT.

ORIGINAL AIR.

SHE comes in a dream of the night,
  When the cumberless spirit is free,
A vision of beauty and light,
  And sweetly she smiles upon me.
And with the dear maid as of yore,
  Through scenes long remembered I stray ;
But soon the illusion is o'er—
  It flits with the dawning of day.

Though low be the bed of her rest,
  And sound is her sleep in the tomb,
Her image enshrined in my breast,
  Still lives in its brightness and bloom :
And link'd with the memories of old,
  That image to me is more dear

Than all that the eyes can behold—
Than all that is sweet to the ear.

And like the soft voice of a song,
    That trembles and dies in the air,
While memory the strain will prolong,
    And fix it unchangeable there ;
So deep in remembrance will lie,
    That form, ever lovely and young ;
The lustre that lived in her eye,
    The music that flow'd from her tongue.

ALEX. SMART.

## JOHN FROST.

AIR—" *The young May moon is beaming, love.*"

YOU'VE come early to see us this year, John Frost,
Wi' your crispin' an' poutherin' gear, John Frost ;
    For hedge, tower, an' tree, as far as I see,
Are as white as the bloom o' the pear, John Frost.

You've been very preceese wi' your wark, John Frost,
Altho' ye hae wrought in the dark, John Frost,
    For ilka fit-stap frae the door to the slap,
Is braw as a new linen sark, John Frost.

There are some things about ye I like, John Frost,
An' ithers that aft gar me fyke, John Frost ;
    For the weans wi' cauld taes, crying "shoon, stockings,
      claes,"
Keep us busy as bees in the byke, John Frost.

An' to tell you I winna be blate, John Frost,
Our gudeman stops out whiles rather late, John Frost,
    An' the blame's put on you, if he gets a thocht fu',
He's sae fleyed for the slippery lang gate, John Frost.

Ye hae fine goin's-on in the north, John Frost,
Wi' your houses o' ice, and so forth, John Frost ;
   Tho' their kirn's on the fire, they may kirn till they tire,
But their butter—pray what is it worth, John Frost ?

Now your breath will be greatly improven John Frost,
By a whilock in some baker's oven, John Frost ;
   Wi' het scones for a lunch, and a horn o' rum punch,
Or wi' gude whisky toddy a' stovin', John Frost.

*William Miller*

## I LO'ED YE WHEN LIFE'S EARLY DEW.

I LO'ED ye when life's early dew
   A' fresh upon your bosom lay ;
I preed your wee bit fragrant mou',
   An' vow'd to lo'e ye in decay.

Ye now sit in the auld aik chair ;
   The rose hath faded frae your cheek ;
Wi' siller tints time dyes your hair—
   Your voice now quivers whan ye speak.

Yet joy it is for me to hae
   Your wintry beauty in my arms ;
The faithfu' heart kens nae decay—
   It's simmer there in a' its charms.

An' kindly is your smile to me,
   Altho' nae dimple round it plays ;
Your voice is aye a melody,
   That breathes to me o' ither days.

Fill hie the cup, my gude auld May,
  In ruddy wine I'll pledge ye yet ;
While mem'ry lingers o'er the day,
  The happy day when first we met.

An' this the pledge 'tween you an' me,
  Whan time comes hirplin wreath'd in snaw,
Like leaves frae aff an aged tree,
  May we to earth thegither fa'.

## THE BURNSIDE.

I WANDER'D by the burn side,
  Lang, lang syne ;
When I was Willie's promis'd bride
  And Willie's heart was mine.
I wander'd by the burn side,
  And little did I think,
That e'er I should gang mournin'
  Sae sadly by its brink.

We wander'd by the burn side,
  Late, late at e'en,
And mony were the vows breath'd
  Its flowery banks atween :—
We wander'd late, we wander'd aft,
  It ne'er seem'd late nor lang,
Sae mony were the kind things
  That Willie said and sang.

But, waes me for the burn side,
  Its flowers sae sweet, sae fair;
And waes me for the lasting love,
  That Willie promis'd there :
The flowers forsook the burn side,
  But ah ! they didna part
Sae cauldly frae its bonny banks,
  As truth frae Willie's heart.


Now I gang by the burn side,
  My sad, my leefu' lane,
And Willie on its flowery banks
  Maun never look again.
For ither scenes, and ither charms,
  Hae glamour'd Willie's een,
He thinks nae on the burn side,
  He thinks na on his Jean.


Oh ! blessin's on the burn side !
  It's a' the bless I hae
To wander lonely by its brink,
  The lee lang night and day—
But waes me for its bonny flowers
  Their sweets I daurna see,
For Willie's love, and Willie's wrang,
  Wi' tears blind aye my e'e !

*W. Ferguson*

## HERE'S TO YOU AGAIN.

*Air—" Toddlin' hame."*

LET votaries o' Bacchus o' wine make their boast,
And drink till it mak's them as dead's a bed-post,
A drap o' maut broe I wad far rather pree,
And a rosy-faced landlord's the Bacchus for me.
Then I'll toddle butt, and I'll toddle ben,
And let them drink at wine wha nae better do ken.

Your wine it may do for the bodies far south,
But a Scotchman likes something that bites i' the mouth,
And whisky's the thing that can do't to a Tee,
Then Scotsmen and whisky will ever agree ;
For wi' toddlin' butt, an' wi' toddlin' ben,
Sae lang we've been nurst on't we hardly can spean.

It's now thretty years since I first took the drap,
To moisten my carcase, and keep it in sap,
An' tho' what I've drunk might hae slockened the sun,
I fin' I'm as dry as when first I begun ;
For wi' toddlin' butt, an wi' toddlin' ben,
I'm nae sooner slockened than drouthy again.

Your douse folk aft ca' me a tipplin' auld sot,
A worm to a still,—a sand bed,—and what not ;
They cry that my hand wad ne'er bide frae my mouth,
But, oddsake ! they never consider my drouth ;
Yet I'll toddle butt an' I'll toddle ben,
An' laugh at their nonsense—wha nae better ken.

Some hard grippin' mortals wha deem themsel's wise,
A glass o' good whisky affect to despise,
Poor scurvy-souled wretches—they're no very blate,
Besides, let me tell them, they're foes to the State ;
For wi' toddlin' butt, an' wi' toddlin' ben,
Gin folk wadna drink, how could Government fen' ?

Yet wae on the tax that mak's whisky sae dear,
An' wae on the gauger sae strict and severe :
Had I but my will o't, I'd soon let you see,
That whisky, like water, to a' should be free ;
For I'd toddle butt, an' I'd toddle ben,
An' I'd mak' it to rin like the burn after rain.

What signifies New'rday ?—a mock at the best,
That tempts but poor bodies, and leaves them unblest,
For a ance-a-year fuddle I'd scarce gie a strae,
Unless that ilk year were as short as a day ;
Then I'd toddle butt, an' I'd toddle ben,
Wi' the hearty het pint, an' the canty black hen.

I ne'er was inclined to lay by ony cash,
Weel kennin' it only wad breed me mair fash ;
But aye when I had it, I let it gang free,
An' wad toss for a gill wi' my hindmost bawbee ;
For wi' toddlin' butt, an' wi' toddlin' ben,
I ne'er kent the use o't, but only to spen'.

Had siller been made in the kist to lock by,
It ne'er wad been round, but as square as a die ;
Whereas, by its shape, ilka body may see,
It aye was designed it should circulate free ;
Then we'll toddle butt, an' we'll toddle ben,
An' aye whan we get it, we'll part wi't again.

I ance was persuaded to "put in the pin,"
But foul fa' the bit o't ava wad bide in,
For whisky's a thing so bewitchingly stout,
The first time I smelt it, the pin it lap out ;
Then I toddled butt, an' I toddled ben,
And I vowed I wad ne'er be advised sae again.

O leeze me on whisky ! it gies us new life,
It mak's us aye cadgy to cuddle the wife ;

It kindles a spark in the breast o' the cauld,
And it mak's the rank coward courageously bauld ;
Then we'll toddle butt, an' we'll toddle ben,
An' we'll coup aff our glasses,—"here's to you again."

*Alex^a Rodger*

## THE IRON DESPOT OF THE NORTH.

THE iron Despot of the North
　　May on his vassals call,
But not for him will I go forth
　　From my old castle hall.
Though sabres, swayed by Polish hands,
　　Have battled for the foe,
There's one, at least, Oppression's bands
　　Shall ne'er see brandished so !

I fought in Freedom's farewell field,
　　I saved a useless life ;
No weapon from that hour to wield,
　　In a less noble strife.
When hostile strangers passed my gate,
　　On Hope's red grave I swore,
That, like my ruined country's fate,
　　This arm should rise no more.

I flung into the bloody moat,
　　A flag, no longer free,
Which centuries had seen afloat,
　　In feudal majesty.
The sword a warrior-race bequeathed
　　With honour to their son,
Hangs on the mouldering wall unsheathed,
　　And rust consumes my gun.

The steed that, rushing to the ranks,
　　Defied the stubborn rein,
Felt not on his impatient flanks,
　　The horseman's spur again.
And I, the last of all my line,
　　Left an affianced bride,
Lest slaves should spring from blood of mine,
　　To serve the Despot's pride.

*Will. Kennedy*

## THE KAIL-BROSE OF AULD SCOTLAND.[1]

### (NEW VERSION.)

AIR—" *The Roast-beef of Old England.*"

THE Genius of Scotland lang wept ower our woes,
But now that we've gotten baith peace and repose,
We've kits fu' o' butter—we've cogs fu' o' brose :
　　O ! the kail-brose of auld Scotland,
　　And O ! for the Scottish kail-brose.

Nae mair shall our cheeks, ance sae lean an' sae wan,
Hing shilpit and lank, like a bladder half-blawn ;
Our lang runkled painches will now, like a can,
　　Be stentit wi' brose o' auld Scotland,
　　The stiff, stughie, Scottish kail-brose.

---

[1] This modern version of the potent effects of the National dish, Kail-brose, fairly, in our opinion, excels the original by Deacon Watson ; but our friend Mr. Inglis must not be unduly elevated at our preference, because the Deacon of the Tailors lays claim, professionally, to fractional proportions in the *genus homo*, though really his song is worthy of Nine hands, the quantity of squatters who are required to fill the clothes of an able-bodied member in common society.

Our Sawnies and Maggies, as hard as the horn,
At e'en blythe will dance, yet work fell the neist morn ;
They'll haud baith the French and their puddocks in scorn,
    While fed on the brose o' auld Scotland,
    Large luggies o' Scottish kail-brose.

There's our brave Forty-second, in Egypt wha fought,
Wi' Invincibles styled, whom they soon set at nought ;
But the Frenchmen ne'er dreamt that sic wark could be
    wrought,
    For they kent na the brose o' auld Scotland,
    The poust that's in Scottish kail-brose.

Again, at the battle o' red Waterloo,
How they pricket and proget the French thro' and thro' ;
Some ran, and some rade—and some look'd rather blue,
    As they fled frae the sons o' auld Scotland,
    Frae the chiels that were fed upon brose.

To tell ilka feat wherein Scotsmen hae shone,
Is vain to attempt—they're so numerous grown ;
For where will you meet wi' mair muscle and bone,
    Than is bred on the brose o' auld Scotland,
    The rib-prapping Scottish kail brose ?

Then join me, all ye to whom Scotland is dear,
And loud let us sing o' the chief o' her cheer ;
Let cutties and cogs show our hearts are sincere,
    While we welcome the brose o' auld Scotland,
    The braw halesome Scottish kail brose !

*Robt. Inglis*

## IT'S DOWIE IN THE HIN' O' HAIRST.

It's dowie in the hin' o' hairst,
　At the wa'gang o' the swallow,
When the winds grow cauld, when the burns grow bauld,
　An' the wuds are hingin' yellow ;
But, O ! its dowier far to see
　The wa'gang o' her the heart gangs wi'—
The deadset o' a shining e'e
　That darkens the weary warld on thee.

There was muckle luve atween us twa—
　O ! twa could ne'er be fonder ;
An' the thing below was never made
　That could hae gar'd us sunder.
But the way o' Heav'n's aboon a' ken—
　An' we maun bear what it likes to sen'—
It's comfort though, to weary men,
　That the warst o' this warl's waes maun en'.

There's mony things that come an' gae—
　Just seen and just forgotten—
An' the flow'rs that busk a bonnie brae,
　Gin anither year lie rotten ;
But the last look o' that lovely e'e,
　An' the dying grip she ga'e to me,
They're settled like eternity :—
　O, Mary ! that I were with thee !

*Hew Ainslie*

## I'VE SOUGHT IN LANDS AYONT THE SEA.

Air—"*My Normandie.*"

I'VE sought in lands ayont the sea
A hame—a couthie hame for thee,
An' honeysickle bursts around
The blythsome hame that I hae found ;
Then dinna grudge your heather bell,
O fretna for your flowerless fell,
There's dale an' down mair fair to see,
Than ought in our bleak countrie !

Come o'er the waters, dinna fear,
The lav'rock lilts as lo'esome here,
An' mony a sweet, around, above,
Shall welcome o'er my Jessie, love,
My hame wi' halesome gear is fu',
My heart wi' lowing love for you ;
O haste, my Jessie, come an' see
The hame—the heart that wants but thee !

But mind ye, lass, the fleetfu' hours,
They wait na—spare na fouk nor flowers,
An' sair are fouk and flowers to blame,
Wha wishfu' wastefu' wait for them.
O bide na lang in swither, then,
Since flowers and fouk may wither, then,'
But come as lang's I hae to gie
A hame, a heart to welcome thee !

*William Thom*

## I WOULDNA—O! I COULDNA LOOK.

I WOULDNA—O! I couldna look
 On that sweet face again,
I daurna trust my simple heart,
 Now it's ance mair my ain.

I wouldna thole what I ha'e thol'd,
 Sic dule I wouldna dree,
For a' that love could now unfold
 Frae woman's witchfu' e'e.

I've mourn'd until the waesome moon
 Has sunk ahint the hill,
An' seen ilk sparkling licht aboon
 Creep o'er me, mournin' still.

I've thocht my very mither's hame
 Was hameless-like to me ;
Nor could I think this warld the same,
 That I was wont to see.

But years o' weary care ha'e past,
 Wi' blinks o' joy between ;
An' yon heart-hoarded form at last
 Forsakes my doited een.

Sae cauld and dark's my bosom now,
 Sic hopes lie buried there ;
That sepulchre whare love's saft lowe
 May never kindle mair.

I couldna trust this foolish heart
 When it's ance mair my ain ;
I couldna—O ! I daurna look
 On Mary's face again !

*William Thom*

## I KEN A FAIR WEE FLOWER.

I KEN a fair wee flower that blooms
   Far down in yon deep dell,
I ken its hame, its bonny hame,
   But whare, I winna tell.
When rings the shepherd's e'ening horn,
   Oft finds that soothing hour,
Stars on the sky, dew on the earth,
   And me beside my flower.

It is not frae the tints o' day
   My gentle flower receives
Its fairest hue, nor does the sun
   Call forth its blushing leaves ;
In secrecy it blooms, where Love
   Delights to strew his bower ;
Where many an unseen spirit smiles
   Upon my happy flower.

Ah ! weel ye guess, that fancy gives
   This living gem o' mine
A female form o' loveliness,
   A soul in't a' divine !
A glorious e'e that rows beneath
   A fringe o' midnight hue,
Twa yielding lips, wi' love's ain sweets
   Aye meltin' kindly through.

'Tis a' the wealth that I am worth,
   'Tis a' my praise and pride ;
And fast the hours flee over me
   When wooin' by its side.
Or lookin' on its bonny breast,
   So innocently fair,
To see the purity, and peace,
   And love that's glowing there.

Wi' saftest words I woo my flower,
　　But wi' a stronger arm
I shield each gentle opening bud,
　　Frae every ruthless harm.
The wretch that would, wi' serpent wile,
　　Betray my flower so fair,
Oh, may he live without a friend,
　　And die without a prayer !

A. MacLeggan

## PHŒBE GRAEME.

ARISE, my faithfu' Phœbe Graeme !
　　I grieve to see ye sit
Sae laigh upon your cutty stool
　　In sic a dorty fit !
A reamin' cog's a willin' rogue ;
　　But, by our vows sincere,
Ilk smilin' cup, whilk mirth filled up,
　　Was drained wi' friends lang dear !

Ye needna turn your tearfu' e'e
　　Sae aften on the clock ;
I ken the short hand frae the lang
　　As weel as wiser folk.
Let hoary time, wi' blethrin' chime
　　Taunt on—nae wit has he
Nae spell-spun hour—nae wilin' power
　　Can win my heart frae thee.

O, weel ye ken, dear Phœbe Graeme !
　　Sin' we, 'maist bairns, wed,
That, torn by poortith's iron teeth,
　　My heart has afttimes bled.

Fortune, the jaud, for a' she had,
  Doled me but feckless blanks ;
Yet, bless'd wi' thee, and love, and glee,
  I scorn her partial pranks.

As drumlie clouds o'er simmer skies
  Let anger's shadows flit !
There's days o' peace, and nights o' joy
  To pass between us yet !
For I do swear to thee, my fair,
  Till life's last pulse be o'er,
Till life depart, one faithful heart
  Shall love thee more and more.

Fair be thy fa' ! my Phœbe Graeme,—
  Enraptured now I see
The smile upon thy bonnie face,
  That wont to welcome me.
Grant me the bliss o' ae fond kiss,
  And kind forgiving blink
O' thy true love, and I will prove
  Far wiser than ye think !

A. Macleggan

## WIFIE COME HAME.

WIFIE come hame,
  My couthie wee dame ;
O ! but ye're far awa,'
  Wifie come hame.

Come wi' the young bloom o' morn on thy brow,
  Come wi' the lown star o' luve in thine e'e ;
Come wi' the red cherries ripe on thy mou,
  A' furred wi balm like the dew on the lea.

Come wi' the gowd tassels fringing thy hair,
　　Come wi' thy rose cheeks a' dimpled wi' glee ;
Come wi' thy wee step an' wifie-like air,
　　O ! quickly come an' shed blessings on me.
　　　　　　Wifie come hame,
　　　　　　　My couthie wee dame ;
　　　　　　O ! my heart wearies sair,
　　　　　　Wifie, come hame.

Come wi' our luve pledge, our dear little dawties
　　Clustering my neck round, and clambering my knee,
Come let me nestle and press the wee pettie,
　　Gazing on ilka sweet feature o' thee.
O ! but the house is a cauld hame without ye,
　　Lanely and eerie's the life that I dree ;
O ! come awa', and I'll dance round about ye,
　　Ye'se ne'er again win' frae my arms till I dee.
　　　　　　Wifie, come hame,
　　　　　　　My couthie wee dame ;
　　　　　　O ! but ye're far awa',
　　　　　　Wifie, come hame.

*James Ballantine*


## THE HIGHLAND DRILL.[1]

Come Corplar M'Donald, pe handy my lad,
Drive in a' ta stragglers to mornin' paraad !
*Greasorst!*[2] or you'll maype get "through ta wood laddie."
Ta Kornal will not leave a soul in your pody !

---

[1] The spoken passage in this song is taken from the "Laird of Logan," and contributed to that work by Mr. Carrick. We do not know whether to admire most the prose or verse portion. The description is so true to life, that we think the burly, consequential tones of the sergeant sound in our ears.

[2] Make haste ; pronounced *kress-horst.*

Faall into ta ranks tere ! ye scoundlers fall in !
I'll mak' ta one half of you shump from your skin !
You're raw as ta mutton, an' creen as ta cabbage,
I'll treel you to teath with your weight heavy paggage !

Advance to ta left tere ! faall pack to ta right !
Tress straight into line, or I'll treel you till night !
You sodgers ! ye're shust a disgraish to your clan,
An' a ferry hard pargain to SHORGE, honest man !

You Tuncan M'Donald ! you fery great sot,
You're trunk as ta cap, or ta stoup, or ta pot !
You'll ket a night's quarters into ta plack hole :—
Now, silence ! an' answer to call of ta roll.

Sergeant (bawling at the top of his voice), "Donald M'Donald,
*Mhor ?*[1]—(no answer, the man being absent)—I see you're there, so
you're right not to speak to nobody in the ranks. Donald M'Donald
*Rhua ?*"[2] "Here." "Ay, you're always here when nobody wants
you. Donald M'Donald, *Fad ?*[3]—(no answer)—oh, decent, modest
lad, you're always here, though, like a good sodger, as you are, you
seldom say nothing about it. Donald M'Donald, *Clausan Mhor ?*[4]
—(no answer)—I hear you ; but you might speak a little louder for
all that. Donald M'Donald, *Ordag ?*"[5] "Here." "If you're
here this morning, it's no likely ye'll be here to-morrow morning ;
I'll shust mark you down absent ; so let that stand for that. Donald
M'Donald, *Casan Mhor ?*"[6] "Here." "Oh damorst ! you said
that yesterday, but wha saw't you?—you're always here, if we tak'
your own word for it. Donald M'Donald, *Cam beul ?*"[7] "Here."
—(in a loud voice). "If you was not known for a tam liar, I would
believe you ; but you've a bad habit, my lad, of always crying here
whether you're here or no ; and till you give up your bad habit, I'll
shust always mark you down absent for your impudence : it's all for
your own good, so you need not cast down your brows, but shust be
thankful that I don't stop your loaf too, and then you wad maybe
have to thank your own souple tongue for a sair back and a toom
belly. Attention noo, lads, and let every man turn his eyes to the
sergeant."

---

[1] Big or great.    [2] Red-haired.    [3] Long.    [4] Big ears.
[5] Applied to a man having an extra thumb.    [6] Big feet.
[7] Crooked mouth.

You Ronald M'Donald! your pelt is as plack
As ta pra' Sunday coat on ta minister's pack!
So you needna stand cruntin' tere shust like ta pig,
For ta Captain *shall* send you on duty fatigue!

An' as for you, Evan M'Donald, you see
You'll go to ta guard-house tis moment wi' me;
Your firelock and pagnet 'll no do at a',
An' ta ram-rod's sae roosty it winna pe traw!

An' Struan M'Donald, stand straight on your shanks,
Whenever ta sergeant treels you in ta ranks;
An' hoult up your head, Sir, and shoulter your humph!
I *toot* you've peen trinkin', you creat muckle sumph!

You, Lauchie M'Donald! you skellum, ochon!
Your hair's neither pouthered nor letten alone,
An' the tin o' your pig-tail has lost the shapan,
An' your frill is as brown as the heather o' Pran!

Oigh! Dugald M'Donald! your small clothes are aye
As yellow as mustard in April or May;
I tare say you think it a creat cryin' sin!
To puy ta pipe clay, an' to rub it hard in!

An' now you'll dismiss like goot bairns till to-morrow,
I'm sure you're my pride, an' my shoy, an' my sorrow;
It's a' for your goods if I gie you a thraw,—
For the sergeant ye ken has the sharge of ye a'.

*David Vedder.*

END OF VOL. I.

*Printed by* R. & R. CLARK, *Edinburgh.*